Dear Joan

" Ulli-Nanauatmeji "

Alice Noyes

Metallak

Metallak, his legacy

By Alice Daley Noyes

FIRST EDITION
December, 1988

Copyright 1988
Printed by Liebl Printing Company, Colebrook, New Hampshire
Design and Editing by Jordan Associates, Colebrook, New Hampshire

Foreword

Our Country is rich in heritage and history, and yet, how much do we know of our native American predecessors? Take Metallak for example, the perfect Native American Indian role model. He attended college, surveyed for a railroad, tamed a wild moose, made all his own clothing and tools, and was highly respected by all who knew him. Yet he died a pauper, a man without a country. How do we explain such a paradox?

I feel that the loss of his tribal support and the fact that he was, by all evidence, a "loner," gives credence to a character very much in conflict with the old and the new, even while accepting the inevitable. If it appears to the reader that he has rather a small role, it may be that I became over-zealous in my attempts to convey the heritage of his people as a tribute to his memory, and there are times when he becomes like a small cog in a wheel.

I soon discovered that information was minimal, and documentation almost nonexistent. To further complicate identity problems, most of these particular Indians took baptismal names and abandoned family names, making it almost impossible to trace one family for several generations. Then, too, the records at Odanak burned three times, so we must depend on secondary documents, old correspondence, etc. Luckily, Dr. Gordon Day (National Museum of Man) has researched these Native Americans for many years and presented numerous abstracts on the subject, so he was my primary reference on the subject.

Thanks to Dr. Day, Metallak's membership at the village of Odanak was ascertained in the census taken in 1812. The spelling of the name at that time was "Matelok."

Father Maurault, whose work I had translated, was an excellent source on religious practices of the natives.

Stephen Laurent was invaluable to my research by checking my vocabulary and obtaining an early dictionary written by his father, the late Chief Joseph Laurent.

Another important contact was John Moody, a Dartmouth graduate who works extensively with the Abenakis in the region, and helped in the preparation of Dr. Day's book.

Because of the long and sketchy gaps in Metallak's life, I have classified the story as fiction. However, a good portion is true, to the best of my knowledge. Keoka, his first wife, is prominent throughout the book, and through her scandalous behavior allows me to incorporate some paganistic practices not completely abandoned by the tribe. She was the only character in the book I was unable to control, and there are times when she completely takes over, almost as though she knows her life will be short but exciting. She bears Metallak four children, one of whom is killed by wolves, after which Metallak swears vengeance on the wolf family. Their marriage ends in the tragedy of Keoka's murder, and Metallak is banished from his tribe under suspicion.

Later on, he lives at Megalloway and marries Molly Oozalluc, and all evidence concludes that this marriage was very happy. The story also touches on the King Philip's land grant, which I believe was written by Metallak's father, Pial, and recorded in Grafton County, New Hampshire, in 1796. I have made reference to the education of the Abenakis at Dartmouth, and incorporated their participation in the War of 1812, which is also documented at Odanak. Metallak lost one of his

I

sons in that war; shortly afterward the stigma against his name was cleared, but his life continued to be difficult. He became totally blind and dependent on his daughter, who loved him deeply. However, he hated the confinement and paid a guide to lead him away from her home to his old friend, Moserill. Unfortunately, the guide abandoned him and Metallak became a town pauper in West Stewartstown, New Hampshire, where he was auctioned off once a year at town meeting. Nevertheless, his reputation as a hunter and guide spread far and wide, and Metallak's name bears a legacy in itself.

Maintaining a tribal identity has been difficult, if not impossible, for many Native Americans of the Northeast. Unlike the western tribes, New England's Indians lacked treaties with the U.S. Government, their ancestry was riddled by intermarriage, and their heritage a mystery to most of them. I began to attend the meetings of the now defunct New Hampshire Indian Council and watched firsthand the struggle to maintain some segment of their former identity. I was amazed to learn there were forty-six tribal origins represented in New Hampshire alone. Perhaps, in some small way, this book will shed more light on this subject.

Alice Daley Noyes
November 1988

II

Dedication

To My Dad: who was always ten feet tall, even though he measured 5"3".

Joseph G. Daley
1906-1966

Courtesy

Margaret Laurent, Book Review
Stephen Laurent, Vocabulary Assistance,
son of Chief Joseph Laurent, author of "Abenaki & English
Dialogues"
John Moody, Historian
Evelyn Bell, Librarian, Andover, Maine
William Copeley, Assoc. Librarian, New Hampshire Historical
Society, Copy of King Philip Land Grant
Gordon M. Day, National Museum of Man, Canadian Ethnology
Service
Kenneth C. Cramer, Archivist, Dartmouth College Library
Chief Watso, Odanak Village
Shaman Pee Mee, New Hampshire Indian Council, access to
museum in her home
Charles T. Morrissey, Editor, Vermont Life Magazine
Ben Conant, South Paris, Maine
State Librarians, of Maine, New Hampshire, Vermont
William Bellerose, deceased; former resident of Odanak
(interviewed at age 96)
J. C. Kenneth Poore, deceased; son of the sexton who buried
Metallak (interviewed at age 95)
Norma Ouden, deceased; Professor, UNH
Alice Flanders, Interview

Points of Interest

Metallak Mountain, Township C, Maine, elevation 2,848 ft.
Metallak Pond, Township C, Maine, elevation 1,867 ft.
Metallak Stream, Township C, Main, source: Metallak Pond
Metallak Brook, Township C, Maine
Metallak Island, Township 4, Range 1, Maine (Upper Richardson Lake)
Mount Metalak, Millsfield, New Hampshire, elevation 2,699 ft.
Upper Metalak Pond, Township 5, Range 3, Maine
Lower Metallak Pond, Township 5, Range 3, Maine (both absorbed by Aziscohos Lake)
Metalak Island, Lake Umbagog, Errol, New Hampshire (now Dutton's Island)
Metalic Point, Upper Richardson Lake, Township 4

Metallak's signature

Disclaimer

We have classified this book as fiction, although historical information herein is based on facts obtained through my research. There are some points that were difficult to verify and if any readers can correct or clarify information in this book, I'd be happy to hear from them.

Alice Daley Noyes
"Circa 1906"
1362 North River Road
Manchester, NH 03104
603/668-2637

Vocabulary

Arsigontegok: Village name
Adirondacks: Bark eaters
Amariscoggin: Androscoggin
Ammonoosuc: Narrow fishing place
Arpent: 191.8 English feet
Asobakw: Labrador tea
Azeban: Raccoon
Bastonais or Pastoniak: Coming from "Boston" (whites)
Kchi Niwaskw: God; The Great Spirit
Ket-a-gus-wowt: Milky Way
Kikas: May
Kissanda: Monday
Kwini-teguh: Connecticut River
Loup Garou: Were-wolf
Naamas: Clyde River
Nakilhot kisos: Sunset, at sunset
Nakkahigas: June
Ne-bi-son-be: Water which has different taste, mineral water
Niboiwi: In the night
Noison: medicine
Nulhegan (or Kulhegan): River–wooden trap
Nunkasoon: Soon to be a woman
Nunksqua: A woman
Nunksquaw: A young woman
Magua, Maguak: Coward, Cowards
Manogemassak: Little people who lived in rivers
Mon-fo-mon-o-bog: Lake Memphremagog
Moskuas: Muskrat
Moz-aianbe: Male moose
Odziohozo: He makes himself from something
Ogawinno: Bear; the sleeper
Ototemon: Brother and sister relationship
Papoeis: Child
Pemola: Flying creature of immense power
Pelawinno; Pela8inno: Tortoise
Pejepscot: Part of Androscoggin
Pe-ton-bowk: Lake Champlain; waters that lie between Abenakis and Iroquois
Piz wat: Good for nothing

Pton gon: Treasury
Quabacook: Merry Meeting Bay
Shaman: Medicine Man
Skwedai-nebi: Fire water
Slologan: Swampy place
Tabaldak: The Owner (created all living things except Odziohozo)
Tmakwa: Beaver; Tree cutter
Tkinogan: Cradle board; Something that binds
Vessie: French, bladder bag
Wa-ba-ban: Northern lights
Wattap: Root to sew with
Wigwam: Summer lodge
Wli-nanawalmezi: May you have good health
Wuskowah: Pigeon
Wigbee: Thong wood
Wski-alemos: A young dog

CHAPTER ONE

Metallak struggled painfully to a sitting position from his bed on the floor, his gaunt bony frame half hidden by the faded blankets he clasped about his chest. His chest heaved as he drew long, uneven breaths from the effort as he struggled to remain sitting. His keen ears detected the faint buzz of voices in the adjoining kitchen, but he couldn't make out what they said. He tried to clear his dry, raspy throat, which brought Matilda running in from the kitchen.

"Why, Metallak, you're awake," she said, feeling his wet brow. He could smell the strong odor of lye soap on her rough hands as she gently adjusted his covers and placed a pillow behind his back for support.

"Now I'll be right back," she assured him, "with a clean basin of water." Metallak knew that she was a big woman in spite of her light step, even though he'd never seen her. He had met Matilda and Leonard Fellows after he'd lost his sight, but they were good, kind people and he was grateful for their help in his hour of need.

"Thank you, 'Tilda,' he murmured, after she set the basin down and began bathing his face and hands. His breath came easier now and she was less uneasy. This proud old Indian had given them quite a turn last night, and one of these days he wouldn't be so lucky. If only she knew how to contact his daughter in Canada, perhaps they would make peace with one another before he passed on. But she was helpless, unless Metallak decided to tell them where Parmachenee lived. Not once since that frightful night ten years ago when Metallak appeared out of nowhere had he mentioned her name. It seemed he had shut her out of his heart forever. From the other settlers, Matilda had learned of his deep affection for this child of the forest, who could never bear to be parted from her father for very long. Why had he turned his heart against her? She kept up a nervous chatter as she bathed him, the first time Metallak had ever been unable to bathe himself.

"Why, Metallak, when you turned up sick, half the town turned out; wanted you to know that if you need anything, they'd get it for you. Some of them are still waiting to say hello."

For the first time in his life, Metallak was grateful to be blind, unable to see his visitors. He could not bear to face the pity of the townspeople for an old Indian who would soon die as a pauper and be forgotten.

"Couldn't we make you more comfortable in a bed, Metallak?" Matilda asked for the umpteenth time. As always, Metallak shook his head no.

"Metallak has a fine bed," he told her, patting the floor, "and one day soon Metallak will sleep under the stars."

Matilda scolded him sharply, always embarrassed when Metallak spoke of death. "Now, Metallak, you're much better today, and you know summer is coming soon and Parmachenee will be hoping to hear from you. Won't you tell me where she lives?"

Metallak shook his head no again, but trembled at the mention of Parmachenee's name, which gave Matilda goose bumps. How he yearned to hold her hand once more, this child of the past and the future, to hear her soft harmonious voice humming a song from her youth. Beads of perspiration stood out on his forehead and his palms grew moist as he regretted the folly of an old man's blunder. Parmachenee had promised to accompany him after the harvest, but he had left in the night, sneaking out like a thief. How could Parmachenee forgive him when he couldn't forgive himself? Besides, he was ashamed to be seen like this, and with no legacy for his grandchildren, all because of his own folly.

Seeing the agony on his face, Matilda quickly changed the subject.

"Couldn't I give you a haircut just this once, Metallak?" she asked, feeling in her ample apron pocket for a pair of scissors. Despite his weakened condition, she heard Metallak's chuckle.

"Never had a haircut yet, don't need one now," he said, reaching up to pull out any long protruding hairs, then

2

smoothing down his shaggy mane with his hands.

Matilda bustled out of the room, satisfied that Metallak could still smile. Somehow, one way or the other, she'd get word to Parmachenee that her father was dying. She began busily stirring up a soup over the fireplace.

Metallak wakened to the aroma of warm chicken broth and suddenly felt hungry. He loved Matilda's homemade bread dipped in hot broth. He could hear whispers from the kitchen.

Matilda stirred the broth over the fire, murmuring quietly to her husband and the visitors. "Stubborn as a mule. He refuses to tell us where Parmachenee is; keeps talking in his sleep about the lost legacy." She sighed and shook her head helplessly.

"Wish we could get our hands on that halfbreed," Leonard said. "We'd get him to tell us where he hid all that money." From the pine sideboard he took down the bowl he had carved for Metallak, handing it to his wife. Matilda filled it with broth and carried it in to him. Leonard watched as Metallak held the bowl to his lips, drinking the broth almost greedily, and couldn't help but wonder if the tough old Indian would outlive them all. It was uncanny the way he hung on, a man that age. According to the town records, Metallak was close to 120 years old. That didn't seem possible, but there was other evidence too. Take old Granny Stailbird, for instance. Said she'd known Metallak since childhood and they'd been friends ever since. Leonard mulled all this over as he donned his frock, preparing to do the chores. The day wasn't long enough for all the chores a man had to do on a farm, even a small farm. Metallak spoke to him as he opened the door.

"What day is this?" he asked, curiously.

"Why, 'tis Monday, Metallak," Leonard answered. "Kassanda," Metallak said to himself. "And what month?"

"The month of May, Metallak." Leonard was puzzled. "What makes you ask?"

"Kikas," Metallak replied solemnly, "the month of planting." Then he sank back down on the floor, exhausted from the exertion of bathing and eating. But something bothered him and forced him to speak again.

"Leonard has not forgotten?"

Leonard shifted his feet uncomfortably, but spoke up in a firm confident voice. "Metallak, a promise is a promise. I give you my word you'll be buried sitting up just like you asked, and facing the East." Then Leonard made his way out the door, already late with the afternoon milking.

Matilda took advantage of the late afternoon sun to do some tatting, after making Metallak comfortable and drawing the covers up around his shoulders. It seemed, with three boys to raise and feed, there was never time to do anything except mending. Somehow, today, she yearned to do some fine needle work to relax her nerves. And besides, she felt a new tablecloth would make her small home more attractive, handy as Leonard was with a pine board. She appreciated the wainscoting he had painstakingly carved for the walls, and the fine hutch that held the few pieces of china they possessed. Still, a pretty tablecloth would go nicely on the long trestle table that had to seat fifteen during the busy haying season.

Metallak woke much later, some inner sense telling him that Matilda was hovering about. He tried to sit up, but his body failed him. He sank back.

"Metallak dreams," he apologized, while she wiped his brow bathed in sweat. She spoke in soft soothing tones and soon he slept again.

He slept in short naps, fitfully. The ghost of Keoka came again and again to haunt him, her mocking smile playing tricks on his memory, taking him back to another time, another place.

The year was 1782. Metallak had been lost in his own thoughts that fateful day, driven by impatience to be home. It was his duty as the firstborn of Chief Pial to help lead his people. Rumors of the turmoil that threatened to tear his village apart had hastened his early departure last night from Moor's Indian School in the small hamlet of Hanover, New Hampshire. A word to his friends about his plans and they, too, eagerly departed with him. Together, they hoped to persuade their people to side with the settlers and resist the harsh demands of the British who ruled their tiny village with an iron hand. Metallak wanted no part of Tom Hegan's bloody raids on the lonely, unprotected cabins of the white settlers, or his underhanded deals with the British.

More determined than ever to put an end to Tom Hegan's treachery, he dipped his paddle faster and faster, his jet black hair waving lightly in the strong breeze that rippled over the water. His

4

three loyal companions traveling north on the Kwini-teguh, the white man's Connecticut River, stole a sullen look at each other as they dipped their paddles hurriedly into the water. Small rivulets of perspiration ran down their backs and faces, leaving stains, as they tried in vain to keep up with Metallak, who relentlessly strove to make better time. They hoped he would tire soon.

Loyal as they were to Metallak, they yearned to leisurely enjoy the sights and sounds around them, after three years of tiresome schooling. They found New Hampshire's little colony of North Stratford practically unchanged, still a vast wilderness of forest. But as they scanned the horizon for Green's Trading Post, they saw more and more small clearings up in the hills, a sure sign that more white settlers had arrived here.

Observing the many small clearings dotting the heavily wooded landscape, Metallak knew he was right. The whites came now in great numbers and his people dwindled. Where would he lead them when his father passed on? Would there be a corner of the earth where the Abenakis could live as their ancestors had? He thought not. The future was clear to him. They must befriend the whites and share the bounty of the hunting grounds. There was plenty for all. If only he could persuade his father to see things as he did. For too many years the Abenakis had been used, first by the French, then by the English, in this war against the colonies. He still remembered the first scalp he ever claimed, proudly displaying it from his lodge. It was that of an old settler, trying to protect his family as they gathered wood. The old settler had shown no fear and Metallak had spared his life out of respect. The females in the cabin had not been so lucky. Metallak remembered the sight of the tiny infant sucking at his mother's breast, crudely caught up and thrown against a tree, his brains spilled on the ground, by his own father's hand. Oh, yes, the villagers had been proud of the daring raid, and especially of Metallak, who had taken his first scalp at the age of thirteen. Far into the night they had celebrated, consuming the white man's fire water until it all disappeared and they fell in a drunken stupor to the ground, unable to find their lodges. Those who did not drink themselves senseless hid the weapons, fearing a drunken brawl.

The coming of the missionaries had changed all that. Metallak had come to know and love God, as well as his neighbors. Never again would he lift the hatchet except in self defense. But not

5

all of his people had been converted by the missionaries. These renegades were craftily banded together by Tom Hegan, who continually stirred up hatred against the whites.

"They take our furs and skins for nothing!" he would shout. "Soon our women and children will go hungry. Let us strike back, before it is too late!" Thus inciting the people, he would urge them to make more raids. When this failed, he would tempt them with the lure of money.

"It has reached the ears of Tom Hegan," he told them in confidence, "that the British pay well for the prisoners who are strong and can be sold as servants."

The lure of easy money tempted the young braves, who eagerly volunteered. With the money, they could buy a gun like that of the whites. Perhaps they could buy clothing too, or a horse. Then too, there would be bright colored ribbons to bring to their nunksquaws. Their eyes filled with greed as they listened to Tom Hegan tell them how easy it would be as he brandished his black war club. Before long war whoops would be heard all over the village as they made ready for another raid. And the elders, who did nothing about it, just shrugged their shoulders helplessly. All this Metallak had learned from a messenger who sought him out at Moor's Indian School, urging him to come home.

Suddenly, the four young men stiffened, listening intently. Then they heard it distinctly: a shrill cry. It was a howling, eerie cry, like that of a coyote in pain.

Gratefully, Metallak's companions brought the canoe to shore under cover of the tall shore grasses. Disembarking and standing quietly in the shadow of the tall shrubs, they watched and listened. A tiny figure racing through the tall grasses toward the river bank was all they saw. A stream of dark hair seemed to hide half her body like a cloak of cloth, all that one could see above the tall grasses. Easily outdistancing her pursuers, she stood poised at the water's edge, glancing nervously in back of her. A tall bearded trapper gripping a whip lumbered after her, shouting all the while to his two companions.

"Dirty squaw. I'll pay ten dollars apiece to the man who brings her back."

For another moment she stood poised at the bank of the river hesitating, her arm clasped to her chest. One arm, they noticed was withered and hung limply from the elbow down. She glanced their way once, her desperate brown eyes betraying her fear.

6

If she saw them, she gave no sign. Then she plunged into the icy river.

It was early in Kikas, the month of planting, and the waters of the Kwini-teguh still had an icy chill from the long winter. The young men watched the dive and marveled at the skill of the small swimmer, whose head finally appeared halfway across the river.

Now the trapper had reached the river's edge, breathing heavily. "You'll pay for this, you dirty little squaw!" he shouted.

Like his friends, Metallak was filled with indignation at the scene. Three men against one small nunksquaw was a cowardly battle, especially when one of them carried a whip. Still, he didn't want to get involved in a family quarrel when they were so close to home. He studied the face of this crude white man with interest. Like his native brothers, Metallak's own face was smooth as the day he was born. He was always amused that his white brothers sprouted hair on the face just as the soil sprouted grass. And even after much scraping with the razor to remove it, the hair would reappear again, almost overnight. The trapper's long shaggy brown beard spiked out in all directions, like a porcupine. As he spat angrily on the ground, some of the spittle stayed in his beard. His two companions shrugged and started back to the trading post. They had no canoes and already the tiny squaw was a bobbing speck in the distance. The trapper followed them slowly back to Green's, mounted his horse and left.

The young men scanned the other side of the river for signs of the small women. When all was quiet, they carefully concealed their canoe and carried their few skins to Green's to bargain for new blankets, knives and supplies. There had been precious little time for hunting these past few years, but each had contrived to gather a few skins. Although they feigned disinterest in the bits of conversation they overheard from the two old trappers by the stove, they listened intently.

"I don't blame her none. Heard him myself. Told her not to touch nothing and knocked her down. I don't have much use for a man that takes a whip to his own horse."

"She sure had spunk, trying to cut that horse loose."

Metallak listened well, learning that the trapper's woman was called Keoka, that she'd never been seen around these parts before. "How many skins for the blanket?" he asked, pointing to a bright red blanket.

"Well, I'll be jiggered," whispered one of the old trappers, "he speaks English."

His companion sucked on his pipe, nodding his head.

Green knew immediately that these Indians had been educated, probably at Moor's. The Abenakis had made him a wealthy man, and he didn't want any trouble. "Nice skins you got here," Green told them. "I'll throw in a knife a'piece along with the blankets. Say, you men from Odanak, Canada? Aren't you the one called Metallak?" he said, adjusting his glasses carefully.

Metallak nodded curtly, saying nothing. In a low voice, Green cautioned the young men.

"Take my advice and stay out of this. That squaw ain't from around these parts, and that trapper looks like a mean one to tangle with." Green didn't want any hot headed fighting around his trading post, stirring the whole town up. Not with the son of the Abenaki Chief in the middle of it.

"We will make no trouble here," Metallak promised. He seemed almost grateful to Green for his advice. They were still two weeks from home, and he wanted no delays.

As they made their way to the canoe and packed it, Sebattis did most of the talking, sensing Metallak's reluctance to get involved.

"What do you say, Metallak? That trapper will kill her if he finds her."

Metallak paused, looking at his other two friends, Francis and Plausawa.

"I say we find her," Francis said. "Make sure she's all right." Plausawa nodded his agreement.

"Does the son of an Abenaki Chief turn his back on a woman in trouble?" prodded Sebattis.

The bait worked. Metallak's high cheekbones flushed, and his black eyes flashed anger. He looked at the three of them, who were waiting expectantly for his decision. "All right," he conceded, "but we leave at the crack of dawn, with no more delays."

They crossed the river in the same direction they had last seen the nunksquaw. Friends once more, Metallak's anger disappearing as quickly as the clouds above. After disembarking, they carefully scouted the area. Here and there, a patch of ice appeared on the dark forest floor, rich in evergreens and fir. They saw a covy of partridge suddenly take flight and cautiously approached, circling the area.

Defiantly, the woman rose from her hiding place and confronted them, a knife in her good hand. They admired her lack of fear as she faced them.

"Keoka will not go back!" she said in English. They were momentarily taken aback by her beauty, her delicate frame, and most especially by her long cascading chestnut hair. As she spoke, she eased back slowly toward the water. "Keoka will die first!"

Metallak was relieved that they had found her so quickly. He spoke quietly, so as not to frighten her. "I am called Metallak. These are my friends. Over here is Sebattis, over there Francis and Plausawa." He could see that Keoka was obviously chilled through. Her stained and meager garment clung to her, still wet.

"Do not fear us," Plausawa put in quickly. "We saw the trapper with the bushy face chasing you, saw you swim across the river."

"Like a fish," added Sebattis with a warm smile.

She continued to stare. The young men wore homespun breeches and white men's tow shirts. Their feet were clothed in tattered moccasins, like her own. The haughty one with the stone face called Metallak was evidently the leader, his short black hair and piercing black eyes commanding attention. Like a tawny mountain cat, he moved gracefully, as though it required no effort. Sebattis was built like Metallak, tall and lithe, but there the resemblence ended. His brown hair and blue eyes were a sharp contrast to the deep black hair and eyes of the others. Francis and Plausawa bore a strong family resemblence. Like Metallak, they wore their hair hanging loose, but their features were slightly fuller, more coarse than Metallak's, especially their noses and lips. They smiled broadly at Keoka, inviting her confidence.

She sensed that she would have to gain Metallak's approval if they were to help her escape. Yet his eyes seemed to look right through her, causing her to blush as he stared. She did not know that this proud and haughty Indian was tongue tied at the sight of her long wavy hair, loose to her waist. The waves were like ripples in a stream, some small and some strong lively ones, wet and glistening in the sun. Never had he seen such hair as this. He found his tongue finally.

"Keoka...Keoka...that name is Sauk, is it not? How does it happen that a Sauk nunksquaw keeps the lodge of a white

9

trapper?"

Keoka lifted her head proudly, but they all saw the slight quiver of her chin.

"Broken Arrow took Keoka from the Iroquois."

Metallak wondered how she came to be with the Iroquois, his enemy, who lodged at Lake Champlain. Their territory was far from that of the Sauks near the land of the great lakes.

Her charms were not lost on Sebattis, who felt she needed a sympathetic ear. He spoke in a soft soothing voice.

"Small one is a good swimmer, even with a weak arm."

Keoka stiffened at the mention of her withered arm. Ashamed, she stared at the ground as she spoke.

"Keoka's arm is like that of an old woman now. It has been so for many moons now, after Keoka fell sick."

For a moment, all were silent. Plausawa and Francis dared not speak and break the spell, so beautiful was the small nunksquaw, like the story of the corn maiden who came to life. Keoka raised her head, watching their expressions from under her deep brown lashes. Sebattis spoke first.

"What do you say, Metallak? Surely the Nebisonbe water may help Keoka's arm. We are nearly there now," he added, as though in surprise.

In spite of Metallak's stern face and preoccupation with his own village, the plight of the small nunksquaw was not lost on him either. He only hoped his friends would not begin fighting over this beautiful half-breed who couldn't be as innocent as she appeared, not if she had been the trapper's woman. And what would they do when they got there, leave her there alone while they made their way north? How did they know they could trust her?

"We must make haste," he finally said to Keoka. "You will have to keep up with us without whining or complaining. Do you wish to go or not?" He immediately regretted his choice of words, envying Sebattis and his easy manner of speaking. A deep strawberry hue spread over his face as he waited for her answer.

Once again Sebattis sought to persuade her, annoyed with Metallak's abrupt treatment of the fragile woman. "The water of the Nebisonbe is known to have great healing powers," he told her. "Perhaps Keoka's arm can be cured."

Keoka knew she could trust Sebattis. After all, was

he not a half-breed like herself? No doubt this was why the arrogant stone face looked down on her, like the villagers. But the desire to make her arm whole was very tempting. She avoided Metallak's cold eyes as she spoke, determined not to let him know how much she wanted to go.

"The trapper will not find us there?"

"No white man will ever find the waters of the Nebisonbe. It is hidden well and known only to my Abenaki brothers," Sebattis assured her.

"Keoka will accept your help," she told them meekly.

Without a word, Metallak motioned with his head, and Sebattis and Francis went for the canoe while he busied himself covering their tracks. They did not fear the fat trapper, but felt it best to make haste.

Keoka followed Metallak, stepping carefully into his tracks. She was determined to keep up with his long loping strides. All the same, she was angry that he forced her to take such long steps. Did he not see that he was much taller than she? Sebattis saw to it that she rested frequently, when he stopped to brush away all evidence of their tracks with a pine branch, or leave tell-tale tracks heading in another direction.

At last, a few miles southwest of North Stratford, they approached the secluded area of the Nebisonbe springs.

"Broken Arrow will never find you now," assured Sebattis, as Metallak scanned the area for signs of strangers.

"Even so, do not forget our agreement," Metallak reminded them. "We leave at first light." Though he seemed to ignore Keoka, he too had noted how quickly she traveled, breaking no twigs and making no complaints. A woman who could walk this quietly would be safe now from the trapper.

"Why not bring Keoka with us?" Sebattis suggested, as though the idea had just occurred to him. "We can bring the water with us, and bathe her arm on the trip. When we get to the village, she can visit the healing waters near St. Francis."

Metallak's face remained impassive as he considered the suggestion. Inside, he was furious with Sebattis. It was so like him to become infatuated with the first nunksquaw he met. Having a female along would only slow them down.

"Perhaps Keoka will return to the Sauks now?" he

asked her, looking straight into her eyes.

Again, Keoka had the feeling that his deep scrutinizing black eyes were looking right through her, that he would detect the smallest untruth. She busied herself rubbing the withered arm while she gathered her thoughts, avoiding his questioning eyes. She had to act quickly, knowing this might be her only chance at happiness. She didn't want any of them to know she had been banished from the Sauks by the Grand Council because there were so many complaints of her wanton behavior. In fact, she had welcomed her captivity with the Iroquois after a raiding party. It was better than being an outcast in the Sauk village, looked down on with scorn and ostracized by the young women her own age.

Keoka's face was very solemn as she spoke, almost in a whisper. "In my heart, I will always be a Sauk. That is true," she said, not mentioning that her mother had been a white captive. She chose not to remember those years after the passing of her father when she and her mother were treated like slaves, forced to run errands and beg from the others. No wonder her delicate mother finally died of this heavy toil, a small girl huddled against her too-thin chest trying to warm her cold body. Keoka's heart was too empty to grieve, like a stone that had no tears. She vowed instead that this would never happen to her, that somehow she would escape. Her cold behavior caused the villagers to think the child was marked, avoiding her whenever possible. Keoka chose to remain in the lodge of her mother and fend for herself, like a wild dog of the village. Slowly she came to realize that she possessed great beauty which was a far better weapon than the arrow. When the young braves sought her favor, they brought gifts. Keoka wisely hid these gifts, knowing the other nunksquaws would be jealous.

A small sigh escaped her lips as she continued. "The Iroquois took Keoka captive three summers past during a raiding party. And then one day, a trapper brought a much needed kettle to the Iroquois village. He waged the kettle for Keoka. This pleased the Iroquois and they gladly took the kettle. The trapper was kind to Keoka," she added, looking at them.

"When he fell sick, Keoka cared for him many moons before death took him. Then Keoka, too, fell sick. Many days Keoka does not remember, until the Iroquois found me wandering. Now Keoka's arm is like this." She paused and looked at the arm. "Soon the trapper's brother, Broken Arrow, came to the Iroquois village and claimed Keoka for his own. The Iroquois no longer wanted a slave with one arm, so they were pleased to be rid of me."

"So the bushy face is called Broken Arrow," Metallak spoke almost to himself.

"It is rumored that years ago, when he was hit with an arrow, he pulled it out and broke it in two, an act of much bravery. He is feted and honored by the Iroquois whenever he visits their village," she explained.

For the first time, Keoka saw a glimmer of compassion in Metallak's eyes when he spoke. "My people have named the Iroquois well," he told her. "Iroquois maquak, cowards!" He turned to the others. "It will be as you wish, if Keoka chooses to accompany us."

Taking his bedroll, he moved up to a higher level to bed down, leaving the others to spread fir bows to make a bed for Keoka. Although he was annoyed with the delay, he could not leave the nunksquaw at the mercy of the fat trapper. It would be like leaving a small bird in a trap. He was puzzled by this tiny woman whose face was sad one moment and seemed to light up the next. No doubt she yearned for the village of her youth, but they had no time to take her back home, unless she chose to go on her own. What if she chose to accompany them? He could only hope that she spoke the truth and would not add to the turmoil already facing his small village. Already she had intrigued the three young men who traveled with him. He wondered what the reaction of his parents would be, and knew they would disapprove, especially if they saw her walking as boldly as a man, instead of toeing in like all the other females. Well, it would not be whispered that he, Metallak, was captivated by her charms. He tried to ignore the quick pulsing of his heart when he thought of the fragile, brave little woman with the shining crown of hair, but her smile mocked him again and again in his sleep. He didn't know that Keoka, too, was having difficulty sleeping.

After greedily eating the corn given to her, Keoka lapsed into deep thought. Hidden in this lovely thicket high above the Connecticut, she felt safe. Far below, she could hear the gurgling sounds of the river, even though she could not see it. She was completely hidden in a strange new beautiful world. She lay awake for some time pondering her past, tears sliding down her small profile as she thought of her mother. Then she brooded about her youth. Was it her fault that the gods had made her so beautiful that all the young men wanted her? She shivered when she remembered the deadly game that had claimed the lives of two young warriors. She had meant it all as a joke, when she blindfolded the two young men that beautiful summer day. Faster and faster, they turned in circles at her command.

"Who will hit the branch?" she had asked, throwing a branch into the air."

Surely she did not know they would take aim and accidently kill each other from under these blindfolds instead of raising their bows and arrows to the heavenly skies above. The village elders were cruel to blame her for this harmless play. After all, a girl of only seventeen summers cannot be expected to know all. For many days after this tragedy, she had been unable to speak or eat. Even the village dogs were treated better than she was. But now she was three summers older. She would not make the same mistake twice.

In that moment, she made her decision. The Abenakis did not know of her past. Here she could start a new life, away from the black shadows of the past. Finally she slept.

The next morning, after a breakfast of fresh trout and cold clear water, they climbed a high bluff rising above the river. The area had a strange odor that Keoka had never smelled before, like the smell of boiled goose eggs. She could see a pond in the valley below, with a mirror-like surface. Dozens of water lilies were floating on the top. As gracefully as a doe, she ran lightly down the bluff to reach the pond below. She peered into the water at her face, an old habit of vanity. The face that looked back at her was pleasing. She smiled and dipped her weak arm into the water, then pulled it back out and stared, disappointed. In her voice there was accusation as she greeted the others.

"Keoka's arm looks no better."

Sebattis chuckled. "Small one chooses to use water from the slologan pond . . . swamp water. Come, follow me." She followed Sebattis still further down a deep ravine into a cluster of pine trees and thick overgrowth. There, completely hidden in a thick grove of pine trees, was a spray of water coming from a crude spout fashioned out of birch bark rolled up like a cone.

"How is it that fresh bark is placed around the water?" she asked in wonder.

"How do you think, small one?" asked a voice from high above. Then she saw Metallak in a tree and knew he had placed the fresh bark to channel the water more easily. In a moment he was standing beside her while the others busied themselves gathering

14

water for the journey. Keoka recognized the familiar vessie, the bladder bag, which her own people used to store water.

"Drink of the water and rest the weak arm under the waterfall," Metallak ordered. Meekly, she followed directions, not wishing to arouse his anger. For the first time, he had shown no resentment that she was there. Last night she feared she had angered him, the way he left so abruptly to bed down. After several moments, he massaged her arm, gently but firmly. His heart once again hammering so loud he feared she would hear it. Confused that he found her so attractive, he dropped the arm abruptly, instructing her to bathe once again in one of the six little hollowed out basins which held much of the discolored smelly water, staining the rocks a brassy yellow.

"Keoka has found a gold nugget," she exclaimed, picking up one of the stained yellow stones and studying it. It was exactly like the nugget that the trapper so cherished and fondled in the evening when he thought she was asleep.

"It is only fool's gold," Metallak said sternly, walking away. He hoped that Keoka did not expect his people to live as the white man did, as she had lived with the trapper. They lived very simply off the land, and the white man's gold was unknown to them.

Metallak sniffed the air suspiciously, then put his ear to the ground. He rose quickly. "Horses," he told her, "many of them. Let us go quickly."

Keoka ran to help fetch blankets and load the canoe. No doubt it was the trapper who had an uncanny knack for tracking. Then, too, he had learned much from Keoka. The others had heard the sound too and noiselessly made ready in a short time. As they placed the canoe in the water, they caught sight of three horses galloping toward the mirror pond of lilies. Quietly, they descended to the canoe, rowing rapidly under cover of the overhanging trees to make their escape.

CHAPTER TWO

As the men rowed expertly away from the cove, Keoka watched the water's edge. Sure enough, a head appeared. They had been spotted. She ducked low in the canoe as a shot was fired, hitting the water and creating a spray of water to douse them. Rounding the bend, away from sight of their pursuers, they moved to the other side of the river, then slowed the pace. There was no way now that the trapper could catch up with them.

"We are safe now," Sebattis announced to Keoka with a smile.

"You are certain?" She questioned, nervously looking in back of them.

"The fat trapper would no doubt sink his own canoe if he tried to overtake us," added Francis with a laugh. Plausawa joined in, pretending to spit in the water as the trapper had done.

"It seems the trapper wants you back, even with only one arm," Metallak said quietly, staring at Keoka. "Could it be that you are hiding something from us?"

Keoka flushed a deep crimson. "Keoka has nothing to hide," she said as she lifted her chin proudly. "If you do not trust me, I will swim to shore and make good my own escape." She stood in the canoe and poised for the dive, still watching the river's edge.

"Sit down before you overturn the canoe," Metallak said. "You are here and we will say no more about it. Perhaps one day our scouts will take you back to your village," he added a little more kindly.

As Keoka huddled back down in the center of the canoe, Plausawa shyly handed her a pouch of corn. "Do you miss your people?" he asked kindly.

"Keoka has no people," she said quietly. "My mother is dead and my father died many years ago. There is no reason for Keoka to return to the Sauk village." She spoke without emotion, but her face reflected pain and despair. Metallak was sorry he had spoken so harshly to her.

Keoka knew what bothered him, and spoke of it aloud. "I am sorry," she said, "that a white man has discovered the secret place of the waters."

Metallak was uncomfortable under her gaze. He

frowned, a habit of his youth when he was embarrassed. "Long ago, another white man was here," he finally answered, not wishing her to think she was the cause of his misery.

"Tell us about it again, Metallak," Plausawa pleaded, "of the only white man ever to drink of the waters."

As if by magic, Metallak's frown disappeared and his tone became more friendly as he spoke. Sebattis leaned back gracefully, enjoying the brief respite.

Keoka listened eagerly as Metallak recounted the Pow Wow of his early youth. The white man, a soldier with guns, had been wounded in battle. Metallak's father Pial had found the wounded man slumped over on his horse and brought him to the springs. First he blindfolded the man, who was too sick to know or protest.

"My people were angry," said Metallak, "but every day my father bathed his arm until the wound grew well and strong. The grateful soldier gave my father his horse when he returned to his people. But when he asked to bring away some of the precious water, my father made a vow." Keoka watched Metallak's voice as he spoke. His features were set, as though chiseled in granite as he gravely recalled the vow. His eyes grew luminous and bright as he spoke.

"No white man shall ever prosper from the medicine waters of the Abenaki."

All was quiet for a few moments after this, until Francis asked, "What became of the soldier?"

"Once again he was blindfolded and taken to North Stratford. He made a pact with my father never to discuss the medicine waters."

Watching his face as he spoke, Keoka pitied any white man who ever tried to profit from the use of these waters. Instinctively, she knew that Metallak would hunt him down and punish him.

Keoka soon learned the routine of her companions in the canoe. Except for the brief carries when the water was low or the stones too large, they made good time, and seemed to be climbing higher and higher into the mountains. Slowly, Keoka began to relax, and no longer looked in back of them for signs of the trapper. She would turn from one man to another with eager questions about their village. With such an apt pupil, they even gave her lessons in their native tongue. In a short time, she had learned many Abenaki words and laughed with them when she made a silly mistake. Her easy laughter

17

made the trip a pleasant one, and the days passed quickly. Even when they made camp in the evening, they would hover at Keoka's side, which annoyed Metallak. He wondered if the silly nunksquaw was ever serious about anything. Besides, she obviously preferred the company of the others, who outdid themselves to earn one of her winning smiles. Each one, of course, thought her mysterious smile was meant just for him and each harbored his own secret hopes for the future.

Metallak never joined in, choosing to take guard duty most of the time. He had little patience with these silly games or with Keoka. If the fickle nunksquaw preferred the company of the others, let it be so. The son of an Abenaki Chieftain would not chase after her before the others. But more and more often, he felt his eyes drawn to her tiny figure. He could not forget her, or her crown of thick chestnut hair, for even a moment. He felt the need for fresh meat, and they camped early that night. Perhaps it was only hunger that made his temper short.

Sebattis brought down a deer in a short time, partly for meat and partly so Keoka could have a new garment. First he made another vessie by cleaning and blowing up the bladder, then hanging it up to dry. When it was dry, he knew it would remain at the size he had blown it. From the extra piece, he fashioned a cover for it. He staked out the deerskin on poles, cleaning and scraping it carefully so as not to make a hole in it. Even Metallak helped by rubbing the skin with the brains of the dead animal to soften it. Francis and Plausawa combed the woods for the most delicate wattap to seam it together. Sebattis made a big show of presenting the skin and the root threads to Keoka. "We thought perhaps the small one would like a new tunic," he told her, his blue eyes sparkling. Keoka looked down at her stained and torn tunic, made from left over pieces that the trapper grudgingly allowed her to keep. But now she would have one cut perfectly from one large skin. She blinked hard, but one small tear escaped and made a path down her face. She was puzzled by all this kindness.

"Why do you help Keoka?" she asked.

"Are we not friends?" countered Sebattis. "Do friends need a reason to be kind? Does Keoka still not trust us?"

"Keoka will always be your friend," she said loyally. She hugged the skin to her body, hoping secretly there would be enough to make new moccasins for all of them. She would need only three small pieces, one for the sole and sides, another for the tongue and top, and a third for a wrap around ankle flap. That evening

18

Sebattis massaged her arm even longer than usual, detecting a great deal of improvement in the withered flesh, which was beginning to respond.

As for Keoka, she found Sebattis very handsome, his looks a welcome change from his Indian brothers. Like her, he was carefree and impulsive.

"Sebattis will take a wife one day?" she asked quietly.

Sebattis hesitated. After many moons in school, he longed only to run free like the deer and moose of the forest, where there were no clocks or Greek books to read. "Sebattis had planned never to marry," he told her seriously, "but for Keoka's hand, Sebattis would change all his plans."

She laughed a melodious tinkling laugh. "And does Metallak wish to have his freedom too?" She was puzzled by Metallak's lack of interest and hoped to learn something from Sebattis. It seemed that he was always deep in thought, scarcely aware of his companions.

"Metallak will never be completely free, even after he takes a wife. He is the eldest son of Pial, leader of the Cowassucks. One day Metallak too will lead his people, as his father and grandfather before him."

Keoka looked up in surprise. Perhaps that explained why Metallak was so serious most of the time.

"A wise leader never talks much about himself," continued Sebattis. "Metallak will make a fine Chief. Always he thinks first of others, never of himself. Even now, he goes to the village to assist his father."

"The Iroquois say the Abenakis are bark eaters," Keoka said. "They even call them Adirondacks."

"Better to be a bark eater when game is scarce than a man eater like the Iroquois," Sebattis told her proudly.

"Only the Cowassucks live in this Abenaki village?"

"No, small one, there are many tribes at the village, all Abenaki. There are the Penacooks, the Sokwakis, the Missiquois, and many others who escaped to St. Francis after the coming of the whites."

Keoka was deep in thought. It would be interesting to be a Sagamore's wife. She would be clothed in fine skins and furs, perhaps even have a slave. She would receive important

19

visitors who wished to smoke the Calumet and make alliances with the Cowassucks. She would have many privileges.

"Perhaps Metallak prepares himself by spending many hours alone in thought, as he does now on yonder hill," she said.

"Keoka is wise," Sebattis said. "Metallak is already a brave of twenty five summers. And Pial grows old. But why does Keoka speak only of Metallak? He is already spoken for."

Keoka's eyes stung when she heard this. She should have guessed Metallak was spoken for. She thought again of the garments she had worn these past few years, skins so badly scarred or torn that the trapper was unable to sell them, moccasins full of holes back at the Sauk village that the other wives threw away. She remembered well the scornful looks of those who looked down on the white half-breed. Only the children had been kind, and frequented her lodge to hear stories. In return for their kindness, Keoka had learned to tell the best stories in camp, full of adventure. The little ones always clamored for more.

"Keoka is very tired tonight," she told Sebattis, not wishing to talk any more. She lay awake for a long time, pondering what to do.

After a restless night, she decided to make the most of her good fortune. There would be many young braves at the village. Surely one of them would ask Keoka to become his wife.

They set off early the next morning. By now, all the young men were intrigued with her mischievous smile and affectionate nature. It was a pleasure just to watch her walk, as silently as they did, with straight feet, not toeing in awkwardly like the other women of the village. Most of all, they enjoyed the rippling waves in her hair that gave off a soft reddish hue when the sun cast itself over her.

Keoka enjoyed the breathtaking view of the mountains in the distance. They looked like giant hills, each one sweeping down to the ground only to be flanked by a bigger, larger hill in the distance. They seemed to rise up to meet the Milky Way and lose themselves in the clouds, their color a deep bluish green in the distance. She thought longingly of her mother, who would have enjoyed this beautiful view. She had worked so hard to be a good wife and mother, whose only wish had been to be reunited with her people. Often they had whispered of this when the two of them lay awake, unable to sleep. Keoka knew only that her grandfather's name was Charles and that he lived near the waters of the Gods, near great waves, waves that could pick you up and throw you to the winds if they wished. "One day I will take you there," her mother always promised. "They are very rich and they will be kind to you." But her mother had grown sick and died after a mysterious sickness had spread through their village.

Keoka realized that they had come to a stop and climbed out of the canoe. "It is only a short portage to the lake with the island," Sebattis explained. The men selected crosspieces to place across their shoulders, evenly supporting the weight of the canoe. Keoka strapped extra supplies to her back, trying to keep up with them. Once, at the sound of a branch cracking, she looked furtively in back of her, still half expecting the trapper to appear. But there was nothing. Looking back, her gaze met long rolling hills and little valleys, dotted with small clearings of new settlements. She climbed gratefully into the canoe as they made their way across the large lake with an island right in the center. From here, they traveled up the Naamas River.

"White men call this the River Clyde," Metallak explained, as he expertly navigated the canoe. Keoka couldn't believe what a jovial mood he was in. He continued.

"Soon we will come to Mom-fo-mom-o-bog, great pond place. From there, it is not far to our village." Last night he had admitted to himself that this had been a most enjoyable trip. So far, the small one had not been a burden and made no complaints, even after a long hard day. He forced himself to think of Mali, trying to forget how his heart skipped when he looked at Keoka.

"Keoka has heard of this great pond place," she said, eager to respond to Metallak's friendship. "It is the land of many moose, is it not?"

"Keoka is right," Metallak answered, studying her. "Did the trapper hunt moose at Mom-fo-mom-o-bog?"

She nodded. "Keoka has heard the trapper talk many times of the fall moose hunt." She shivered slightly. "Do you think he waits there for us?"

At this, they all laughed and then finally became serious again.

"He is only one, and we are four," reminded Sebattis. Metallak added, "This is the hunting ground of my people. Many secret coves are well known to us. Keoka need not fear that Broken Arrow will find us."

Still, they made good time with their canoe. The trapper had a gun, and they did not.

One morning, Francis told her they were almost at St. Francis.

"St. Francis is your brother?" she asked him.

At this, they all laughed, even Metallak. Then he patiently explained. "Long ago our small village was called Arsigontegok. Then one day Governor De La Barre gave a gift of land to the Abenaki people for planting corn at Chaudiere Falls. This bargain was sealed on the birth date of St. Francis, January 29. In gratitude to the good fathers who helped us, and in honor of St. Francis, my people made a beautiful collar of wampum. This the good fathers sent to France to be placed on the tomb of St. Francis of Sales. In later years, other belts of wampum were sent to France, one to honor the Mother of God. The French, wishing to honor our gifts, sent us statues for our little church. Most of these were burned or stolen when Rogers attacked our village."

The look of intensity on Metallak's face told her more than the speech. He was devoted to these good fathers who helped his people.

"Keoka does not know this word saints," she finally admitted shyly.

"Father Roland will welcome Keoka to our church," Metallak answered. "And soon Keoka, too, will know of the true God, who watches Abenaki brothers, white men . . . even bad ones, all at the same time." He knew his parents would expect this, and watched her face anxiously.

Keoka was even more puzzled than before. Still he had not mentioned Pemola.

"This God is a friend of Pemola?" she finally asked.

They made no attempt to hide their smiles at her silly chatter. Deeply hurt, Keoka turned her attention to the great view before her. After days of traveling through the deep forest, she was taken aback by the view in the valley far below as they reached the height of land. No doubt it was the work of Odziohozo, the Transformer. He had reached into this vast forest and lifted out a great portion of the earth, leaving the valley far below to stretch endlessly before them, just as he had channeled the other rivers and basins. A flock of geese flew gracefully over them in V formation. Keoka envied them their freedom and beauty. Somehow, she knew she would like this country.

She decided not the mention Pemola again, but she would ask this Father Roland of the spirit world if he knew of Pemola. What did these braves know? Had they ever seen this strange new God? The air grew cooler here and she was glad when they stopped to make camp.

They made camp near a big beaver dam. The fir boughs were tipped with frost when they woke in the morning. Keoka was grateful for the extra blanket she found spread over her, but wondered who put it there.

She hurried to the warmth of the fire, where Francis and Plausawa were busy cooking fish, dropping them into a steaming kettle. She felt a blanket being placed on her shoulders and knew it must be Sebattis.

"Keoka should have guessed it was you, Sebatt...."

As she turned, she was momentarily taken aback to find Metallak, and not Sebattis, standing behind her. Seeing her quick blush and confusion, he motioned her to be silent as he whispered, "Yonder the beavers are holding council to seek justice. It is amusing to watch them."

They tiptoed closer to the beaver pond to watch. Keoka scarcely dared breathe as Metallak stood close to her. She drew the blanket closer over her shoulders, enjoying the quiet intimacy between them. She could see the large family of beavers behind the thick barricade in the water.

The council members sat silently in a semi-circle while the leader addressed the jury. He gesticulated wildly with his paws, stopping now and then to look from one beaver to the other smacking his tail against the water for emphasis as he paused in his oratory. Keoka giggled.

"Shhh," Metallak whispered, "they will hear you."

The guilty beaver was apparently accused of not holding up his end of the workload, judging by the motions of the leader and the untouched wood at his end of the dam, evidence of his laziness.

The jury conferred at length, with heads drawn together in strict confidence. Next they proceeded to form a line. The guilty beaver hurried toward shore, looking for an escape route, but there was none. As he lay there in fright each of the beavers took his turn at smacking the guilty beaver with his tail, making a great smacking sound. Then he was left all alone.

23

At first Keoka thought the guilty beaver was dead, so still did he lie. But he slowly slunk off into the water, battered and sore, to hide in shame at the side of the pond. Metallak addressed Keoka without moving.

"The beaver is truly wise, and settles his own quarrels well." He did not add that the beaver was much revered by his people, that he himself had been named for the beaver.

"Does the jury never make a mistake?" she asked him.

"Did you now see the look of shame on the face of the guilty beaver?" he returned. Keoka shivered as she returned to the warmth of the fire. She hoped Metallak would never learn that she had been cast out by her people. Even so, she had found a soft spot in Metallak. Truly he cared for her and perhaps would change his mind about this one he was pledged to marry.

As Metallak took leave of Keoka, he too thought with guilt of Mali but he brushed the thought from his mind. Besides, he had done nothing to feel guilty about, except try to keep Keoka from freezing. But his small act of kindness had not gone unnoticed by his friends, who nudged one another and whispered by the fire. Could it be that Metallak was interested in Keoka?

But Metallak remained quite aloof for the rest of the journey, and Keoka sometimes thought she had imagined the day the beavers held court. On the thirteenth day of their sojourn, they turned the canoe deftly into the cove on the lush green banks that bordered their little village. The old familiar odor of drying skins and fresh venison wafted through the air.

Placing the canoe face down with a log over it for safety, they climbed to the top of the bluff in back of the little church overlooking the St. Francis River. There they stood for a moment taking in the sights.

The entire village, it seemed, from old men to small boys, was clearing and sweeping the roadway. In the cool freshness of mid-morning, women giggled and whispered as they decorated the street altar with their best beads and necklaces. They paid scant attention to the strangers on the bluff.

Keoka could see many lodges in the village, most of them long, rectangular buildings. Some were made of logs, others of skins, very much like the villages of the Sauk people. She knew that several families probably lived in one lodge, and wondered where she

24

would be placed. She had never seen this strange object that the women fussed over. It looked like a large wooden block covered with pretty pieces of cloth, and the small images sitting on it had faces like humans. Around the necks of these faces, they hung beads and necklaces that glittered in the sunlight. She hoped that she, too, could join in this fun.

"Watch this," said Plausawa, as he sent a stone skimming into a circle of young boys. It spun like a top before it came to a stop. The boys' keen eyes soon detected the young men, and soon they were all surrounded, the villagers chattering.

"Metallak is back. John Baptiste, too, with Francis the Greater and Francis the Lesser." There was much cheering and back slapping. Keoka felt very awkward as she looked on. She felt many eyes on her, and envied the young men as they were welcomed home.

The women stared at Keoka curiously, this small woman who stood apart from them and shamelessly walked just as the men did, with feet outstretched in front of her. "Who is this strange one?" they whispered among themselves. Mali Oozalluc looked closely at this beautiful girl with the strange hair that seemed to sparkle in the sunlight, but stubbornly refused to lie straight, like the hair of some of their white friends. She had waited three years for Metallak to return. Surely this girl was only visiting for the Feast Day.

The Chief came slowly forward while two of the elders ran for the missionary, Father Roland, who was working as hard as the villagers in preparation for the Feast. The young men pretended not to notice the looks of envy from their younger brothers, or the interest of the nunksquaws, hiding behind giggles and whispers.

"My children, my children, this is indeed a pleasure," said Father Roland, his red curly hair clinging to his tiny cap. "Now we have cause for a double celebration tomorrow. Let us give thanks to Our Lord."

Solemnly the villagers crowded around in a semi-circle for a prayer of thanksgiving that these scholars of Wheelock's Indian School had returned in time for the Feast Day. Father Roland smiled at Keoka.

"And who is our honored guest?"

"Small one is called Keoka," said Metallak, stepping forward to stand at Keoka's side. "We ask that you make her welcome in our small village."

The women gasped. Never before had four young

men brought a single nunksquaw home unchaperoned like this. But when Metallak recounted her ordeal with the trapper at the hands of the Iroquois, their enemy, they clucked their tongues in sympathy, and invited Keoka to join them in their activities.

Keoka smiled shyly as she joined a group of women. Never before had she seen such feverish cleaning activity in her life, except in the white settlements, where some women were foolish enough to beat their rugs or hang them outside. It was whispered that they even scrubbed their floors with sand.

"Keoka will help too," she said, able to make herself understood to the other women with her mixed tongue of English and Abenaki. She was ashamed that she had no beads to contribute for the altar.

"We make ready for the Feast of the Blessed Sacrament," explained Mali Oozalluc, studying Keoka carefully. "We will carry the street altar in a long procession through the village tomorrow. All must be in readiness before sundown."

Although some of the women hung back, jealous of her beauty and having an uneasy feeling that Keoka was much too comfortable around the young men, Mali Oozalluc persuaded them in her favor.

"Let us all make Keoka welcome as one of our own. It is Metallak's wish. Did you not hear him say that her life has held much sadness, that she needs to have friends now?"

Soon they all joined in, welcoming Keoka and examining her hair closely. If Mali did not fear this strange nunksquaw, why should they? Everyone in the village knew that Mali hoped to share Metallak's lodge one day, and had prepared many baskets and rush mats in his absence. They finished their work and joined together in a hymn before going to their lodges, bidding Father Roland good night at the door of his small church.

Keoka watched these activities with surprise. Never had she seen a path swept through the entire village, or a street altar all decorated. The altar was truly beautiful, with white vestments, and silver images set in among the wood carvings. And all of them wore sparkling jewels, even the sad one who hung on the cross. Never had she expected a Missionary to look like Father Roland, or act like him. Although he dressed strangely for this warm weather, wearing long black garments, he was just as kind as Metallak. He did not laugh as the others did when Keoka asked foolish questions. She was certain he

26

would understand about Pemola.

"Keoka will share Mali's lodge," Mali told her. Although her voice was warm and inviting, Mali was disappointed that Metallak had brought this other one, but perhaps he was only being charitable. Was there ever a time that Metallak did not bring home the wounded or the maimed? Besides, Keoka needed kindness after the ordeal with the trapper.

All of Mali's relatives made Keoka welcome in the lodge. There were colored mats for sleeping, some of them hand embroidered. On the center pole hung a kettle of soapstone. Other pins in the center pole held baskets of all sizes and shapes, woven with great skill and patience. Keoka already envied Mali the comfortableness of her lodge. Each family in the lodge had their own fire, and their own door flaps facing the north and the south. Keoka felt safe here, and slept well on the new mat Mali had given her.

At the first opportunity, Metallak made his way to his own family lodge, eager to see familiar faces and the same old amulets and furs on the walls. At the sight of his aged but dignified mother who still walked straight and had all her teeth, pride filled Metallak's chest.

"Have you clothing?" he asked in Abenaki.

Silently she handed him a package. He opened it and held up the new shirt and leggings in appreciation. They were a pale fawn color and of the softest doe skin. The shirt was cut in the fashion of the white man's clothes, with sleeves attached, but delicately embroidered along the shoulders with multi-colored moose hair and quills. And there, on the left breast, was embossed the bald eagle, in honor of Metallak's family sign of beauty, grace, and strength. Always it would be their family totem. In a still smaller package, he found a soft, pliant pouch about ten inches long, made from the ears of a moose, and carefully stitched up the sides. It would be perfect for carrying tobacco or supplies. Hurriedly donning his new clothes, he smiled his gratitude to his mother.

"Metallak still rescues captives," she remarked casually.

Metallak blushed, knowing that his mother favored Mali over all others.

"You will like her, mother. Please give her a chance to prove herself."

They stood awkwardly for a moment before his mother spoke.

"Very well, my son, if that is your wish. But remember, you will one day lead your people. You must give them no cause to gossip."

Metallak changed the subject, relieved that his mother would give Keoka a chance. "Metallak also has a gift," he said, and drew from his pouch a necklace of pearl, held together with sinew of the moose. Shyly, his mother took the necklace and started to pull it over her head.

"No," she said, suddenly making a decision. "Molly Messel will make a sacrifice for the Blessed Sacrament. Let the jewels first be worn by the Infant Jesus in the procession before they appear on Molly Messel's unworthy neck."

Metallak nodded approval. Looking at her gentle expression, he was reminded of the Madonna herself. Her graying hair was parted in the middle and drawn carefully back to expose her beautiful black eyes and high cheek bones. Tiny earrings adorned her small ears.

Walking past her, he went to stand in one corner of the lodge, where the rocks and barks were kept. Here was the Cowassuck library of important events and visitors, who came to smoke the Calumet or to deliver a branch of wampum. Scratched out on the rocks were the names and dates of these events, and Metallak knew them all by heart. Some records, of course, were kept by the good fathers, like The Peace Treaty of 1685 which guaranteed his people protection against the Mohawks by the English. All this he knew from the good fathers, but now at last he could read these documents himself, as well as any white man, after three years at Moor's Indian School.

From the time he was a boy, this had been his favorite place in the lodge, and he had studied the writing carefully to learn more of his Otoamon, his brother and sister relationship, often called by his tribal brothers as totem. Sometimes, the inner layer of bark from the birch tree had been used to record the names of the brothers and sisters born to one mother. These fragile rose colored papers Metallak handled with great care.

"Always Pial finds Metallak among the rocks," said his father, who had entered silently and observed Metallak among the rocks and papers.

Metallak stood and drew forth a pearl handled knife, exquisite in shape, and grooved to fit the hand of its bearer. He would tell his father later how he had won it in a game against his white brothers in a canoeing contest.

"Pial is proud to carry such a fine knife," said his father. "Come now, let us appear at the door of our lodge, so as not to offend any visitors."

Metallak pulled on some old moccasins and joined his father, but he was puzzled that his mother had not prepared that which he truly needed more than any other, footwear. As he turned to follow his father, his mother handed him still another package. No doubt this was the moccasins.

"Old Molly did not make this gift," she said mysteriously, and gave Pial a significant look. It would be his duty to inform Metallak that while Mali Oozalluc had patiently waited for him to return, she had made many preparations for their own family fire in the lodge one day. Molly's heart longed for more grandchildren. After all, what else was an old woman good for, except to help bring up the grandchildren?

Pial curtly grunted his assent, turning abruptly to go outside. These matters of women could wait. With the Pastoniak, the settlers, clearing land on both sides of the Coos in their corn fields of the upper Kwini-teguh and their loyalty sworn to the English, there were grave matters to consider.

Metallak knew that the mission was divided into two camps, those like his father, on the side of Joseph Louis and the rebel sympathizers, and those of the English loyalists. He knew, too, that his brothers had marched against the English during the Revolution, and like them he would support his white brothers who wished to live in peace. Pial had grown old and weary of the deceit and promises to his people. He was growing weary of Tom Hegan's activities; the threat of war. He looked forward to Metallak's help, now that he was educated in the white man's ways. The British, it seemed, were suspicious of every movement, and Metallak dared not speak his innermost thoughts where they stood in front of the lodge. They were approached by a sentry.

"You are the one called Metallak?"

Metallak nodded. "You are to appear to Luc Schmid tomorrow morning," he told him.

"But tomorrow is the Feast Day," Metallak answered. "Nonetheless, you will report to Luc Schmid. These are my orders."

Metallak nodded his assent and the sentry moved

on. He wondered what Commandant Schmid would ask of him, and whether he would have to leave before the Feast Day celebration.

His father decided they must speak alone as soon as possible.

"Come, my son, let us go to our sweat lodge," he said, and Metallak eagerly headed in that direction. Here they could relax and speak privately without intruders. They approached the small, round hut made of wickerwork, covered with skins and barks. It was all prepared. There in the center were the heated stones. Soon, Old Molly would pour cold water over them to make steam and cause them to sweat. Later several of the young warriors would use the bath, but for now Metallak and Pial had some privacy and could speak openly in their native tongue.

"Tell me, my father," Metallak said when they were finally alone. "How is it that Antoine is Grand Chief of the village, and not Joseph Louis?"

"The English no longer trust Joseph Louis after the escape of Major Whitcomb."

"Joseph Louis let Whitcomb escape?"

"This much Pial knows. They made camp only twenty-four arpents from here, on a small island in the St. Francis River. After supper, they all bedded down. Joseph Louis even shared Whitcomb's pillow, a small sack of flour. While all was quiet, Whitcomb fled to a canoe with paddle and gun already inside. Somehow, Whitcomb took the flour, too." Pial scrubbed himself with the rough fir tips and continued.

"When our Abenaki brothers sought to hunt down Major Whitcomb, Joseph Louis stopped them, saying it was God's will that Major Whitcomb's life be spared. Our brothers listened to Joseph Louis, respecting his authority. But after they returned to the village, some betrayed him and told Luc Schmid that Joseph Louis made a deal, maybe even arranged the whole escape."

Metallak leaned back and enjoyed the steam bath, the first he had felt for three long years.

"And what do you think, my father?"

"Could be many things. Joseph Louis never got over the deadly raid by Rogers and the horrible death of his first wife. Perhaps he fears for his second wife. Then, too, being Chef-de-la-Priere in our village makes Joseph Louis grow soft and preach always the word of God."

"At Wheelock's School, it was rumored that Joseph Louis had been banished from the village."

"This is true. For a long time Joseph Louis was banished from the village. But, in spite of all, there has been much disruption here. These treacherous acts always point to our people, and the English grow more suspicious each day. Some families have even turned against each other. Knowing this, the English sent for Joseph Louis to re-unite his people."

Metallak sipped his tea. "Then why is Joseph Louis not Chief?"

"Well," his father explained, "Joseph Louis finally took the oath of allegiance to the King to show the English his loyalty. Then he was made welcome in our village again. To prove his loyalty further, he took Colonel Carleton's scouting party into the northern grants so that finally the soldiers found the eastern part of the Bayley-Hazen road." Pial chuckled quietly at this, knowing many false attempts had been made by their English friends to locate this elusive road.

They sipped the hot fir tea, which was always drunk when one used the sweat lodge if he wished added strength.

"Last winter," Pial continued "Captain Fraser came from the Department of Indian Affairs to see Joseph Louis. Told him if he could stop all this plotting in the village they would make him Grand Chief."

"How is it that Joseph Louis refused such an honor?"

"Joseph Louis refused, but begged that Antoine, his half-breed son, be appointed in his place. That is how it all came about. It must have been a big surprise to Francis the Lesser, Plausawa, too, to learn that their younger brother has outranked them." Pial finished his tea, then decided the time had come to discuss this woman called Keoka.

"But what of Metallak? How is it that Metallak brings home a strange one, as small as a child, who knows not of our God or our people? Surely it is only an act of kindness."

Metallak was glad the darkness of the hut did not disclose the redness of his face when Keoka's name was mentioned. He was angry, too, that he still felt like a boy in his father's commanding presence.

"Her life had been filled with sadness," he said

31

quietly, "yet she never complains. Already her arm looks better."

"But there is no involvement between you?"

Metallak cleared his throat, feeling uncomfortable. "When Metallak is near her, he thinks of no other," he confessed. "Besides being brave, she is very beautiful and closer to my age than Oozalluc." Because there were so many young women named Mali, he preferred to use her last name, Oozalluc.

"But Keoka is not of our people," Pial protested.

"One day, I will lead our people as you have done before me. Surely I have the right to choose my own wife."

"Her beauty blinds you to the truth, my son. But real beauty cannot be seen by the naked eye. Oozalluc has such beauty, but one has to search for it, like a rare and precious stone, to be cherished forever."

"But surely you look forward to grandchildren, my father?" Metallak challenged. "Oozalluc is already past her thirty-fifth summer."

"But she is strong and buxom, my son," laughed his father. "She will bear many sons."

"I have only known Keoka for two short weeks, father. Please give me the summer to make my decision."

"That is a wise thought, my son. Meanwhile, Pial will send scouts to Keoka's people and ask them to come for a visit."

"But she has no people left there. Her father died many years ago, and later her mother. She is alone in the world." Metallak felt very uneasy about Keoka's past, and preferred to believe what she told them. He hoped his father would not challenge him.

"Very well, Metallak," Pial said slowly. "Let us watch and wait. That is the habit of wise ones. Never forget that Metallak wears the totem of the bald eagle, king of all birds."

Relieved, Metallak chose to let the matter rest. He departed, to meet his father later at their lodge. He was relieved, too, that so far he had not encountered Tom Hegan. Perhaps his father had already cast him out of their small village before he stirred up more trouble. Somehow, Metallak felt that his father would have preferred his own son to be more like Tom Hegan, ruthless and unfeeling. Though he never spoke of it, Metallak knew Pial was secretly proud of the fear and respect that Tom Hegan commanded, especially among the white settlers. As long as he remained with them, the whites would never again try to destroy the village of St. Francis. In this, his father

32

was wrong. Tom Hegan would only betray them at the first opportunity. Metallak was glad to let the matter rest, at least for tonight, and joined his father at their lodge. It seemed good to be in old familiar surroundings.

Early next morning, Metallak approached Luc Schmid's lodge. He stood respectfully at attention while Luc Schmid remained seated. They studied each other. Luc Schmid was thinking that now was the time to test the loyalty of this educated Indian, whose athletic prowess was the object of many wagers in camp. Metallak, too, was thinking: "This man would be a good friend if he were on my side. He is sure of himself and a good commander." Luc Schmid spoke first.

"I wish two prisoners delivered to General Haldimand at once, Metallak. Can I count on you and Sebattis? You will accompany my sentries as guide and Sebattis can pilot the bateau."

Metallak countered the questions. "Commandant, my father tells me that you will not permit the fall hunt. Our people will be hungry before the snows come."

Luc Schmid narrowed his eyes. He had been thinking for some time about this situation, and had already decided to ask permission for the fall hunt. They all needed meat. He decided to test Metallak.

"There will be a gift of four ducks for the General. You may pick them up at the Despin farm before you leave. When you deliver the prisoners," he instructed, "wait for a return letter to me from General Haldimand."

"What may I tell my father of the fall hunt?"

Luc Schmid lit his pipe, puffing slowly. "If the prisoners are delivered safely, the letter will permit the fall hunt. Plan to leave tomorrow, after today's festivities. I will await your return." He tapped his pipe as he studied Metallak, who stood impatiently to be dismissed.

"My men tell me you have rescued a beautiful half-breed, that you gaze upon her with fondness and affection. For her own safety, I would advise a speedy return. My men have not seen a beautiful woman for many months." With that, he returned to his papers.

Metallak stood for a moment, angry that Keoka

33

should be used as bait against his return. Did the English forget that an Indian's word was one of integrity, without trickery? He left quickly, the blood pounding against his temples in anger. As he returned to the lodge, he saw Oozalluc and thought guiltily of the moccasins in the package. They were nicely stitched, and also embroidered with the emblem of the bald eagle. He would give anything if he truly loved her. Even if she had been attractive, and many years younger, his heart did not hammer when she stood close as it did when he approached Keoka. Yet he felt comfortable around her, knowing he could tell her intimate secrets and she would understand. Though some said she looked like a fat pumpkin ready to harvest, Metallak knew that she was a good woman, and a true Cowassuck. But marriages were no longer planned by the parents, and he was entitled to some choice in the matter.

He spoke abruptly to all of them, the words of Luc Schmid ringing in his ears. "I am allowed to remain for the feast day, but leave at first light to deliver the two prisoners. Then, if all goes well, the fall hunt will be permitted." He brushed past them into the lodge without waiting for a reply, not bothering to conceal his anger.

Ashamed of his rude behavior, Old Molly stared at the ground, not daring to meet the eyes of her husband. Oozalluc looked away painfully, certain that Metallak wished to avoid her. Pial, too, was offended, thinking Metallak must learn to control his temper or he would never be Chief.

Metallak sat with his head in his hands, ashamed of his conduct. After only one day back at the village, he had once again let his temper get out of control, to no purpose. He knew that following the celebration his people hoped to depart for Indian Stream to their summer quarters on the Kwini-teguh. The lush green meadows and forest were filled with the finest moose and deer, to say nothing of the fishing. He, too, hated the confinement of this tiny village and longed for the freedom of the ancestral grounds.

He felt trapped–forced to stay here with his people, where they felt safe and secure, even though he longed to explore the hills. But he felt even more trapped by his parents, who expected him to marry Oozalluc and set a good example for his people. Why should he spend his life doing what others wanted? He had gone to the white man's school, as his father asked. But he would pick his own wife, no matter what the consequences.

Keoka

CHAPTER THREE

Metallak joined his family for a breakfast of fresh salmon smoked over an open fire on long sticks. He refused to meet their inquisitive eyes, especially those of his father. His mother smiled as though nothing had happened, handing him a large fish and chattering about the coming activities. After she had returned to the lodge to change her attire, he remained at the fire with his father.

"This is good news you bring, my son, about the fall hunt."

Metallak agreed, eager to make amends. "With the summer harvest of corn and squash and fresh meat, there should be plenty until the fall hunt after we have returned here to the village" Metallak bravely continued.

"Why do we have to return here for the fall and winter? Why not stay in the hunting grounds where we have our freedom?"

"I, too, have considered this," Pial said. "But here the long wooden lodges protect us well from the snows, as well as from attack."

"But surely, my father, you do not plan to fight the settlers along the Connecticut? They are many and we are few. With the supplies we can get from Green's Trading Post, there will be plenty for winter without more raiding."

"Let us hope so, my son."

Inside, old Molly finished dressing. She wore a delicate white mantle with small blue and white trade beads adorning it over her plump but dignified figure. A crown of beads was drawn back over her forehead and intertwined with her hair in the back. She contemplated her duties for the day, and prayed that nothing would go wrong. Being a village trustee sometimes made enemies, especially among the young women, who had to be watched carefully. There were always some who, by their speech and actions, seemed to invite trouble.

She knew all too well what would happen if skwedai-nebi was brought in for the festivities. The white man's rum was evil

36

and caused disruption, sometimes even fighting. In the back of her mind she knew that she worried most about Metallak, who had a weakness for this intoxicating drink. She hoped he would set a good example on this special occasion and not anger his father. It would mean so much to her if they could get along peacefully. It seemed their explosive tempers always drove them apart, until they were almost strangers to each other. But after their long talk in the sweat lodge last night, she began to take hope. Perhaps now they would be friends.

She busied herself making asobakw, Labrador tea, to offer her guests. Curious eyes followed the appearance of Keoka and Oozalluc as they approached her lodge. Indeed, they made a sharp contrast. Keoka's hair was neatly pulled back into one large coil that draped down her chest like a rope. Oozalluc had pulled her own thick black hair into two fox-like tails at the side. Somehow, they had contrived to find bright ribbons to adorn their hair. The two of them giggled as they sauntered self consciously through the village, aware of the many stares of the villagers. Keoka had scrubbed her tunic, which molded to every curve in her small body, even without a belt. Only her crown of hair and blue ribbons completed the ensemble. Oozalluc, too, wore a plain garment, with lovely embroidery in the four corners, embellished with a lovely beaded belt in yellow and blue. Some of the villagers gasped as Keoka brazenly walked with her shoulders proudly held back, her feet straight ahead. As he watched them, Metallak thought Oozalluc's rolling gait with her feet toed in and her shoulders hunched forward looked far less appealing. He couldn't help but compare Keoka's tiny frame to Oozalluc's thickness as they drew closer. Remembering Luc Schmid's words, he searched the area with his eyes and they rested on two soldiers, indolently leaning against a tree, watching. He drew in his breath. Perhaps Luc Schmid only spoke as a friend when he urged him to return quickly.

His mother greeted the two women like old friends, complimenting them on their appearance. Once again they giggled, embarrassed at the sudden attention. Flecks of bronze seemed to dance in Keoka's eyes; she was so excited as she sipped her tea.

"Keoka has never had Labrador tea before," she commented as she sipped the tea daintily. "Tea leaves grow here at St. Francis?"

"Here we have many fine leaves to make tea," Oozalluc answered. "There is an abundance of checkerberry, and the wintergreen. For everyday, there is the hemlock, too."

"Will Oozalluc show Keoka where these leaves grow?"

"Perhaps Keoka would like to come with us the next time," offered Oozalluc. She had noticed with a sad heart that Metallak had eyes only for Keoka, but was pleased to see that he wore the new moccasins. She did not blame Metallak. Keoka was an attractive young nunksquaw, even though she did look scrawny and underfed.

Oozalluc discussed her cooking duties with Old Molly, who was busily appointing other trustees to watch the entrances to the village.

"Keoka wishes to help too," offered Keoka, feeling left out in all the activity. Old Molly hesitated, but decided they should not offend this strange young woman her son was fondly observing.

"Keoka will watch over the games," she told her. "Also, you will help keep the little ones busy. But remember, the warriors cannot have skwedai-nebi on this special Feast Day. This would bring discord to our village, and interfere with our games. All must be happy today. Keoka will report to a trustee if she sees this evil drink being passed. This is Keoka's duty."

"Keoka is honored to accept this duty," she said, with a modest smile. Never before had she been chosen for anything virtuous, but here in this tiny village she would make a new start. Soon the women would admire her just as they did Old Molly and Oozalluc. She was delighted with her good fortune.

As they walked to the village center, Oozalluc offered Keoka some bear grease to rub in her hair, but Keoka distainfully sniffed, shaking her head in refusal. Seeing the hurt look in Oozalluc's eyes, she immediately regretted her refusal.

"Keoka does not like fat in her hair," she tried to explain, patting her lustrous wavy hair.

"Surely Keoka wants to look like the others?" questioned Oozalluc.

"Keoka does not like the smell of bear fat," Keoka told her, hoping Oozalluc would forget it. She did not wish to tell Oozalluc that she had once been afflicted with the lice which crawled through her beautiful hair and only after many washings with the snake root did she get rid of this evil condition. The trapper had been very angry when this happened, and would not allow Keoka to enter his lodge until the lice were all gone. He instructed Keoka to wash her hair often and never again to put bear fat in her hair, or even the red ocher to get rid of the insects. Now that she was used to this cleansing of the hair, she liked it very much and bathed in the river whenever she could.

"Keoka is silly," Oozalluc retorted, not arguing, but determined to discuss this vulgarity with the village elders at the first opportunity.

"Keoka's hair was forgotten as they approached the village center, where all was in readiness for the beautiful procession. Many Canadian farmers and their families had come to watch this annual celebration of the Infant Jesus carried through the village. Antoine greeted them, looking truly magnificent in his regal head-dress of feathers, with a bear claw necklace adorning his chest. He rose slowly.

"Antoine will speak now," he said, raising the talking stick for silence. Immediately the villagers grew still. Antoine took great pride in his ability to place names and dates in his head.

"Today we will speak of another time," he began, "a time when the mighty Abenaki nation was unbeaten, when our brothers joined our people from the village on the banks of the Chaudiere, with Father Bigot's help. Game was plentiful and our warriors were many. Our hearts fill with grief as we recall the powerful sickness of pox that followed like fire and killed many. Our many warriors became few. And those that remained were driven from the hunting grounds by the Pastoniak. Remember Paugus and the fall of his mighty Pequakets at Lovewell's bloody hands sixty summers ago." His voice grew stronger and more excited.

"Remember the blood-thirsty Rogers, and his treacherous raid on our village. Pray for the sinners that burned our sacred church and caused the death of our loved ones!" Keoka could hear lamenting and sniffing all around as he spoke. The deadly Rogers must have been a vicious enemy indeed. Suddenly she saw Tom Hegan rise to the platform and grab the talking stick away from Antoine. For a moment, they grappled and she thought Antoine would fall. Tom Hegan's handsome face seemed to undergo a transformation as he took on a wild, crazed look. His voice carried across the entire village.

"Remember, too, how many of the treacherous intruders were ambushed and killed on their return home!" Out of the corner of her eye she saw Metallak and Sebattis crowding up to the platform, to pull Tom Hegan down. He brandished his hatchet and pulled from his pouch a scalp lock, which he held up to the crowd.

Keoka looked around her. The villagers were cheering. Some got on their knees and made the sign of the cross.

Metallak could see Father Roland approaching the platform. He and Sebattis boldly jumped to the platform, forcing Tom Hegan backwards. Metallak tore the talking stick from Tom Hegan, shouting. "Have you lost your senses? This madman will lead you to more death and destruction!" Gradually, the villagers quieted, staring at the ground in shame.

"We'll meet again," Tom Hegan whispered, as he jumped down and made his way into the crowd. Breathing hard, still very angry, Metallak handed the talking stick to Father Roland.

"Let us pray for our Savior," he said quietly.

At this, a loud cheer rose among the villagers, and each took his place in the long processional line, their anger forgotten. But Metallak had seen with his own eyes how easily they could be stirred up, and knew he would have to confront Tom Hegan if his people were to live in peace. Very soon the villagers would have to make a choice, bloodshed or peace.

Joseph Louis, as Chef-de-la-priere, took his place directly in back of Father Roland. Ordinarily, it was his duty to preside over evening prayers and note that each Indian carried out his religious responsibilities. Now he would take the most honorable position of the procession.

Next in line were all of the Chiefs or their delegates, standing side by side in rows of two. They carried long lances, holding themselves rigidly at attention, heads high. There were representatives of the Cowassucks, the Missisquois, the Sokwakis, and the Penacooks, and many other tribes having relatives at the village. There was even a large delegation from their brothers at Three Rivers, who lived not far away on the St. Lawrence.

Keoka took most interest in the third division. She could see Plausawa, Francis, and Sebattis. Where was Metallak, she wondered? She gasped when she saw him, opposite Tom Hegan.

"Do not worry," Oozalluc reassured her, moving closer. "They will not bring disgrace on the procession. Besides, do you not see Sebattis and his friends marching close to Metallak? He is among friends."

All around them they could hear whispers. Surely there would be a fight today, between Tom Hegan and Metallak. Many of them looked forward to this diversion, and hoped to place a small

40

wager on the battle.

A Shaman could be seen moving through the crowd, hovering over shoulders to pick up the gossip. He let it be known that he favored Tom Hegan. The villagers listened attentively, while they speculated. Most of them agreed Tom Hegan would win.

On the other hand, Metallak was not a warrior to dismiss lightly. For many years they had followed Pial in peace, and many of them looked forward to his son taking over. Metallak wore an air of elegance and princely blood as he moved about in his new deerskin leggings and shirt, the front vee neck exposing a chest of thick muscles. In contrast, Tom Hegan wore clothing confiscated during a raid, no doubt: tight black leggings and a silk blousy shirt. Metallak thought he looked more like a white man than an Abenaki.

For a time, the two men ignored each other before their eyes flickered and met, but each looked away quickly. Buried memories of the past worked their way to the surface, and though their faces were unreadable, they longed to settle their differences.

Old Molly hovered nearby, chattering nervously about the festivities. She knew all too well of the ill will between her son and Tom Hegan. One she had borne, and one had been left on her doorstep. Though they bore a strong resemblence of tall lean figures with flashing black hair and eyes, she knew inside they were as different as night and day. Try as she would when they were boys to teach them to be fair and just, Tom Hegan had been hard and greedy, just as he was now. He had a cruel nature that couldn't be curbed, even by Metallak's generosity. Though she often reminded Metallak that Tom Hegan had lost his mother in Rogers raid, she couldn't understand his lust for bloodshed. Stubbornness was a trait they shared, and each had a way of setting his jaw and raising his chin that frightened Old Molly. Except for Tom Hegan's pale eyes, they looked enough alike to be twins. Perhaps that explained her husband's fondness for Tom Hegan and his reluctance to put a stop to the stealthy raids. Once when she had mentioned the strong resemblence between the two boys, Pial had silenced her curtly. She had never mentioned it again.

She remembered vividly that day of their tenth summer, when Metallak won the annual footrace, and Tom Hegan had vowed to get even. Shortly afterward, some white prisoners were brought into the mission village. Most of them were sold, all but one, a small girl prisoner with hair the color of bees honey.

Metallak had begged his mother to keep that one

41

and adopt her. She had blue eyes, as blue as the skies. She followed Metallak around like a puppy dog. Tom Hegan was more jealous than ever and plotted. One day when Metallak went off fishing, Tom Hegan stayed behind and caught the girl, teasing and tormenting her. A group of his friends joined him and they tied her to a tree, shouting encouragement as Tom Hegan threw knives closer and closer to her head. She screamed hysterically, begging them to stop. When they grew tired of this sport, they left her there.

When at last Metallak returned, he found her still sobbing, tied to the tree. After carefully undoing her bonds and carrying her home, he found Tom Hegan and gave him a good trouncing. The little girl was later returned to her home in New Hampshire for a ransom, but Tom Hegan never forgave Metallak for the public disgrace he endured following this episode.

Pial had questioned Old Molly about the incident, seeing no harm in Tom Hegan's sport. This had confirmed Old Molly's suspicions that the boys were closer than cousins. Metallak had been deeply hurt that his father scolded him for his weakness where prisoners were concerned.

"A good leader must never be weak," his father told him many times. "Our first loyalty is to our own people, who have suffered much at the hands of the whites."

To show his father he was not weak, Metallak had doubled his efforts at endurance, spending long hours–sometimes days–without food, always bringing home the most game, which he shared generously. The two boys took care not to join the same hunting parties, avoiding each other when possible. When the time came for education, Tom Hegan had refused to attend Reverend Wheelock's School and learn the white man's letters and words. Instead, he had nurtured his hatred of the whites and used Metallak's absence to his advantage, stirring up the people whenever he could, urging them to make raids on the settlements. Pial watched and waited, wondering which of his sons would one day lead his people.

Finally Tom Hegan spoke, hoping Metallak's temper would get the best of him. Then perhaps Old Molly would see what a troublemaker he truly was. His father, too, often praised Metallak, while he, Tom Hegan, provided for his people by risking his life every time there was a raid.

"It is rumored that Metallak has grown weak, like an old woman. Perhaps he will stand with the nunksquaws while the

42

warriors take part in the games."

Metallak's frown made a deep furrow in his forehead. "You will find Metallak is not a helpless little girl," he said, not turning his head.

"I wonder–I'll wager the little heathen half-breed could put Metallak to shame, even with one feeble arm."

This time Metallak turned and was heard by several bystanders. His square chin drew back and his eyes cold as stone, he warned his old enemy.

"Keep your filthy hands away from that woman, I warn you."

Tom Hegan chuckled, as though he knew a great secret. "Perhaps she already finds me more attractive than the great stone face."

"You only attract one kind–the kind that crawls under stumps."

"And what kind is the little heathen? A saint?" Tom Hegan chuckled again, enjoying his little joke. Metallak clenched his fists, which were wet with perspiration.

All others fell in now, the elders, the women and the children, following Father Roland through the village. At the appropriate time, guns and cannons were set off, and then Father Roland led them in singing their favorite hymns. The harmony of their voices echoed through the vast forest, as they sang a lilting melodic chant that rose and fell like the wind, in a slow tempo.

In seeing the splendor of this devotion, tears came to the eyes of Father Roland, gratified at the piety and devotion displayed by these natives for the little Jesus. He would write his superiors this very evening, describing the festivities.

Keoka watched this activity with amazement. Never before had she seen such devotion, not even for Pemola. She, too, wished to learn the hymns and learn of the Invisible God who brought the entire village together with harmony and laughter.

At last the feast could be consumed. Pieces of blessed bread were liberally distributed. This was the gift of the good father, and all the leftover bread would be saved for their hunting trips, or to mix with their medicines, as an added precaution against the evils of the forest. The boiled sweet corn had been reduced to a soft pulp, which was served along with boiled beaver, venison, and other special cuts of meat. Young wives hurried to pass out more food in the large

43

soapstone bowls. No one must be hungry on such a day as this. Keoka and Oozalluc sat near the trustees, a place of great honor, as they chatted with the other women.

"Now for the games!" announced Father Roland, and once again a cheer arose. Proudly, the older warriors looked to their sons and nephews to demonstrate all their skills. Many proudly placed a small wager on those who were known to be gifted. The single women enjoyed this part of the Feast Day, cheering and encouraging their favorites, wishing them luck. Keoka joined in gaily, cheering for Sebattis and Metallak, wishing she had something of value to make a wager.

Suddenly, she found her arm gripped in a powerful vise, as someone whispered in her ear. "You cheer for the losers, little one. Cheer for Tom Hegan instead." She looked up into pale amber eyes filled with laughter, his head already thrown back in victory. She edged away, fearful of this man who hated Metallak and who incited the people. Again he whispered in her ear as she pulled to get away. "Tom Hegan will win a prize for the little one. Besides, you waste your time thinking of Metallak; he is already spoken for." As she looked where he pointed, she saw Metallak, his head drawn close to Oozalluc's, deep in discussion.

"I must go to the children," she told him, as he slowly released her arm. She could see brown tobacco stains on his teeth as he smiled, taking in every inch of her small body. She hurried off, feeling dirty, pouting because Metallak was still pledged to Oozalluc. If only she could make him jealous, perhaps he would notice her. The children beckoned, and she followed them to the edge of the village, where a tall tree had been staked into the earth and surrounded with dry wood. Eager young boys brought fuel for the fire, with Keoka proudly supervising. Then Father Roland came to bless the fire and ignite the log. Flames shot out as the dry punky wood ignited, and circled the tall tree, the flames rising higher and higher.

"Let us begin," said Father Roland, glad to see the natives enjoying the festivities. This was one of his favorite games, not played in the village for many years. The young men, arranged in a semi-circle about twenty feet from the fire, would throw balls at the tree top. The one to succeed in bringing down the most branches would get a prize. Metallak took his place in the circle, angry thoughts crowding forward, almost choking him in his anger. Had he not pleaded with his father to make Keoka welcome? How could she been seen

44

whispering with his enemy, Tom Hegan?

Sebattis brought down two branches, earning a loud cheer from the children. Plausawa was able to bring down three, amid much yelling. Tom Hegan and Metallak had each brought down four branches, and there remained but one branch. As they threw together, the final branch was dislodged amid screams and cheers. Each of them was awarded newly painted miniature bears, or Ogawinnos, their insignia.

In front of all the villagers, Tom Hegan gave his bear to Keoka, who stood uncertainly with the bear in her hands. "Take it, Keoka," the children shouted, so she smiled at them, planning to give the bear as a prize for one of their own little games. Observing this, Metallak placed his own bear in his pouch and walked away indifferently, though he was deeply hurt. Keoka had shamed him publicly by accepting this gift from Tom Hegan. Keoka watched him walk away anxiously. Surely Metallak would not mind that she kept the bear for the small children. She grew so absorbed in the games and excitement, she forgot her duties. Soon the young warriors were passing around a vessie of the rum. One could hear their laughter increase and their quiet behavior grow loud and coarse. Keoka decided to fetch Old Molly as soon as the children had a drink.

She went to find her own vessie, carefully marked for the children, and passed it around. Grateful, the children took in great gulps of the drink, their little bodies bathed in perspiration. Soon many of them began coughing and hiccupping, puzzling Keoka. She sniffed the vessie suspiciously, and drank some herself. The drink was hot and stung her throat, making her cough, too. She felt light headed and warm. As she went to fetch Old Molly, her feet wobbled and the ground moved around, making her dizzy.

Someone quickly went for the elders, seeing the children falling down, some of them sick and vomiting. Metallak came running over as he saw Keoka weaving in the crowd. He gripped her arm angrily, looking around for Oozalluc. "Have you gone mad?" he asked, his face hard as a rock.

"The great stone face is angry," Keoka said, suddenly finding this very amusing. She laughed as though she found this a great joke, unable to stop.

Metallak slapped her, trying to sober her, then she began crying. Old Molly appeared at his elbow, her face weary with disappointment. This, the same old story, took place when the

45

skwedai-nebi was drunk. It had always been so. She confronted Keoka, only to find her giggling helplessly. "Go to your lodge now and we will speak of this later."

Meekly, Keoka allowed herself to be led away to Oozalluc's lodge to sleep off the effects of this evil drink. "Old Molly is disappointed," scolded Metallak's mother with disapproval. Keoka continued to giggle, unable to stop herself, while Molly continued. "We have welcomed Keoka as a daughter. Still she does not behave like one of us."

While the nunksquaws helped with the children, Metallak stalked off into the crowd, his frown deepening with anger. He should have known it was trouble to bring the half-breed back with them. Why had he let Sebattis talk him into it? She had disgraced the entire village and brought shame on his parents. He was grateful that Pial was officiating at the games and had not seen Keoka drunk.

Sebattis joined his old friend in sympathy. They walked silently until Sebattis defended Keoka. "Do not think too harshly of her, Metallak."

Metallak spoke in a stern, unforgiving voice. "She has brought disgrace on our people."

"I'm not so sure, my friend," Sebattis retorted. He could see Francis and Plausawa running toward them, in great urgency.

"Metallak, I must tell you something," Francis said, huffing and puffing from the exertion. He had searched the village far and wide for Metallak to tell him what had happened.

"It wasn't Keoka's fault," put in Plausawa. One of the children saw Tom Hegan exchange drinking bags. You can ask him yourself! Keoka thought she was giving the children the drink she prepared for them. Tom Hegan has even whispered the secret to another, as his filthy tongue loosens with the skwedai-nebi."

Metallak's face had grown cold with rage, his eyes showing no mercy. His ears rang with a strange feeling that made him dizzy. Blood pounded in his temple as the vein on his forehead grew larger and larger. "Metallak, wait!" pleaded Pausawa, as he stalked off to find Tom Hegan.

He could see a circle of men that attracted a good deal of attention, and headed that way. Soon he could hear Tom Hegan's silky voice.

"It seems we have no competition for the games. Metallak is ashamed to risk losing in front of the villagers." They all laughed, one of them clapping Tom Hegan on the back. "This Feast Day is one to remember," he said, raising the vessie to his lips and taking a deep gulp.

He felt the vessie torn from his hands and thrown to the ground, then saw Metallak's face filled with rage. "Metallak goes too far!" he blustered taking a swing at Metallak's chin. Metallak side stepped and struck Tom Hegan in the jaw, knocking him down. Tom Hegan leaped to his feet like a cat, facing Metallak. All the pent up anger of years gone by surfaced as they struck each other, again and again. Metallak felt a strange exhilaration in his blood, as though his body would never grow tired. Sebattis and his friends prevented any interference by Tom Hegan's renegade friends.

The villagers shouted as they fought, some trying to break up the two warriors, others shouting encouragement. But the skwedai-nebi had taken its toll on Tom Hegan, and he finally dropped in a heap on the ground. The crowd cheered, but for Metallak, the beauty of the day was ruined, and he wanted only to be alone. Oozalluc, never far from Metallak, saw him walk toward the river. Later, she would bring him food and listen, if he chose to talk. She knew his pride had been deeply hurt by the small one who walked like a man. Perhaps Metallak would reconsider and ask Oozalluc to become his wife. Surely now he must know that Keoka was not one of them.

The celebration continued. The young warriors bearing the insignia of the Ogawinno, the bear, lined up on one side, and the warriors of the Pelawinno, the tortoise, on the other. These insignias had been carefully stitched to the shirts of the young warriors by the young women preparing for the festivities. Since the alliance of their two tribes long ago, the mission had been so divided. Each man wore his insignia proudly as a sign of great honor.

For this running game, Sebattis easily took first place, winning a claw necklace of large bear claws donated by the young warriors for this occasion. They feasted ravenously once again before the singing and dancing of the evening hours. Before Nakilhot-kisos, sunset, there would be one last ceremony.

Oozalluc found Metallak with his head in his hands, deep in thought. By now, even Oozalluc knew that Tom Hegan had caused all the trouble.

"I am a fool," he told her bitterly. "I blamed Keoka without even asking what happened. What kind of a leader would I make?"

"You only thought what we all thought," she told him in a soothing voice. Inside, she was hurt. He still had thoughts for no other but Keoka. He hadn't even noticed her new garment or the beaded belt which took six months to make. "Come, let us join the others," she said.

Shame-faced, Metallak accompanied her back to the village, glad it had grown dusky. He could hear his father speaking. "Let us give an account of the Pton-gon."

Keoka had awakened and found the day had disappeared. Slowly it dawned on her that she must have drunk of the evil drink skwedai-nebi. Deeply shamed as the events of the afternoon came flooding back, her face burned. She remembered going to get the children a drink, and then how the ground had wobbled under her feet. She wondered if she had dreamed the part about Old Molly scolding her. And she couldn't understand how it all happened so quickly. Feeling forlorn and frightened, she sought out Sebattis. Maybe he could tell her what happened. Finding him at the edge of the crowd, she whispered, "What is the Pton-gon?" sleepily rubbing her eyes.

"Pton-gon means treasury," he whispered back, with a smile. One look at Keoka and it was clear that she was unused to the fire water. "Does your head ache?" he asked.

She nodded, grateful that he still spoke to her. In the dusky light, she could see Metallak standing next to Oozalluc and shrunk closer to Sebattis, ashamed to be seen. By now, dozens of curious eyes saw them together, saw the brazen way she stood close to Sebattis. It seemed the entire village knew about the fire water, but many of them still blamed Keoka. She should have tasted it before giving it to the children. Old Molly kept her eyes downcast as the whispers reached her ears. Perhaps the villagers blamed her, too, for allowing this to happen. Word had already reached her of Keoka's friendliness with the warriors, young and old, and how she seemed to put them under a spell, each one eager to please her.

"But the children praise her," Old Molly pointed out, as though that closed the argument. "Children know goodness when they see it."

48

But inside, Old Molly's heart was heavy. She had seen how hurt Metallak was this afternoon, and how much he cared for Keoka. But she knew that Keoka would not make a fitting wife for a Chief, and his life would be filled with hurdles and jealousy with such a beautiful wife.

The Council of six men and seven women helped Pial with stripping the altar and returning necklaces, bracelets and beads of wampum. They reported that all was intact, that the village treasury now contained nine necklaces of wampum and thirteen branches of wampum. Pial read the branches of wampum to the crowd, by his interpretation of the color and size of the beads.

"May the resting place of the Abenakis be respected," he said in a strong clear voice. A loud cheer arose, and the cannon boomed once again.

"May the outer covering of their bones be respected," he added, holding up the branch of wampum. Again they cheered. All was intact, and was returned now to the keepers of the village Pton-gon. The necklaces of wampum were evidence of their alliance with other tribes, as well as with the whites, and would be guarded carefully, some even kept in the village church.

"And now, let us make our guests comfortable," said Father Roland.

"Please take me to the lodge before I am seen," whispered Keoka. Sebattis remained beside her, pleased that she had come to him instead of Metallak. "It was Tom Hegan who put the fire water in the drink," he confided. "The villagers know it was not Keoka's fault."

"So that is how it happened," she said slowly. "Does Old Molly know?"

"Metallak knows, and if she has not heard, surely he will tell her," reassured Sebattis, seeing the relief in her eyes. He drew her closer and put his arm around her, amazed that her body was so tiny, yet so firm. She leaned against him, grateful for his friendship and, lifting her head, she kissed him on the cheek. Neither of them saw the stealthy movement in the trees or the jealous eyes that watched them.

"Sebattis is a good friend," confided Keoka, "but Keoka's heart is with Metallak. Do you think he hates me?"

Sebattis felt his heart sink. Somehow he had known all along that she preferred Metallak and yet he had hoped. "Metallak
49

is a fool if he lets Keoka get away," he told her simply. She shrunk back against Sebattis, seeing Tom Hegan approach.

"It seems we half-breeds have a lot in common," he said, with a nasty smile. He picked up Keoka's braid absentmindedly and held it to his face. "We have enemies as well as friends."

Keoka shivered, afraid of him for some reason. Under the careless banter, she could sense genuine hatred. Did Tom Hegan know something of her past? Had the trapper reached him somehow and offered a reward for her return?

Sebattis spoke through his teeth in a low frightening voice. "Get out of our way and stay away from this woman. If any harm comes to her, you will answer to me as well as Metallak."

Tom Hegan stepped aside, still bitter about the fight. "I, too, like the looks of Keoka. Perhaps she would like three men instead of just two?" With a sly laugh, he moved away into the night.

"Stay away from him while we are away," cautioned Sebattis. Keoka promised and hurried inside.

Metallak brooded, hoping to see Keoka, but ashamed to face her. He hadn't meant to slap her, it just happened. It was just that he had wanted so much for the others to like her, and the disappointment had driven him mad. He didn't blame her for seeking out Sebattis. He would never strike a woman, even in anger. He sighed with remorse as he stood awkwardly beside Oozalluc, avoiding her eyes.

"Oozalluc still makes good moccasins," he told her, as he shifted his weight from one foot to the other. "We leave tomorrow to bring the prisoners," he added, not knowing what to say.

Oozalluc knew that his heart already belonged to the small one who shared her lodge. Had he not warned Tom Hegan that no harm should come to her?

"Oozalluc will help Keoka learn our ways," she said, knowing what he wished to hear.

Metallak felt the tension leave his body and the anger fade away. Oozalluc was a strange and wonderful woman. In the moonlight, she was almost pretty.

"She is young and surely she will never drink of the

fire water again," added Oozalluc, seeing the sudden luster in his eyes.

"Wli-nanawalmezi," he said, squeezing her hands gratefully.

"Wli-nanawalmezi," she replied, wishing him good health also. He never saw the tears slide down her face as she hurried away to her lodge.

Metallak and Sebattis set out at dawn with their bateau and two prisoners, uncomfortable with the English sentries aboard. They said little, but surveyed the prisoners under hooded eyes, taking in the dirty tattered clothing and the gaunt, tired faces of the two men, who slumped pathetically in the bottom of the boat.

The sentries secured the bonds of the prisoners once more, placing the two moose horns for General Haldimand around their scrawny necks under Captain Mure's scrutiny. With lewd remarks, they examined their bodies for signs of abuse or tight thongs about their arms. Then they nodded to Captain Mure, who looked forward to the reward money if these prisoners were safely delivered in good condition.

"I hold you to your honor for their safety," he solemnly reminded Metallak and Sebattis. "If they escape, you will be punished. But do not make sport with them either. If they are not delivered in prime condition, they are worthless to us."

"You need have no fear, Captain," assured Sebattis, looking nervously at Metallak, hoping he would not take offense from the crude Captain. He began to whistle a light-hearted tune to change the atmosphere.

Metallak looked straight ahead, ignoring the Captain. He felt the blood pulsating against his temples as his head pounded with rage. "I am an Indian," he thought, "and still a savage in spite of my education. But the Captain is civilized," he thought grimly, "so he is free to sell these men into bondage for his own evil purposes."

He could remember a time in his boyhood when the English had paid his brothers handsomely for the hairpieces of the Pastoniak, as much as fifteen dollars each, in competition with their enemies, the French.

The French, though, had befriended them, issued them firearms, and fought side by side against their enemies. They did not think of his people as savages, but instead, adopted their hunting habits and married their women. Some of them even sent their young ones to live among the Indians as their foster brothers, to learn their language and customs. Metallak called them Coureurs-de-Bois, these brave young men who spoke in his own native tongue, and learned to trap and hunt as well as many of his own brothers. He himself had trained three of these foster brothers and took great pride in their performance and skill in the forest.

But England had emerged the victor, and they had all sworn allegiance to the great King across the sea, who now controlled their waterways and hunting territories.

Metallak resented the sentries who shared his bateau, but he wanted no more bloodshed. Never again would he make raids on the colonies, or kidnap the children of the hardworking farmers along the Kwini-teguh. After the delivery of these prisoners, he would depart to his old hunting grounds, the ancestral grounds of his people, where the wilderness was too dense even for the Pastoniak to settle or the sentries to follow him. Here he could gaze upon the heavens with solitude, near the sacred burial grounds of his people. He had grown fond of his white brothers, but still longed for the stillness and solitude of the forest. Here the wild animals shared his love of privacy in their own private domain.

Then, too, he wished to be alone with his thoughts. He had noted the lines of age around his father's eyes, and the stiffness to his stately gait. Although they never spoke of it, he knew that one day soon he would be Chief of all the Cowassucks, and he wished to remain at peace with the whites who came by land and by sea to the hunting grounds of his people.

But sitting here in the bateau eyeing the prisoners, Metallak knew his people were far from making peace. He was ashamed to be part of this vile transaction of human bondage, aided and abetted by his own people. If he could only persuade his people to stay in the hunting grounds, and not return to the village, they would owe no allegiance to the British. He, Metallak, would show them they had nothing to fear, and win their trust and confidence. He knew this would not be an easy task, with Tom Hegan making enemies everywhere, casting suspicion on the entire tribe.

A few miles upriver, they disembarked from the

bateau and walked across the fields to the Despin farm to collect the ducks for General Haldimand. He loosened the bonds on the prisoners' arms so they could help with the ducks. The sentries saw this, but said nothing. Gratefully, the prisoners extended their hands out to receive the ducks.

"My brothers call me Metallak."

"My name's Josiah," one of the men spoke up. "This here's Gilbert. Had us a place in North Stratford when we was took prisoner."

"Near Green's Trading Post?"

"Up the river a piece," Josiah said, as he stepped into the bateau. Metallak recalled how desperate Keoka had been when they found her near Green's Trading Post. These men, too, would like to escape. He wished he could help them.

He guided the bateau with ease, as they passed through the low banks of the St. Lawrence, the wide cultivated plains extending for miles in the distance. Sebattis would help him when they reached Three Rivers, when the tide from the huge river would be more difficult to control. They made camp along the east bank of the river, on a bed of dry fir boughs, after a meal of fresh salmon. For once, the prisoners had enough to eat. The two sentries had gone for a walk and the prisoners visited as they watched the Indians make camp.

"Why is it the Abenakis always camp on the east side of the river?" asked Josiah.

"It is the way of my people," Metallak said. "The westerly wind blows hard, protects us from the insects."

"Well, I'll be," said Gilbert, glad to know how to avoid the insects. "Can't wait to tell my son about that one." He cleared his throat and looked at Metallak, hoping for a sign that he would help them.

Sebattis, too, glanced at Metallak, but he busied himself making camp. He had given his word and their people would go hungry this winter if the prisoners were not delivered. He could only hope they would be returned home after a short period of captivity. Then he had an idea.

At length, in a few days' time, they approached the narrow straits of Quebec, with its high embankments, a hub to activity and trading with all manner of boats. Even the prisoners looked about curiously. The large city was impressive looking down on them with high, peaked buildings.

As they disembarked, the prisoners were yanked to their feet and stood uncertainly. Metallak had been hoping for a chance to slip them a little corn. He reached out a hand to Josiah, pressing a small sack of corn into his hand. "Perhaps we will meet another time," he said with a knowing look that he hoped Josiah understood. He could only hope that Josiah would find the small map inside the pouch, outlining their passage back through the forest, should they get a chance to escape.

"Mind who does the talking here!" snapped the sentry, prodding the men forward toward the city above.

Metallak and Sebattis remained patiently near the bateau, hoping the sentry would return soon with the letter. They enjoyed the sights and sounds of Quebec as people bustled to and fro to transact their business. Many were farmers, but others were well-dressed businessmen. Ladies passed by–wearing bright colored hats with plumes.

The sentries returned late that evening in jovial spirits, smelling of ale and wine, escorting two ladies who giggled nervously.

"Excuse me, my dear," one of them whispered. "Business, you know," as he approached Metallak and Sebattis.

"Well, here 'tis," he said, waving the letter. "Guess you're to be allowed hunting privileges this fall, after all." He coughed and added in a loud whisper to the lady, "Provided some of us git to go along for our own provisions as well." This delighted the lady, who giggled again.

With a hearty laugh, he told them that they were free to return on their own. They wished to spend a few days visiting old friends. Gratefully, Metallak and Sebattis accepted, eager to be away from these obnoxious men.

They set out at dawn's light and reached the village in three days time, going directly to Luc Schmid with the letter. Both men shifted their feet nervously. Metallak had deliberated for some time about his speech, and he chose his words with care, using his very best English.

"My father's people have given their loyalty to the King," he said. "But always they have planted their corn in the rich meadows of the Cohos, and fished the waters of the Kwini-teguh. They long to return there now."

Commandant Schmid thought for a moment,

tapping the letter. "You are free to go," he said, pleased with the report he received. "And those who choose to remain here at the village may plan for the fall hunt."

"Commandant Schmid is a good man," said Metallak gratefully. "I will go now and tell my father." Eagerly, he and Sebattis left the lodge.

Before they parted, Sebattis and Metallak made plans to search for the prisoners at the first opportunity. When Metallak disclosed the contents of the small pouch, they both had a good laugh, hoping the sentries would be outwitted.

Metallak sought out his father with mixed feelings. He was proud to be the bearer of good tidings and knew his father would be pleased. He was worried about Keoka, though, and couldn't forget the Captain's veiled threats about his soldiers. He knew, too, that she was different from the other nunksquaws and hoped she had not caused more disfavor to fall upon herself with the villagers. His eyes scanned the area, searching for her.

He rushed toward his father, briefly telling him the good news then set off in search of Keoka. He combed the entire village, but she was not to be found. Oozalluc confessed that she had not seen her since morning.

Pial walked among them spreading the news, asking who would accompany him for the summer. "My people," he said humbly, "our English brothers have given their word to Pial that we may spend the summer season in the ancestral grounds of our fathers."

A loud cheer rose from the people.

"It is Pial's wish that we walk in peace among our white brothers who share the meadows along the Cohos. There is plenty for all. Let us remember, Pial's people are few, but the whites grow stronger every day. Let us enjoy the fields that are empty, plant our corn as always, and pray for a good harvest. Let Pial's people show our white brothers that we walk in peace."

Tom Hegan shouted out in anger, protesting: "That is the way of cowards! Let us make an example of the white settlers who dare to intrude on our hunting grounds!"

"Enough!" silenced Pial. "There will be no more raids on the white settlements. Pial has spoken."

At this, Tom Hegan went storming off to pack his things, muttering vile threats under his breath. He would get even with Metallak for this if it took forever. There must be a way, but how?

55

Suddenly, an evil gleam filled his pale amber eyes. The little heathen! He had seen her make her way to the river, and she was all alone.

From her hiding place, Keoka had watched this feverish activity of the villagers making ready to leave. She heard the wives speak of the strange lodges of the whites, and giggle at the strange cumbersome garments they hung on their clothes lines. Feeling left out, she made her way to the river to take a swim in the privacy of a little cove. The cold water stung as she plunged into the water, making her tingle all over. After a long leisurely swim that refreshed her, she climbed out, looking for her tunic. It had disappeared. Frantically, she searched everywhere, imagining the humiliation and shame of being seen without clothing. Then she heard a familiar voice.

"Lose something, Keoka?" She saw Tom Hegan coming toward her, his face leering with lust as he devoured her small body with his eyes. She reached out for her tunic but he pulled his hand back, grasping her by the wrist.

"Give Keoka her tunic!" she spat at him as he twisted her arm. Tears filled her eyes as he twisted her arm, but she made no sound, determined to show no fear. He flung her down as she spat in his face, swearing at her. "You dirty little half-breed, I'll teach you–"

She leaped to her feet like a cat, but he caught her hair and pinioned her against a rock. The coarse demented look in his eyes frightened Keoka as he pressed her against the rock, still pulling on her hair. He lowered her to the ground, making her shiver with fear. She raked her hands across his chest and then his face, drawing blood and leaving deep gashes. It only seemed to excite him feverishly as he panted with lust. She picked up a stone and held it, waiting for her chance. As he lowered his leggings, she flung it at him and jumped into the river.

Frantic at not finding her and thinking the worst, Metallak had headed for the river, knowing that she loved the water. Perhaps she had taken a canoe and left them forever. He wouldn't blame her. From high above, he saw Tom Hegan attack her and started running. He would kill him with his bare hands. He reached the river's edge just as Keoka plunged in, never taking his eyes off Tom Hegan. There he stood, blood dripping from his face and chest. He began running when he saw Metallak. "You haven't seen the last of me!" he shouted back at them.

Metallak plunged into the water to see if Keoka was

hurt. She came to him and flung her arms around him, sobbing against his chest. He lifted her out of the water, carrying her to the privacy of the cove, and cradled her in his arms.

"Keoka must leave," she sobbed. "Keoka has no friends."

Gently he stroked her hair, holding her close, embarrassed that she wore no tunic but unable to take his eyes off her. Her soft curves were wet and glistening with water, and his hands trembled as he touched her. He was powerless to move, his heart pounding with excitement. He turned her dainty face to his own and kissed her gently. "Metallak is your friend," he whispered, kissing her again and again. She looked up at him gratefully, and put her arms about him. With her body pressed so close, he was blind to the color of her eyes, thinking only of her tantalizing little body. He could feel her tiny heart beating under his as the sun blazed on his back, the smell of fresh sweetgrass in her hair intoxicating him with desire. Their bodies merged together in passion as he stroked her tiny body, and buried his face in her hair, kissing her soft pale skin through the hair. Keoka responded to his gentle touch that tingled her body with pleasure, much different than the crude efforts of the trapper. Once again she felt that the earth was moving, that she was suspended in air as their bodies moved in beautiful symmetric rhythm to the primitive pounding of their hearts. The fiery bodies of the heavens came together as their passion intensified, then all was still.

Metallak smiled down at the small delicate creature who looked up at him, and playfully peeked under the mantle of hair that shielded her chest. She blushed and pulled his own short hair, making him jump. He longed to stay here with her forever, but felt the cool air as the sun went down. "We must dress," he told her softly, jumping up. "The villagers make ready to leave."

"Will Keoka come with Metallak's people?" she asked hesitantly.

"I have spoken to my father," he said. "He has told me that all the nunksquaws will do the same share of work, and follow the example of the village elders. I have promised that you will not drink again of the rum."

Keoka stood and pulled on her tunic angrily. "And what would the village elders say about this afternoon, Metallak? I suppose they would say I tricked you into coming here and dragged you into the water. Surely Metallak has never set a poor example."

Metallak blushed, ashamed of his conduct and sorry that he had hurt her feelings. He held out his arms but she brushed them aside.

She walked rapidly up the trail, digging her heels angrily into the loose topsoil. It was one thing to be scolded by a village elder, but another to be reminded of good behavior by a handsome young brave, the future Chief of the tribe. Would she never be included and accepted, even here in the new village? She had hoped Metallak would stand by her now that she had given herself to him with such careless abandon. Perhaps this was just another victory to him that meant nothing.

"Keoka, please think about this. I am not the leader of my people yet."

She turned suddenly. "Will Metallak marry Oozalluc this summer?"

He shook his head no. "After today, Metallak will marry only Keoka."

"Even if it means going against your people?"

"Metallak will never love another," he told her simply. "Keoka will make the elders proud," she said eagerly. "I can help with baskets, supplies, and small children too. In my village, too, we had to harvest the nuts and berries," she said. "Keoka can bring down game, too."

"But that is not woman's work," he explained patiently, hoping she would understand. "It is more fitting that Keoka help with the small children. Promise you will do this for me. And after your instructions by the Good Father, we will be wed. Until then, it must be our secret."

She thought for a moment and then slowly nodded her head. She would try hard to please Metallak this summer. She gave him her most serious look. "You have been kind to me, Metallak. I will try to follow your advice."

He squeezed her hands, overcome with happiness. Surely she preferred him above all others, and wished for the approval of the elders a much as he did. If his father were not Chief, he would run away with her this very minute, even without their approval. But he wished to lead his people one day with his wife by his side. And Keoka would make a lovely bride. She sensed his uncertainty and asked in a small voice, "What if your father says Keoka must stay here?" Metallak looked into Keoka's eyes, so dark and serious, and remembered how

58

badly she had been treated these last few years.

"If my father says no, then Metallak, too, will stay at the village this summer," he told her.

Keoka's eyes lit up with emotion, reflecting the dazzling lights of the sun. Once again she stood on tiptoe and kissed Metallak on the cheek. Then just as suddenly, she was gone, joining in a game with the children. Neither of them knew they had been seen and overheard. One had tears in her eyes as she walked away. The other was insanely jealous, and determined to stop this silly affair.

Metallak walked away in a half daze, nearly bumping into his own mother. "This is not good," his mother scolded. "Keoka is not yet finished with the teachings of the missionary. She is better off here than to come with the villagers this summer."

"Keoka would be a big help with the little ones," Metallak said persuasively. "Small one speaks English, too, as well as Metallak."

Chief Pial joined them and nodded his assent, saying nothing. He also had seen the look in his son's eyes. But his mother added. "The elders will watch Keoka carefully. She will have to work hard."

"She has given her word to please the elders," promised Metallak, running off to find Keoka and help her get ready. Soon the entire village knew that Keoka was joining them. The elders felt this unwise, but they were so happy to be leaving the village for the summer that they wanted no discord among their own people. After all, it was Metallak who had helped gain their freedom. They would try to make allowances for the small ignorant one. But they clucked their tongues in disapproval as they folded and packed the heavy skins while Keoka busied herself packing small stones and colored plumes for the children to play with.

Oozalluc kept to herself, unwilling to face the pity in her friends' eyes. No doubt the entire village knew there would be no wedding between Oozalluc and Metallak. Still, she refused to give up hope. She had carefully observed Keoka when Metallak was away with the prisoners. Perhaps she would take up with another young warrior and Oozalluc would win Metallak back. But try as she would, she couldn't forget the kiss she had seen pass between them earlier, and the radiant look in Metallak's eyes, or the look of triumph on Keoka's face. Sighing, she busied herself packing.

CHAPTER FOUR

When they arrived at Memphremagog, the lake of many fingers, they found moose standing belly deep in the waters, feeding from the watercress. The great clumsy beasts crashed through the water and retreated into the woods in all the excitement. But in the early dawn hours, when all was quiet, Oozalluc knew the hunters were already waiting in their canoes. She could hear the familiar moose call as someone called through a cone of rolled birch bark. The long "ooooo" sound soon brought a bull moose toward the water, and there were sounds of others approaching. Keoka, too, had heard the sound, and daringly crept toward the water to watch.

Pial carefully dipped his birch cone into the water, letting it run back into the lake, like the sound of a cow moose urinating. As the bull moose plunged toward the sound, he raised his bow, and brought the beast down with one arrow. Keoka longed to be out there with the men and show her skill with the bow and arrow, but dared not.

"Good size," Pial said proudly as several men helped him drag the Mozaianbe out to shore. "This male moose stands horse high, and look at the horn spread." "Almost the size of a good corn stalk," teased Metallak, as he skillfully extracted the nose and mouth, keeping the choice pieces for his family, then skinning the animal with a long curved knife. He would leave the rest for the women to take care of, as well as the skin to scrape and cure. He could hear other crashing sounds of moose falling, and knew the hunt was bountiful. He looked back once, pleased to see that Keoka had gone forward to help the women with the meat.

That day, they feasted ravenously, eating the boiled meat in great quantities, as they always did after the hunt. Later, they would cure some slowly over two forked stakes raised four or five feet over the fire, to be saved for emergencies or during the long winter.

The women worked hard at the skins, which were spread on poles over eight feet high and eight feet apart. Carefully, they scraped the skins with their sharp stones, trying not to tear the skins.

It was hot, heavy work, but Keoka heard no

complaints. Every evening after the toil of the day, she would run off for a long swim, washing her hair and cleansing her body. Then she would run through the woods to help dry her long tresses, afraid of the disapproval of the elders if they caught her washing her hair, rather than bathing it with fats as the others did. Oozalluc suspected she was sneaking off to wash her hair, and confided in the elders, who shook their heads in disbelief. Many of them felt she was possessed by an evil demon. Surely no decent woman would refuse to use the precious bear fat to make herself beautiful. Instead, she chose to let her hair fly about indignantly, like a wild animal. Among themselves, they whispered and gossiped. What could be done about this wanton young woman?

Little did Keoka know that her furtive activities were being watched, or what a lovely picture she made in her wet clinging tunic. The Shaman, filled with lust at the sight of Keoka, was determined to win her friendship. He would rub his long dirty fingers together with hope, imagining that he touched her smooth small body and stroked her glowing hair. His greedy mouth drooled with anticipation, thinking how warm she would keep him on a cold winter's night. One night soon, he would make love to her. As she stepped out of the water–he sighed with desire and went off to seek a vision.

Metallak longed to take Keoka in his arms, as he had that day at the village. But here it seemed so difficult. Inquisitive eyes followed them about everywhere, giving them very little privacy. Metallak was tortured by having her so close to him, yet so far. He longed to take her in his arms and run away, far from the prying eyes and gossiping tongues that surrounded them. He told himself over and over he must behave like the son of a Chief, especially now. Here in the hunting grounds of their ancestors, they still feared an attack by the whites and moved about cautiously. He must win their trust and confidence, no matter what the cost. Until then, an occasional kiss –a stolen walk in the woods–was all they would be allowed. But for today, they would be together, it was all planned. He and Sebattis would leave together, to go fishing, and Metallak would join Keoka and the children as they gathered cattails, with none the wiser.

He followed them as a hunter stalks his game, watching the carefree play of the children as Keoka, too, stopped to play their silly games. He wondered where she found the patience, annoyed by their silly chatter. He could hear Keoka telling them in

her soft voice how the young shoots would be dried and made into flour for the coming winter, or boiled down to make a syrup. Oh, yes, they too could help, she assured them. The small flowers and seeds would be eaten, and the soft protective down would be saved to wrap the small infants and cleanse them. Keoka's eyes glowed when she told them this, almost sure that she carried Metallak's child. She must have the softest down to protect his little body. She allowed the children to waste nothing, not even the stems, which would be woven into rushes and mats, or used as darts. The children ran on ahead, as Keoka slowed her pace. Just as Metallak lowered himself from a nearby tree, he saw Oozalluc approaching, pleasantly greeted by Keoka. Angrily, he left to go fishing.

By day and by night, they enjoyed lake fishing, using hooks of bone or wood. Keoka grew braver every day, and often sought out the company of the young braves, avoiding the women whenever possible. She was careful not to do this when Metallak was around, but hoped he would be envious and seek her out. Night after night she fell asleep, pretending that his strong body held her close, making love to her as he had that day at the cove. But she knew Metallak was ashamed of her, unwilling to show his love for her in front of the others. She would show him she didn't care. The young men loved her company and outdid themselves trying to please her. Plausawa made the mistake of telling his friends about her skill with the bow and arrow, and they often teased her about this. It wasn't long before the women heard too, and their tongues wagged over this new development. Keoka felt they were avoiding her, except for Old Molly and Oozalluc, who stood by her loyally. Although Metallak made himself scarce, Keoka was determined to see more of him.

"Where is Metallak?" she asked Plausawa one evening. "Metallak hunts Moskuas," he answered, and pointed to where Metallak was busily scooping dirt into the ground. Curious, Keoka joined him. "Why does Metallak cover the Moskuas?"

"So the small one does not know all about hunting after all," he teased, drawing her close.

Secretly, he was delighted that she joined him, and for once, there were no curious eyes around. "Come," he whispered, drawing her back into the protection of the trees. Feverishly, he pulled her against him, kissing her eyes, her nose, her small mouth, touching her tiny ears.

"Metallak has thought of nothing but this for a

63

month," he told her, his pulse racing. Keoka smiled in victory as she drew off her tunic and held him in her arms, sensuously touching and stroking his body, as they passionately possessed each other with tender love.

Darkness protected them as they returned to the tunnels of the Moskuas, and Metallak instructed her eagerly. "First we close off the tunnels, all but one. Then when the Moskuas climb out of the ground, he is clubbed in the head." He showed her the club made from the dried roots of a large tree.

"Keoka will use the club on Metallak instead, if he avoids my company," she whispered.

Though his face betrayed nothing, Metallak felt his pulse quicken, and his heart begin to hammer.

"Until you are accepted by the villagers, our love must be secret," he whispered back, almost angrily. Do you think it is easy for Metallak?"

Keoka said nothing, longing to tell him about the child, but sensing that this was not the time. Surely when he knew that she carried his child, he would wed her, no matter what the elders said.

Metallak nudged her as a muskrat peeked up out of the ground and quickly was clubbed to death as he tried to escape. Keoka enjoyed this new game, and helped Metallak carry their game into camp an hour later, proud of their bounty.

The women jealously whispered among themselves, as they watched Keoka. She should remain with the other nunksquaws, where she belonged. Why should they clean all the heavy skins while she ran off with the men to kill muskrats? Tomorrow she would gather herbs with Moll Ockett. They would see to it. It was not fitting for Keoka to join only the men, laughing and playing games.

Secretly, Keoka longed to explore the forest, and was delighted when Moll Ockett invited her to help gather herbs for the coming winter. It was decided that Oozalluc would go too, and the three women set off for a nearby mountain early in the morning. They were laden with baskets.

Keoka looked forward to their excursion, humming lightly to herself. It was a great honor to accompany Moll Ockett, the village doctress.

Moll was highly respected by the village elders, and yet, somehow, Keoka felt completely at ease with her. Moll did not always worry about what was fitting or proper, and her comings and goings were never questioned by the villagers. Keoka was certain that some of the other nunksquaws were envious when they heard that she had been invited. As they climbed higher, she recognized the mountain ash and the bush honeysuckle.

"That is a pretty plant," agreed Oozalluc, following her eyes to a ripe plant laden with rich purple berries on a short bush. Oozalluc had seen the goodly supply of cattails Keoka had managed to find. In spite of the hard work and heavy bundles, the children all had a good time. Oozalluc had grudgingly admitted to herself that Keoka was trying, and deserved her help with the villagers. In spite of the pain in her heart, she could see why Metallak was so taken with Keoka, and had to admit, she was attractive in an odd sort of way. Moll Ockett pointed out witch hazel shrubs, the high bush cranberry, and the bright red sumac that would be handy for sore throats and fever during the long winter.

Keoka saw her pass by some and went to gather them, anxious to help, but Oozalluc came running over to stop her. She touched her hand to her mouth in dismay when she noticed that Keoka had already picked one.

"But Moll Ockett passed by and didn't see these," pointed out Keoka.

"Moll Ockett always passes by the first three plants, and takes only the fourth," explained Oozalluc. "We must never take more than one from each plant group. Surely Keoka does not wish to offend the underground world?" She shook her head, aghast at Keoka's ignorance.

Keoka shook her head no, embarrassed that she had made such a silly mistake. She was glad Moll Ockett hadn't overheard the conversation. From then on, she watched and observed, only picking what she was told. In spite of her first mistake, she enjoyed the day and envied Moll Ockett, who seemed to know everything about the plants and shrubs. As they descended from the high rocky ground, they gathered the yellow bark of the barberry.

"At home we used this for jaundice," offered Keoka, and Moll Ockett nodded approvingly. "And so we do here also." Later she showed Keoka the Life of Man herb, often used for run-down conditions. The pouches they carried became rough and clumsy to carry and they sat near a cool mountain stream to rest.

"Never forget the roots," Moll Ockett continued as they chatted. "Roots are always valuable in healing the sick, especially the red roots of the black willow which help cleanse the blood." Keoka nodded seriously, absorbing all that she heard. They chewed on their dry meat and drank before heading back to the village. As they passed through an open field, Oozalluc picked up two potato balls from the ground. She pricked herself with a rose bush to show Keoka how quickly the potato ball would stop the bleeding. Moll Ockett was picking the white blossoms of the Yara, which were so good for diarrhea when steeped in hot water. They glanced at the setting sun and hurried to camp, frightened of the wolves.

"Where will Moll Ockett store the plants?" asked Keoka, looking at their large bundles.

"Perhaps one day Keoka will help us grind them up with sharp stones," she heard Moll Ockett reply. Keoka nodded enthusiastically, hardly able to believe her good fortune. So far, Moll Ockett had not scolded her once all day, and treated her as an equal. Keoka hoped they would become good friends.

The village elders were pleased with Keoka's progress as the three of them recounted their adventures that evening. Word even reached Metallak that Moll Ockett was pleased with Keoka, much to the amazement of some of the jealous wives.

Metallak was so relieved that he immediately went to find Sebattis. With Keoka in safe hands, perhaps at last they could search for the prisoners. Sebattis, too, was restless and couldn't believe his ears when Metallak told him they would leave at dawn. "What will you tell your father?" he asked casually, wondering how many knew of their plans.

Metallak could smell the rum on Sebattis' breath, and answered shortly. "Only that we wish to do some trapping and fishing, that we will join them at the seashore." He looked hard at Sebattis, but the words wouldn't come.

"I know, I know," Sebattis told him. "No drinking on this trip." He showed Metallak the empty cup. "It is all gone anyway, just a little I had put away." Eagerly, they parted to get ready for the trip.

Early next morning, Metallak passed by Oozalluc, surprised that she wore a little bear around her neck which he had given her long ago. He was even more surprised when she held out a new rifle to him as he passed.

"It is whispered that Metallak longs for a gun," she said with a smile, "a good rifle for hunting." He was overcome with

66

emotion to get such a fine gift and stood tongue-tied, partly because of the gift and partly because Keoka stood watching not far away.

"It is but a small gift between old friends," Oozalluc continued. "Our white friends pay well for moccasins and baskets."

Staring at her foolishly, Metallak noticed that she looked almost attractive in the morning light, with her sparkling dark eyes, her glossy hair tied into two thick plaits at the side. Somehow, her face didn't look as round as before. He blushed, wondering what Keoka would think.

"Metallak is grateful to Oozalluc," he stammered. "Keoka has also told me of your kindness and loyalty." He wished fervently he hadn't mentioned Keoka's name when he saw the pained look in her eyes.

"Oozalluc will continue to honor Metallak's request to make the small one welcome," she said simply and walked quickly away, tears burning her eyes.

Metallak raced over to Keoka to show her the gun, not understanding her sudden jealousy. "Why does Oozalluc bring Metallak gifts?" She pouted, waiting for his answer.

"We are old friends," he said simply. "Surely Keoka does not mind?"

"Oozalluc is fat . . .an ugly old woman, who dreams only of Metallak."

She saw the stern look that came over his face, turning it hard as a rock with no mercy, his eyes cold. "Oozalluc will always be a friend to Metallak. She has been kind to Keoka too, sharing her own lodge and food. What more does Keoka want?"

Angrily, he stalked off, not telling Keoka where he was going. She regretted her rash outburst, knowing that in spite of her youth and beauty, Metallak was very fond of Oozalluc. What if he changed his mind and decided to wed Oozalluc after all? Feeling confused and lonely, she ran into the woods to cry. Already her body felt swollen, and she wondered if anybody had guessed her secret. She longed to tell Metallak her secret but she never seemed to get the chance. This morning she had waited for him, only to end up arguing with him. After a long cry, she felt better.

"Metallak," said Sebattis in all seriousness, "would

67

you recite the next psalm please?" He held his hands up studiously, like Reverend Wheelock.

With a wild shriek, Metallak threw his friend into the water, chanting a prayer as Sebattis climbed back into the canoe. Carefree as the birds and beasts of the forest, they revelled in their freedom from the village. Neither of them had mentioned school all summer, but they remembered well the long tedious hours, rising before sunrise to attend prayers and then to recite the scriptures aloud. Like a daily ritual, this had been followed by a question and answer period from the Assembly's Catechism, especially if there were guests visiting. Impatiently, they had struggled through the classes from nine until noon, and again from two until five.

The strict discipline had been hard for both these young men, even though they were long past their boyhood. But they had adapted well, making Reverend Wheelock proud. In order to help pay their way, they had become good farm hands, doing all manner of chores, summer and winter. Metallak quickly trained many of the animals to do his bidding, even to eat from his hands.

Like boys, they shared the new gun, bringing down a plentiful supply of game, meticulously saving the skins. Metallak selected the choicest furs among them for Keoka, imagining her long cascading hair flowing down against the fur around her shoulders. Trying to forget her for a moment, he would lie back gazing at the heavens, but even the clouds took on the appearance of Keoka, and he would imagine that she looked down on him, smiling her elusive smile.

"Metallak has a silly smile on his face," Sebattis teased. "Could it be that he dreams of Keoka?"

"And you, I suppose, will become a priest one of these days," Metallak responded.

Sebattis laughed, a hearty laugh. "No, my friend, I'm afraid I would not make a very good priest. But I do not wish to marry either. Not for many years. I value my freedom too much."

"I wanted to get away hoping to forget her," Metallak confided. "But I can't even though my parents do not approve." He turned to Sebattis. "What would you do?"

Sebattis pondered for a few minutes, deep in thought. "I will not give up my freedom for any woman. How can I give you advice? I would say only this, my friend. Take your time and make sure Keoka is the right one."

"You are right, old friend. I will take my time. Let

68

us continue our search today. I am afraid the prisoners were unable to escape after all." Carefully, they had followed the route the prisoners should take if they made their escape, with no sign of them. For two weeks, they had searched in vain, but Metallak hated to give up.

Toward dusk, they come upon footprints that looked bloody. Sebattis spotted the remnants of a shredded moccasin. Cautiously, they tracked the footprints for almost an hour, seeing nothing unusual. Both of them wondered the same thing. Was it an Indian brother or a white man who left the bloody footprints? Then they heard a soft moan, just a few yards away, and discovered two men lying half hidden under a large oak tree. Their feet were bare and bloody, their legs covered with insect bits. The men recognized the two prisoners, even with a dirty stubble of beard and sunken eyes. For a moment, the men stared, not recognizing Metallak.

Metallak helped them to their feet, as they stared incredulously.

"Is it really you, Metallak?" whispered Josiah. "Please help us." He tottered on his feet and tried to smile.

"Are you alone?" asked Gilbert suspiciously, looking around for sentries.

"You are with friends now," Sebattis answered. "It was not our idea to take you to Quebec."

"That's what we figured when we found the map," Josiah said, feeling better. He tried to sit up.

"You are safe now," Metallak told them, giving each of them a drink from his vessie. "But you have gone without food for too long." He took some smoked meat from his pack for them to chew while he brewed a thick broth in the small skillet he carried, and Sebattis gathered hemlock leaves to treat their insect bites. The men sipped the broth, feeling better already. "You ain't goin to turn us in, are you?" asked Gilbert.

"You are as free as we are," Metallak assured them. "The sentries will never find you here."

"Tell us about the escape," said Sebattis as he mixed bark and water to cleanse their legs and feet, which were gouged and bleeding. He tore up one of their shirts into square pieces of cloth and wrapped their feet as he often wrapped his own.

"They sold us to a farmer this side of Quebec," Josiah said.

"One day one of the field hands broke his ankle,"

69

added Gilbert, "and the two of us carried him home."

"We was ahead of the others, and we just took off through the woods."

"That was near three weeks," Gilbert put in. "Ain't had a good meal hardly since then."

Metallak was puzzled about the loss of their moccasins. "What happened to your moccasins?"

"Boiled 'em and drank the broth," said Josiah.

"That was two days ago, the last food we had 'til tonight," his friend added.

The following day, they made their way to the Cowassuck village at Memphremagog, where the prisoners confessed they had become lost and wandered for days. "This place is a nightmare of rivers, goin' in all directions," Josiah told them.

"Worse than a swamp," added Gilbert. "Can't find your way out."

"This country is not easy on strangers," agreed Metallak.

The villagers were surprised to see the prisoners being returned, but treated them well. Moll Ockett busied herself brewing herbs and barks to give them strength, allowing Keoka to help cleanse their wounds. Metallak hovered nearby, unable to take his eyes off Keoka, glad to see that she and Moll Ockett had become good friends. Keoka sympathized with the prisoners and her heart swelled with pride that Metallak had rescued them. She blushed as she looked up and found his eyes resting on her. She rose quickly, suddenly feeling a little faint in the hot sun, and hurried off to her lodge.

"Metallak," Josiah spoke up, "we'll pay you thirty dollars a'piece if you bring us home to North Stratford."

"When do you think you'll be able to travel?" put in Sebbatis, before Metallak could refuse the money. "Tomorrow morning," they answered at once, their faces pleased.

"It is agreed," Metallak told them, and set off to find Keoka. He couldn't wait to tell her about the money. He would have taken them home for nothing, and this was an unexpected surprise. Here and there, people chattered about going to the seashore for a

70

different diet. He, too, looked forward to the change in diet. Moll Ockett passed by, staring at the ground, ignoring him.

Surprised, he ran after her, asking if he had offended her in some way.

She studied him carefully as she replied "Moll Ockett is not easily offended, but what of the small one who eats for two? Does Metallak not wish to father his own child?"

Metallak's mouth dropped open in amazement, not believing his own ears.

"Surely this cannot be so!"

"Why don't you ask Keoka?" He followed her glance and saw Keoka picking berries in the far distance. Without even thanking Moll Ockett, he began running, the words ringing in his ears. "Father his own child?" But surely there was no child, he couldn't believe it. He, Metallak, the father of a child! Keoka saw him running toward her, and wondered what was wrong.

At last Metallak came to a stop, scooping her up in his arms, nearly spilling her container of blueberries. Then he set her on the ground, staring intently. "A strange rumor has reached Metallak's ears," he told her, "that Keoka carries his son. Is this true?"

Keoka stared down at the ground, embarrassed. "Yes, it is true," she whispered, afraid to meet his eyes.

"We will be wed as soon as the prisoners have been returned," he told her proudly. "Soon the whole village will know our secret. Does anyone else know, besides Moll Ockett?"

"Only Moll Ockett has guessed," she told him, knowing she might be cast out of the village if the others learned.

"Do not fear, little one. In a few days, everybody will know." He brought her close and whispered in her ear, and she nodded. They would meet again while the village slept and make plans.

That night, Metallak revealed his plans to Pial, telling him also of the reward money.

"And what if word of this reaches the British?" his father asked anxiously.

"We are no longer on British soil," Metallak reminded his father. "And we had nothing to do with their escape. Is that not true?"

Slowly, his father nodded, convincing himself that he worried for nothing, that the British would never suspect Metallak. After all, it was he who delivered the prisoners in the first place. Old

71

Molly worried in silence. She had never been able to control her son where prisoners were concerned. She might as well hope and pray for the best.

Late that night, Metallak found Keoka as they agreed, not far from the village. He carried a robe of fur to make their bed comfortable and was pleased to see that Keoka had already made a soft bed of boughs. Holding her in his arms, they talked far into the night. He recounted his adventures with Sebattis, and Keoka eagerly told him of her progress with Moll Ockett and the elders.

"The children love me, and follow my orders. Moll Ockett has taught me the use of many herbs too." She looked shyly at Metallak. "Are you pleased with Keoka?"

Metallak smiled down at her, holding her tenderly, the mother of his unborn child. "Metallak does not want to leave Keoka, even for one day." Sighing with happiness, Keoka turned to him. All summer she had wondered if Metallak would turn against her, making her an outcast again. Frightened, she had imagined that she would have to flee for her life. Her heart gave a hard thump. "Moll Ockett says we travel soon to the seashore, where the waves are higher than a man's head." Her eyes were bright with excitement.

"Sometimes even higher than that," he assured her. "Keoka will like the soft white meat found in the seashells. It is very sweet."

"My mother grew up near the place of great waves on the coast," she confided. "We used to talk of my grandfather named Charles. Mother said he married a small woman like me, that he loved her so much he had a great portrait painted of her likeness, and hung it over the fireplace."

When Keoka spoke of her mother, her eyes took on a dreamy far away look. Metallak put his arms around her protectively. "Perhaps one day you will meet this grandfather, and not know who he is."

"My mother always wanted to come home, to bring me with her." Her eyes filled with sadness as she continued. "But she grew very ill one winter. She whispered his name, but I could barely hear her. It sounded like Pickford or Bickford. I only know that I carry the birthmark of my mother, and her mother before her. It is here, in back of my right ear." She showed him the tiny half moon hidden under her hair in back of the right ear.

"No wonder Metallak has never seen this," he

laughed. "It is hidden by Keoka's hair." He kissed the tiny half moon and stroked her beautiful chestnut hair, inhaling the fragrance of sweetgrass.

Keoka sighed and stood up. She must return to her lodge before dawn and her unseemly conduct was discovered. Metallak took her in his arms, whispering. "Metallak will join you at the seashore," he promised.

The serious look on his face made her laugh. "Perhaps Keoka will stay at the seashore, with the tall waves," she teased, and ran quickly away to Oozalluc's lodge.

Metallak and Sebattis left quietly with the escaped prisoners before dawn, not wanting to publicly announce their plans. They followed the Clyde River until they came to the island with the pond.

"There's Derby," shouted Josiah, recognizing familiar territory at last. He knew from there it was just a short portage to the waters of the Nulhegan and then home.

As they approached home, they took in the sights hungrily, the old familiar landscape of Monadnock Mountain, blackish green foliage of the black spruce almost hiding the great stands of red maple, beech, and sugar maple trees. Huge white pines stood out, towering above the other trees majestically.

Coming down the Nulhegan, Gilbert said. "There's somethin' puzzlin' me. Why do you call this river Nulhegan?"

Metallak laughed at this remark and Sebattis finally answered.

"Nulhegan is a white man's word. The Abenaki word, Kul-he-gan River, means wooden trap."

"Feels more like a death trap," shouted Gilbert as they churned through the swift strong rapids once more. He admired their Indian friends as they maneuvered the canoe and managed to stand upright through the powerful current as they were tossed about. Several times they stopped to make shore carries before they finally reached North Stratford, where the Nulhegan joins the Kwini-teguh. A great lump came to Gilbert's throat at the sight of his home, a small cabin on the banks of the river just north of town.

He recognized his brother Elijah, and began shout-

73

ing and waving. Elijah was just about to cross the Nulhegan from Mine-head. They could all see the white cloth hanging in the window across the river. That meant there was mail to be picked up. Letters were scarce in this neck of the woods and the whole town turned out when the mailman came to town. But when Elijah heard the shouts and saw the frantic waving, he blew his tin horn, bringing most of the townsfolk of the tiny little hamlet to the banks of the river.

Mrs. Blodgett threw her arms around her husband, her hands white with flour. The two little ones peeking from behind her wide skirt giggled shyly as Josiah scooped them up and danced a little jig on the riverbank. The townsfolk were overjoyed, not quite believing the prisoners were alive and well. They confessed they had given them up for dead. Mrs. Blodgett couldn't seem to stop wiping her eyes.

"Come on over to my place," offered Samuel Lamkin. "The missus will make us a lunch." They all walked up the hill to the nearby Lamkin place, Metallak and Sebattis feeling terribly out of place. Much as they appreciated all the help, most people felt a little nervous around Indians. Mrs. Lamkin made hasty pudding for the hungry men, the best she could put together on short notice, and everyone gathered round for the captives' story.

"Why, if it warn't for these men, we'd be dead and that's a fact," Josiah told them. "There was days we had nothin' to eat but beech leaves and what bark we could pull from the trees."

"We did have plenty of water," agreed Josiah, chewing on a hunk of tobacco. "And then one day Gilbert gits the idea of fishing' with the end of a pin, so we give it a try."

"And it worked too," added Gilbert quietly.

"And then one day we came across a fire with a hot coal or two left, must of been theirs," he said, gesturing toward Metallak and Sebattis.

"And that's the day we boiled our moccasins for a sip of broth." He shivered, remembering how bitter they had tasted. "Well, the long and the short of it is, we owe these men sixty dollars. Can anyone lend us the money?"

Their friends shook their heads grimly. Some of them even laughed

"Land sakes, we can't even pay our taxes," put in Mrs. Lamkin. "Why, the widow Rhodes was struck off just last month for a dollar and thirty cents."

Mrs. Blodgett whispered to her husband in the corner. These men had kept their word and she wanted her husband to keep his. Somehow, they had to come up with the money. Josiah cleared his throat.

"I've got an idea," he said, turning to Metallak and Sebattis. "Can you men meet us at Green's in the morning?" Josiah knew that Green had plenty of cash money. He would mortgage his home if Green would agree to take up the mortgage.

Metallak and Sebattis agreed to meet them at Green's, and gratefully left the crowd to make camp on the riverbank. All the chatter was giving them a headache. It seemed their white brothers could only be happy when they all spoke at once. Metallak could not imagine anyone living in this state of confusion, glad that his red brothers had more common sense.

When they got there in the morning, it was all arranged. Green, being a trading man and eager to please the Indians, knew a good deal when he saw one. Elijah drew up the paper on the back of an old envelope. It seemed like nobody in town had a piece of paper, it was that scarce. Green asked Metallak, an educated man, to read it aloud. The writing was very small and Metallak had to squint to read it.

July the 19th, 1781, oure friend Indions brought in Prisoners of our men which desarted from Canady which S'd Indions found in the woods and brought in which S'd Prisoners promised to pay S'd Indions 30 dollors apece which prisoners was not able to pay and one Elijah Blogget paid the S'd sum to S'd Indions for the redemtion of Gilbert Borged and Josiah Blogget which was 60 dollors.

When Green handed the men the money, the townspeople cheered and passed around the jug of rum. This was a moment they would all remember. Knowing their fondness for the rum, Metallak and Sebattis declined.

Happy to conclude their transaction, they took their leave, among many hearty handshakes. Mrs. Blodgett pressed hot cakes and home made bread into their arms for the journey. Green followed them outside.

"We will always be in your debt," he told them. "If you ever need anything, please come to me or Jeremiah."

They headed north, planning to head inland later,

making their way northeast to the seashore. Occasionally, they spotted smoke from a lone cabin in the wilderness, or from slash burning, but for the most part, it was a quiet journey. They enjoyed the quiet solitude, each deeply contented that they had outwitted the British. Little did they know that the townspeople still celebrated, and told the story to news-hungry traders. That very day, in fact, word reached Tom Hegan's renegade camp up in Indian Stream of Metallak's victory and the return of the prisoners.

"So," he chuckled, an evil gleam in his mirthless eyes, "our friend has made a big mistake. I wonder what our British friends will pay for this knowledge?" He laughed aloud, a coarse vulgar laugh. "Metallak is a traitor!"

The villagers enjoyed their sojourn to the seaside, especially Keoka. The tangy salt air and the sight of the great lashing waves excited her. The soft clinging mud of the beach was warm under her feet as she ran across the shore, looking for pretty shells. The ghost of her mother haunted her here, and she tried to imagine a little girl playing among the rocks where the waves slapped against the shore with such force. She loved the taste of the sweet meat in the clam shells.

Not far away, where the great ships came in, was a white settlement. Their tall houses crowded about the busy pier. Keoka was entranced with the high circular building made of stone. Like a rugged warrior, it withstood the hammering of the angry seas, day after day. At night the winking blinking lights from the windows guided the sailors to shore.

Each day when she peeked about the settlements, she found several baskets of strawberries along the river bank. So far, she had not been discovered by the white community. The elders looked approvingly at the fruits of her labors, pleased with the berries. Old Molly too was pleased.

But many of the other nunksquaws were jealous. Why should Keoka be allowed to explore the white territory, while they busied themselves with household chores? Here at the shore, Keoka's hair had been forgotten by the elders. She no longer swam in secret, but was allowed to run about the water like a child, just because the children clamored for her company. Like a fish, she took to the angry waves. Instead of tossing her about, they picked her up tenderly and finally deposited her at the shore, laughing with the children. Angrily, the nunksquaws plotted, and finally laid out a plan to get even. They knew that under cover of darkness, Keoka often went swimming without her tunic. They giggled with anticipation as they speculated. What if Keoka's tunic disappeared?

They watched and waited, carefully observing Keoka's habits. Some of the nunksquaws even offered to help with the children, hoping to win her confidence with this false attempt at friendship. Unsuspecting, Keoka welcomed their advances, thinking how proud Metallak would be when he returned. Her eyes glowed when she thought of the child. This child would be treated like a prince by the villagers, and not be shoved about like a beggar. He would grow strong and handsome like his father.

That night she laid her tunic carefully under a rock and played in the water, unable to believe her good fortune. Closing her eyes, she dreamed of her wedding to Metallak and being able to speak of the coming child. She felt at peace for the first time in many years. Then she heard voices.

"Keoka will soon turn into a fish," said one angrily.

"Perhaps she looks for the Manogemassak," suggested another.

Keoka listened quietly. She had heard stories of the Manogemassak, the Little People who lived in the rivers, traversing the waters in their stone canoes. Try as she might, she had never seen these underwater creatures, whose faces were as thin as ax blades, and who spoke in squeaky voices. Even when she swam silently, so as not to frighten them away, they hid from her.

From behind the safety of a rock, she pouted. Was it wrong for her to enjoy the freedom of the waters as the young braves did? Was she not the best swimmer in the whole village? She saw them pick up her tunic, giggling softly as they ran from the shore. And she had thought they wanted to be friends! Angry tears filled her eyes as she drew her hair about her shoulders.

CHAPTER FIVE

She knew that somewhere, they watched and waited, knowing she would be unable to find her tunic. Well, she would show them that she didn't care! Defiantly, she walked from the water, drawing her hair down about her shoulders, and continued toward her lodge, completely nude.

The Shaman was overcome with emotion. Her soft curves held him spellbound in the moonlight as he followed her with his eyes. Those who sat outside their lodges taking in the night air stared with their mouths open, not believing their eyes.

For Keoka, it was a nightmare. She felt cheated and scorned, a deep shame suffusing her body in the darkness. But still she felt the eyes that burned into her, even after she finally sought refuge in her lodge, covering her body with a skin draped on the lodge pole. Shivering and hurt, she sobbed for a long time. No one came to her lodge, not even Old Molly. Probably they all believed the worst, even Oozalluc and Moll Ockett. Finally she dried her eyes and took up her needle. She would make herself another tunic and prove to the village that hers had been stolen. But she had hardened her heart against the nunksquaws. She would never trust them again. By the light of her tallow candle, she sewed late that night, finishing her tunic.

Next morning, she went about her duties as usual, ignoring the stares and the whispers of the elders who were gossiping.

"Keoka brings shame to our village," scolded one.

"And shames Old Molly, who befriended her," said another.

"Like an evil creature from the big swamp."

Moll Ockett said nothing, knowing how jealous the nunksquaws had been of Keoka's beauty. Except for Oozalluc, they had been unfriendly, rejecting Keoka's advances by ignoring her or making cruel jokes. Keoka had been doing more than her share of work without being reminded. Perhaps she, Moll Ockett, could do something to help. Under cover of darkness, she visited the Shaman that night. True, she had been baptized into the Catholic faith and had great respect for the Good Fathers who called her Mary Agatha, but she still consulted the village Shaman occasionally.

The Shaman was delighted that Moll Ockett had

78

consulted him. With the approval of such a highly respected doctress, the villagers would surely cooperate. And none would ever guess that he coveted the wild princess for himself. In hushed whispers, they conspired until midnight, then Moll Ockett quietly left his lodge.

"Do not forget the lock of hair," he reminded her. She nodded her head.

The Shaman withdrew into the privacy of his lodge, squatting by the fire, contemplating. Now was his chance to regain power and control in the village, the stature he had lost since the coming of the missionaries. There must be no mistake. It would be his greatest victory. Then the villagers would come to him once again for advice and medicine, as they had in the old days. He rubbed his dirty fingers together with greed. To rid them of the responsibility of this wanton half-breed he himself would marry her as a sacrifice to his tribal brothers. He would have their gratitude and Keoka at the same time. Just the thought of holding her warm bronze body close gave him shivers. He moved closer to the fire, and sipped his hot tea.

There was a time, his grandfather had told him, when the responsibilities of the Shaman made him a very important man, more important even than the Chief. He alone could detect a trespasser in another band's hunting territory, and it was his job to take action, by sending sickness or bad luck to this trespasser. But this was only part of his many duties. He was expected to know the mysterious properties of many plants, herbs, roots and berries, and their use in the treatment of diseases and wounds, to rid the body of the demons present. All this he did with the aid of his animal helper.

But with the coming of the missionaries, the people had lost faith in him, calling on their Invisible God and the priest for assistance. Little by little, they had ceased to come to his lodge for advice.

He paced the floor as he feverishly made plans. He must take care that Keoka had no assistance. Perhaps they would be lucky and Metallak would not return until it was all over. He was much too protective of this small one who conducted herself so brazenly in public. His eyes narrowed and he giggled to himself. Sometimes the small one swam in the nude, rendering him unable to carry on his visions, just as she had last night. Try as he would to transport himself into the vision, Keoka would interrupt his thoughts, and he would be unable to think clearly. He must rid her of this demon that possessed her. Surely her body had been invaded by the devil.

For once he would get even with Metallak, the pride of the village. It seemed as long as he could remember, Metallak could do no wrong. He was admired by young and old alike for his prowess on the hunt, and his generosity and kindness to others. It was even whispered that he might make a better Chief than his father Pial. But at last he had exposed his weak spot, his love for a fallen woman. If this affair continued, Metallak would bring shame on the village as well as his parents.

Metallak has not patronized the Shaman's lodge since the coming of the missionaries, and openly professed his disapproval of the Shaman's activities and predictions. He called them superstitions, old wives' tales. He practiced instead this silly business of confession to the Invisible God rather than consulting with a Shaman of his own tribe.

As he contemplated, he drew on the skins of his animal helper, the great bull moose, who would help him drive the evil Spirits from Keoka. He took great care never to wear these skins in daylight, so as not to reveal the identity of his animal helper. There were those who suspected, of course, because he never partook of the male moose meat. To partake of the flesh of one's animal helper was taboo, and Shaman Ignatius did not wish to meet with misfortune or tragedy. He would start with an amulet, and shake this over Keoka's head as she slept. If this did not work, he would seek a vision.

His joy at this opportunity to redeem his powers was profound, like a miracle the Good Father spoke about. He would emerge from this grave of loneliness a new man. At last he slept, but his sleep was tormented by the vision of a lovely young woman with long flowing chestnut hair. He longed to run away with her, but she scorned him for another. He awoke next morning bathed in sweat from this vision. He was even more distraught when he heard rumors that Metallak and Sebattis had arrived. He could only hope that Moll Ockett would not betray their plans.

The two young men had loped off in opposite directions, seeking their own summer lodges. Metallak was eager to see Keoka, and show his parents the reward money. He breathed in great breaths of the salty air.

There seemed to be a great commotion in front of

one lodge, far in the distance. He began running, observing that somebody was tied to a post. A second one seemed to be lashing out at her with a whip.

As Metallak drew closer, he could hear the shouting.

"Tom Hegan is Polly's husband! Keoka had better remember this lesson, or much worse will happen!"

He recognized the hair first, Keoka's beautiful hair leaning against the tree. And there was blood on her back, oozing from the ugly welts made by the whip. Metallak ran toward Polly, snatching the upraised whip from her hand.

"Go to your lodge or I will use this on you!" he exclaimed.

He could see Keoka's head slumped down, as though she was unconscious. Immediately he ran to loosen her bonds and placed his shirt over her shoulders for modesty, then carried her to his father's lodge.

Polly Sussop was still screaming, as she followed them up the path. "Keoka is evil!" she shouted. "She swam with Tom Hegan, Polly's husband."

Metallak ignored her. Small children trailed behind them, bewildered. Never before had they seen a whip in the village. If they did not behave well, they knew the worse punishment would be having their faces blackened with soot and being made to sit in public and display their shame before all the village. But a whip they had never seen. And Keoka had blood on her back! Some of them were crying, thinking that Keoka was dead. Who would want to hurt their best friend this way?

Old Molly came running to her lodge, hearing the shouting and commotion, clasping her hand over her mouth when she saw Keoka in Metallak's arms. He carried her inside and tenderly placed her on a fur rug, on her stomach. Keoka whispered.

"Please go away." She turned her head from Metallak, ashamed, and he looked toward his mother. Old Molly bent down, examining Keoka's back, then straightened.

"Go find Moll Ockett. Ask her to come and bring medicine." She looked closely at her son. "Old Molly will stay here."

Metallak was glad to have something to do and ran out of the lodge, then ran back in, snatching up the whip. He would see that this whip was never used again. He found Moll Ockett, who went quickly to Old Molly's lodge, saying nothing. She had seen the whip in Metallak's hand and didn't want to arouse his wrath against anyone else.

A crowd had gathered in all the excitement. Seeking their support, Polly Sussop lost no time recounting how she found Keoka swimming with Tom Hegan. "But Polly taught her a good lesson," she went on, telling about the whip. They listened attentively, clacking their tongues, until Old Molly joined them and they were suddenly silent. She spoke quietly.

"Old Molly is ashamed to hear the gossip. The elders say let the missionaries settle this affair. It is not for us to say who is right or wrong. Perhaps Tom Hegan is guilty too." She turned to Polly.

"Where is Polly's husband now?"

Polly hung her head, hating to lose face before the other wives. She sobbed.

"Tom Hegan told Polly he wants Keoka for a second wife. Before Polly could speak of this to him, he left the lodge." Tears slid down her face. "Polly did not see him again until I saw him swimming with Keoka."

"Pial will speak to Tom Hegan and learn the truth," Old Molly said firmly. "Let us go now to Polly's lodge." After brewing some hemlock tea and calming the distraught wife, Old Molly sought out her own son, speaking to him with sadness in her heart.

"Do you not see that Keoka is a strange one, my son? Today was not the first time she swam with a young brave. Only last week she walked through our village with no tunic, bringing disgrace on our family and our village. She has refused to tell us why, but her tunic has disappeared. And now, today, when Tom Hegan pays us a visit, she lures him into the water."

Metallak said nothing, but she was the look of pain on his face. She continued. "Your father has questioned two guides who come from the Sauk country. They described one such as Keoka who was banished from her own tribe for bad conduct, and they were pleased about her captivity with the Iroquois." She continued on grimly. "It is rumored at Green's Trading Post that the fur trapper hunts Keoka down like an animal, that he even offers a reward for her capture." She paused. "Perhaps the missionaries can help."

"Then we leave this very night," said Metallak, determined that the white trapper would never see Keoka again. Besides, he knew that if he remained overnight, he would kill Tom Hegan. He had warned him that no harm should come to Keoka, and he meant it. He

82

was sure that Tom Hegan did not want to support two wives, he was baiting Metallak for a fight to disrupt the tribe and split up their people. Much as he longed to even the score, he would choose another time and place, and he would show no mercy to the sneak. He wondered if Tom Hegan was in cahoots with the trapper, who promised a reward for Keoka. Where else would Tom Hegan had gotten the whip?

"I hope the missionaries will instruct Keoka to behave properly," his mother continued. "Already she has brought unhappiness to our village." Old Molly held her tongue and said nothing more. But inside, she was distraught. She knew her son loved this strange little one, who seemed to use poor judgement. No good would ever come of it. And she feared that Keoka would never be accepted as Metallak's wife. But then again, there was no excuse for Polly to use a whip. She was just as guilty as Keoka. As for Tom Hegan, his conduct was shameful, offering to take a second wife. He knew very well that this old pagan custom was frowned upon by the priests and the elders. She hoped Pial would disown him publicly.

Metallak wished to make all haste, choosing not to face the villagers, especially his father. The more he thought about it, the angrier he became. As hard as he tried to push the thought from his mind, it was there in the back of his mind. Had Keoka invited Tom Hegan to swim with her? Again and again the question tormented him, while he packed his canoe.

In the darkness, Moll Ockett came to him, telling him that Keoka needed rest and kindness. "The nunksquaws have been cruel to her," she confessed. "They even stole her tunic, forcing her to walk naked to her lodge." She sighed. "Keoka has tried hard, Metallak, but the nunksquaws are very jealous." She said no more, not revealing her talk with her.

"You are a good friend," he told her gratefully.

In the darkness and still of the night, he placed Keoka in his canoe and headed for St. Francis. Within days, they would be there, where not even the fur trapper could find them.

Keoka, bruised and sore, was strangely quiet as she huddled in the bottom of the canoe. Metallak, too, said little, hoping she would sleep, remembering Moll Ockett's orders. She looked so tiny and helpless, and her eyes had an emptiness he had not seen before. They were together and nothing else mattered. He disembarked hours later and they rested for a few hours, in each other's arms.

Metallak applied some of Moll Ockett's salve to her

83

back after they slept, letting his hands linger on her waist.

"Keoka will speak the truth only to you, Metallak," she said in a small voice. Metallak looked at her strained face and the black shadows around her eyes.

"Metallak should not have left," he said, holding her.

"Keoka did not know Tom Hegan was there," she continued. "Not until he was swimming beside me in the water."

"I thought so," Metallak said angrily. "Tom Hegan will always be a sneak and a coward. And if his jealous wife ever comes near you again, she will bear the marks of her own whip."

Keoka leaned against him gratefully. "Does Metallak truly love Keoka?" she asked timidly.

"Metallak loves Keoka and the child she carries," he told her solemnly, "more than anyone in the world."

Once again, he saw Keoka's eyes light up as they had in the past, full of eagerness and curiosity. She glowed with the bloom of motherhood in spite of all that had happened.

When they reached the mission village, they sought out Father Pierre, a new priest at the village. When Metallak explained that Keoka was bearing his child, he welcomed Keoka and confided to Metallak that he looked forward to enlightening her about the true God.

Awkwardly, when they were alone, Metallak attempted to explain Keoka's behavior and the disfavor she had caused. But the priest only smiled and told Metallak that Keoka shouldn't be blamed for doing what seemed perfectly natural to her.

"She does not know what is evil and what is not," he explained. "We will consider her past forgotten and begin again. That is the way of the Lord." Metallak nodded, pleased that at last someone understood Keoka.

"First Keoka must be baptized," he told them. Keoka submitted meekly to this water bath, and chose the Christian name Mary Eunice. Like most of the other women, she admired the Virgin Mother and the small Christ child, and wanted to adopt her name.

"I baptize you in the name of Mary Eunice," the priest told her proudly.

"Malyeunice. . . Malyeunice. . ." said Metallak, trying out the sound of the name. Like all Abenakis, it was difficult for him to manage the letter "r", which was not part of their alphabet, and Father Pierre knew that in a short time Keoka would be called Maly or Molly, which was so much easier for them to pronounce. Somehow he had a feeling that Metallak would go on calling her Keoka, which was truly a beautiful name.

Father Pierre sympathized because he had difficulty with the Abenaki tongue, and found it nearly impossible to create the "ooo" sound made by the natives without any movement of the lips, coming wholly from the throat. When he studied the dictionary left at the mission by Father Rasle, he discovered that he had assigned a figure "8" to designate this sound, such as that found in Pele8innos. He simply pronounced it as Pelawinnow, although he loved the sound of the flowing poetic speech of the natives.

Keoka was a bright pupil who learned quickly from Father Pierre. She promised faithfully to worship his new God, Kchi-Niwaskw, but in her heart, she still thought of her God as Odziohozo, who created himself from dust, then managed slowly to grow legs of such powerful strength that he was soon able to make brooks and streams merely by extending them. With his arms, he dug great bodies of water, piling great mounds of dirt into mountains. Keoka herself had seen him, after he transformed himself into the great rock at Pe-ton-bowk, the large lake basin separating the Abenakis from the hated Iroquis, called Lake Champlain by the whites. Even Broken Arrow had heard of Odziohozo. Once he had even told her of the native practice of leaving tobacco on the rock as a gift if one should pass by in a canoe, out of respect of Odziohozo. She was pleased that Odziohozo had seen fit to bring his wife to Lake Champlain also. Naturally, she was a much smaller rock, not nearly as important as her husband. She puzzled about this Invisible God who chose to hide himself. Yet Father Pierre and all the others spoke highly of him, and offered prayers every evening on their knees. They even made carvings of God's helpers, the disciples, out of tall trees. These tall trees made a pathway, called the Stations of the Cross, where some of the villagers prayed every night.

In vain, Keoka searched for a sign from Pemola. If the *new* God could fly even faster than Pemola, then why did he not reveal himself? She finally asked Father Pierre, who seemed such a good listener.

"Tell me about Pemola," he said. "I have not heard of him."

Eagerly, Keoka told him of Pemola. He did not laugh at her or make her feel silly. Her eyes filled with awe as she spoke.

"Pemola lives high on the mountains. His body is like that of a man, but he flies like the eagle."

"Tell me more," Father Pierre encouraged.

"His yell may be heard from far far away. Yet Pemola hears all who whisper his name as he passes over." She looked furtively up to the sky lest Pemola should be listening.

"Is Pemola kind?" asked Father Pierre.

"Keoka is frightened of Pemola," she confided. "With his body heat, he is able to set fire to villages. Even the bravest warriors do not climb the high peaks where Pemola lives.

Father Pierre sat down and had a long talk with Keoka, and she listened carefully. It seemed that his God did not create beings that were half-bird, half-human, but one or the other. This business of Pemola, who could fly from one pole to the other in just one day, was only a myth, a beautiful story.

She was glad she had not mentioned Tabaldak, the Owner, who created all living things, except for Odziohozo of course, but in her mind, she questioned the words of this strange man, and the little book he carried. The words were strange to her, and she hoped she would be able to read soon.

But Keoka was wise. She wished to marry Metallak as soon as possible. Thus, she learned her prayers quickly, adapting herself to Father Pierre's teachings with such charm that he marveled at her progress. He found it difficult to believe the stories he had heard of her conduct. She was just a child who needed instruction.

In a short time, Pial's people returned to St. Francis also, and Metallak sought out his parents to tell them he would be married in three weeks.

Soon the entire village knew of Metallak's plans to marry Keoka. Metallak welcomed Father Pierre's support with his parents, who finally gave their grudging approval. Still, the village was heavy with the silent disapproval of the elders and the jealousy of

86

the nunksquaws. In spite of all they had done, Metallak had chosen Keoka. And what was worse, Father Pierre had publicly announced that he approved of Keoka swimming every day and washing her hair. He encouraged them to do the same, and to give up this silly practice of rubbing bear fat in the hair. They began to wonder if Keoka had cast a spell over the Good Father.

Try as she would to be demure and modest, Keoka found it hard to change completely. When she was around the men, her laughter was contagious, drawing them closer to her and making the other young women jealous. What did the men see in this small skinny one who drew the men as the honey draws bears?

Oozalluc accepted the news gracefully, offering to help make preparations, even though her heart was heavy with grief. She did not want the pity of the other nunksquaws, and tried to keep busy all the time. She was pleased though that Keoka shared the long lodge with Metallak's parents, so she would not have to hear and see all the preparations for the wedding.

Shaman Ignatius trembled when he heard the news. It could not be possible. For weeks he had plotted to have Keoka for himself, and now he had been foiled again! His eyes glittered with hatred for Metallak as he conspired with the elders, who had decided the priest was against them and they must take matters into their own hands, for the good of the people.

"There is one among you who can help," he whispered to them in grave confidence. "Metallak's old enemy, Tom Hegan." Then they whispered far into the night, one of them going to wake Tom Hegan and take him into their confidence.

Although Tom Hegan dared not show his face in the village, he was camped not far away. He, too, was plotting against Metallak, and joined forces with the Shaman.

"Leave Metallak to me," he assured the elders. "He will know nothing and see nothing from his jail cell." His pale eyes lit up for a moment as he thought of Metallak being confined by the British. And it served Keoka right for rejecting all his advances. Who did she think she was, this ignorant half-breed?

"Metallak need only be jailed for a few days," the Shaman assured the elders, who squirmed now with apprehension. "Once Keoka's spirit is cleansed, we will go on with the wedding plans." He rubbed his hands eagerly as he presented his plan, persuading them it would be a simple matter for him to cleanse Keoka's spirit of the demons who obviously possessed her. It would take only one night, two at the most. But they must take care also that Metallak's family did not learn of the plan. They would only consult Father Pierre, who would surely disapprove, and take Keoka into hiding.

As for his own plans, Shaman Ignatius said nothing. Once he had Keoka in his clutches, they would escape together. Keoka would be so grateful for his protection and Metallak's indifference that at last she would see the light and choose to spend the rest of her life with him, the most important man in the village! Besides, this was a chance to restore his reputation at last and exhibit his great powers. Surely if he failed now, he would become a laughing stock among the villagers. He shook the gourd rattle which held a small lock of Keoka's hair. So far, his efforts had failed, but this time things would be different.

The elders listened. Although they were loyal to the missionaries and loved the Infant Jesus, perhaps they needed the precaution of additional measures. After all, they assured themselves, Keoka would not be hurt and Shaman Ignatius had promised he would need only one night to cleanse her spirit, driving the Devil from her body once and for all. They conferred at length, whispering. Pial grew soft in his old age by permitting this affair to continue. It was up to them, the elders, to do something about her unseemly conduct. Surely the Devil himself possessed her.

One by one, they gave their nods of consent, returning silently to their lodges. They would await word from Tom Hegan before taking action.

For Tom Hegan, it was far easier than he anticipated. The British not only paid him for his tale of Metallak's treachery, they immediately placed Metallak in confinement.

Metallak, thinking that Luc Schmid had another favor to ask, went to his quarters agreeably, only to be clasped into irons by the same two sentries who had accompanied him on the trip. Luc Schmid was not there.

"So, it is Metallak we have to thank for the return of the prisoners," snapped one of them, deliberately grinding his heel into Metallak's foot as he shoved him to the cell.

"Perhaps he too should be shipped to Quebec," laughed his companion.

Metallak, still in shock at being thrown into the jail cell, said nothing. He would demand an explanation the moment

Luc Schmid returned. He would not give these weasels the satisfaction of conversation. Besides, his father would notice his absence and make inquiries. In no time at all, he would be released. He tried to remember if he had told anyone where he was going. For a moment, he panicked, wondering how long he would be kept here. But then his courage returned. If he had to, he would break out of this filthy place. Although his stomach knotted with hunger, he refused the dirty smelling stew they left in a tin plate. Again the next day he refused the bread crusts, spitting on them.

At this, the sentry drew back angrily, throwing the food to the floor.

"The prisoner is not hungry," he announced. "He will go without food for three days." He took a deep swallow of wine, making Metallak's mouth water. "Perhaps in three days time, Metallak will learn some manners." He stalked out, slamming the door, leaving Metallak to pace the dirty cell.

He could not reach the tiny window high up in the cell, but cooled his body with the sweat on the stone walls. He cursed himself for not having accepted the food, his body craving nourishment. He heard a movement, and looked up. Something was being lowered through the window on a rope. In the semi-darkness, he picked it up and unwrapped the message eagerly.

"This time, my friend, you will not be there to save the half-breed."

Metallak heard a sly laugh as he threw the rock to the ground. That dirty traitor! He should have known it was Tom Hegan who reported him to the British. But how had he learned of it so quickly? Surely Moll Ockett did not betray him. It must have been one of the villagers. He refused to believe it could have been his own father. And yet he knew how his father had listened to Tom Hegan in the past, and how upset he was about the coming wedding.

Shaman Ignatius quickly spread word that—with Metallak confined—he would cleanse Keoka's spirit that very night One by one, the conspirators passed by his lodge for details, then wen about their business so as not to arouse suspicion.

"I must be alone with Keoka," he told each of them "You must trust me completely." Feeling less guilty, they returnec to their lodges, glad they did not have to participate in this ghastly ritual even though they gave their approval. Secretly, they all feared that Chief Pial would learn of their plans, or that something evil would come to pass. Some went that evening to the Stations of the Cross to pray for forgiveness.

Secretly, Shaman Ignatius made his plans. It would not be difficult to find Keoka alone. He would simply wait by the river, as he often did, and watch Keoka take her nightly swim without her tunic. He shivered with greedy anticipation. On this evening, he daringly picked up her tunic, and stroked it eagerly as she swam unsuspectingly not far away.

When she emerged, he was ready, hiding in the bushes. He pulled it quickly over her head, blinding her, while he pulled a rope about her waist. He pressed the skin of the tunic into her face, choking her breath, whispering vile threats while his dirty hands fondled her body. Though Keoka kicked and fought, she was unable to see or move and was no match for his powerful strength. Choking and exhausted from struggling, she felt him stroking her body, whispering insane obscenities, as he raped her. Then she remembered nothing, until she woke up.

Early next morning, Father Pierre came looking for her. She had not arrived in time for morning prayers or lessons and he was concerned. She had made such remarkable progress. Finding no trace of her, he searched for Metallak, but was unable to find him also. Old Molly and Pial looked puzzled, staring painfully at the ground, thinking that Metallak and Keoka had slipped away in the night without a word to anyone. They were embarrassed to face their friends, who kept their grave faces stoicly blank. Old Molly and Pial would know the truth soon enough.

The young women gossiped openly. Only a brazen young woman would live with a man without the blessing of a marriage. Again and again they told Oozalluc that Metallak was nearly as strange as Keoka, that she was lucky to be spared a wedding with such a man. Hesitantly, Oozalluc agreed, not knowing what to say. She, too, was very puzzled by all this. Keoka had gotten along so well with Father Pierre. Why would she give up her wedding day? And why hadn't Metallak told his parents?

Sebattis was puzzled when word of their disappearance spread through the village. Even though he knew how infatuated Metallak was with Keoka, he didn't believe his old friend would go off without a word to anyone. Feeling that something was amiss, he began scouting the area. As dusk drew darker, he had searched the entire village without a trace of Metallak or Keoka. But he had made certain that Metallak's canoe was still where he left it. And he knew his old friend would not take off on foot. And his new gun was still in his parents' lodge. Though he assured Pial and Old Molly that Metallak had waited far too long for Keoka, he was worried as he continued his search. Then he remembered the sentries. Perhaps they had seen or heard something. He made his way to the jail, where one of them sat stupidly on the steps, grinning.

"What do you want, my friend? To share a cell with your brother?" Thinking this a great joke, he laughed and took another swallow from his jug. Slowly, the truth dawned on Sebattis. Metallak was in jail! As the sentry tenderly touched his gun watching, Sebattis walked away, bidding him a happy evening. He made his way to a grove of trees, made himself comfortable, then watched and waited. Sooner or later the sentry would leave or take a walk. Sure enough, about two hours later, the sentry lifted his gun and began his evening walk, singing to himself. There remained only one sentry inside the jail, and Sebattis picked up a rock. He would make quick work of the sentry, using the rock only if he put up a fight.

In a short time, he had tied and gagged the sentry and located Metallak, who was never so glad to see his old friend. He gripped his hand in thanks, then bolted out the door, whispering to Sebattis that he must have food.

They made their way silently to Pial's lodge, Old Molly gasping when she saw Metallak's angry face and learned that he had been in jail all this time. Then she confessed that Keoka had disappeared.

Metallak tore out of the lodge in a fury, suspecting the worst. Sebattis followed closely behind, just as worried as Metallak. He knew how happy Keoka had been about the wedding preparations, and neither of them believed she had left the village of her own accord. Metallak kept remembering the message thrown into his cell. "This time, my friend, you will not be there to save the half-breed." He would kill Tom Hegan with his own bare hands. As they ran about the village combing the woods, he confided the message to Sebattis.

"I promise you this, my friend," pledged Sebattis. "If I find him first, I will show no mercy."

Metallak hunted as one possessed, and found remains of a campfire near an old barn, and signs of a hasty departure. "I will find you, Keoka," he said to himself, "and God help Tom Hegan!" Sebattis made a motion at his elbow, toward a curl of smoke in the distance.

When Keoka regained consciousness, she found herself dressed again, lying on the ground. She could hear whispers all about her.

"First we need to have a deep pit," whispered the Shaman, "away from the village near the swamp. Fill the pit with leaves. . . branches too, to make a slow flame. Call me when all is ready." Keoka closed her eyes, feigning sleep, hoping he would not put his vile hands on her again. As she pretended to sleep, she watched him flitting about, shaking his gourd muttering secrets to his animal helper. Every few moments, he would turn to assure himself that Keoka was still there. How he coveted his prize. She would soon be his forever and they would leave this village. Together, they would raise children and start their own village.

Though she tried to stay awake, Keoka found herself napping from exhaustion and hunger. Finally, she felt herself being dragged again. She rose to her feet, following along meekly.

When she saw the great pit and fire, she gasped. She had not imagined that even Shaman Ignatius would burn her alive! A long tree had been dropped over the pit lengthwise and she was tied to the tree at the outer edge. Although she was terrified, she showed no fear, longing to spit once more in the Shaman's ugly face.

Some of the painted faces did not approve. "The flames may catch in her long hair," they pointed out.

"The fire will not harm Keoka," the Shaman promised as he bound her with still more rope. "The slow flame will drive the Evil Spirit from her body. Then perhaps Keoka will be cleansed at last."

Keoka stared vacantly at the strange faces illuminated by the glow of the fire. Some were dressed in animal garments and already they were shaking rattles and murmuring incantations. Surely this must be a nightmare. She would sleep and never wake again. It would be good not to have to please the elders of the village, or be ridiculed by the women. And never again have to be used by the trapper or the Shaman.

Faster and faster the Shaman danced around the pit of fire, shaking his gourds and calling out Keoka's name. She hoped he would slip and fall into the pit. She was uncomfortably hot, but there was a breeze that blew over her, giving some relief. Keoka was lifeless, sometimes coughing up the smoke that rose about her, sometimes just lying in a daze.

One by one, the villagers left, growing frightened for Keoka's life. The Shaman looked grotesque, even to them, as he danced madly about the fire. And the small one showed no sign of life, or movement. They feared the wrath of Metallak, should he find out, and pledged never to reveal who was there on this night.

Keoka prayed to the Invisible God of Metallak's people. Perhaps he would lift her up to the sky away from her tormenters. But she took no chances, adding several prayers to the Devil. She knew the Good Spirit could hear her, but she feared the Evil One must be placated. She promised to pray to him faithfully if he would spare her just this once. She would even give up swimming if the Devil so desired.

Metallak and Sebattis arrived in time to see several men sneaking out of the village. They followed silently and found the Shaman was alone. Metallak shook with rage. How dare they attack a helpless woman this way? They were not better than the Iroquois Maguak. If Keoka was seriously injured, he would seek out every man involved and see that they died a slow death over flames, as Keoka had suffered.

They roped the Shaman and dragged him backward without a sound. Still muttering incantations in a half-trance, he appeared terrified when he recognized Metallak and Sebattis.

As they neared the fire, Shaman begged for mercy in a high shrilling voice. "It was all Tom Hegan's idea. I tried to stop them, please believe me Metallak." Tears slid down his filthy face.

Ignoring him, Metallak raced to Keoka, he cut lose her hands and cradled her in his arms, murmuring over and over

93

'Keoka, my love, do you hear me? Please wake up Keoka.'' Finally her eyes fluttered open and she recognized Metallak and collapsed in tears, choking and coughing.

"The villagers think Keoka is evil. Please let Keoka die."

"Keoka is not evil," Metallak told her, tears in his own eyes, "and Metallak will not leave her, ever again."

Metallak and Sebattis showed Shaman no mercy as they tortured him with hot sticks. Metallak held one to his eye, and Shaman's scream of agony could be heard in the village far away.

"Let us go now, my friend," suggested Sebattis, after they had draped his unconscious body over the fire to breathe smoke.

"Perhaps the good villagers will believe Keoka has grown horns," remarked Metallak with a grim smile.

"And her tiny feet have tripled in size," observed Sebattis. They turned and left hoping Shaman would die a slow death.

Several weeks later when Metallak and Keoka returned home, the villagers were overcome to see them both in good health. When the Shaman had been discovered, he had been so demented he was unable to tell them what happened. Some of the elders had grown fearful and confessed to the Good Father. He had been shocked, and prayed for them. But they feared the worst. Perhaps Keoka had fallen into the pit or perhaps the Evil Spirit had released her and she would return again to haunt them. Shaman Ignatius had been publicly disclaimed by the Good Father, and lived like a hermit at the far end of the village. The children ran from him, frightened of his ugly face with only one eye, and of his frantic gibberings that didn't make sense.

By now, it was apparent to everybody that Keoka carried Metallak's child. Old Molly cried with joy, and hugged Keoka, pleading with her to stay in the village. The elders too, in a fervor of guilt, begged them to stay, convincing Metallak that they had grown to admire Keoka, that Tom Hegan would not return again to cause trouble.

In this fervor of guilt, they made up an enormous dowry of baskets, bowls and mats for the happy couple. Oozalluc, stout-hearted and cheerful, presented them with a tiny pair of moccasins for the unborn child. In the flurry of activities, some of the villagers still expressed misgivings.

"Metallak could have had the most beautiful

nunksquaw in the village, but instead he picks this small scrawny one,"
said one of the aunts.

"He is your eldest. Surely you do not approve such
a match," said another.

"Enough!" Pial told them. "Pial's son has spoken.
He has chosen this nunksquaw of the Sauks.

We are proud of our alliance with the Sauk people
and soon Keoka will be part of Pial's family.

Once again Metallak made a trip down river to
Green's Trading Post to buy a gift for his bride, a beautiful blue blanket.
A tall homesteader dressed in deerskins and moccasins approached
him, and he recognized Jeremiah Eames from his last visit. Jeremiah
spoke quietly.

"You're hiding that Sauk, aren't you."

Metallak said nothing, studying Jeremiah.

"We are in your debt, Metallak, and I speak as a
friend. Take my advice and be careful. The trapper still hunts for her
and offers a reward."

Metallak nodded gratefully. He respected Jeremiah
and knew he could be trusted. Years ago, his people had expected
trouble when Fort Wentworth was built just a few miles down the road.
But the fort had never been used, never even fired a shot, mostly
because of Jeremiah Eames' influence. Metallak pulled nervously at
his hair, smoothing it down, then confided in Jeremiah.

"Metallak and Keoka will be wed within the month.
The son of Pial would be honored if Jeremiah would come to the
wedding as a guest."

"Well, I'll be darned," Jeremiah said, with a hearty
laugh. "Never figured that would happen. Best wishes to the both of
you," he said, extending a hand.

Metallak's grip surprised Jeremiah as he shook
hands. "From this day forth, we are friends. When Jeremiah visits
our village, he will sleep in Metallak's lodge."

The entire village was caught up in the spirit of the

wedding. This would not be an ordinary wedding. The future Chief of the tribe, the eldest son of Pial, must have a fine wedding. There was new clothing to be stitched, extra bowls to carve for the feast, to say nothing of the baskets that would be needed.

Pial and Old Molly gratefully accepted many fine gifts in honor of the occasion. Pelts, wampum and new furs filled their lodge. Pial took great interest in the weather and watched the skies carefully. The young couple must pledge their troth for three successive dawns. If rain fell, the ceremony must start all over again. The entire village prayed for good weather, in order that the wedding take place on time.

But good fortune befell the young couple, who walked into the lake up to their chins and faced the rising sun three days in succession. There before Pial, they pledged their vows. Keoka loved this part of the ceremony. She was most at home in the water and felt it was all a dream. At last they completed the final vow and returned to shore to be married in the eyes of the church by Father Pierre. The villagers waited impatiently for the feasting and celebration.

Still in their wet clothes, they stood proudly before Father Pierre and repeated their marriage vows. Father Pierre recited the vows proudly.

"And you, Metallak, do you take this woman Keoka to be your lawfully wedded wife?" Metallak picked up Keoka's hand tenderly and repeated humbly.

"Metallak takes thee Keokum." Without thinking, he had reverted to the old native practice of indicating intimate possession by adding "um" to her name. The villagers were touched by this display of affection and tears slid down Old Molly's cheeks. Then, suddenly, it was all over, and they were surrounded by well wishers and relatives. Metallak found himself shaking hands with Luc Schmid and eyed the sentries in the crowd uneasily.

"Relax, Metallak" Luc Schmid told him with a laugh. "My sentries will not bother you today. They were fools to believe Tom Hegan in the first place."

Metallak's face grew hot, but he smiled amiably. He was pleased to know that Luc Schmid still trusted him. He turned to his little wife, smiling.

The struggle had been difficult for Keoka. For three days she had been on her best behavior, docile and obedient, but a sudden wild impulse took over. She looked mischievously up at

Metallak and ran toward the water. Turning back to see if he followed, she laughed, the same old contagious laugh, then dived under water and swam quickly away from him. As he plunged in after her, the wedding guests shook their heads in dismay.

"This is an Evil Omen," said the aunt, clucking her tongue in disapproval.

"Already she runs from Metallak," Oozalluc commented thoughtfully. "In many ways she is like the renegade plant that runs wild, the poison ivy."

"Sshhh," cautioned Moll Ockett, lest somebody should overhear them. She knew that Oozalluc had made a worthy observation, even though she always supported Keoka in public. She too wondered what would happen with this strange marriage, but she dared not voice her thought aloud.

Keoka slowed and allowed Metallak to overtake her, wrestling playfully with him in the water. Then they made their way back to shore, dripping and laughing, and the villagers followed them uncertainly back to Metallak's family lodge, all carefully prepared for the festivities. The young nunksquaws gasped when they saw the pelts and skins covering the walls. Baskets of fresh berries hung on the center pole, along with Keoka's new skillet. A large bed of fir boughs occupied one corner, covered with soft white furs, skinned by Metallak himself. Petitions divided each portion of the long lodge, so Metallak's lodge was like a small house by itself.

"Let us all join in the feast," Father Pierre invited.

The villagers fell to consuming the sumptuous feast so lavishly spread outside the lodge. There was soft, boiled meat, broiled meat, and strips of venison, breads with or without berries, and several kinds of fish.

Keoka was too excited to eat, unable to believe she was truly Metallak's wife, the owners of the beautiful pelts and skins on the walls. Metallak, too consumed very little, his eyes on his beautiful bride. She was flushed and excited from the activities. He went to whisper in her ear. Taking down two beautiful pelts from the wall, they stole out silently by the side flap in the lodge, wanting only to be alone.

Metallak turned to his bride, taking her hand, leading her to a lovely hidden thicket where the sweet clover and moss softened the rough stones. There he spread their furs and held out his arms to his wife. Removing the damp wedding dress from her, he wiped her cold skin with the robes. He thought she had never looked

97

more beautiful with the fullness of carrying his child. After all that had happened, he still couldn't quite believe they were married at last, with the approval of his parents. The sight of her lovely body excited him and he pulled her against him impatiently. She, too, was excited, feeling like a lost butterfly. She was beautiful to him now, but would he tire of her when she grew big with child? Would he scorn them as her mother had been scorned?

They fell into each other's arms and made love with the careless abandon of children, murmuring words of tenderness to each other and when they were exhausted, they finally slept, wrapped in each other's arms. Although the grass rustled around them occasionally with the breezes, neither of them stirred until the following morning. Keoka woke to find Metallak looking down at her, tenderly stroking her beautiful hair, pulling bits of grass from it. His powerful arms wrapped her in an intimate embrace as he whispered to her again how much he loved her. He felt clumsy, unable to tell her how he loved the dancing lights in her eyes, the sensuous sway of her tiny body.

Keoka sighed with sheer happiness. For the first time in her life, she had a chance. She rolled quickly away from him, laughing again. "Has Metallak forgotten that Keoka eats for two?"

He grasped her wriggling body firmly in his arms and whispered. "We will eat sooner if you please your new husband."

Keoka opened her mouth to protest, but he kissed her so tenderly that she forgot she was hungry. The sun was high in the sky when they finally stretched lazily, and began to don their clothing. As they approached the village, the little ones came running to greet them. Happy to see her little friends, Keoka stretched out her arms in welcome. Metallak picked up a small toddler and set him firmly on his shoulders. Laughing and joking, none of them saw the glassy stare of a shabbily dressed one-eyed onlooker. He stood nearly hidden under a large oak tree, muttering obscenities as he stared at Keoka's swollen body. Though his arrow was raised and ready, he dared not risk hitting one of the little ones. Wiping the ooze trickling down his face from his disfigured eye, he moved away silently into the forest. There would be another time, another chance, he told himself.

CHAPTER SIX

For weeks, Keoka would wake suddenly in the night and sit up apprehensively, making sure Metallak was still there beside her. This movement always woke Metallak, who wondered what was bothering his lovely bride.

"What is Keoka afraid of?" he asked gently one night.

"It was only a dream," she answered shyly, embarrassed. Metallak would never understand that she wanted to hold on to each precious moment, afraid that disaster would befall them and she would be taken away from him. Perhaps the trapper would finally locate them, or Tom Hegan would find some dreadful way to get even with Metallak. She never felt really safe unless Metallak was holding her closely.

Metallak shrugged and went back to sleep, thinking perhaps he had been too demanding of his loving wife. Probably she should get more sleep with the coming child making her so tired and jumpy. But she was irresistable even in her sleep, and he couldn't keep his hands away from her. So far, she had not tired of his lovemaking, which brought him pleasure beyond his own belief. Secretly, he was delighted at the ardent response of her own lovemaking. Though he sometimes wondered how much experience she had in this mysterious art, he quickly shut it out of his mind. He refused to admit that the trapper or anyone else had possessed his loving wife in such an intimate fashion. He thought only of how warm and inviting her arms were, and how gentle her touch that aroused him to such heights of ecstasy.

They kept to themselves a good deal of the time, but occasionally joined the villagers to take a meal with them. One morning after a lazy breakfast while Keoka chatted with Moll Ockett about the coming child, Metallak handed her his bowl to refill and she looked up at him in surprise, taking it grudgingly. She sat indolently back against the center pole, asking.

"Has Metallak grown tired so early in the morning?"

Amid the titters and giggles of onlookers, Keoka saw his chin tighten and his eyes darken with anger. He stood
99

oking down at her, saying nothing.

Keoka rose to her feet angrily and went to the
ettle, slopping the contents as she re-filled the bowl and handed it
o him. Still he stared at her, saying nothing, his face a mask of
tone, cold and unfeeling. How dare he order her to wait on him in
ront of all the village. Was she no better than a slave to him, now
hat she was no longer slim and pretty?

Without thinking, she threw the dish to the
round and ran off to a grove of trees to hide her shame.

The villagers were incredulous, some tittering,
ome gasping, others praying under their breaths. Metallak
tood uncertainly, unable to understand this behavior and very embarrassed before the others. Pial raised himself to his full stature,
acing his son. "Come," he said.

As he walked beside his father, Metallak
tubbornly refused to speak of the incident. His father contin-
ed to speak. "Metallak must train Keoka to obey." He faced his
on. "Dishonor will stain your name if you allow this disrespect to
ontinue. A good wife should always obey her husband. Keoka
as set a bad example for the others. Did you not hear them
aughing? A future Chief must earn the respect of all the villagers,
ot just his wife."

"Metallak must do this thing alone," he replied,
ngry that his father gave him advice. "I do not care what the
illagers think!" Angrily, he strode away in the direction Keoka had
one.

His head hammered with anger with each step
hat he took. He could never outguess Keoka. It might take minutes
o find her, or a whole week. One never knew with this woman.
his much he knew. She had brought shame on her husband and
amily. She would answer to her husband for this. It was well that
e could not overhear the comments of the elders as they gossiped.

"Metallak cannot manage even a small one. It is
ell that he did not marry a big one," said one with a dry smile.

"Metallak's lodge is not good enough, not
nough furs," commented another as she stirred the big kettle.

Pial sat alone inside his lodge brooding, but Old
Molly brought him comfort as always. "Do not think too harshly of
Keoka," she said. "She must get used to the ways of the Abenaki
ith our help."

"I think our son will regret this marriage," Pia said bitterly. She left him alone with his thought, knowing it would be useless to try to reason with him.

All day Metallak searched for Keoka, with no luck. Concern for her began to overcome his anger. What if she had been hurt, or taken captive? Suddenly he stopped. Keoka would go first to the water, if only to hide her tracks. Why hadn't he thought of this before? He calmed himself. Perhaps she had gone to wash her beautiful hair for him, the quarrel forgotten. Perhaps even now, she had returned to their lodge, looking for him.

Determined not to panic, he sat by the banks of the river in deep thought. Why had Keoka become so angry with him? Could he not ask his own wife to refill his bowl? Shaking his head with frustration, he lay back exhausted, and took a short nap. In his sleep, he was sure he heard Keoka's tantalizing laugh and sat up quickly. The ground was wet with dew and soon it would be light.

Keoka saw the glassy stare of the Shaman behind a tree. At first she thought it was wolf, and gripped her stick nervously. When she heard his lecherous laugh, she recognized him and began running. When she tripped over a root, he overtook her pinioning her to the ground. Like a cat, she hissed at him.

"Get away from Keoka, or you will lose both eyes next time."

The drool on his face sickened her and she felt like vomiting as he replied in a sly cunning voice. "It is rumored that Keoka has already killed two braves. I wonder if her husband know this?"

Keoka gasped and drew back from him, frightened. What if he told Metallak and the others?

"I am your friend, Keoka. I will keep all your secrets, for a price." He eyed her body greedily and she shivered.

He chuckled with victory as he felt her body relax. He touched her small body intimately, with possession feeling the roundness of the unborn child. "A small promise, that is all I want," he spoke soothingly. "If Keoka meets with me now

and again to discuss the coming child, I will keep her secret."
Keoka heaved a sigh of relief as he made no attempt to ravage her
body, apparently content to speak of the coming child.

"You have Keoka's promise," she whispered,
trying to wriggle away.

He fondled her for a moment before he rose,
cackling and coughing. Through this little half-breed, he would re-
institute some of the long forgotten customs with his people.
He would start with Metallak's child.

"When the time comes, I will let you know," he
said and moved away like a shadow, his demented giggle echoing
through the trees.

Furtively, Keoka backed away, still not trusting
him. Perhaps he hoped to gag and tie her again, and burn her at
the stake. She longed for the safety of Metallak's strong arms,
and regretted her show of temper when he asked for more food.
As she hurried toward the village, she hoped he would forgive her,
and all would be forgotten. Surely the Shaman would not bother
her in front of Metallak.

From his place high in a tree, Metallak scanned
the area. A man in his position could not return to the village
without his bride, not after all the warnings he had been given.
He must find her! The only sign of life was the movement around
the lodge of the Shaman, who lived pretty much as a hermit these
days. Then he spotted Keoka, far in the distance, heading back
to the village. He breathed a sigh of relief and made his way to
the ground. In a short time, he too walked haughtily toward
his lodge, blushing from the many hidden eyes that watched.

As he entered their lodge to confront her, he
found her stretched out innocently under all the white furs, fast
asleep, as though exhausted. He sat beside her, too uneasy to
sleep and too angry to leave. Although he bristled with anger, he
was filled with longing as he looked down on her, sleeping peacefully. He told himself he would teach her to be a good wife when
she was rested, reminding himself of all that she had suffered at
the hands of the Iroquois and the trapper. She needed patience,

as Old Molly advised.

When Keoka finally woke, he said not a word. His face remained like stone carved in the mountains. He held out his bowl once again to Keoka, watching her response.

Keoka thought carefully, contemplating the bowl. They were alone now, so there was no cause for embarrassment, and Metallak was a man of much importance in the village. He had only to speak a command and it would be done. With Metallak at her side, she need never fear the Shaman. Besides, she was ashamed of her conduct and only wanted his forgiveness. But Metallak must not ever treat her as a slave.

"The wife of Metallak should not cook," she said shyly, as she found food to feed her husband. "Soon Keoka will become a fat, ugly old woman, and Metallak will leave her. Keoka would like a slave to cook and clean the lodge of Metallak."

Metallak was momentarily stunned. He had thought Keoka would wish to be alone with him, as he did with her. He answered slowly. "But surely we have no need for a slave. Metallak wants only Keoka in his lodge."

"She could have her own lodge to sleep in," she said with a tantalizing smile. "Perhaps Oozalluc would like to come here and cook and clean."

Metallak was furious with Keoka. He grabbed her by the shoulders and shook her, his face stern and angry. "Oozalluc will never be a slave here!" Tears ran down her face as he continued to shake her. He stared at her, breathing hard, as he finally released her.

Suddenly she looked very vulnerable and helpless to him as she sobbed.

"Keoka has been a slave for many years. My arm is still not strong like that of the others."

Metallak wavered at the sight of his small, frail wife. Truly, one so small should not work as hard as the others. Finding a slave should not be so difficult.

"Metallak will find a slave for Keoka if that is her wish," he said simply. She threw herself into his arms, as passionate as she had been on their wedding day. For the moment, he forgot everything but Keoka, intoxicated with desire for his wife.

They said no more about the slave, but early next morning, Metallak went to his father's side of the lodge. After a long discussion, it was agreed. Metallak would be allowed the wife of a dead warrior to help out. In this way, he would be helping the tribe by feeding and caring for her.

Keoka was delighted when Metallak brought Cecile to their lodge, and greeted Metallak lovingly. She took a skin down immediately to work on a pair of moccasins for the little one.

"Already my wife finds work to do. Cecile will cook," he ordered the slave, proud of his new stature and of his loving wife. He should have realized that Keoka lacked the strength to lift the heavy skins or to scrape and clean the heavy skillets. Cecile, on the other hand, was built like a man, with muscular arms and legs. She lifted the skillet as easily as Metallak himself. Keoka's hands were much too delicate for this heavy work, useful only for sewing or painting. Perhaps she would learn to embroider with his mother's help, and her handiwork would be the talk of the village.

Though there was some grumbling and jealousy among the wives, most of them wisely kept silent. They wished to retain Metallak's friendship, so he would remain with them always. He was their strongest warrior and one never knew if the whites would come again with guns, or if the supply of food would be short. They would try to be tolerant of his ignorant wife.

Life resumed its routine and Keoka tried hard to be worthy of Metallak's good name. She carefully observed Cecile, even while scolding her, as she cooked and cleaned. She took a great interest in sewing, sometimes meeting with the other wives of the village. They agreed among themselves to show her all they knew about stitching and quilling. Each day, Keoka would take her bone needle and take up the skin with determination. But before long, the effort of concentration and the hard work of piercing the heavy skin would make her impatient and she would pull violently, sometimes ripping the skin and making it scarred or useless.

"Perhaps Keoka should learn to embroider," suggested Old Molly to the indignant women who gasped when she ruined a skin. "Old Molly will help her." Gratefully, they gave over this duty to her mother-in-law.

Old Molly worked patiently with the porcupine quills, with theer barbed sharp ends cut off. "Always wet the quills first like this," she said, moistening them in her mouth. "Then draw them straight like this." She flattened the quills by drawing them between her thumb and a flat round edge piece of moose bone. Slowly and carefully, straightening each one, she inserted them perpendicular to the skin they were holding.

"Keoka will try one now," said Keoka, grasping this task quickly. In no time, she had learned to make the sign of the bald eagle, for Metallak's shirts and moccasins.

"Keoka learns quickly," Old Molly told her proudly one day. "Now we will work on shirts for Metallak." Once again, Keoka resumed her attempts to sew. But she found the skins heavy and awkward, and quickly made rents and tears in them. Once again, the other wives grew angry at the waste of the skins, and refused to have her work with them. Soon, none but Old Molly and Oozalluc would allow her to sew with them. Other young wives had already learned that they could tear the skins to get out of doing their share of the work. The older women lost no time in expressing their disapproval to the village elders.

Metallak had resumed his hunting activity, coming home every three or four days to see his wife, unable to stay away longer. He was pleased to see her expression when he unfolded the lovely furs and pelts. He was determined that none should have furs as elegant as Keoka. They framed her bronze body perfectly, her lustrous hair making a picture as elegant as a regal fox of the forest. If he heard rumors of her behavior, he ignored it. He wished only to spend all his time alone with his bride when he came to the village and cared not what others thought or said.

"Look under the floor into the bark pits," she told him proudly on his last return. He saw with pride that the huge bark bins beneath the floor were filled with corn for the coming winter.

"Take care that Keoka's arm does not get too tired," he cautioned Cecile, not knowing or caring that Cecile had done all the lifting and carrying. Carefully, he chinked and prepared the lodge for the coming winter, as Keoka patiently smoked the meat he brought home.

Sometimes he would catch her making sketches in the dirt or on rocks, which she would quickly hide when he caught her, afraid he would think her to be silly and childish. Metallak said nothing, but one day he brought her some fine pieces of birch bark. "Perhaps Keoka will make a sketch for our lodge," he told her.

She was delighted with the gift, and threw her arms around him. He did not think her silly after all, and she no longer had to draw in secrecy. Metallak showed her how to wet the bark and make her drawings by knife point. After her drawing was completed, she dipped a hot rag into a dye mixture he had contrived, giving the etching a rich dark color. Thus, the outer layer of bark became a background for the lighter area which was sketched with the knife. Metallak was amazed at the beauty of her handiwork, as she made ready to grease it to help preserve it.

"Does Metallak like the drawing?" she asked shyly.

It was a male moose, with a large horn-spread, ridden by a mighty warrior. In the background, mountains rose in the distance.

Metallak stared at the drawing, puzzled by the face of the warrior, a proud warrior who looked distainfully down from his high perch. "Who is the warrior?" he asked at last, facing Keoka.

"Does Metallak not recognize himself?" she asked with a mysterious smile.

Metallak proudly showed the etching to his friends and relatives, then hung it on the wall of their lodge for all to see. He was secretly delighted that Keoka drew him as a bold warrior, afraid of nothing. And it proved that she thought of him, even while he was away from her. He began to think about the possibility of taming a moose. With the village so short of horses, it might be worth a try. He began planning how he would capture the moose, what steps he would take to tame him. He would show his wife that he was as strong as the warrior in the drawing.

The daily routine of village life was dull for Keoka, and she was most happy when skipping from lodge to lodge, spreading gossip or showing off her newest and most elegant furs. The young wives welcomed her and gasped at the bounty she received from her husband. Many of the other husbands did not hunt until they were nearly out of supplies, and their wives envied Keoka.

Keoka generously shared the excess, keeping the choice pelts and cuts of meat for Metallak and herself. Old Molly showed her how to burn the hair off the lips of the moose and prepare this delicacy for eating, after several hours of boiling.

"Keoka has worked so hard," he would caution with pride. Soon his wife's handiwork would be the most sought after in the village, if she continued to weave rushmats like this.

Cecile said nothing, always loyal to Keoka, but she had observed the stealthy transactions with the other women, as Keoka traded Metallak's game for a beautiful basket or a floor mat. Sometimes Keoka drew them a sketch for payment, which they treasured.

It did not take Old Molly long to see through this trickery, or Oozalluc either, though they seldom spoke of her bad habits. Following Moll Ockett's example, they continued to wait, hoping she would learn in time, and become a better wife. Old Molly especially could not bear to hurt Metallak's feelings, but she felt he was extravagant with his selfish wife. Patiently, she came to Keoka's lodge day after day, basket in hand.

"Old Molly will help Keoka dig the wattap today," she would say, offering a basket. "We have many fine roots in these hills." And she would point out the finest roots to sew with, showing Keoka how to soften them first by wetting them, and which sinews of the game to keep for Metallak's fishing lines.

"Old Molly is kind to Keoka," Keoka would say, always grateful for the advice, promising to do all that she was taught. But she forgot her promises just as quickly, joining in with the children at their games, or going for a visit in a neighbor's lodge and forgetting to go home until her fire was burned out.

"We need fresh coals," Cecile would tell the neighbors, carefully carrying home a few and blowing them into a flame. While this caused a good deal of tongue wagging. Keoka was not at all embarrassed.

But for Metallak, Keoka never forgot to make herself radiant, putting on her best trinkets and fare to greet him. Although she felt clumsy and fat, Metallak seemed not to notice, and she was grateful that he still found her attractive. He refused to let her carry the heavy wood as the other women did, and made her rest often. There were plenty of small boys around, and Cecile was as strong as a man.

The villagers were not blind to her beauty or her generosity, and had to admit there was a certain charm about her. They forgave her small faults and looked for the good. All but Shaman Ignatius. She had ruined his one chance at regaining his stature with the tribe, and now he would be forced to work through her son. Perhaps he had been unable to control the willfulness of this devilish creature, but the small one would be a different matter. He would bide his time and train the young one to do as he was ordered. Carefully, he observed the comings and goings of Metallak, and knew almost to the minute when Keoka was alone. If only that slave were not around. There seemed to be no way of getting Keoka completely alone, to speak of the coming child. They would start with a simple potion, and by the time the child was running about, they would be great friends. The child would do his bidding, much to Metallak's humiliation. Then perhaps he too, would know how it felt to be a laughing stock in his own village.

Metallak was still blinded by love for Keoka. He ignored her laziness and the dead embers in the fire when Cecile was elsewhere. He thought Keoka was even more beautiful than ever, and still the best storyteller in the village. The small children loved to gather and hear her tell of Azeban, the raccoon, and his silly antics. It seemed he was always getting into trouble.

Metallak would sit back and listen, thinking what a wonderful mother Keoka would make. He began fashioning a Tkinogan, a cradleboard, for the small brave. He chuckled and told himself it must be a brave, and not simply a female. He shaped and whittled the cradleboard every day, making an adjustable footboard, so the little warrior could kick as he grew. By the age of nine months, perhaps even sooner, he would be walking, the first born of Metallak. When it was finished, he proudly displayed it from the center pole of their lodge, urging Keoka to find sphagnum moss to line it for the papoeis.

One thing bothered Metallak. They were not

invited out much that winter, and his parents seldom came to visit. Except for Sebattis, they were alone most of the time. Surely his parents were pleased about the coming papoeis? And Metallak had enough pelts and furs to buy blankets and ammunition for his brothers in the spring. Oozalluc, too, was a stranger to their lodge.

Metallak did not know of the gossip concerning Keoka's increasing laziness, or how easily the young men were captivated by her quick laughter, causing so much jealousy among the nunksquaws.

"There is a gathering in Oozalluc's lodge," she told him one nights. "Others play games . . . sing too." Tears filled her eyes. "We were not invited."

Once again, Metallak's face became chiseled in granite and Keoka regretted her words. "Then they are no longer welcome in the lodge of Metallak!" he thundered. He had made a decision. As soon as the baby was born, they would leave. If Keoka's beauty caused the others to resent her, he would take her away where none could bother them or inturde. They would go to the fertile banks of the Androscoggin, where he had spent his boyhood. Here the salmon were plentiful, and the long lazy river a pleasure to behold. When his people saw how well they got along with the whites, they would join them. In time when they saw what a good mother Keoka was, they would accept her.

Keoka dared not tell Metallak about the Shaman following her about and whispering of the coming child. She was afraid he would tell Metallak about her past. More and more she kept to her lodge, going out only for necessities. Besides, she was clumsy and big with child. Metallak had grown impatient, being shut up in the lodge and eagerly made plans for the winter hunt.

Keoka bravely saw him off, but she brooded fretfully all that day and sure enough, Shaman Ignatius appeared at her lodge that very evening, looking dirtier than ever. He spoke softly of the ancient rituals for a newborn such as her very own. This would assure the small brave of protection in Metallak's absence, he promised. He stroked her arm gently as he spoke, and then left. Day after day he returned, speaking again and again of the ritual and how important it was. Not once did he mention Keoka's past.

Keoka began to have doubts in her mind. She had never really been convinced that the Invisible One protected

109

her as he did the others, and listened more carefully to the instructions of Shaman Ignatius. After all, why should she take chances, and expose her unborn baby to harm?

Before Metallak returned from the hunt, she gave birth to a fine male child. The tiny infant bore the strong features of his father, according to Moll Ockett, and the gentle hair of his mother. The villagers rejoiced in such a fine boy, and spoke well of Keoka's bravery during the long ordeal of delivery. When Metallak returned and saw his tiny son in the cradle, he was overcome with emotion.

"It is Paugus returned from the grave," he told her seriously. "We will call him Paugus after my grandfather."

"I too, like the name Paugus," Keoka told him, and so he was named.

Importantly, Shaman Ignatius visited their lodge, carrying the treasured white clover, called "that which follows every man's footsteps." He had sorely missed this ancient ceremony since the coming of the missionaries, who disapproved of this practice. He ground the clover into a fine powder and then stirred the powder into fresh water.

Metallak looked on with disgust, angry with Keoka for permitting this silly old custom. But she had begged and pleaded for several days and he could not bear to see her so sad. If it meant so much to her, surely it would do no harm. She had not asked for new skins or furs, only for this silly ritual. It was as though the Shaman held some power over her, and Metallak couldn't understand it. Surely the Shaman would never again try to harm Keoka, not if he wanted his life spared. What was she afraid of?

"Paugus will drink from this water for four days," Shaman instructed. "Only in this way will he have a strong memory, a tribute to the first born of Metallak." Such was Metallak's dislike for the Shaman that he stood directly in back of him and watched carefully. If any harm came to the child, he would seek revenge. The Shaman saw how jealously Metallak guarded the child, and was more jealous than ever of Metallak's good fortune. Why should he have a beautiful wife and handsome young child? It was unfair. He whispered words of incantation unheard to the others as he stirred the potion, then took his leave.

Keoka heaved a sigh of relief. She had kept her promise and she hoped the Shaman would keep his. For the first time in many weeks, she began to relax and enjoy her new son. She fed him often, wanting him to grow strong and lithe like his father.

After a long winter of confinement, the first rays of sun on icy patches and sprigs of green peeping through brought joy to the entire tribe. Small quarrels were forgotten, and with the careless abandonment of children, they ran on the icy slopes and greeted spring with renewed life.

Metallak had not forgotten his plans. He approached his father and told him they would soon be leaving.

"But the tribe needs Metallak," Pial protested, "and the streams swell with fish."

"We will stay for the spring run of fish," agreed Metallak. They all needed the change of the spring run of salmon and alewives. The bark pits in their lodges were empty and they were all hungry.

Taking a group of young braves, he headed for the Kwini-teguh, where they fished for a week, using three pronged fishing spears and wears to traps the fish. They returned to the village jubilant with seventy-five bushels of fish to be smoked, some of the salmon weighing as much as a three year old child. Metallak ran quickly to his lodge to assure himself that his son was well, and scooped him up in his arms with pride. Then he drew his small wife to his side and told her to make ready, they would soon leave the village.

Keoka packed eagerly, looking forward to the change and the freedom, even granting Cecile her freedom. She knew that Metallak loved her deeply to leave his people, and she recklessly made gifts to the villagers.

Oozalluc, for one, was glad to see them go. It was painful for her to see Metallak love another as he did Keoka, and embarrassing to listen to the gossip about her, that she was lazy and slovenly, and very lucky to have a happy good natured child who required practically no care.

Slim and commanding again in appearance, Keoka took full advantage of the attention from the young braves, who outdid themselves performing for one of her smiles. It was disgusting.

"It is well that you go for now," Old Molly advised them. "Old Molly will pray for you, and keep the fire in Metallak's lodge until he returns."

Metallak had gathered plenty of birch bark for the canoe in the winter, when it was hard and tough, separating easily into layers. In the spring, he built them a canoe two feet wide and twenty-two feet long. Inside the bark were rails of birchwood sewn with spruce roots to two edges of the bark. Then he placed a log on the bark to help shape it, and the outside he shaped by raising the sides and driving stakes around the edge. Finally, he inserted cross pieces of maple in between the rails. He had carefully lined the inside with strips of cedar and now he would coat the outside with pitch. Three weeks had been lost in building the canoe, but it was well done, and he was proud of it. He knew it would last many seasons.

He packed their canoe tightly with blankets, food, skins and skillets. Keoka carried Paugus in his Tkinogan on her back. Both of them looked forward to their new life together, and left with good feelings toward all. In no great hurry, they made their way down to Lake Memphremagog, then down the Naamas River to the Nulhegan, and on down to the Upper Ammoonsuc to the Androscoggin. They searched for some time before finding a fine wooded spot overlooking the slow moving lazy river. Metallak picked a spot in a stand of beautiful red oak, where they would have shade in the heat of the summer as well as privacy. The area was rich in timber, beautiful black poplar, birch, hemlock and fir. Here and there along the swampy ground were tall white cedars. He began making a blaze in a tree.

Keoka watched him curiously. "Why does Metallak write on the tree?"

"It is the way of our people, to leave a message for others," he told her, carefully cutting the message and filling it in with charcoal. Keoka could read her letters already, thanks to Father Pierre. She could see the picture of the bald eagle and another message on the tree above Metallak's, in Abenaki.

July
1759

We go lodge on
Mamfloobagogg
Pial

Metallak here go
Androscoggin
April
1783
Metallak

Metallak read the message left by his father years ago and printed his own in English.

"Why did you not write Keoka's name?" she pouted. Metallak laughed and added her name to the bottom of the message.

He built them a wigwam by bending a few saplings into a conical shaped wigwam, with a large center pole. He fastened the saplings with roots, then covered them with skins. But here without the other villagers, it seemed very little protection against the wolves, and Metallak was anxious to make them a log home.

There was a large stand of maple trees near the lodge. Together, they tapped the trees, making a diagonal slash, then inserting a hollow elderberry twig. With birchbark pails, Metallak collected the sap, while Keoka patiently boiled it down in her new skillet. He held a piece of fat pork on a long stick, ready to immerse it should the kettle start to boil over. They made a good supply, boiling sap for several days. Before long, the dandelions were in full bloom with bright yellow blossoms and Metallak could hear Keoka singing her gathering song as they dug from the ground.

He protected his little family with pride. Paugus was growing rapidly, and already Metallak made plans. He would

113

be Chief one day, like his father. Surely by then, Keoka would be accepted by the villagers. But for now, he would enjoy his family. During the lazy summer months, they all laughed and played, living like nomads under the sun. Metallak cleared a field for planting corn and squash. Keoka and Paugus sat and watched Metallak fertilize each little hill with a small fish.

"Perhaps it is too soon to plant," Keoka observed. The sun went down early and the nights wre still cold.

"Metallak has watched for a sign," he told her. "The oak leaf is now big like the ear of mouse." He pulled a leaf from an oak tree and showed her. "When the leaf is this size, it is time to plant."

Keoka never ceased to marvel at Metallak's knowledge of the woods. He seemed to know where to find everything. She wanted to surprise him and combed the riverbanks searching for sweetgrass while he planted, but found none. She grew discouraged and finally confided to Metallak.

"There is no sweetgrass on the Androscoggin. Keoka has looked every day."

"There is plenty of sweetgrass," he told her impatiently, and next day took her to the swampy marshy banks where they found some of the satiny olive-green sweetgrass, with pink bases. It was very tiresome work pulling each blade, mixed in as it was with the other grasses. He helped Keoka gather some for making baskets in the long winter months when they would be confined.

He brought her soapstone too, and hung it from the center pole in their lodge. This, along with the good clay from the Androscoggin, would make sturdy vessels and pottery. He would help Keoka until she learned to properly pound the vessels as she shaped them in the heat. Already she had made them bowls to eat from, and etched a little design into them.

Around the clearing of the fresh cut field, the woods were thick with berries; strawberries, raspberries, even blueberries. These Keoka often added to her bread, or just served them plain. She was becoming a good cook, and Metallak searched long and hard for the choicest game and the softest furs to reward her. They seldom quarreled in their new home.

They always rested on Sunday. Metallak had been taught by the Good Fathers never to work or hunt on

Sunday. It was a day of rest. Keoka admired his loyalty to his religion, but still took the precaution of placing an offering of grease on the fire whenever she cooked, to thank Tabaldak for their good fortune. She did this furtively so that Metallak wouldn't see her make this offering. He would scoff at her and call her a pagan. But she felt so alone here away from all the villagers, especially when Metallak was away hunting. The howling of the wolves often frightened her, and she would draw Paugus closer to her.

"Keoka will carry a stick at all times," Metallak told her when she complained, and brought her home a stout walking stick. "Always return to our lodge before darkness and light a fire." She felt much safer with the stick and ventured farther and farther away from the lodge seeking the juciest and ripest berries.

Sometimes Metallak would come home early to surprise her. In her soft, melodic voice, she would be talking to little Paugus, telling him an old legend from her childhood. Paugus understood none of what she said, but giggled appreciatively.

Tonight she was telling a story that was one he too, remembered from his childhood. He sat back contentedly in front of his lodge and listened.

"Long long ago," Keoka began, "there lived one Indian alone, far away from the others. This old Indian did not know of fire, and lived on roots, barks, and nuts. The poor lone Indian grew lonely, and lost his appetite."

"As he lay there thinking, there came to this old man a vision of a beautiful woman with long golden hair, unlike any he had ever seen before. He sang to her of his loneliness and begged her not to leave him. At last the beautiful woman told him that if he did as she said, she would remain always with him. She took him to the dry grass, and instructed the old Indian to get dry sticks and rub them together until a spark flew out. Soon the small grass burned over. Then the beautiful woman told him, "when the sun hides, take me by my hair and drag me over the ground." The old Indian did this because she told him wherever he dragged her, grass would spring up and he would see hair between the leaves, and that he should use the seeds. The old man did as she said, and now all Indians know where the silk on the cornstalk comes from."

Paugus gurgled deeply as though he understood, and then Metallak entered his lodge, a proud and happy man.

The following day, Keoka gathered berries longer than usual and had just straightened up from her spot in the bushes when she noticed a wolf leering at her from behind a tree. Furtively, she turned and saw two more off to her left, just behind her. Quickly, showing no fright, she removed Paugus's cradle board from a nearby tree where it hung from a branch and with him safely on her back, she walked hurriedly, towards home, the heavy stick in her right arm, the birch bark carrying a pail full of berries in her left. She swung the stick from side to side as she walked, hoping to frighten off the wolves, who now had increased in size and they brazenly trotted behind her. Terrified, Keoka broke into a trot and used the stick as a weapon, lashing out at them and yelling. They would slink off for a moment, then rejoin her as she ran. At last the lodge was within sight. Keoka breathed a sigh of relief and lashed out at them again. She began to scream "Aiiieee", hoping Metallak would hear. He came running out of their lodge, gun in hand. But when he saw the size of the pack, he didn't dare risk hitting Keoka and picked up a stick to help stave them off.

"Run for the lodge," he told her, running out to meet the oncoming wolves. As Keoka ran to him, out of breath and hysterical, she tripped on a root, half hidden in the twilight. It sent her sprawling at Metallak's feet, the baby exposed on her back as he slid from his moss bag.

Instantly, the pack fell on them, one of them biting into the neck of Paugus, opening a large vein. Blood spurted everywhere, like a fountain. Metallak dared not fire, but drew mighty blows with his stick, killing two of the wolves from sheer rage and frustration, smashing them in the skulls. The others slunk off towards the woods.

Keoka scrambled to her feet, then screamed when she saw Paugus in Metallak's arms. He was lying still, no more movement to the lively little arms and legs. No more bubbling smile. Keoka began tearing her hair out and lashing herself with cuts and scratches.

Metallak held the child in front of him and faced the heavens as he spoke, his voice quivering with rage. Keoka had never seen his face more like granite or his color so white. "Hear Metallak speak!" he yelled. "Metallak puts a curse on the wolf family!" His arms dripping with the blood of his first born, he laid the child down and took up his hatchet. Quickly, he severed the heads of the two dead wolves, mounted them on stakes, and planted them into the ground.

"From this day forth, no wolf is safe from Metallak!"

Keoka had never seen Metallak in such a state. She was frightened, and sat like a ghost holding the dead child, rocking back and forth. She placed Paugus in his father's arms gently.

"Soon Metallak will have a new boy son," she told him. "When the snows come. Has Metallak not noticed how much Keoka eats these past weeks? The wolf family will not get Metallak's second son." She hung her head in shame that she had tripped.

"Metallak does not blame Keoka," he said. "One day we will have many sons, to replace our firstborn." Tenderly, he carried their little Paugus into the lodge and laid him gently on a rug. He prepared a sheath of bark to carry the infant to Father Pierre for a Christian burial.

The villagers were grief-stricken at this evil which had befallen Metallak. Some wondered if Keoka had brought a curse on her own son. When they saw her face, their hearts went out to her and they consoled her as best they could. Old Molly tried to make Keoka rest, but she was unable to eat or sleep. Metallak sat by his son, not leaving his side for an instant.

Molly made lovely little moccasins for the burial ceremony, and Keoka laid out his finest deerskins for this long journey, for which Paugus was placed in a sitting position, his favorite plaything placed in his hands, a cowhand rattle. Father Pierre blessed the ground and prayed for the soul of the little child. "He is an angel," he assured the parents. "Even now he looks down on us from heaven." That evening as he visited the

117

grave, he found Keoka furtively setting a tallow candle over the grave.

"What are you doing, my child?" he asked. He had tried for many years to discourage this pagan practice of having a light over the grave for seven days following a burial.

"Keoka is lighting the way for Paugus," she said simply, tears streaming down her face. "Does Mon Pere think Paugus will find the way?"

"I'm sure of it," he told her, and prayed with her to the Virgin Mother to look after the child. Finally, he left her alone to grieve. It had been a long and disturbing day, with the women moaning and lamenting over the grave, their grief uncontrollable. He was unable to reason with them when they reached such a state and simply retired to his lodge.

When she left her baby, finally, she walked blindly into the outstretched arms of the Shaman who had patiently waited to catch her alone.

"Get away from here!" she screamed at him, pounding his chest with rage. "Your powder did nothing to protect little Paugus. You are evil!"

She ran from him, wondering if he had placed a curse on her newborn. She never saw the tear trickle down the dirty face from the one pale eye he possessed. He too, was shaken by the death of the child, whose death would do nothing to improve his stature in the village. Once again, he would be scoffed at and ridiculed. He muttered into the night that Keoka was still possessed by the Devil, who had caused the death of the small one.

"One day there will be no one around to protect her," he promised himself, rubbing his hands together, his teeth chattering. "I will wait."

Keoka gradually overcame her grief and talked of the new papoeis. Oozalluc made little shirts and moccasins and talked often of the coming child to keep Keoka's mind on the living. In her own quiet way, she gave solace to Metallak too, by her soothing presence and calm way of discussing their future. Metallak was grateful for her friendship, knowing that she had forgiven him for choosing another. But both Metallak and Keoka were impatient to leave. They missed their little lodge on the Androscoggin and Metallak longed to take revenge against the wolf family.

family.

They were well prepared for winter. Already, baskets of dried berries hung in the lodge, and tubs of frozen meat lay in the river. Again and again Metallak took up his gun and his knife, leaving a trail behind him as he ravaged the forest for wolves, planting their heads on a stake for satisfaction. But it was never enough. His tiny son lay deep in the earth forever.

When Metallak returned from his mid-winter hunt, Keoka presented him with a new son. "Keoka has called him Andwilumpi", she said proudly. Metallak felt warmth creep back into his heart as he looked down at the soft wavy hair of his newborn and the fine even features of his face. Gently, he picked up the little one and kissed him, then carefully placed him next to his mother.

"So Keoka too has been busy," he teased her, his eyes alive and warm again.

Keoka rose and hugged her husband, glad to see him in such a happy mood. His somber black eyes frightened her because they were so often filled with sadness. But Andwilumpi was playful from the start, and quickly won their hearts. Keoka often sang to him and repeated the old Indian legends even before his eyes could follow her movements. Soon they nicknamed him Olumbo, and once again Metallak would sit outside his lodge and listen to his wife's soft voice. Pride would not allow him to sit inside and listen to these absurd tales, but still they amused him and he enjoyed hearing them. Sometimes Keoka would even make up stories he had never heard, which were much more interesting. He perked up his ears.

"Olumbo had a brother just one short season ago. This brave little brother has gone now to the land of Wa-ba-ban, the pretty lights of the sky. Here he followed the Spirits' Path, along the Kat-a-gus-wowt, Milky Way, to the land where children play all day long. There small warriors have many lights on their heads, and wear belts all colors of the rainbow. Paugus is very happy in the land of beautiful lights."

Metallak swallowed the lump in his throat and wiped a tear from his face. Keoka must never lose this second son. He would not allow it. He would carry the tiny warrior himself when they walked in the forest. Already, the woods were filled with the heads of the wolves he avenged for this dreadful deed.

119

Never would his hatred be satiated for these wild beasts.

Sometimes, though, he grew angry with Keoka. She was so like a child herself, carefree and irresponsible, often neglecting her household chores to play in the sun. Try as he would to instruct her religiously, she persisted in many of her pagan beliefs.

"Keoka behaves like a child," he chided her, watching her prepare Tmakwa for their evening meal. She was carefully removing the small bone from the back paws of the beaver. He knew she would save all the animal's bones to be thrown back into the water, out of respect.

"Keoka tries to be a good wife, to save Metallak from madness or misfortune," she retorted, continuing with her task.

"Everyone knows that is only a superstition, an old wives' tale."

Keoka was angry. No matter how hard she tried, she couldn't seem to please Metallak and turned to face him.

"Metallak believes in the same superstition as Keoka. That is why he never takes two shots at the same beaver, afraid the beaver will return to life again."

"Metallak does not waste ammunition," he replied quickly, looking away from her probing eyes. It was true that he always refused to fire a second shot because of this old superstition. After all, the beaver was the insignia of the great Abenaki nation. He felt a deep respect for this animal and hunted him only every third year, so the beavers could continue to breed. He regarded them as possessively as the whites did their horses.

Keoka boiled their beaver, as great tragedy might befall them if she roasted it, and then, as always, she carefully carried all the bones and threw them into the nearby water. She was determined to prove that Metallak was just as superstitious as she herself.

"Why does Metallak go to confession?" she asked innocently as they ate.

"Keoka knows well that Metallak makes peace with God every year."

"Perhaps Metallak is afraid of Loup Garou."

"Metallak afraid? Never!" he snapped back, waking up the baby.

120

"Keoka has heard of Loup Garou," she continued, going to pick up the drying child. "If a warrior does not got to confession for seven years, this beast appears, especially to strong warriors like Metallak. The warrior will try to strike the beast back if he can. And if one drop of blood comes from the head of the beast, the warrior will be liberated."

"Keoka talks like a silly old woman," he told her, walking away in anger. How did Keoka guess that he was plagued by this nightmare? Time and time again, he would wake in a cold sweat, raising his club to hit this wild beast, the old wives' tale coming alive in his dreams. He had been thinking lately that perhaps he and Keoka should make trips twice a year to the mission village to make peace with God.

Neither of them admitted it, but the truth was that they were lonely for someone to talk to. Metallak especially missed his parents and his people, and yearned for their company. Although there were white settlements nearby, they were strangers to him and he didn't know how to go about seeking friendship.

As Olumbo grew, he and Keoka often traveled with Metallak on his treks through the forest. Although Metallak loped ahead of them impatiently, he enjoyed their company, and was very proud of Keoka's skill with the bow and arrow.

"Metallak has found a secret place to show Keoka," he told her one day.

"Keoka will like this secret place?" She smiled mischievously.

He smiled, "Perhaps we will find a gift hidden in the forest for Keoka."

She ran eagerly to him. "What is it, Metallak? Please tell Keoka."

He smiled at her enthusiasm, as eager for a gift as Olumbo would have been. "Keoka will see for herself," he told her, surveying her small form in her deerskin tunic. Green would go well with the tunic, he was sure.

They approached a high bluff along the east side of Dead River Pond.

"From here, we climb like the mountain goat," he told her, taking Olumbo in his arms.

Keoka followed, scratching her head in bewilderment. Why was he taking her into these rocky clefts? She paused a moment, and then lost sight of him.

"Metallak," she called, her voice echoing.

"Here, in the cave!" His voice sounded hollow, and thin.

Keoka found the opening and slipped inside, adjusting her eyes to the dim light.

"Metallak's hidden cave is bigger than his lodge," she commented, looking at the length and breadth of the cave. As her eyes adjusted to the light, she ran from one side of the cave to the other, spotting the mottled red walls, the different shades of green, and the rich brown with more streaks of green running through it like a tiger with stripes.

"Keoka is in the land of Wa-ba-ban," she whispered, her eyes lustrous. Now she would have many jewels to wear about her neck, her arms, even from her waist.

Out of the walls Metallak chipped out great hunks of colored rock, handing them to Keoka. She stuffed them into the pouches she carried, still in a daze at such good fortune. When Metallak was all finished and the pouches would hold no more, he turned to Keoka. She spoke softly.

"Metallak is kind to Keoka."

"Keoka is like a Queen of the forest," he told her seriously. "She should always look like a Queen." He stared at her curiously. "Does Keoka not remember this is the month we were wed?"

"Metallak has remembered!" she exclaimed, throwing her arms around him there in the Jasper cave, Olumbo chuckling amiably at all this excitement. He picked up a piece of bark from the floor and sucked on it.

"Our son grows hungry," Metallak said, suddenly sounding stern again.

Quickly Keoka gathered him up and opened her tunic to him, glad she still had milk enough for this child. This child must grow strong and tall like his father. She found a cozy spot in the grass for him to nap while she and Metallak lunched on a rabbit. Metallak rose suddenly, looking above them at the sun.

"We must go now to the other cave," he told her, waking Olumbo. "But Keoka must never speak of these caves to anyone. Greedy people will sometimes kill for such riches."

"Keoka will never speak of the caves," she promised solemnly.

Not too far away, he revealed a much smaller cave, warm and dry, a safe place to store his furs until trading time. Keoka gasped when she saw the piles of furs already stocked.

"What will Metallak do with all these furs?"

He put his arm around her and stared at the skies. "One day Keoka will have a lodge such as those of the whites. This lodge will have a root cellar, stairs, a place for cooking . . . sleeping too. Perhaps even two windows. Above all, it will have a door that cannot be pushed open by a wolf," he added.

Keoka's eyes danced with sheer happiness. "Metallak is the best husband in all the Abenaki nation," she told him proudly.

"When Metallak goes again to trade in Andover," he told her, "Keoka will come too, and our son," he added, winking at Olumbo.

Keoka thought this had been the happiest day of her whole life and often when she was alone, she would relive the happy moments in the cave.

From their little lodge on the banks of the leisurely Androscoggin, backed by the craggy mountains and surrounded by graceful sweeping elms and oaks, they talked eagerly of the coming trip.

Early one morning when the sun shone more brilliantly than any other, they set out with their furs for Andover. In some places, the wide sluggish river would grow narrow and seem to be falling. Metallak navigated these small falls with ease, as Keoka and Olumbo kept the canoe in balance.

Metallak loved the river of his boyhood, and knew all its secrets.

"Far away," he told her, " where the water of the Amariscoggin mingle with the waters of the Kennebec, many rivers flow into one great bay, an old meeting place of all the

123

Close to there are the huge Pejepscot Falls. Metallak has been there often."

Keoka sat listening quietly. Very seldom did Metallak share memories of his past. One day she would tell his children of these waters, just as Metallak described it. They came upon a smaller river, the Ellis River, where they branched off to Andover, then onto the small settlements. Olumbo clapped happily at the sight of the cattle grazing in the fields. Keoka could feel the curious eyes of the children and villagers who watched their arrival. Some came closer to see their choice furs and pelts. Small children pointed at them, surprised to see real Indians. Keoka kept her eyes down as the men stared at the visitors. Finally one of them spoke.

"Moses Merrill," he said, holding out a hand to Metallak. "Mind if I look over your pelts?"

Metallak liked the looks of Moses, in spite of his big nose. He had a kindly look about the eyes and didn't waste words. "I am called Metallak," he told the big man, extending his own hand. "How do, Moserill."

Moses stooped and examined the skins and furs for about five minutes, then straightened and faced Metallak. "Tell you what," he said, chewing tobacco placidly. "These are good furs, best I ever saw. Hardly no marks on 'em." Metallak said nothing, but his chest rose with pride. "You and the missus and boy stay with us and sup, and we'll talk.

Word had spread of this tall, powerful Indian who kept to himself and Moses knew that he alone was responsible for killing hundreds of wolves, wolves that killed off their cattle and threatened their families.

Metallak was intrigued by Moserill's dog, who obeyed his master always, stopping dead in his tracks when Moserill spoke. He was a large, wolf-like dog, majestic in appearance, with a huge white chest and narrow gray body.

"So you like my dog, eh?" Moserill laughed, rumpling his fur. "Brought him all the way from Connecticut when he was just a pup." He began telling Metallak about Old Three Toes.

"We been bothered by this wolf for a long time," he said. "Can't seem to lay a finger on him. Outguesses us every time, like he's laughing at us. Never seen nothing like it.

124

Killed off half the sheep in the valley so far."

He chewed his tobacco and spat. "Tell you what," Moserill finally offered. "You find Old Three Toes for us and I'll git you a dog like that."

"Metallak will find Three Toes," promised Metallak, looking carefully at the dog. Secretly, he was elated. He would have given half his furs to have such a dog, and all he had to do was find a wolf.

"Now I'm a man of my word," added Moserill, guessing Metallak's thoughts, as he passed the cheese. Metallak had already refused twice, but apparently Moserill though he was just being polite. He disliked the strong smell of this strange food, but hated to offend Moserill. Taking a small piece, he managed to slide it down to the dog under the table. Keoka hoped Moserill hadn't noticed.

It was all arranged. Keoka would stay on with Mrs. Merrill while Metallak and Moses went hunting.

Early next morning, taking two hunting dogs, Moses led them deep into the forest where the wolf had last been seen, and on the third day, they found tracks.

"That's him," said Moserill excitedly. "Them's his tracks." Carefully, Metallak examined the tracks.

The old wolf was cagey and knew he was being tracked. He doubled back, causing them to walk miles for nothing, as he climbed higher and higher. The men, both in good physical condition, stopped only long enough to chew a piece of jerked venison and take a drink.

The wolf grew hungry too, and the temptation of the two hunting dogs overcame his reluctance to show himself. He grew more brazen, stealing up on the dogs at every opportunity. At last he attacked one of the dogs, the two of them rolling over and over, biting and gouging each other. Moserill dared not fire, afraid of killing his dog. As he raised his rifle, the wolf fled to the woods again and the dog lay dead in the path. The wolf left a trail of blood, probably from the dog bites. They sat on a dead log and waited. When the wolf slunk out that night to tear at the carcass, Moserill raised his gun to fire, but the old flint lock jammed and the wolf stood poised to lunge at Moserill. Metallak raced toward them with a raised club and threw it at the wolf, then when the wolf jumped at him, he delivered several strong blows, finishing the job. After a great deal of admiration for the size of the beast, they set out for home, dragging the wolf behind them.

The townsfolk of Andover were astonished. Some had even come to believe that Old Three Toes was more legend than fact. When Moses explained how Metallak had saved his life, everyone wanted to shake his hand in thanks.

The town had a celebration that night, and the jug was passed again and again. Metallak tried to keep pace with Moserill, taking a drink every time his friend took one. The last thing he remembered was a crazy dance. He could see Keoka dancing provocatively as the townsfolk clapped their hands, but he couldn't seem to catch her. She seemed to float right away from him.

The next morning he found himself asleep on Moserill's floor, his head throbbing with pain. He met Keoka's reproachful eyes with shame, knowing that he drank far too much of the rum. He wanted to return to the privacy of their little lodge, to solitude and peace. He was filled with guilt when he gazed at Keoka, already beginning to show signs of the child she carried.

"Metallak does not remember last night," he confessed and she smiled at him, saying nothing. She had discovered that her husband was not perfect after all.

"Lots of Indian raids here," Moserill told them at breakfast. "Two little girls was kidnapped just last summer." Metallak looked at Keoka and the two of them spoke together. "Tom Hegan!" Metallak knew that Tom Hegan was still raiding, his hatred of the settlers never cooling. Just hearing about his raids made Metallak's blood pound furiously. His eyes grew black with anger when he remembered the cell back at the mission village. He listened patiently while Moserill explained that the town would pay him to protect them from this madman.

"Metallak will take the job," he told them, longing for revenge. "I will patrol the waters and forest around the village. We leave now to set up lodgings and bring supplies."

Keoka was silent on their return trip home, which puzzled Metallak. Usually she found something to chatter about, entertaining the baby. He said nothing, respecting her privacy, but wondering what was troubling her. As though she felt his eyes on her, she looked up and spoke.

"Metallak will fight his own Abenaki brothers?"

"It is not right to raid white settlements, or take their children," he said, avoiding her eyes. "Soon there will be many whites in our old hunting grounds. Our son will not have the privacy of the forest as we do. We must think of the whites as our brothers and seek friendship with them." He surveyed the virgin forest around them, as though to burn into his memory forever the sight of the beautiful timber untouched by axe or plow.

"Metallak will be paid ten shillings a month," he added proudly. "One day Keoka will have a fine lodge." Olumbo began babbling, "Lumbo lodge, Lumbo lodge."

Keoka's good nature returned at the sight of her son speaking his first words, and she began drawing a sketch of a lodge for Olumbo. As for Metallak fighting his own Abenaki friends, she said nothing. He had made his choice and she would stand by him.

The days passed quickly and Keoka tried not to worry about Metallak. Sometimes he was gone for a week at a time and her heart would hammer with fear, but he always returned, usually late at night under cover of darkness. Often he would find Keoka with Olumbo in her arms, where they had fallen asleep together. Guiltily, she would jump up and place Olumbo on his mat, ashamed to have Metallak know how lonely she had been.

True to his word, Moserill delivered the pup to Metallak, and the whole family was delighted with him.

Olumbo sat quietly for hours watching his father train the dog to leap in and out of his canoe without touching the sides. Then he taught him to carry game and sit protectively by his son. Often they would curl up together and nap in the sun. In spite of this, Metallak worried that his son might be attacked by wolves. He bargained for a second dog with Moserill. Then at last he began to relax his vigil, knowing his son was safe.

Olumbo called this dog Moslem after his father's friend Moserill, which delighted Old Moses. Before long, he had a little brother to play with also, named Parmagunnit. While Keoka was busy with the newborn, Metallak trained the second dog. This dog Metallak sometimes took on his weekly treks through the forest while he continued to train him. A whole year passed with no more attacks on the little village.

Metallak put by a good store of money and developed a strong friendship with Old Moserill. Metallak found Moserill to be a good hunter and a good companion on a hunting trip. He said very little but always seemed to know what Metallak was thinking about. He took a great interest in Keoka and the children, which pleased Metallak also.

Two years later, in 1788, Metallak welcomed his daughter, who pleased him beyond measure, his own beautiful daughter. She seemed to be smniling even at birth, and he named her Parmachenee, Smiling Water. For her, he fashioned a special Tkinogan, of the finest ash. Her jet black hair soon fell out, and in grew the fine chestnut silky hair of mother. Metallak knew she would be a beautiful woman one day.

He paid little attention to Keoka, who had grown quiet and withdrawn with so little companionship for five long years, except for the occasional trips to Andover with Metallak. Yet when she complained to her husband, he grew impatient.

"Keoka has a fine lodge, and many fine skins to wear. What more do you want?" Frustrated and angry, Metallak left the lodge. She had refused to go to Andover with him last week, even though she was lonely. He would never understand women.

Keoka wept quietly in her lodge. How could she tell Metallak that she didn't feel welcome in Andover? It seemed to her that the women avoided her, as always. Sometimes they whispered when they thought she wasn't looking. More and more she turned to the children for companionship. Making certain that Metallak was not around, she drew a little rum from the jug in the corner and sipped on it.

Like many of the farmers, Moses had a still at his farm, and had taken to giving Metallak great quantities of rum, which Metallak stored at their lodge although he never drank in his own home, as he had promised himself many years ago. Only recently, Moses had questioned Metallak about the rum.

"How do you like the rum?"

Metallak hesitated a moment, then spoke bluntly

128

to his old friend.

"The rum is fine," he said, "but Metallak wonders why there is so much brook in it."

Moses shook his head, puzzled. He knew the rum was fine and good. He couldn't imagine why Metallak thought he'd watered it down. Unless somebody else was watering it down. Once he opened his mouth to speak of this to Metallak, then changed his mind and said nothing. The best thing to do in a case like this was to mind your own business.

Finally, Metallak came to know what was going on, when he chanced to come home early one day and found Keoka with a cup in her hands. She was smiling to herself and Parmachenee was crawling near the fire. He grabbed the child first, then slapped the cup out of Keoka's hand.

"Too much rum is dangerous!" he shouted. "Keoka almost hurt Parmachenee."

Guiltily, Keoka got up and began starting their evening meal, stumbling in her efforts.

"Keoka is lonely," she said, tears in her eyes.

Metallak stalked out of the lodge and didn't come back until late that night, when he was calm. "Keoka is right," he finally admitted. "It is time we visit our friends and relatives. Keoka will have no need of the rum now."

"Does Metallak promise?" she asked, delighted to hear the news.

"We leave tomorrow," he told her. She had grown even more beautiful than ever before, he thought. Her eyes danced with joy at the thought of the games, feasting and celebrating. Furtively, she made plans. She would bet many wampum beads against Metallak's prowess and skill, and win back even more.

Outside their lodge, Metallak was bending down the poplar saplings to make a loop for the boys to sit in, let it go spinning up, and then gently down to release them again. It was a good swing. As she watched, Keoka never doubted that her boys would be the fastest runners in the village. The boys too were excited about the trip and helped their parents get ready.

They traveled up to the village at Mon-fo-mom-o-bog by canoe and on up the Nulhegan River to the Clyde River, the longest trip their children had ever been on. Keoka talked to

129

them excitedly of village activities. Olumbo would not leave Moslem, and held him on his lap.

Keoka took more interest in her wampum than she did in the childrens' appearance, and the villagers were amazed to find Metallak's children in ragged shirts and worn moccasins. Old Molly set to work immediately to make new ones.

CHAPTER SEVEN

Old friendships were renewed, and Old Molly was delighted with her grandchildren. Metallak tried to persuade his father to join them when they returned to the Androscoggin. For hours, they sat discussing this, and Metallak knew his people longed for the freedom that he and Keoka enjoyed. Inside, his heart sang. A few more days and they would be persuaded to come back with them. They would make another village and once again, his family would be with their own people. They would all learn that the whites were not to be feared, that they could all live together in peace. He was about to leave his father's lodge when Tom Hegan stepped through the door. Metallak rose in anger, his hand clasping his knife as did Tom Hegan.

"That is enough!" interrupted Pial. "While you are both here in the village, there will be no fighting. This you will promise me as Chief of the tribe." The stern commanding voice of the old man made itself felt. Without a word, Metallak left the lodge, refusing to meet Tom Hegan's eyes. For hours he sat and meditated before he returned to his lodge. Tom Hegan's timing couldn't have been worse. No doubt he came to tell Metallak's people that Metallak had betrayed them, had taken a job for the whites.

The thing that really hurt Metallak was that his father still welcomed Tom Hegan to his lodge. As long as he continued to remain loyal to this half-breed, there would be no peace between them. Even now, he was probably filling Pial's ears with lies, or making promises he didn't intend to keep. His wife, Metallak noticed, had grown as coarse and unkempt as her husband, always covering her dirty face with jewels, sometimes even wearing them in her nose.

They had brought a guest with them this summer, a strikingly beautiful niece named Madeleine of seventeen summers. Her flawless beauty and agility reminded Metallak of Keoka, although her black hair was not nearly as pretty.

Keoka, too, disliked Tom Hegan being there in the village. She dared not venture far from the lodge alone, wondering if he would try to harm her or the children. Still, she couldn't avoid

131

the females and found that Madeleine loved to flaunt her good fortune with the young braves who sought her favor. She seemed to find any number of excuses to visit their lodge and consult with Metallak, who found her visits amusing. This infuriated Keoka, and she ignored Madeleine most of the time. As though determined to cause trouble, Madeleine tripped Keoka one day as the women returned from gathering wood.

"This one is so small I did not see her," she said laughing, to her friends.

The giggling made Keoka's temper snap. She jumped up and faced Madeleine, hissing quietly in a half whisper.

"If the clumsy one is wise, she will stay away from married men, or great misfortune may follow her."

By now a crowd had gathered and many of the women laughed nervously.

"What kind of misfortune, small one?" Madeleine tittered.

Keoka raised one eyebrow and whispered again. "You will find out," then slapped Madeleine in the face, leaving her hand print, and Madeleine ran home to her Aunt Polly, telling her only one side of the story.

Polly listened in stony silence, remembering the past. All too well she remembered that day years ago, when she found her husband swimming with Keoka. But she had gained nothing by whipping this evil one. The elders had disapproved and shamed Polly. Even her husband had been very angry when he had learned of Keoka's disappearance. And now Keoka chose to pick on her niece Madeleine. She chewed her tobacco, deep in thought. Surely there must be a way to get even.

"Do not speak of this to my husband," she told Madeleine, looking around to make sure they were not overheard. "We will get even with the evil one ourselves." All afternoon she sat and plotted, eager for this chance to get even with Keoka for all the embarrassment she had caused.

But rumors of the incident in the village had reached even the ears of Tom Hegan before he returned home. He too, plotted and connived for a way to get even. Anger burned in his chest at the thought of Keoka rejecting him, Chief of several tribes, desired by all the women of the village. Instead, she had chosen Metallak, a weakling who coddled his prisoners and befriended the whites. But it was whispered that Metallak found his niece attractive. He would soon find out. He chose his words carefully that night as he spoke to his wife in their lodge.

"Metallak has lived too long among the whites," he remarked casually. "It is rumored that his wife has has picked up their crude habits." He spat on the ground. His wife nodded solemnly, saying nothing.

Madeleine, flushed and angry, looked at her Uncle, wondering how much he knew. Somehow, she felt he had another reason to speak of Metallak and Keoka, and she was sorry she had gotten involved.

"Let us invite Metallak and his wife to visit," he said with a knowing smile. "After all, Metallak is still one of the best looking men in the village," he continued. "Is this not true?"

"And Keoka likes to gamble," Polly replied, grasping his plan. "It is whispered that she even drinks of the white man's rum."

"Well, well, let us share our bounty with them," Tom Hegan said, tapping his fingers greedily.

Pial and Old Molly heard the rumors with grave misgivings. They had hoped that Metallak and Tom Hegan would forgive and forget as the years outgrew their differences. There were so few of their people remaining they should be loyal to each other. Pial urged Metallak to reconcile his differences with Tom Hegan and forget the past. "Our lodges are meager and small," he said. "And the tribes along Memphremagog are loyal to us. When game grows scarce, we will all share together as brothers. Tom Hegan's hatred would be a threat to all of us. I ask that you make amends before it is too late for all of us."

Metallak said little, thinking and brooding. Did his father really think he could be friends with a man he despised?

"All I ask is that you try, Metallak, to set an example before your people."

Metallak nodded curtly, saying nothing. Apparently his father knew nothing about Tom Hegan's raids in Andover. Very well, he would not betray their secret either, and would keep up a pretense of friendship for his father's sake. But never again

133

would he trust Tom Hegan.

He finally gave his consent to Tom Hegan's invitation, persuading Keoka that he went only to obey his father. He assured her it would stop the gossip that she was jealous of Madeleine. Grudgingly, Keoka gave in, checking her appearance several times before she finally ventured out with Metallak.

Madeleine, certain that Metallak came only to see her, waited on them herself, giving Metallak the choice cuts of meat and biggest helpings. With false heartiness, she filled Keoka's cup with rum several times, hoping she would appear ridiculous and embarrass Metallak.

As the warmth of the powerful drink relaxed Keoka, she began to enjoy herself, thinking perhaps she had misjudged Madeleine. Even Polly seemed amiable this evening.

"Polly is a good cook," Keoka complimented. "One day you must all join us at Metallak's lodge to share our bounty also."

"We are honored by your visit," said Polly graciously, a malevolent smile on her greasy face.

As Madeleine refilled Keoka's cup, she leaned forward and whispered in her ear.

"Later on we gamble."

Keoka began to giggle and laugh, and as Tom Hegan played the drum quietly, she did a little dance in the center of their lodge.

Angry with Keoka's behavior, Metallak rose abruptly. "The sun sets early," he said. "And the fire grows cool in our lodge."

"Keoka does not wish to leave yet," she pleaded with her husband.

"Then Metallak leaves alone!" he thundered, passing out the doorflap.

With Madeleine's encouragement, Keoka stayed well into the night, gambling away her beads and jewels, even some of the little chipped rocks from the secret cave.

"Metallak will get more for Keoka," she said excitedly. "From the secret cave."

Tom Hegan leaned forward eagerly, asking many questions about the secret cave. But Keoka giggled helplessly.

"It is a secret," she laughed. "Keoka has promised."

Polly lost no time slipping out of the lodge to spread the gossip that Keoka gambled and drank of the rum in her husband's lodge. Even her husband had grown disgusted and returned to his own lodge alone. The village buzzed with gossip. Never before had a married woman behaved so brazenly in the absence of her husband.

Next day Metallak was curt and abrupt with Keoka, stalking off without telling her where he was going or when he would be back. The villagers too ignored her, their scorn hurting her deeply. Alone in her lodge, she brooded, thinking that Madeleine was practically the only friend she had in the village. When Madeleine appeared at the door of her lodge, Keoka greeted her warmly.

"Keoka has fresh hemlock tea for Madeleine," she said, rising to pour the fresh tea. Madeleine noted Keoka's sloppy appearance, and her tearstained eyes.

"Madeleine wishes to help Keoka," she told her disarmingly. "Madeleine would be happy to watch the little ones so Keoka can visit old friends."

"That is very kind of Madeleine," Keoka returned. "And Keoka will win plenty of wampum to repay Madeleine." She thought quickly. "Already Keoka has a gift for Madeleine," she said, taking from her pouch some of the colored jasper chipped out by Metallak.

Madeleine's eyes lit up with joy and greed. "Keoka is truly kind."

Each day Keoka took to going out, gambling her wampum away. There were always other fallen women or some of the young braves willing to gamble. But she seemed to have lost her skill. The pile grew smaller and smaller. Keoka grew frightened that she wouldn't be able to buy rum and frantically made plans to gamble even more, making arrangements when Metallak was away from the lodge.

Old Molly heard the gossip and cautioned her son. "The entire village gossips about Keoka," she said.

"They say Metallak's wife neglects her own children to drink and gamble. This is sinful, my son." Molly hung her head, sorry that her words hurt Metallak.

Metallak listened in stony silence, neither denying nor confirming what his mother said. He wanted to scream that it wasn't o, but he knew his mother spoke the truth. Angrily, he turned and eft the lodge, his jaw set with determination.

He entered their lodge and towered over Keoka's mall frame, demanding an explanation.

"The entire village, it seems, talks of nothing but Keoka! They say that she drinks of the rum, neglects her children, and gambles away all that Metallak provides. Is this true?" He stared at her, daring her to deny all that he said, yet hoping that she would.

Keoka humbly stared at the floor, nodding her head.

"So it is true! Keoka wishes to shame the lodge of Metallak, and of his father, Chief Pial!"

"No, no it is not true," she sobbed, but Keoka is so lonely, and I wanted to make you proud with my winnings. And Madeleine offered to watch the children for me."

"So! It is the work of Tom Hegan again," he stormed. "From this day forward, Madeleine does not enter this lodge!"

Keoka nodded her head meekly.

"And there will be no more drinking or gambling!"

"I give you my word, Metallak," said Keoka, cleaning up the lodge. Relieved, he left their lodge, hoping she would keep her word.

He hated to leave the village just now, noting his father's slowing footsteps and tiredness. He still walked straight and tall, but seemed more gaunt and pale this summer. One night his father asked him to come to the sweat lodge for a talk.

"Metallak remembers Jeremiah Eames, of the white colony in Stratford?"

Metallak nodded, remembering this man's loyalty even when he knew that Metallak had helped Keoka to escape.

"Eames had made several visits to see me," Pial continued, "to ask that his friends may purchase the Indian Stream territory. They promise always to be fair, never to take from us the pleasure of hunting of venison or the fishing of the streams. He has promised that the Cowassucks will be allowed all the ground they need to plant corn, or track the moose. Most important, they promise to protect us from other whites. They come fast now, and some have hatred of their red brothers. It is Pial's wish that Metallak make up deed with the white man's words, giving the land to Eames. One day when Pial is no longer able to travel the forest, Metallak will give this deed over to Eames. Metallak and his people will always be free to hunt the ancestral hills of our fathers, and our grandfathers.''

Metallak sat deep in thought. Although he liked most of his white brothers, he hated to see their encroachment on the ancestral grounds of his people. Soon there would be less game and less privacy for his people. He looked at his father, who studied his face anxiously.

"I will do as you wish, my father. It is a wise course of action." Deep inside, he felt at peace. At last his father had seen the light, that they must share with the whites if they were to survive. Surely this meant that his father no longer tolerated the evil raids by Tom Hegan.

Next day, Pial called a meeting of the Grand Council to explain what he planned to do one day with the Abenaki hunting grounds. The elders listened carefully, but some of the young braves protested vigorously.

"Pial grows weak like an old woman," said one angrily. "Perhaps he has need of the skirt," said another, laughing.

Pial rose to his full stature, lifted the talking stick, and slowly spoke.

"Do the young men see on yonder hill that tall green pine? Note how bravely it stands braced against the rocks, laughing at the strong wind. That is Pial of many moons ago. But now Pial is like an old shivering maple in the cold of winter, the covering leaves gone, the old branches crackling with age under the heavy weight of many snows. One day soon there will be no more sap in that old maple. It is so with Pial. But Tom Eames is just like our Indian brothers. More so. Eames will help our people . . . protect them from greedy whites. Eames has given Pial his word on this."

Pial sat down heavily and passed the talking stick to Metallak.

"Hear me, my brothers," said Metallak. "One day Metallak will lead you as my father has done. Harken to the words of my father. Have we ever been without fresh meat or corn for the long winter? Have we known hunger such as our white friends, when great snows come and bellies are bloated with hunger? Have we lost face with the whites since the dreadful day when my grandfather Paugus gave his life in Lovewell's charge? Do we skulk through the forest and hide like rabbits in the tall grass, like some of our red brothers? Hearken to

137

Metallak's words. Did you not send Metallak to the white man's school to learn more of the white man's ways? There is room in Indian Stream for all of us to live together, with no more battles. As for the village at St. Francis, it is a place of refuge where no white may enter, save for the British.''

Some young braves muttered under their breaths, but most of them lifted their lances. They cheered in loyalty.

The elders conferred with each other quietly. It was true, was it not, that Pial had been a good and wise leader? They would think on this deed to the white men as Pial grew older. They too wanted no more bloodshed.

Madeleine was angry that Metallak refused her the hospitality of his lodge and blamed Keoka for his rejection. She took to luring Keoka's children to visit her lodge, offering them sweets and playthings. Soon Keoka took advantage of her spare time, slipping slowly into the old ways.

When Metallak would return to his lodge in early evening, there would be no fire to greet him, no smell of cooking food. Finally, Keoka would return, all apologies and smiles, and quickly made his supper. But Metallak no longer trusted her. His face grew taut and he wore a frown most of the time, puzzling his children even more than it did the villagers.

One night he returned home to find Madeleine in his lodge. Angrily he ordered her out.

Madeleine sauntered out slowly, saying "Madeleine is always in her lodge. Why does Metallak not pay her a visit?"

Metallak avoided her eyes. "Metallak has a wife already."

"Keoka often visits other lodges, sometimes even with men. Why not Metallak?"

"What does your evil tongue try to say?" he demanded, a menacing look in his eyes.

"Why don't you look in Tom Hegan's lodge if you don't believe Madeleine?" she taunted.

Metallak struck her across the face, cutting her lip. "Madeleine lies!"

Madeleine wiped the blood trickling down her lips

138

and backed away from Metallak. Hatred flashed in her eyes.

"Keoka is good for nothing–Pizwat!" she said, and spat on the floor. Nervously, she backed out of the lodge, afraid she had gone too far.

Metallak continued to stare vacantly after she had left. Suddenly, he realized that his mother stood at his shoulder with a bowl of hot tea.

"Drink this tea, Metallak," she said. "Hot tea will make you feel better. I will feed the little ones." She took the children with her quietly.

Finally, Metallak stormed out of his lodge, angry and disgusted with Keoka for bringing disgrace on his name and on the names of his children. But it could not be true. He would not let it be true! Madeleine was just a troublemaker. He remembered the tantalizing smile on her face when she told him to look in Tom Hegan's lodge. Surely it could not be true!

Without realizing it, he had made his way to Tom Hegan's lodge, where Polly sat outside smoking a pipe. As usual, her appearance was offensive, her hair uncombed, her face greasy and dirty. She was throwing bits of fat to the dogs, who yelped for more.

"Does Metallak enjoy the night air?" she questioned, puffing noisily on her pipe. "Or does he look for Keoka?" Now at last she could get even with this small spider who caused so much pain.

"Polly has seen Keoka?" he asked hopefully. Perhaps he had misjudged Polly that day long ago with the whip. He offered her red osier for her pipe from his own pouch. She tamped the tobacco carefully down into the stem bowl and whispered.

"Perhaps Metallak should look inside," she whispered, afraid to have her husband hear. "Keoka spends all her time with Tom Hegan. And tonight he ordered me to leave the lodge." Tears trickled down her dirty face as she continued. "Keoka is a bad wife. Polly speaks the truth."

Metallak no longer heard. He had stealthily opened the flap in the side of the lodge and looked inside. In the semi-darkness, he could see Keoka stretched out with Tom Hegan in front of the fire on a bear rug, the white bear rug he had brought Keoka himself! Her moccasins lay at the edge of the lodge.

Cautiously, he made his way out without a sound. He would deal with Keoka later. Crawling back to Polly, he said. "Polly will never speak of this night, do you understand?''

The glitter in his eyes was frightening, even to Polly. She dropped her pipe in fright, wondering if she should confess that she and her husband had deliberately given Keoka too much rum, causing her to fall asleep. Instead, she dropped her eyes in fright. "Polly has seen nothing, she will tell nothing.''

Metallak walked quickly back to his own lodge in a daze, overcome with nausea and burning in his throat. Why had Keoka done this to him, in his own village, with his own worst enemy?

From another part of the village, another watched and waited, biding his time. He had lost face among the villagers. No longer was he an important part of the clan, but was scoffed at, even by the children, all because of this evil creature. He had been unable to drive the demon from Keoka, and yet he admired her courage and strength. Together they could have had a good life, but she preferred to scorn his love. First Metallak, and now Tom Hegan. He brooded, thinking about revenge. Sooner or later, his chance would come.

Metallak lay by the fire contemplating his future as Chief with no wife and three small children. How would he manage? He thought for hours, then broke his own vow never to drink in his own lodge. He drank greedily from the jug in the corner, seeking a vision that would help him. But even the rum could not dull the pain of betrayal, and even through the walls of his lodge, his mother heard him sobbing.

When Keoka crept in to join him in the early dawn, he turned to her, and said in a drunken stupor. "Leave this lodge now, tonight! Keoka is no longer Metallak's wife. Go away and never come back!'' He motioned to the sleeping children in the corner. "Metallak will find a good woman to care for them.''

Keoka began to cry and protest. "Keoka fell asleep. It was the wine that Polly put into my cup. Keoka grew very sleepy and I could not rise from the floor. Polly gave me a mat and told me to sleep. I did not know the hour was late.'' She begged Metallak. "Please give Keoka another chance.''

"Keoka has had many chances–but she is evil.'' Keoka could barely understand his slurred words. "Metallak has two enemies now–the wolf family and Keoka!'' He turned his back on her.

Keoka crept about the lodge, picking up her supplies, extra petticoats, and good tunic. She would go to Oozalluc's

140

lodge. Surely tomorrow, when he was sober, Metallak would come to his senses. She would ask Polly to explain what had happened.

"Let Keoka take Parmachenee," she begged.

Even in the half light, she could see the glitter in his eyes when he sat up.

"No! Go now and leave Metallak in peace."

Lightning lit up the sky and soon thunder joined in an evil omen. Keoka was frightened. Even the Gods in the sky were angry with her. She fled into the storm, picking her way through the mud, her tunic soaking wet. She must find shelter from this torrent of rain. Desperately, she scratched at the door of Oozalluc's lodge and crept inside.

"Please let Keoka stay," she pleaded. "Metallak has thrown Keoka out." She cried loud sobbing cries.

Oozalluc knew that Metallak would never be unjust. She had seen and heard the gossip about Tom Hegan and Keoka.

"Keoka is no longer welcome in Oozalluc's lodge," she said. "Leave now or I will wake the village elders."

Keoka ran from the lodge, hysterical with fright. Lightning flashed about her, as she looked for shelter. She ran toward the river, but seeing the flicker of a candle in the Shaman's lodge turned and ran the other way. She ran headlong into waiting arms that gripped her like a vise. She tried to see through her rain soaked hair but was unable to identify her captor. She felt herself being pushed down into the mud and felt the hands about her neck, closing off her breath. She lashed out with her fingernails to no avail. She felt herself sinking, sinking into a black pit of darkness. Metallak could feel someone shaking him by the shoulders. He sat up and clasped his knife, holding his breath.

"Put the knife away, my son," his mother told him in a soft voice. "Pial awaits Metallak. Come quickly." Instinctively he rose, the grave tone of her voice sobering him. He followed his mother to the next fire in the long lodge, where his father stood waiting.

Slowly, his father came forward. Never had Metallak seen his face look so somber, or his eyes filled with such pain. His father spoke simply and to the point.

"Pial has bad news, Metallak. It is Keoka. But first I must know this. When did Metallak last see Keoka?"

Metallak tried to think, to quiet the pounding in his

head from the rum. He could not seem to remember, his mind was a total blank. Then it all came rushing back, the argument, sending her out into the rain.

"Keoka was found early this morning not far from here. She had been strangled," Pial continued. Pial studied Metallak's face as he spoke. He saw disbelief, shock, horror. He continued quietly. "Tell Pial what happened last night."

Nervously, Metallak pulled at his jagged black hair, his temples pounding. Keoka could not be dead, it could not be true. He felt his teeth chattering as he replied.

"Metallak found Keoka in the lodge of Tom Hegan last night. When she returned to our lodge, I ordered her to leave forever," he confessed.

"What time was this?"

"Just before dawn came, Niboiwi, when light comes down through the heavens.

"Does anyone else know of this?"

Metallak felt unable to think, to feel, and still his teeth chattered. "I pledged Tom Hegan's wife to secrecy. There is no one else."

His father showed little sympathy. Metallak stared at him, unable to believe his father could speak of this so calmly. "Pial goes now to the Grand Council, to see what others will say," he said. "Pial does not make decisions alone. Metallak knows this. Already the young braves are angry. They say a true warrior does not kill his wife, even an evil wife like Keoka.

He watched his father walk away, a broken man, his shoulders slumped with grief.

"Where is Keoka?" Metallak demanded of his mother, who burst into tears.

"In Oozalluc's lodge, where they prepare her for burial," Old Molly confessed. "You must not go there." He led his mother back to his lodge still in a half trance, not believing what had happened. The children were running about searching for food, and Parmachenee was wailing for her mother. Metallak sat with his head in his hands, unable to think or speak.

Old Molly scooped up Parmachenee and took the children with her, giving Metallak a clumsy pat on the shoulder as she left.

"Metallak did not harm Keoka. A mother always

knows these things."

But she had seen the empty jug beside Metallak's mat and had heard the angry voices in the night. Her heart was heavy with fear for her son.

The village was consumed with gossip and disbelief. Never before had such a thing happened. Men sometimes struck their wives in extreme anger. There were those who even took a second or a third wife, but to kill a wife was unforgiveable. Even the Good Father warned against punishment by death.

Metallak's lodge was as silent as the grave. The emptiness in the lodge nearly drove Metallak mad. Everywhere he looked, he saw Keoka's face. He tore the etchings from the wall and rolled them up, tears running down his face. Why hadn't he given her just one more chance? He looked up to see his son come running into the lodge.

"Mother is dead," cried Olumbo, great sobs racking his small body. "Shaman Ignatius said the demons took her. Make them give her back, please?"

"Olumbo must not listen to wagging tongues of old men and old women," his father said sternly. "One day Olumbo will be a great warrior."

"Make mother come back," pleaded Olumbo with all the logic of his five summers. Metallak felt helpless and filled with self pity as he looked at his son's tear-stained face. Parmagunnit followed suit and cried "Mother, Mother!" Oozalluc heard their cries and came running in to help. A tear slid down her face when she saw Metallak with his head in his hands ignoring the cries of the children.

"Come play games with Oozalluc," she invited, holding out her arms. Her eyes met the anguished eyes of their father on her way out. Grateful for her help, he said nothing, oblivious to all but his own pain.

Oozalluc confided to his mother as she passed by her lodge. "Metallak did not do this evil thing. We must find the real killer."

Oozalluc said nothing about her own part in Keoka's tragic death, but the truth haunted her. Why had she turned Keoka out of her lodge into the storm? Deep down, she knew it was jealousy and she hoped God would forgive her. She lavished attention on the children, her heart filled with guilt.

"Old Molly does not know what to do," replied his mother, rocking back and forth at the fire. "Surely the Grand Council will speak soon, before sundown. But Old Molly feels their wrath at Metallak. All along they have been against this marriage, and now the worst has happened." She hoped and prayed that Tom Hegan would be expelled from their village forever. He was the cause of all this grief and the loss of her son's wife. Then fear filled her heart. What if Metallak decided to take his own revenge? Hurrying, she brought hot tea to her son, telling him what news she had overheard.

"Do not fear the worst, Metallak. Pray for the truth to appear. Metallak has many loyal friends in our village. Only the jealous ones speak out against him, their evil tongues wagging that Metallak has picked up the ways of the whites in the Indian School." She faced her son. "But most say that Metallak is a good man, and could not do this evil thing." She kissed him quickly on the cheek, then ran out of the lodge.

Metallak just sat and stared, not seeming to hear or see anything but blackness. He could not even feel anger, only a deep deep shame. He had turned his wife out into the storm, into the arms of a killer, brought disgrace on his parents and his village, and now his little family had no mother. He must restore honor to his family name - but his heart was too heavy to think.

At last his brother came to bring news. "Pial speaks well, but some are against us," he reported. "They say that Metallak is strong headed and sets a bad example." The two sat silently for some time.

Just before sunset, Metallak was called to the lodge of the Grand Council for their decision. It was not easy for Pial to give this grave news to his eldest son, but it was his duty as Chieftain.

"The Grand Council has made their decision," he said sadly. "All day we have talked of the past, recalling our favorite son, the extra burden he always carries when we move about, the generosity he shows with his hunting bounty, the quick flash of his arrow. All these things we remember. But never before has an Abenaki brave committed such a serious offense. Is it wise, question the elders, for such a man to lead his people? Many of us believe you are innocent, and hope that the truth will come out in time. Until such time, the Council has reached a decision. Metallak must be banished from the Cowassuck tribe, never to lead his people until his name is cleared."

Metallak held his head high, his face deeply

flushed. Never to be Chief of his people, and to be unjustly convicted. The unfairness of their decision filled him with rage. His eyes glittered as he spoke.

"The Council is wrong. Even now, the traitor walks among you, a sneak and a liar. Metallak will find him and justice will be sought. May this traitor be cursed forever!"

With that, Metallak turned and left, going quickly to his lodge. There was not much to pack. They would travel light and live off the land and the water. Clumsily, he tried to pack fresh moss into a vessie for Parmachenee, who was always wet.

He did not hear Oozalluc's footsteps behind him. Never had he felt so humiliated and so alone, angry at the world, even at Keoka for leaving him in such a helpless situation. Why had she forsaken his lodge for another? He longed to tear Tom Hegan apart, limb from limb, until there was nothing left but his bones. But what good would that do? Surely Tom Hegan did not kill Keoka, when they had been together only hours earlier.

He drove his fist into the ground in despair. Oozalluc spoke quietly in a soft soothing voice.

"Metallak is a brave warrior and is well known for his kindness and honesty. Soon the truth will come out and clear Metallak's good name, and the real traitor will be found. But for now, let Oozalluc keep the little ones until Metallak makes a place for them"

Gratefully, Metallak turned to her, tears in his eyes. "Metallak trusts Oozalluc, who has always been a loyal friend," he said. "I ask that you treat them as your own children until I return to clear my name."

"Oozalluc is honored," she replied, tears in her eyes too.

His mother joined them, a package of dried bread and a pouch of corn in her arms. Her voice broke as she tried to speak.

"Together, Old Molly and Oozalluc will care for the little ones. Soon, with God's help, we will learn the truth about this evil deed, and Metallak will return to lead his people."

Metallak held his sons and told them he would go to make a new home for them along the Androscoggin.

"No, No!" cried Olumbo, terrified that his father too, would be lost to him. "Take me with you, father, please!" His chin quivered as he held back the tears.

"I will come back for you, my son," Metallak told

145

him. "I leave the dogs both here in your care until you join me in our new home. But first Olumbo will learn many things - to bring down a bird - to speak the white man's tongue - to hunt with a bow and arrow. Then Metallak will come for Olumbo."

"Olumbo will work hard," he promised solemnly, holding his head high like his father. Little braves never cried, no matter what. He would help look after his little brother and sister, an important chore.

Metallak did not tarry. He held his sleeping daughter one last time, touching her lightly on the nose, gripped his sons in a tight hug, and with only a nod for his mother and Oozalluc, slipped through the side door without once looking back. The sooner he got away from here, the better.

Keoka's funeral was a very somber affair. There was very little lamenting or shedding of tears. Because of this stranger, the villagers had lost a strong warrior, their future Chief. And she was not even an Abenaki. Some spoke in whispers for the sake of Metallak's children, but others spoke more openly about the tragedy.

"Keoka never belonged here, but Metallak would not listen," his aunt was overheard to say.

"Let us ask the Good Father to offer prayers for Parmachenee, that she does not follow in her mother's footsteps," said another.

In the Abenaki fashion, Keoka had been wrapped in a long section of birch bark and placed in the earth. One day her sons would cleanse and scatter her bones, as children should. The pouch that she carried was given to Olumbo, her eldest son, who guarded it as carefully as his mother had. It was the only thing he had left to remind him of his mother, who had been gay and carefree, never whispering evil things about others as these old ladies in the village did.

Metallak's mother wore a black mantle of mourning and socialized very little. The village was plagued by sadness, and uncertainty. Who knew what would happen when the whites moved into the Indian Stream territory? Pial had depended on Metallak to deal with the whites and now Metallak was gone, perhaps forever unless his name could be cleared. Some of them watched each other warily, wondering if perhaps Metallak was right and a traitor walked among them.

Shaman Ignatius lost no time asserting his old powers again. "Ignatius warned you of the demon in Keoka, but

146

nobody listened." He drew little attention with this feeble bid for power. He had been unable to help cleanse Keoka's spirit of evil, in spite of all that he promised. He grew surly and unkempt, the lack of respect for his position penetrating to his soul.

Oozalluc watched and listened, seeking a clue to this terrible act of injustice. Surely the real killer would reveal himself sooner or later. What had Keoka been doing in Tom Hegan's lodge, and why did Metallak turn her away? Oozalluc waited for a chance to see Polly alone, and finally approached her when they were out gathering wood.

"Did Polly not see Keoka entering her lodge that fateful night?"

"Polly saw nothing, nothing!" retorted Polly, breaking into a nervous high pitched laugh. "Tom Hegan would not touch a dirty woman like Keoka." She hurried away from Oozalluc with her little armful of sticks.

Oozalluc did not give up so easily. She spoke to Pial one evening when bringing him some of her leftover stew.

"It is rumored that Keoka visited the lodge of Tom Hegan on the night of her murder," she said bluntly. "Even now, Polly denies it."

Pial pondered her words for some time. He too had heard this gossip, and remembered well the old bitterness between his son and Tom Hegan. But strangely enough, Tom Hegan had not spoken out against Metallak as some of the others did, and he had no reason to accuse him of any crime. As a Chief, he must not show disloyalty to anyone, and weighed his words carefully.

"Oozalluc speaks with a twisted tongue," he said. "Tom Hegan is still a guest here, head of many small bands of Abenakis along the waters of the Umbagog and Mom-fo-mom-o-bog. Because the white settlers fear Tom Hegan, we may traverse the land in peace."

Oozalluc left with tears in her eyes, making her way to her own lodge. Perhaps the whites feared Tom Hegan because of his dreadful attack on Bethel in 1781, but he and Metallak were old enemies, and Tom Hegan was jealous of Metallak's popularity with the whites, and with his own red brothers. And it was common knowledge that Tom Hegan's niece Madeleine had been very interested in Metallak, encouraging Keoka to drink and misbehave.

Oozalluc forgot all her problems as the children ran

to greet her, throwing their arms about her. They took great comfort from her kindness in this time of sorrow. She couldn't run quickly through the tall grass as their mother had, but she could bait a fish hook and mend moccasins better than anyone they knew. She taught them to speak in the white man's tongue, and form their letters. This progress delighted their grandparents.

Oozalluc found a wet nurse for Parmachenee, and for Parmagunnit now four years old. Soon she would try giving them goat's milk or even milk of the cow. She did not believe in prolonging the breast feeding as some of the others did, now that his mother was gone. The busy chatter of the children filled her heart with joy, but she grieved for Metallak, who must miss the children sorely. She guarded them zealously lest someone should try to harm them as they had their mother.

She didn't trust Shaman Ignatius, and went out of her way to avoid him. She had caught the malevolence in his remaining bloodshot eye when he chanced to encounter Metallak's children. She had even heard that he made strange prophesies about them. They would be evil like their mother. Oozalluc should rid herself of them. Only today she had passed him lurking behind her lodge and overheard the incoherent muttering.

"Those little ones left in Oozalluc's care. . . Shaman's duty to drive the evil from their bodies . . . seek a vision, vision." She had shivered and hurried on past his voice, determined not to leave the children unattended for one moment. She cautioned the boys never to speak to him or go to his lodge.

Madeleine was anxious to leave the village, now that Metallak was gone. But she wasn't sure how to persuade her Uncle. Then she had an idea, and approached him.

"Metallak plants his corn crop and rules all of Indian Stream, perhaps even the territory of Tom Hegan," she hinted, with a smile.

"No one enters the territory of Tom Hegan, especially a traitor!" he retorted, ordering his band to pack up and make ready to travel. Word spread of their leaving, but few came to see them off.

Polly seemed in a great hurry as she clutched her roll

and made her way to the water, but Oozalluc managed to knock it out of her hands as they passed, then gasped when she saw the tiny moccasin, one that she herself had made and given Keoka as a gift.

"Where did Polly get that moccasin?" she demanded.

"Polly found it in the mud," she stammered, at a loss for words.

A crowd had gathered in a semi-circle. Tongues wagged anew and heads drew closer.

"It is true, then, that Keoka visited Tom Hegan's lodge."

"Let us see what the elders make of this," muttered one of them.

Polly hung her head. "Polly did not wish the villagers to know of her shame," she whispered. "But Polly did not harm Keoka."

"Where is Keoka's other moccasin?" asked one of the elders.

"Polly does not know," she sobbed, getting into the canoe.

"What is this sniffling?" her husband demanded. "Give them the moccasin if they want it. It is only a curse on us!" With that, they left.

The whole town talked of Keoka again, and the strange tragedy. How did Polly come by the moccasin? Why did she try to hide it? Was Metallak innocent after all? Already, many of them regretted their decision to banish Metallak.

Tom Hegan's band traveled to several villages before returning to his summer home. The story of Metallak and Keoka was told and re-told. Grand Chief Louis Antoine soon knew of Metallak's banishment. Sebattis was speechless. He had missed his old friend sorely, and never expected to hear such news as this.

Knowing how cowardly Tom Hegan was, Sebattis immediately suspected him of arranging the whole thing, perhaps even killing Keoka himself. Quietly he set about leaving the village, to find Metallak and learn the truth. The villagers must be mad to believe such a story. Sebattis knew better than anyone else how deeply Metallak had loved Keoka, in spite of her faults. He packed quickly, and left at dawn. He would set out for the Androscoggin and find Metallak himself. He knew the territory as well as Metallak did, and he knew his

149

old friend's habits better than anyone else. When he began to find the heads of wolves implanted in the soil, he knew he was on the right track. Finally, he found Metallak's clan symbol emblazoned on a tree.

"Metallak passed here," he read. "Go Andover."

Sebattis canoed up the Androscoggin to Andover and inquired for Metallak. "Moses is Metallak's best friend. They hunt on yonder hill."

Sebattis made his way toward the distant hill, the words rankling him. Metallak had only one best friend and that was Sebattis. Halfway up, he heard gunshots and came upon Metallak and Moses gutting and quartering the meat from a ten point buck.

Metallak's eyesight was keen and he recognized Sebattis even from a distance. He gave a hearty whoop, and for a moment they were boys again, carefree and young. Then Metallak grew somber, remembering the past. They talked until late that night about all that had transpired these last few years. For the first time all summer, Moses saw Metallak's eyes light up with interest. He knew that Metallak grieved sorely for Keoka and the children, though he seldom spoke of it. Moses respected his solitude, and never asked questions. But he knew that Metallak blamed himself for all that had happened. More than once he had murmured in his sleep, "It's all my fault," as he was tossing and turning.

"What news bring you of the village?" asked Metallak, eager for news.

"I tell you, Metallak, Joseph Louis grows more religious every day, preaching more than the village priest. Our old friend Tom Hegan comes to stir up the people, encouraging them to raid, even steal. But many of the villagers no longer listen. He grows angry with his cowardly brothers, as he calls them, and takes solace in the rum."

Metallak grew flushed at the mere mention of Tom Hegan's name. He felt almost certain that he was connected with Keoka's death, but still, it didn't make sense. Keoka had gone to his lodge of her own free will. And his wife was right there at the lodge. How could he have been involved?

Sebattis ventured, "It is rumored that Metallak has been banished from the village."

Metallak nodded, a tortured grim look in his eyes. "Metallak will find the traitor one day," he said.

"Perhaps Sebattis can help."

"Metallak needs no help from anyone!"

Sebattis ignored the fury in Metallak's face. He knew the hostility was not directed at him, but at the unfairness of all that had happened. Metallak could be independent if he wished, but he, Sebattis would keep his ears open. Nothing loosens the tongue like firewater, and sooner or later, he would hear something that would clear his old friend's name.

Later on that evening, in the privacy of his own lodge, Metallak spoke seriously to Sebattis.

"Promise, me, Sebattis, that you will visit my children. I cannot face them until my name is cleared. But I can help in another way." Sebattis could see the anguish in his old friend's eyes as he dragged out two large bundles of furs.

"What would you have me do, Metallak?"

"If these furs were traded, my sons would have warm blankets, perhaps a skillet for Oozalluc." Metallak nervously pulled at a stray hair on his neck. "Tell them I long to see them and hope to visit soon." In his guilt-ridden mind, he imagined a hundred times a day that they blamed him for the death of their mother, that they too, thought him guilty. How could he ever face them, these innocent children who longed for their mother?

A day never passed that he didn't blame himself. Why had he not listened when Keoka said she was lonely? Why had he been impatient with her clumsy attempts to make pottery and baskets? Why hadn't he joined in when she played games with the children? Much as he would have liked to confide in Sebattis, his pride wouldn't allow it. Sebattis had always looked up to him as the future leader of their people. How could he tell him about the burden of guilt that he carried, the nightmares that haunted him with the past? No, it would not be the manly thing to do.

He would keep these things to himself.

"Metallak has my promise," Sebattis assured him, "that I will visit your sons often, and bring Oozalluc what she needs." He wanted to add that what his sons needed most of all was to see their father, but he saw the faraway look in Metallak's eyes. He was not yet ready to see his family.

And so it was that sometimes Sebattis would visit the village, bring Oozalluc news of Metallak, and whatever supplies she needed. Often he took the boys fishing, a week at a time, and they looked forward to his visits eagerly.

151

But there were times when Jeremiah Eames himself delivered the supplies in a horse drawn wagon. It seemed he was enchanted with little Parmachenee and always had a little gift for her. After a time, Oozalluc felt more comfortable with this tall sandy haired stranger who brought news of Metallak. Before long, they were good friends.

"Metallak is well? she would call out, running to meet him.

"Fit as a fiddle," answered Jeremiah. "Lives like a hermit though, talks to no one except old Moses up in Andover. He and Sebattis are his best friends." He tugged at his mustache. "His pride is hurt and it gnaws at him. He doesn't want to face anyone until his name is cleared. Any chance of that?" He looked straight at Oozalluc, thinking that for all her ugliness, she had beautiful understanding eyes.

Oozalluc shook her head no, adding. "I would give anything to learn the truth. The boys long for their father. His daughter does not even know him." She looked toward the beautiful little girl racing to catch up with her brothers as they ran.

Jeremiah said no more, hoping to pay a visit to Pial while he was here in the village. Then he remembered and pulled out a beautiful fur. "This fur Metallak wished Oozalluc to use for her bed," he said, gravely holding it out.

Oozalluc blushed. "Tell Metallak Oozalluc is grateful, that his parents are well." She handed Jeremiah another set of leggings and shirt for Metallak, who refused to wear the white man's dress. She gave him several pairs of moccasins too and told him to keep one pair himself.

After he left, she draped the beautiful fox fur over her shoulders. She would be the envy of the entire village with this beautiful fur. Perhaps Metallak was beginning to think of other people, other things. She loved keeping his children, but they were growing fast. Soon Metallak would miss the passing of their youth.

Still, she knew she would miss them terribly if he ever came to reclaim them. She had grown to love them as her own, and took great pride in their achievements and skills. And with each little disappointment they suffered, her heart suffered painfully too. Parmagunnit grew rapidly and had learned to speak English quickly, articulating his words carefully. He was such a serious little boy, always deep in thought, while Olumbo was quite the opposite, always in a

152

playful mood that captivated the others.

Although Oozalluc tried to ignore it, there wa
something peculiar about Olumbo. Though his intentions were good
the boy was sneaky and often told falsehoods. Oozalluc worriec
that one day he would come to harm because of this habit. She told him
tales of Azeban, the raccoon and the many problems he encountered
because he told untruths, but time after time, she caught him
disobeying her, and taking advantage of his brother. Only thi$
morning she had pretended not to notice, when he ran to greet hi$
younger brother.

"Give Olumbo the fresh trout," he said, holding ou
his hand.

"No!" yelled Parmagunnit, clutching the three
fish.

"Olumbo will play ball with Parmagunnit later," he
promised with a grin, and his brother gratefully turned over the fish
Olumbo carried them proudly to Old Molly, saying "Grandmother
here is trout for breakfast," making her beam with pride. Oozalluc
could not bear to interfere, especially when she saw the big hug from
Olumbo's grandmother. She knew that he needed the hug more than
he needed the fish, more than the love of his brother.

Pial spoke more and more frequently of Metallak
these days, and Oozalluc knew that he missed him sorely. But the
mystery of Keoka's death remained unsolved. He had hoped that long
before this, his son would come to him and all would be as it was. Bu
now he feared that perhaps this would never happen, that he migh
never see his son again.

Oozalluc watched and listened, but learnec
nothing. She knew that the bloom of her youth was fading, and she
felt older than her forty three years, faced with three small children and
no father to care for them. She lived only for the visits from Sebatti
and Jeremiah, when they brought news of Metallak. Sometimes she
made up stories of Metallak, just to please the boys. He had gone back
to the place of his own boyhood to kill off all the wolves so they would
be safe there when they joined him. Their eyes would light up with
hope when she relayed these stories. The little hand carvings tha
Metallak sent were saved for special occasions, when the boys were
especially lonely.

Big tears would fill Olumbo's eyes sometimes
though he tried to be brave. "Olumbo doesn't need a gift," he would

15$

ay in disgust. "Give it to Parmachenee!" throwing it down. But
Oozalluc knew how much he missed his father, and often found him
ater digging in the camp dust looking for the lost toy. Sensing his
grief, Parmachenee and her brother joined in to help him. Oozalluc
breathed a sigh of relief when one of them let out a whoop of victory.
The lost toy was found and all was well.

Sebattis became a regular visitor, and each boy had
a place on his knee. He described their father's lodge, down to the
last detail, even to the huge pile of wolf skulls behind the lodge. They
looked at each other in amazement. Oozalluc, too, had told them that
their father had killed many of the dangerous wolves.

"One day soon I will take you there," Sebattis
promised, "as soon as your father is ready."

"When, Sebattis, when?" they shouted all at the
same time, making him regret his ill chosen words. But he'd been
thinking about it for some time now. If Metallak didn't come to them,
he would bring the children to their father. Oozalluc joined in, seeing
his distress.

"Olumbo is the grandson of a great Sagamore," she
said. "And his brother Antoine is also the grandson of a great
Sagamore." Secretly, Parmagunnit loved to be called by his Baptismal
name Antoine because it made him feel special.

But as they grew taller, these little stories were not so
exciting. They longed to explore the forest and find their father themselves. They beseeched Sebattis to make plans for the visit.

"Are we ever going to see our father again?"
Parmagunnit asked one day out of the blue.

"One day your father will come," assured Oozalluc,
though she was no longer sure. It had been seven long years since she
had seen him, and months now since he had sent supplies. Perhaps
something had happened to him. After the children were asleep, she
prayed that they would see their father this summer. She stood outside
her lodge to take a breath of air and was surprised to see so many lodges
with candlelight. In the far distance, she heard sobbing. Frightened,
she fastened the door to her lodge and got back into bed.

By morning, she knew what was wrong. The village
had been stricken with the small pox again. Many of the elders could
remember the plague of 1755 and the many lives it had cost. The
mysterious disease spread rapidly, even to the children. Strange pink
spots appeared on the fallen victims, who tossed and turned in agony,

in spite of all that Moll Ockett and the priest could do. Most of them died shortly after a terrible hemorrhage of the nose, their bodies having a yellowish tinge.

The village huts were scattered, and those on the outlying areas had not yet caught the terrible sickness. In terror, many fled to St. Francis, seeking safety and help, leaving the ill behind. Oozalluc cautioned the children to stay far from the village, making them a temporary shelter in the woods nearby.

Sebattis urged Oozalluc to leave the village at once, take the children and search for Metallak. Pial and Old Molly must come along too.

"If we stay, the children may die," he told her.

That was all Oozalluc needed to hear. Quickly she went to consult with Pial and Old Molly, and persuaded them to come with her. Pial promised his people he would come to St. Francis after the great sickness had passed. When they urged him to come with them to St. Francis, he wavered.

"It is time to find Metallak, before it is too late," he told them. "Perhaps he too has the sickness and has no one to care for him."

It was a sad parting of old friends clinging to each other, not knowing if they'd ever see each other again, or who would be struck down next by the dreadful sickness.

With tears in her eyes, Oozalluc set off with the children, their grandparents following not far away. She hoped she had made the right decision, and that Metallak would welcome his family, especially the children. She knew that if he chose to keep the children, she would have to return to St. Francis alone. She tried not to think about it, trying to enjoy the children for these next few days. She wanted to remember the way Olumbo's hair clung to his small face, and the trusting smile of Parmachenee when her brothers held out their arms to her. She wiped a tear from her eye as the children chattered happily.

They asked Sebattis a great many questions about their father's lodge. Did he think it would be large enough? Where would they all sleep?

Sebattis found a dozen jobs to keep everybody busy, so they would stop asking questions. He hoped Metallak would welcome his family, but this much he knew. If Metallak didn't want them, he would make a home for them himself. Like Oozalluc, he

155

walked in trepidation, as they drew closer.

CHAPTER EIGHT

Oozalluc was glad they had to travel slow, with the grandparents and children. But in just a week's time, they made camp not far from Metallak's lodge. Sebattis hesitated, and decided to make camp here and then seek out his old friend. He was certain that old wounds would be healed and all would be forgiven between Pial and Metallak. Still, he knew how stubborn they both were and hoped they would use common sense.

He found Metallak in back of his lodge, his head in his hands, deep in thought. Startled, Metallak jumped to his feet and greeted Sebattis.

"Metallak should forget the past," said Sebattis. "The time has come to think of others who still live . . . Olumbo, Parmachenee, and Parmagunnit."

"Metallak thinks of them every day," he said humbly, looking away.

Sebattis studied Metallak for a moment, not certain how to begin.

"Sebattis brings grave news of the village," he finally commented.

"What news?"

"Many villagers are dead of the pox sickness. Others flee to the safety of St. Francis. Your parents have chosen to remain with you. They bring Oozalluc and the grandchildren. Moll Ockett, too, plans to join us later."

Metallak couldn't believe his ears. "Where are my children?" he shouted.

"We made camp yonder," Sebattis told him.

Metallak didn't wait for him to finish, but raced to the pen where he kept his pet moose. He stroked his neck gently as he mounted him. His friend stared at him, dumbfounded.

"How did Metallak tame the moose?"

"Metallak has plenty of time," he said modestly. "Three moose I have trained to the pen. Caught this one a little calf four seasons ago. I trained him young to mind the halter, then put him to ox work. This year Metallak rides him." He stroked the huge beast as he spoke, and held out his hand to Sebattis. Soon they were

157

both astride the moose. Sebattis could not believe the size of the animal and marveled at Metallak's skill. Truly Metallak was a remarkable man, taming a beast like this to do his bidding. He wondered vaguely what Oozalluc and the children would think when they saw Metallak.

"Not far from here we have made camp, at the head of the stream."

Metallak eased the moose through the trees until he saw the small wigwam and heard voices. His heart hammered like a drum beat, and his palms were wet. He drank in the sight of his children greedily, thinking he must be dreaming.

Two boys stood staring, overcome with awe at the sight of their father astride a great bull moose. Parmachenee burst into tears and ran into the lodge, thinking they were under attack.

The men slid off the great beast, and Metallak tethered him to a tree, speaking in gentle low tones. The moose might get nervous in all the excitement. Besides, he was not certain how to greet his family, and he hoped they would make the first move. Oozalluc came forward timidly.

"Metallak looks well, as always. Look upon your little ones, who thrive even now, when others die of pox. This is a sign of great strength."

Metallak grasped her hands, his eyes telling her how much he thanked her for the safety and well being of his children. His parents came forward slowly to greet their son. His mother looked thinner and much older in her faded calico. His father still walked with grace, but his movements were stiff. He grasped Metallak's hand.

"We have missed you, my son," he said.

Metallak swallowed hard and still the words stuck in his throat. He looked around, taking in the sight of his tall sons, the beauty of his dainty little daughter, and the welcome in Oozalluc's eyes. His mother sensed his discomfort and said quickly;

"Metallak has not changed a bit."

"But I see somebody who has changed," he said, scooping Parmachenee up into his arms and placing her astride his shoulders. This eased the tension and soon the boys, overcoming their shyness, begged for a ride on the moose. Oozalluc held her breath, waiting. Metallak put them both astride the huge beast and led them about for a time. But he cautioned them not to try it without him, because the moose was afraid of people.

Metallak helped them to pick up their few

158

belongings and took them to his lodge along Umbagog. He knew they would be safer from the wolves in his fine lodge of wood. And there were plenty of rocks nearby where his father could sit and fish if he wished.

Metallak was surprised that it was so easy to converse with his sons, who had a hundred questions, and laughed easily. Then too, they remembered him well, especially Olumbo. But Parmachenee didn't remember her father at all. She had smiled politely when he scooped her up into his arms, but he felt like a stranger to her. Still, he knew this was a long walk for her small legs. When her footsteps lagged and Oozalluc reached out her arms, he came forth and gathered her up. She quickly went to sleep in his arms, a smile on her face, and Metallak slowed his pace so as not to wake her. Oozalluc looked away, unable to bear the pain. Soon she would have to leave the little ones in the care of their father. She felt that she would die of loneliness. Still, she was grateful that the boys had returned to their father at last. The happiness on their faces made up for all the sleepless nights of worry. She looked up to find Metallak's eyes on her, and looked away, embarrassed. What if he guessed her thoughts?

Instead, she busied herself scolding the boys, who were counting the skulls they found in a mound in back of their father's lodge. Oozalluc had to laugh in spite of herself, as they suddenly dropped one and ran, Olumbo screaming that the wolf had come back to life.

Metallak was grateful that so far, no one had mentioned Keoka, not even the children. If they blamed him, they carefully concealed it, and he was determined to keep them with him from now on. For as long as he lived, he would never leave them again, unless they chose to leave him.

That evening when they gathered together after a busy day, Parmachenee timidly approached her father, this beautiful child of seven summers who reminded him so much of her mother. She had the same wavy chestnut hair and deep black eyes that looked far too serious for her lovely oval face. She was truly the most beautiful child Metallak had ever seen. Again and again he found his eyes on her, studying her delicate movements and thoughtful expressions. She found her voice.

"Will Parmachenee stay here with father?"

"Parmachenee will stay with her father always," he promised, as he gently drew her toward him. He held her for a time, and when she had fallen asleep, he placed her on the floor on a clean bear rug, wondering how he had managed without her all these years.

He sat quietly with the others, enjoying this intimacy with his family and the deep contentment in his heart. They were together at last and nothing else mattered. As for Oozalluc, she looked more beautiful to him every time he looked at her. He saw her eyes following the boys activities several times and wondered what she was thinking.

"They will soon be men," he said, breaking the silence.

"I will miss them very much," Oozalluc blurted out, her voice breaking.

"Surely you do not plan to leave!"

Oozalluc said nothing, not sure how to begin. "Well, they have their father now," she began.

"They have a mother too, and they love her very much." Metallak stared at Oozalluc, thinking she was worn out and sick of the children.

"Metallak will have enough mouths to feed without Oozalluc," she replied.

He rose in anger. "Have you ever heard Metallak complain of his duties?" As he strode back and forth, he regretted his outburst. Perhaps he had upset Oozalluc, the last thing he wanted to do.

"Promise you will stay," he said quietly.

Oozalluc nodded slowly, her heart singing inside. Metallak did not love her, but he cared. He had asked her to stay, and that was enough. They would be good friends, if nothing more. And she would be able to stay with the children. For the first time in many years, she slept peacefully.

They settled quickly into a comfortable routine. Throughout the long lazy summer days, the boys demonstrated their skills to Metallak, eager for his praise. And though Metallak seldom praised, he would give an appreciative nod in their direction, sometimes even a small reward such as a hunting knife. He still made all his own hunting tools and sharpened them daily. This he taught them to do as carefully as he himself, cautioning them that they must never be without tools for hunting, scraping, or cleaning.

He saved the finest furs for Parmachenee, watching for the smile in her eyes when she caught sight of them. Like her mother, she loved to wear pretty things.

Metallak often conversed with his parents and somehow, they managed to forget the pain of their last parting. He no longer had tortured dreams and cold sweats in his sleep, but fell asleep easily now. When Moll Ockett joined them and told them of the painful deaths among their people, he was doubly grateful that his family had escaped. His people were few now, but he had his own little family. He guarded them almost possessively, seldom going far from the lodge.

"Metallak's lodge bears many attractions, does it not?" teased Sebattis, noting how Metallak's eyes often followed Oozalluc's movements.

Metallak quickly blurted out his thoughts.

"Is Metallak blind," he countered, "or does Sebattis follow Moll Ockett about like a child?"

Stubbornly, Sebattis insisted this was not so. "Moll Ockett needs help to gather herbs, that is all."

But Metallak laughed and slapped his old friend on the back. "Perhaps Sebattis will give up his freedom after all."

The smoke of their lodge brought visitors that summer, white visitors. There was Pial's old friend Eames and three others, who came on business.

"We wish to settle the land," Eames told them. "But I give you my word, no harm will ever come to Pial or his people. Eastman, too, will help," he said, including his friend in the transaction.

"We will provide food and clothing for all of you," Eastman quickly added, "and you may stay here as long as you live."

"That is very generous," Pial responded, "but my people wish to have the freedom to plant their corn and beans in the spring here in the sacred grounds of their people. Without the hunting and fishing grounds, my people would starve."

"I give you my word," said Eames, extending his hand. "Pial's people are welcome here always, to hunt and fish, and make their summer crops."

Such a decision was not easy to make. For several days they worked out the details for Eames' deed. Pial handed it to Metallak, proud that his son could read and write. They all sat quietly as Metallak read them the land transfer aloud around the campfire.

To all persons to whom these presents shall come, greeting. Know ye that I, Phillip, an Indian, a native of America, now

161

resident in Upper Coos and Chief thereof, for and in consideration of the sum hereafter named, for which I have received security to my full satisfaction of Thomas Eames of Northumberland in the county of Grafton and State of New Hampshire and his associates, namely, John Bradley and Jonathan Eastman of Concord, county of Rockingham, and Nathan Hoit of Moultonboro, in the county of Stratford, all in the State of New Hampshire, esquires, all my peculiar friends. I have this day given, bargained, sold, released, conveyed and confirmed and by these presents do give, bargain and sell, release, convey and confirm to them the said Thomas, John, Jonathan and Nathan, their heirs and assigns forever all that tract or parcel of land and water, situated within the following boundaries, vix: Beginning on the east side of Connecteecock, now called Connecticut River, at the mouth of the Ammonoosuck River, then up said Ammonoosuck River to Head Pond to the carrying place, then across the carrying place to a small pond on the head of Plumpetussuck, or Dead River, then down said river to

Androscoggin River, then up the Androscoggin River to Lake Umbagog, including all the waters of said Lake and island; from said lake up Androscoggin River to Moleychunkomuck, then along the easterly side of said lake to the outlet of Mosseluckmegantick, then up said river to said lake Mosseluckmegantick, including all the waters and island thereof; then across the carrying place Sqwasuktemick, thence down said river till it empties into Awsisegowassuck River, then up said river to Palmachinanabagogg Lake, including all the waters and islands thereof, thence up Awsisegowassuck River to the carrying place into the Awsiemtecook River, a St. Francis River, thence down said river till it falls into the branch which empties from Lake Mamfloobagogg, then up said river to Skessawennock Lake, thence up said river to Mamfloobagogg, including all the waters and islands thereof, from thence up Massheecoowanggawnall river to the head thereof; then across the carrying place to the head of Walbeogawmuck, then down said river, including all the islands thereof to a mouth of the Ammonoosuc River, the place began at, agreeably to a plan I have this day given to them, their heirs and assigns forever, with the following conditions and reservations, vix: that I reserve free liberty to hunt all sorts of wild game on any of the foregoing territories, and taking fish in any of the waters thereof for myself, my heirs, and successors and all Indian tribes forever. Also liberty of planting four bushels of corn and beans. And this, my trusty friend Thomas, having given me security to furnish me and my woman with provision and suitable clothing which I have accepted in full. I have for myself and in behalf of all Indians, who hunted on or inhabited any of the foregoing lands or waters forever quit, claimed and sold as aforesaid to them the said

Thomas, John, Jonathan and Nathan as a good estate in fee simple, and do covenant with them that myself and my ancient fathers forever and at all times have been in possession of the above described premises, and that I have a good right to and will warrant and defend the same to them, the said Thomas, John, Jonathan and Nathan, their heirs and assigns forever against the claims of all or any persons whatever.

In witness whereof I have here unto set my hand, and seal and signature this twenty-eighth day of June, 1796.

> his
> Philip, Indian Chief
> mark
>
> her
> Molly Messel
> mark
>
> his
> Moosekit Sussop
> mark
>
> *Signed, sealed and delivered in
> presence of Jeremiah Eames and Ely Buck.*

To Metallak, the transfer of land was a relief. Now at last his people would live at peace with the whites in good faith. His children would one day live in these colonies with the white settlers.

It seemed the days of summer were never long enough. After planting their summer crop, he took his sons to the forest every day, training them to be skilled hunters. Although they were fond of his company, they did not take such delight in the solitude

163

of the forest as he did.

But here, in the quiet and soothing atmosphere of the tall timbers, Metallak found it easier to talk to them, and finally broached the subject of their mother.

"Metallak has never found the traitor who killed your mother," he told them bluntly one day. "And now Metallak has no more tribe, just his family." He sat staring for some time, bitter that even if he found the guilty one, many of his tribal brothers were stricken with the sickness and the tribe had dwindled to practically nothing. Antoine made his way to his father and placed his hand on his shoulder.

"Father has Olumbo and Antoine," he said proudly. "We will make our own tribe, my father."

Metallak was never more proud of his sons than at that moment. He was proud too, of their perfect English.

"Antoine speaks like a true warrior," replied Metallak. "Already we have two brave warriors in our small tribe."

"One Princess too," added Antoine, thinking of his little sister. Already the boys knew she was Metallak's favorite, the light of his lodge, but they weren't jealous. It seemed from the time she took her first step, she asked no favors, but accepted what was given, asking no questions. She seemed to sense when her brothers wanted to be alone, and never teased to come along unless she was asked. So her brothers pampered her, often whittling toys or playing hand games with her, sometimes letting her win.

"Parmachenee must walk straight," cautioned Metallak to Oozalluc. "It is not the fashion of whites to allow their feet to turn in."

"Oozalluc will see to it," Oozalluc said quickly, happy to please Metallak in any way. Perhaps she herself could learn to walk with her feet turned out too.

Sebattis helped Metallak put up a larger lodge. Carefully, they lined the windows with bladder skins. The women made soapstone bowls and picked acorns for cooking oil. For the first time in many years, Metallak felt content. He tried to forget the past. Instead, he thought only of his future and that of the children.

There had been no raids on Andover for several years now, but he still traded with Moserill, bringing out his skin and trading for potatoes and other necessities. He was eager to have Moserill meet Oozalluc, and took her to Andover with him the next time he traded. He knew she wasn't beautiful in the way that Keoka had been, but he wanted Moserill's approval and hoped they would be friends.

For some reason, Moserill took to Oozalluc right away, and so did his wife. They urged her to come often and bring the children. Oozalluc, too, seemed comfortable with his white friends, and Metallak was strangely relieved. In no time, Oozalluc had taught Mrs. Merrill to do a special stitch in her embroidery, and promised to make her a straw basket. Mrs. Merrill promised to make Oozalluc a fresh blueberry pie. She even approved Oozalluc's worn calico bonnet, and offered her a new one.

Metallak began to look at Oozalluc differently. He saw, instead of the ugliness of her round face, the beauty of her eyes, and the generosity in her heart. He saw, too, the way all three of his children looked to her for advice. she had grown slimmer in her years of caring for three children. Sometimes she caught Metallak staring at her, and blushed. She longed for the privacy of her own lodge where she could escape his eyes.

"Metallak will build a small lodge soon for Oozalluc and Moll Ockett?" she asked timidly one night.

"Metallak thinks on this," he told her solemnly. "But Metallak wants Oozalluc in the safety of his own lodge. Oozalluc has reared Metallak's children as her own, asking nothing. Now Metallak asks that Oozalluc share his lodge for the rest of her days." He held his breath, waiting for her answer. Though his face betrayed nothing, he feared that she would refuse. Why would she want him now, a man rejected by his own brothers?

She answered him slowly. "Oozalluc is an old woman now, past the age to bear sons for Metallak."

He held her hands in his as he spoke. "Metallak grows old too, and wishes to live with one who shows kindness in times of pain and sorrow, who always gives much and asks very little."

Oozalluc was stunned. Never in her darkest moments when she despaired of the future had she dreamed that Metallak would turn to her. She knew he would never love another as he had loved Keoka, and felt he was being kind to her only out of loyalty. Still, she saw the pain and loneliness in his eyes which only lately had taken on a carefree look. Sometimes he even laughed aloud. Could it be that he actually cared for her?

"Where would Moll Ockett live?" she asked, still

165

dazed.

He laughed. "Has Oozalluc eyes only for the children? Does she not see Moll Ockett departing each day with Sebattis at her side? If we do not hurry, they may decide to marry before us."

"Oozalluc will set a wedding date," she finally promised, immediately taking out her bone needle to make a new dress for the ceremony.

That evening, Oozalluc watched carefully. There was definitely a flush on Moll Ockett's face, she who had sworn never to re-marry, especially to one who took a liking to the rum. Sebattis seemed to take a great interest in everything she said and did.

"How does Moll Ockett know that the crane'bill will staunch the flow of blood?" he asked. "Has Sebattis not noticed that the geranium is the same bright red color as that of the blood? That is why Moll Ockett picked it."

"And the liverwort Moll Ockett brought for Grandfather Pial?" asked Parmachenee, a good listener too.

"Man, too, has a liver," replied Moll Ockett, "with the same shape as the liverwort. Has Chief Pial not grown stronger since he tasted of the liverwort?"

"When did you decide to be a doctress, Moll Ockett?" asked Antoine.

Moll laughed and thought a moment before she spoke. "When Moll was young like you, she did not play with the others, just watched the small insects and ways of the animals. Many thought Moll Ockett was strange indeed. One day Moll Ockett saw a toad bitten by a spider. He wrapped himself in the leaf of a plant to draw out the poison. It was then that Moll Ockett decided to spend her life studying the plants and the animals."

"Will you show me some of the plants too, Moll Ockett?" asked Parmachenee.

"Tomorrow Moll digs for ginseng, to make a strong tonic for Pial and Old Molly. Parmachenee will come too."

And so it was that the following day, Parmachenee brought home the ground nut, and learned a good deal. Sebattis, who had a tooth ache, tried the prickly ash that Moll Ockett supplied.

Parmachenee was fascinated with the beauty of the yellow ladies slipper.

"Ladies slipper makes a strong body, gets rid of the

166

weakness," explained Moll.

Each day she instructed the children, until they themselves could be sent for wiki-pee, the Indian thong wood, wild lettuce, wild onions, and Indian tobacco. While they explored, Oozalluc sewed, making ready for the wedding, although she never spoke of it. But even the children noticed that her face became more beautiful, that her eyes shone with a new light.

Sebattis began building a lodge on the opposite side of the lake, working long hours while Moll Ockett busied herself with the children. One evening she asked him.

"Does Sebattis plan to move into his lodge soon?"

"Only when Moll Ockett comes to share the lodge of Sebattis," he told her. He looked at her carefully, trying to read her thoughts. He knew better than anyone else how independent Moll could be.

"Sebattis will try to give up the rum for Moll Ockett," he added.

Moll Ockett was fond of Sebattis, and knew that he too, was very fond of her. Although she had vowed never to re-marry, she felt uncomfortable sharing Metallak's lodge with his parents and Oozalluc. Besides, Sebattis had been very kind to her during the sickness of the pox.

"Moll Ockett will share the lodge of Sebattis," she said simply. Like children, they set off to sleep in their new lodge.

It seemed the boys found something new to amuse themselves every day. Excitedly, they would come running for Metallak. "Father, look at the pigeons," called Parmagunnit, observing the huge flock of birds overhead. Olumbo came running to look also.

Metallak regarded his family with pride. Everything in the forest seemed to take on more beauty when he viewed it from their eyes. They had mastered the English tongue easily, but he didn't want them to ever forget their heritage of the Abenaki tongue. He joined his sons.

"In our tongue, we call the birds Wuskowhan," he said. They look now for Wuskowhannanaukit, a place of nesting." Later that day he showed them a tree holding a colony of pigeons.

"No doubt Oozalluc has need of some pigeon fat," he told them, "and Metallak longs to eat of the breast of the small birds." He felt strange not even knowing whether his boys had tasted

167

pigeon in the past. There were so many things he didn't know about them, or they about him. He wondered what their future would bring. True, they could always trade their skins and furs with the whites for food, but that was the easy way. He wanted them to be able to get their own game if they could. High up in the tree, the slate gray of the small birds was difficult to see.

"I count fifty," said Parmagunnit triumphantly.

"Parmagunnit has good eyes," his father said. "Fifty five in all." Each of them carried home an armful of birds to Oozalluc, the pigeons an easy target. Oozalluc welcomed the change in diet, and noted the deep satisfaction on Metallak's face after an afternoon with his sons.

It seemed to Metallak that Oozalluc had been there always sharing his lodge, instead of just a few short months. He was always eager to return home now, to a warm clean lodge smelling of good foods and fresh herbs.

Thanks to his mother and Oozalluc, there were always extra moccasins, and skins drying. Oozalluc preferred the thin calico for herself, but always dressed Parmachenee in little gowns of deerskin to please Metallak. She understood his need for silence as well as his need for company, always adjusting to his moods. Silence, to Metallak, was the ultimate balance of body and mind. Sometimes he would sit for hours without speaking a word. Never had he been so content. He would spend long lazy days teaching his sons to make the family emblem on the fir tree, or to properly pitch the canoe with turpentine and resin.

"We are nearly out of pitch," Olumbo told his father one day.

"Tomorrow we make some," he told his sons, "and you will be tired before we are through."

"Gather all the baskets," he told them as he commenced cutting the pine trees next morning. After cutting and piling the trees into a center pile on good clay earth with a little hole in the middle, he showed them the circular trench he had dug down below.

"The juice will flow down here," he explained, setting their containers down deep in the earth, to collect the juices of the pine tree as the pile burned.

"We have tar enough now for a good while," he told them, "enough to tar a canoe every day." Later he would show them

168

how to put a fire brand into the coals and blow this flame against the pitch to melt it just enough to spread it carefully over the seams of the canoe. He took great pride in his birch bark canoes which lasted many seasons, and wanted his sons to make their first canoe soon.

Parmachenee often stayed with Oozalluc at the lodge, her busy chatter a pleasant diversion. She was a docile, happy child who was easily pleased. She was especially dear to Oozalluc, who thought of her as her own daughter. She brushed her glossy chestnut hair until it glowed like her mother's had and fashioned for her beautiful garments that even white children would have envied.

Oozalluc, who always felt crude and clumsy, was fascinated with Parmachenee's gracefulness. She would skip carefully over the ground, always avoiding puddles or marshy ground, finding a clean stump or patch of ground on which to sit, never tearing her clothing. She could run nearly as fast as her brothers already, on tiny feet like her mother's. But sometimes Oozalluc had an uneasy feeling that Parmachenee was more white than red. Although she was anxious to please her father and quickly learned to paddle the canoe, she took great pleasure in the ribbons and shawls that were bestowed on her by Mrs. Merrill. Mrs. Merrill often declared that the child was none other than a princess, and should be dressed accordingly. Parmachenee loved to accompany her father on these visits where the whites often treated her like a guest and showered her with gifts.

Metallak, too, pondered the future and wondered what would become of his delicate daughter. Would she be drawn to the comforts of the settlements, or marry into the tribe?

That evening, he and Oozalluc sat together overlooking the beautiful Umbagog Lake at the narrows where they made their home. Metallak held her close to him and asked softly.

"Is Oozalluc ready at last to marry me?"

"Oozalluc is no longer young," she stammered. She did not tell him that all was in readiness, even the new rush mats for their bed.

"Do deer of the forest have age?" he asked. Oozalluc is like the deer of the forest, who looks after her small doe, Parmachenee."

Oozalluc felt so warm and safe she dared not move. She couldn't believe that Metallak still had his arm around her. Metallak's eyes gleamed with pleasure as he playfully tickled her chin with a leaf. She giggled again. Then she felt herself drawn against him

169

in a powerful embrace. She could feel his breath on her neck, hot with desire. She found herself returning his kisses with passion.

Later, he sat and held her gently against him and leaned over possessively to kiss her ear. Finally he whispered.

"Metallak has been without a woman for many moons now. Let us not wait another night."

Oozalluc shivered as he continued. "Let us meet later, when all is quiet, in the small cove below."

Oozalluc nodded silently, terrified inside. What if she disappointed him? She had no experience making love, except in her dreams.

Metallak sensed her confusion and stood abruptly. "As soon as Parmachenee sleeps," he ordered and walked away to join his parents.

Oozalluc did not remember eating that evening, or anything that followed. Only that Metallak came to her and led her to a cozy spot, made comfortable with furs and boughs. There he held her gently in his arms as he tenderly made love to her, overcoming her fears and inhibitions. Humbly he told her how much he loved her and needed her.

"Oozalluc is more beautiful than the finest lady slipper," he whispered. And indeed, Oozalluc's face was transformed in beauty in the moonlight as tears of happiness filled her eyes. He wiped her tears and kissed her eyelids, drawing her close, consumed with desire. Oozalluc felt completely at home at last, and relaxed in his arms, her own ardor mounting. Once more she tested him.

"Metallak is sure?"

He kissed her as he murmured. "Sshh." Oozalluc left her future to fate as she melted into his arms.

When they woke in the morning, she giggled, embarrassed at her lack of clothing. Finally she voiced her thoughts.

"Surely it would pain Metallak and his parents to see what is left of our small village after the plague of death. How would we marry without a priest?"

"Let us ask Moserill for help. We leave today." So they set off eagerly that morning and sought out Moserill, who was pleased to hear that at last Metallak had forgotten Keoka and made a new life for himself.

"About time!" he exclaimed, laughing.

"We'll send for a man of the cloth," he said

170

heartily. "Send word down river tomorrow, and you're as good as married. Meantime, you stay right here with us."

Oozalluc had never been so excited in her life. After all these years, she had given up her dream of becoming Metallak's wife. She was caught up in the excitement of the others, forgot her age, and shyly discussed it with the children.

"Now father will never be alone again," Parmachenee assured her, and Oozalluc smiled. Parmachenee gathered great clusters of flowers from the clearings for the festivities, conferring in whispers with her grandparents. They were old and feeble, but would make the trip to Andover for the wedding, and see Metallak married to Oozalluc. Nothing could have made them happier in their old age. True, the wedding was many years too late, but it would take place after all. Old Molly talked of little else.

Although Sebattis and Moll Ockett had made their home in the new lodge for some time now, they too had not married in the eyes of the church, and it was decided they would all marry together.

Although Metallak was no longer obsessed by Keoka's death, he never forgot the stigma on his name, and pondered on this for hours. His sons would have to carry this blemish forever, and he worried that Oozalluc too thought about this. "Does Oozalluc truly believe Metallak is innocent?" he asked her one evening.

Tears filled her eyes that he would ask this of her. "Oozalluc knows Metallak is innocent, and one day all others will know it too," she said loyally.

"Metallak regrets this blemish on our marriage," he said lamely.

"Oozalluc has regrets too," she said, "that I will never bear sons of Metallak, that I will slow him down in his treks."

"Metallak has two fine sons already. But he has no wife," he said tenderly, embracing her.

And so, one beautiful summer day in the month of Nakkahigas, June, they were married, and Oozalluc returned to Metallak's lodge as his lawfully wedded wife at last.

Metallak seemed to grow younger each day, in spite of his forty odd years. The boys helped eagerly with the garden, and then they would play, climbing trees, diving into the water, always inventing a new game. At last he felt he had a purpose to his life, and a true friend. More and more he depended on her and often

171

consulted with her about small things. It seemed she always anticipated his needs and made endless treks with him into the forest, not mindful of her appearance, but happy to keep her husband company. Together they would listen to the cry of a loon, or lie in the blanket under the moon's glow. They laughed like children at the animals at play, or the futile efforts of the whites to beat their rugs and fight the dust with such frenzy. It was such a silly way to spend the passing of time.

The settlers at Andover took note of the change in Metallak. The grim somber look seldom crossed his face anymore, and he made a hasty departure when he deposited his furs.

"Oozalluc must be some wife," Moses would tease, and Metallak would proudly answer.

"Oozalluc is the best wife in Indian Stream."

Once in a great while, he would stay with Moserill for a drinking spree.

"Take it home, Metallak," urged Moserill.

"Long ago Metallak made a vow," he said seriously, "never to drink in my lodge. Besides, Metallak might offend Oozalluc."

Moserill laughed and they went back to their drinking. After a long evening, he made his old friend comfortable by the fire.

When Metallak woke in the morning, he regretted his folly. His head pounded and he had no appetite. Moserill insisted he try a slice of bread dipped in molasses.

"This will make you feel better," he insisted.

Much to his surprise, Metallak found he liked the strange mixture that looked so much like pitch.

"I believe Oozalluc would like some of this too," put in Mrs. Merrill. "You go over to Mrs. Akers and see if she's got any left over. She had a whole barrel just last week."

Metallak was delighted. Perhaps he would have a gift to bring Oozalluc. Feeling less guilty about his drinking spree, he set off for Canaan, bringing a few choice furs to trade for the molasses.

He found Mrs. Akers at home and clumsily tried to bargain for the molasses. "Metallak has tasted of the molasses," he began hesitantly.

"Why, Metallak, you just sit a spell and I'll fix up a jug for you," she told him. Gingerly, he sat on the chair while she prepared

172

the jug.

"Now you tell Oozalluc to stop in and see me soon," she said. When she refused to take the furs in payment, Metallak took his leave, carefully folding one fur and leaving it on the steps.

It was dusk when he finally presented Oozalluc with the jug.

"Mrs. Akers sent the sweets to Oozalluc, calls it molasses."

Thereafter, whenever he went to Canaan, Oozalluc would watch for his return.

"Did Metallak fetch molasses for Oozalluc?" she would ask.

"Oozalluc will soon turn black," he would tease, showing her the jug. In return, Oozalluc always sent a basket of blueberries or raspberries to Mrs. Akers. These Metallak would set carefully at the front door where she would find them. Mrs. Akers saved the birch bark container and treasured the hand woven sweet grass baskets. They were hard to come by in the settlements, and Oozalluc received lots of preserves in return for a basket.

Moll Ockett had not been idle during this time. She made countless trips over the countryside, bringing herbs and tea, visiting the settlements and helping the ill. The settlers of Andover and Paris came to think of her as their doctress. She delivered all their babies, and for her services never took more than a penny, placing each penny in the pouch around her neck. Some said she was clairvoyant and could see into the future. At any rate, she was in great demand, and Oozalluc and Metallak saw little of her except in passing an occasional night with them in their lodge when Sebattis took comfort in the rum and she wished to be away from him.

Thus it was that she chanced to learn of Tom Hegan's plans to raid Andover this fall after the harvest, when there would be a large store of food in the settlement, from a frightened member of his clan.

"Tom Hegan tells his people not to trade with the whites, just take what they want. It is whispered that he plans a raid on Andover," she confided to Oozalluc.

Oozalluc knew that Hegan's name brought fear into the townships, especially Bethel where he had savagely raided in 1781. Because of him, many of their people were still not trusted. Metallak was angry that Tom Hegan still frightened his white brothers, instead

173

of learning to live in peace with them. Besides, he still suspected him in connection with Keoka's death and wished to have nothing to do with him. He had been a nagging thorn in Metallak's side, from the time of their childhood.

He set about studying the countryside, trying to guess where Tom Hegan would strike. Then one day it came to him. He would take the enemy by surprise. Surely Tom Hegan would come by water, and he had discovered an old Indian cellar on the banks of the Ellis River, not visible from above. He had found it quite by accident one day after a leisurely swim in the river. It would be perfect. He set out to tell Moserill he would need at least twenty men, ready to ride at a moment's notice. Sebattis would wait upriver to bring word when they came.

The townsfolk remained hidden by the river as instructed, shivering on the cold, frosty banks of the river.

Night after night they waited to no avail, but early one morning, they heard sounds. Sebattis had arrived early and told Metallak there were at least thirty of them.

From their place under the riverbank on the ledge, the settlers remained hidden until the last possible moment. Then with a blood thirsty yell, Metallak sprang up and began to fire. A shower of bullets followed his, and the enemy raiders were overwhelmed, many falling back into the water from their canoes, others managing to escape into the forest.

Into their retreating ears, Metallak shouted "Tell Tom Hegan Metallak awaits him. Metallak's white friends live in peace."

The raiders returned to the north, to recount their heavy losses and lack of success. Tom Hegan raged and swore bitterly, then raged and drank heavily of his rum until he spoke in slurs.

"Metallak is a traitor to the Abenakis. It is well that he has been banished. For this, Tom Hegan will seek justice. Metallak's day will come!" His fishlike cold eyes stared vacantly into space as he spoke.

"Do you not see my empty cup?" he shouted to his wife. "More rum!"

Polly jumped up to refill the cup, terrified that he would grow angry and throw something at her. The fire water had an evil effect on him, making him do strange things. Once she had buried his gun, thinking he might use it on her or the children in a drunken

174

rage. But he caught her and hit her with the gun, breaking her arm. Moll Ockett had come in the night to set the arm for her.

"This arm will always be crooked now," Moll said in disgust. "It is the work of Tom Hegan, is it not?"

"My husband grows angry when Polly asks too many questions," she whispered, looking fearfully at the door. "Ever since the time of Keoka's death. When he drinks of the rum, he grows suspicious of Polly and thinks I mean to harm him."

Moll Ockett studied her, wondering if she spoke the truth. "What does Tom Hegan fear from Polly?" she asked. She saw other bruises on Polly's arms and legs and wondered why she stayed with Tom Hegan.

"He has nothing to fear," she whispered again. "Polly had never told anyone that Tom Hegan disappeared on the night of Keoka's death, only asked him where he went."

Moll Ockett gripped her by the good arm and spoke quietly. "Watch and listen well. If you learn anything, Moll Ockett has much gold, enough to set you free from Tom Hegan forever. You have only to send word that you have the fever, and I will come."

The eyes of the battered wife glittered with hope. "Moll Ockett is a true friend," she whispered.

Moll Ockett confided all that had passed to Oozalluc, telling her not to give up hope. Perhaps one day they would be able to clear Metallak's name. This brought hope to Oozalluc, who wanted more than anything else to clear Metallak's name, not for herself, but for the children. She had said nothing to Metallak, not wishing to get his hopes up.

In the chill air of the fall, they made ready for winter. With the children's help, they set by a good store of berries, corn, and smoked meat. The pen was well stocked with wood for the winter, and this year Metallak looked forward to taking his sons on the winter hunt, when supplies ran low.

For his parents, he purchased a horse and sleigh. Of late, it seemed they tired easily, and sat by the lodge for hours. Sometimes they napped, waking to the demands of the children. They admired the fine pung and horse, and often went for long rides about he countryside. Olumbo would drive the pung with the family, and

175

Metallak would follow along on Big Horn, often with Parmachenee on his lap. He knew that his sons envied them and planned in the spring to fetch home another calf and train him for the boys.

Pial often reflected on his life, at peace with himself and with his son. He could see that the whites favored Metallak and his family, and knew that Metallak would do well, perhaps better than if he had remained with his people. Here they could grow their crops and live in peace.

When the grandchildren clamored for stories, he would tell them of their father's skill with the arrow, of the little white girl he had saved from torture. He even told them a little of their mother Keoka.

"Your mother was a Sauk," he would say, "and she swam like a fish."

Metallak knew that his mother was happy here. She taught Parmachenee to make baskets and moccasins, as she recounted the old legends and tales she herself had memorized many years ago.

She seldom left Pial's side and often helped him to drink broth, but one day he remained asleep, never to wake again. The grandchildren stoutly helped to bury, him, holding back their tears. They would miss the proud and gallant leader who had led his people in peace for many years.

Molly Messel never really recovered from his passing, wishing only to lie at his side. She would sit by his graveside for hours, sometimes talking to herself, refusing to eat or drink. The children sensed her despair and left her alone in her grief.

On good days, Metallak would hitch up the pung and take her for a long drive over the countryside, but in her weakened condition, she took a chill one day and never got up again from her bed of boughs. They buried her beside her husband, marking the graves with heavy stone which Metallak inscribed carefully with their names.

Oozalluc was haunted by her last words, "My son is innocent." She too, knew that Metallak was innocent, but how could she prove it?

CHAPTER NINE

The growing boys grew restless for excitement, and in the summer of 1798, they decided to visit the settlements, Metallak and Parmachenee astride Big Horn, the boys and Oozalluc following in the pung. The boys had grown lean and tall, twelve and fourteen seasons of age. Nine year old Parmachenee was beautiful in her soft deerskin garment, fringes hanging gracefully from her arms and skirt, just like her father's. Her hair was decorated with scarlet ribbons, a last minute gift from Mrs. Merrill.

They made an unusual picture, this handsome family, and caused many heads to turn as they passed. Nearly everyone had heard of Metallak, but he had kept his family in seclusion. They were astounded at the beauty of his daughter, who looked almost white. Instead of the glossy black hair of her two brothers, her silky chestnut hair waved like Keoka's had. Her dainty features accented her beauty, and her dusky skin looked more like a healthy glow from the sun than the leathery brown of her brothers.

As always, Metallak and Oozalluc were reticent with the whites, speaking only when spoken to. The children, though, had none of this shyness and eagerly asked questions.

As they entered the town of Portsmouth, they were amazed at the size and activity of the village. Great clusters of buildings stood facing the busy pier, with many little shops. There were black-smiths, ropemakers, mastmakers, coppersmiths, painters, coopers, seamen and shipwrights, all a bustle of activity.

Out in the harbor, Olumbo counted more than thirty ships, brigs, and schooners.

"What do they carry, father?" he asked.

"Many things from across the sea," answered his father. "Molasses, coffee, even tea leaves."

"Why don't they make their own tea, as we do?" asked Parmachenee.

At this, Metallak burst out laughing. Most of the whites did not know what a tea leaf looked like.

"Look at that," said Parmagunnit excitedly. Men were walking about with hemp around their waists. Others were mending nets. They wore brightly colored hats and great blousy shirts.

177

On their feet were tight fitting boots.

But Olumbo was looking elsewhere, spellbound by the huge ships and their striking colors. He had heard of the gallant ship Ranger and the powerful Captain Jones who frightened off the privateers. He envied the sailors who were greeting their loved ones on shore. It must be exciting to sail away on a great ship. To Metallak and Oozalluc, the old days were gone. No longer was there privacy at the seashore, such as they had known in their youth. Even the whites dug for the clams now and ate of the sweet meat. They picked the strawberries too, which grew in such abundance along the lush banks. From the first little settlement exporting fish, lumber and small produce, Portsmouth was now a big trading center, supplying rum, sugar, cocoa, coffee and salt to the settlers.

Ladies dressed in great billowing gowns and fitted boots passed them, carrying gay little parasols that caused Oozalluc to stare incredulously, suddenly conscious of her own faded and loose fitting calico. She drew her bonnet tighter about her head, fastening the strings.

The whites were equally taken with the sight of this little family, all the children dressed in soft deerskin with lovely fringes.

"What a lovely child," remarked one lady, touching Parmachenee's face and passing on. "And what a waste. Just an Indian. Imagine that beautiful hair on my niece."

"And such an ugly mother," her companion replied.

Metallak clenched his teeth, trying to control his temper. Oozalluc looked straight down at the ground and kept walking rapidly. Finally Metallak followed along.

"White people are cruel, aren't they?" asked Parmachenee, who had overheard the conversation also. She held her mother's hand loyally. But nevertheless, she accepted everyone hospitably, fascinated by the habits and clothing of the whites.

A well dressed elderly couple approached them, the man dressed in a black suit and wearing a frilly white shirt, carrying a lovely carved cane, the lady dressed in a fashionable pink dress. He tipped his hat and Parmachenee smiled.

"Wait until I tell Lady Hester," his companion said. "I have a friend who would love to paint her. I must find him today. Do find out where she is staying, Charles."

Olumbo and Parmagunnit looked at each other incredulously. Did white people paint Indians? Protectively, they stepped closer to their sister, in case these whites should try to make off with her.

The lady adjusted her glasses to her face in order to see Metallak's family better. When she looked at Parmachenee, she gasped as though she had seen a ghost. She fell to the ground and her companion called for smelling salts. Someone handed him a bottle and he quickly revived the lady placing his jacket under her head. She was apologetic and bewildered.

"I'm so sorry, Charles," she said. "I thought I saw a child who looked just like . . ." Her eyes fell on Parmachenee and she fainted again.

Metallak urged his family to keep walking. That woman had been looking at Parmachenee, there was no doubt about it. Even the children had noticed.

What did that lady mean, father?" questioned Parmachenee.

"It is nothing," he told her. "Perhaps you remind her of another child."

"Perhaps she admires your scarlet ribbons," Oozalluc told her with a smile. But she too wondered about the intense interest of the old couple.

Each of them seemed lost in their thoughts for a few moments, but then they were caught up once again in the sights and sounds of the excitement in the village, especially around the pier. They could hear snatches of conversation.

"More bounty than I ever saw on one ship," an old seaman was saying, "worth a fortune."

"Guess we showed the English a thing or two," added his friend.

"What does the sailor mean?" asked Oozalluc, always fearing attack.

"Many settlers do not trade with England any longer," said Metallak, "because it is too dangerous. Sometimes sailors are captured to run other vessels. Many prizes are seized by the winner of the battle."

When they tired of walking, they took shelter outside the town away from the noise where they had tethered their animals, settling down to a quiet evening. Metallak was surprised to hear riders approaching in the fading light of day. He knew of no one that could be visiting him so far from home. Cautiously, he moved closer to his rifle. The boys were excitedly talking of all they had seen and heard.

"I'll work on a ship like the Ranger when I become a man," said Olumbo. "Make good wages and maybe even win prizes in a great battle."

"You know father says we must not trust the English," his brother said. "Many of them regard Indians as savages and take advantage of them." But he, too, was enchanted with the sights he had seen, and the apparel of the rich white people.

Metallak recognized the face of the man descending from the pung. It was the same one they had seen in the streets of Portsmouth, the one called Charles. He was alone and Metallak wondered what had become of the lady who fainted so suddenly. Always hospitable, he stood to greet the stranger. But he had an uneasy feeling about he whole thing.

"Welcome to Metallak's fire," he said cordially.

"So you are Metallak," the stranger greeted. "I have heard you know these woods like the back of your hand. Also that you rid our forests of the wolves, a big help to the settlers. You are well known in these parts."

"Metallak did not know this," he said modestly, "but I am pleased that my white brothers speak well of me."

"We've heard a lot about you, but very little about your family." He turned to Parmachenee, "and my wife is much taken with your little girl. What is your name, my child?" He raised Parmachenee's hand to his lips.

"Parmachenee," she said smiling.

"Enchanting, positively enchanting," he said, standing back and regarding her from all sides. Then he turned his attention to Metallak and the boys, not wishing to offend anyone in the family.

"I have heard that you and your sons are fine hunters also, that you can track an animal almost by smell. I have even heard that you ride a great bull moose."

"Big Horn is a fine animal," agreed Metallak, pointing to Big Horn where he was tethered.

"I have come to make you an offer," said Charles in a hushed tone. "It would please my wife very much. She longs for companionship, you see." They drew nearer to the fire away from the children and spoke in hushed tones.

"Seeing your daughter today has been a big shock to my wife," the man said, "to myself as well. You see, many years ago, we lost a daughter who looked very much like your daughter, especially her hair. She was taken captive by the Indians, no offense mind you now, and we never saw her again."

Suddenly, the pit of Metallak's stomach gave a lurch. He wondered if his face betrayed him. Why hadn't he paid more attention when Keoka spoke of her mother's people? She had mentioned a family who lived near the great tall waves. The father's name had been Charles. What was the last name? He tried to remember. Suddenly he had to know.

"Your name is Charles?" he inquired.

"Charles Wickford," he said holding out his hand. Metallak shook the extended hand, but his heart hammered crazily. What should he do? Surely that was the same name Keoka had whispered to him. Very likely, this man was Keoka's grandfather, and this was the village where Keoka's mother had grown up.

"I carry a miniature of my daughter with me always," the man explained. "You can see what an extraordinary resemblence your own daughter bears to ours." He took out the miniature and Metallak studied it carefully. There was even a birthmark on the right shoulder, a tiny half moon, just like Parmachenee's. Metallak felt a lurch of dismay and fear.

Metallak handed the miniature back, studying Charles.

"As you say, they bear a strong resemblence. I am sorry to hear about your daughter."

Metallak felt he must do the honorable thing and tell this man all that he knew. With a stout heart, he began. "I too have a story to tell you," he said, "that my wife told me long ago."

They sat by the fire and spoke for nearly two hours in hushed tones. Metallak told Charles about Keoka's past with the Sauks, how her mother had longed to return home to this place of great waves, and what a good swimmer and fast runner Keoka had been.

When he heard the whole story, tears ran down Charles' cheeks, tears of sadness and gratitude that at last he knew the truth. When at last he took his leave, it was agreed that Metallak would think about his proposition, and discuss it with Parmachenee the following day. Metallak's sons, too, were welcome to visit anytime Charles insisted.

181

Metallak sat alone by the fire for a long time, until the coals had turned to glowing embers and his family slept peacefully. Oozalluc knew that something bothered him, and went quietly to sit beside him at the fire.

"The stranger has asked Metallak to make many canoes," he told her. "He has offered a good price, too."

"That is good news," she told him. "What else did he ask?"

He sighed and then he began. Squire Charles had begged him to leave Parmachenee in the town of Portsmouth with his wife as a companion. There she would go to the best schools, be dressed in the very finest clothing, and learn the ways of her white brothers. She would visit her parents in the summer months at their lodge on the lake.

Metallak knew this was a rare opportunity for his little one, but she was so dear to him, the light of his lodge. Squire Charles had described the splendid home where she would live, with a large feather bed of her very own. What if she grew so attached to this great home that she never came to visit again?

Oozalluc held Metallak's hand and said nothing. She too would miss Parmachenee, but such a chance was not to be scoffed at. Metallak continued to talk.

"I think this man is Parmachenee's great grandfather," he went on, and Oozalluc looked at him in surprise.

"What do you mean, Metallak?"

"Keoka told me long ago that her mother grew up along the seashore, among the great waves, that she was taken captive by the Indians. I paid little attention, but I remember that name Charles. Then too, he has a miniature etching of the child and she bears a strong likeness to Parmachenee, even to the birthmark on the shoulder."

"Parmachenee will never forget her father, even if she has a very rich great grandfather," she assured him, squeezing his hand.

Worries plagued his mind. What if Parmachenee didn't like the white world? What if she ran away? Who would run to meet his whistle when he rode in from the hunt? Who would sit on his knee in the evening hours and plead for more stories? He would miss her companionship sorely, but he did not wish to be unfair. He turned to Oozalluc.

182

"Metallak must do the honorable thing," he said simply. "Parmachenee must be told of her mother's people."

She looked at him with pride, saying nothing.

"Oozalluc is fine," she assured him. "Sometimes I long for peace and quiet. One day Parmachenee may be left all alone, lost in a world of whites. It is far better that she get acquainted now, and make a place for herself."

"And what of our sons?" he asked.

"They too should go to the white man's school like their father," she told him. "Already they speak with envy of the white man and the settlements. The small village at St. Francis dwindles. One day Olumbo and Parmagunnit will live in a white settlement. Why not send them to Wheelock's School for a few years?"

He thought for a few minutes. Squire Charles had asked only for Parmachenee, although he assured Metallak that his sons could visit. And his sons might be tempted to become sailors if he left them here. Better to take them to the mission village and send them to Wheelock's with their Indian brothers.

"Oozalluc speaks well," he said. "We will return to St. Francis and get our sons into school." He looked at his wife, who looked thinner and more aged than her fifty summers. She never complained of the many moccasins she made, or the appetite of his growing boys, but she needed a rest. As much as he would miss their company, he knew the time had come to place them in school.

Next day, Parmachenee was told first of the kind offer by Squire Charles, and then the story of her grandparents that Keoka had told.

"So you see, Parmachenee, this man is your great grandfather, although he prefers that you call him Uncle, and they are prepared to make arrangements for your education." Parmachenee couldn't believe it at first.

"You mean my great grandfather is a white man?" she asked. "My grandmother was a white captive?" The boys too were entranced with the story.

Metallak told them of Keoka's youth in the Sauk country, and her later captivity by the Iroquois. He told her also that her mother had longed to find this white family and visit them.

"What do you think, my father?" she asked timidly, excited but fearing all these changes. "Will you come often to visit?"

Metallak described the great house, the large

feather bed, and the pretty clothes Parmachenee would have. "Parmachenee will come home to our lodge for the summer months," he told
her.

Parmachenee said little but her eyes lit up with
delight when they spoke of the pretty clothes.

"Parmachenee will be in a fine school," he said,
"and learn the ways of her white brothers."

"Parmachenee has longed to read and write,
father," she said simply. "I will make you proud if you let me stay with
my white family."

"Then all is settled," said Metallak firmly. "Squire
Charles will come for you today. But never forget you are a Cowassuck
and life will be as it was when you join us for the summer months."

"Why is Parmachenee chosen for the school?" asked
Olumbo jealously.

"Was she not our mother too?"

"Olumbo and Parmagunnit will also go to school,"
said their father, and told them of his plans to send them to Wheelock's.

With head held high, he said goodbye to
Parmachenee. She clung to Oozalluc passionately for a moment, and
waved bravely to her brothers, then mounted the horse behind Squire
Charles, excited over the new prospects before her.

Metallak thought back to his own school days, after
he was man grown, rising at dawn and then working hard until evening.
School would not be easy for his sons, and they had grown lazy in the
forest. It was time they learned the habits of their white brothers.

"Let us take Big Horn home to graze," he told
them, "and then go on to St. Francis to make arrangements for
school." This time he allowed his sons to take turns riding Big Horn
and he accompanied Oozalluc in the pung.

They took the trip in easy stages, arriving at St. Francis
a few days later. With the good father's help, they got their sons placed
at Wheelock's School. The boys were impatient to begin their
schooling, but Metallak knew they would come back young men, and
cherished his last few days with them, playing la crosse, fishing, and
showing them old landmarks in the village. He knew they were
different, as different as night and day. Olumbo, the older one, plunged
headlong into everything, while his brother was always more serious
and cautious.

Metallak took Parmagunnit aside and cautioned him

to look after Olumbo.

"Olumbo seeks mischief," his father said. "Try to keep him out of trouble."

"I will look after Olumbo, father. Do not worry."

Metallak and Oozalluc returned to Lake Richardson a few days later with a strange sense of freedom. Even though they would miss the children, they could go on trips and visit old friends. They would have a good winter, secure in their lodge.

Metallak tried not to think of Parmachenee, but night after night he would see her in his dreams, walking down the steps of the great mansion, or climbing into the high feather bed. Would she ever come back to him?

It **was** late September when Oozalluc finally met Blanche Akers. There was a frantic pounding on their door, and Metallak was surprised to see Amos Akers from Canaan standing there.

"The Missus needs help for the birth of the child," he said nervously. "Been over on the other side of the lake, but Moll Ockett's gone someplace else and there's not a minute to waste."

Oozalluc quickly picked up a shawl as he spoke and made ready to go. Her services were often in demand in the white settlements and she enjoyed showing these women how to make dyes, or gather slippery elm bark to thicken their milk. But around childbirth, she got a little nervous. White women always suffered a great deal and took a long time to bring forth the child, not like the women of her own people, who had their babies without ceremony, sometimes all alone in the fields.

"Pung's all hitched up and waiting," he said, and helped Oozalluc up onto the seat. He made haste back to Canaan, obviously concerned for his wife. Oozalluc too was concerned for the friend who sent her the black sticky molasses that she had grown to love. But she remained placid, knowing it might be hours before the child was born. Her lack of concern seemed to calm Amos, and he gratefully helped her down when they reached his little homestead.

Once they were inside, Oozalluc couldn't help but stare. This was the first time she had been in Blanche Akers' home. There in one corner stood the samp mortar, an immense hardwood log almost three feet in length hollowed out at one end, with a stone

185

pestle hung above on a spring pole for grinding corn. Molly thought this would be a great treat to have for rainy days and wondered if she should ask Metallak to set one up for her.

"Right this way," Amos told her, leading the way. They passed through the best room, where Oozalluc saw a tall clock and a small writing desk with a mirror hanging above it. Mr. Akers appeared to be very prosperous compared to the simplicity of most of the little log cabins she frequented.

"This here's the bedroom, and the Missus is right here," said Amos, opening the door and going to his wife's side, taking her hand in his. She gasped with a pain and he quickly turned away, telling Oozalluc he'd be out in the barn if she needed him.

"Oozalluc, I'm so glad you've come," said Blanche. I've never had a baby before and Amos doesn't know much about these things."

Oozalluc felt the baby and told her everything was coming fine, but it would take awhile. Blanche looked pale, lying in the large billowy four poster with netted fringes and dimnity hangings. Oozalluc wondered if she had made them herself. On the bed, she noticed a beautiful coverlet made of squares of many bright colors. Gingerly, Oozalluc felt of it, attracted to the design.

"That's my wedding quilt. Carried it on my lap all the way from Connecticut," Blanche told her in a friendly voice. "I use that comforter for every day. It's made of flannel and stuffed with wool. Why don't you sit on it and make yourself comfortable, Oozalluc?"

As she squatted on the floor, Oozalluc could see another smaller bed under the large bed, so small that she giggled.

"Small bed for the new papoeis," she said.

"Better than the cold loft," agreed Blanche, looking towards the roof. "And it doesn't take much room, just slides right in under this one."

The board floor was sanded almost white, and Oozalluc knew Blanche must spend a lot of her time scrubbing and cleaning. No wonder she looked pale. There was only one other piece of furniture in the room, a large high mahogany chest.

"In the chest," she told Oozalluc, "are all the baby things. Would you like to see them?"

Curiously, Oozalluc opened the drawers, peeking at the tiny garments Blanche had prepared for the papoeis. Oozalluc

186

loved handiwork and admired the small stitches and fine work in these small garments. There were so many she wondered if Blanche expected twins. There were several long gowns, and a tiny little cap. Several pairs of booties threaded with ribbons caught her eye, and one drawer was filled with pretty indigo blue blankets. Molly felt a pang that she had never had a child of her own.

"Oozalluc, I think it's time," called Blanche.

"Oozalluc hurried to the bedside and examined Blanche. The child seemed to be coming slow and Blanche looked tired. She spoke to her in soothing tones.

"Always the first papoeis takes a long time."

"I don't know what I'd do without you," Blanche told her.

"Blanche is a strong woman, stronger than most," reassured Oozalluc with a confidence she didn't know she had. "Before long, the papoeis will be here." She couldn't help but remember that one of the nearby settlements had lost a mother in childbirth just last week. Somehow, she must keep busy, and not think about it.

"Tomorrow Blanche will have a hearty hunger," she told her. "Oozalluc will grind corn in the kitchen, for cornmeal." In the kitchen, she laid out clothes for the infant and a basin to cleanse him. As she made ready to grind the corn, she surveyed the room where Blanche spent most of her time. There was a cobbler's bench in one corner, well worn and marked by the cobbler. Oozalluc knew the whites preferred to have their skins soaked down at the vats in the Connecticut Valley for making shoes, and once a year, the traveling shoemaker would come by and make up the family shoes for another year.

Cautiously, she tried on one of the high button boots standing under the bench. It felt tight, like a binder, and pulled at her skin. She took it off and went to the samp mortar and began to grind corn with the pestle.

Along about twilight, Oozalluc called Amos by blowing on the great conch shell she found by the door. She took it to Blanche and asked her how to use it.

"Just one blow," Blanche said. "He knows the sound."

In a short time, Amos arrived, grateful for the corn meal mush and stew Oozalluc provided. He looked in on his wife anxiously, and then looked at Oozalluc.

"The papoeis will come soon," Oozalluc assured them both, knowing that Blanche was getting weary. "The small one grows impatient and stirs." She sat by Blanche, who was moaning and gasping for breath.

She helped ease the child out as she had seen Moll Ockett do hundreds of times, and within the hour carried the eight pound boy to his father in the kitchen. Blanche was asleep, exhausted by the whole ordeal.

"Blanche is a good strong wife, just like an Indian." she told him. "She will have many sons for Amos."

Well, I'll be," he said, looking down at the tiny form flailing his arms and crying out at the strange new world. He picked up the baby gingerly, afraid to crush him, and scarcely breathed until he had placed him gently in beside his wife.

"We ain't got much money," he told Oozalluc, "but anything we got is yours."

"Already Blanche shares her molasses with Oozalluc. That is enough."

"Why, sure enough," he said. "You take a fresh jug of that home with you when you leave. It's the least we can do."

Oozalluc settled in to stay for a few days, while Blanche recovered. She enjoyed holding the small infant and often held him in her arms so Blanche could rest.

Oozalluc and Blanche became good friends over the next few days, chatting quietly while the baby slept. Oozalluc was curious about how Blanche had managed to carry her furniture to her new home.

"We came all the way from Connecticut," Blanche told her, "in a lumber wagon loaded with barrels and furniture. We had a box for provisions we might need on the road, and a trunk, covered with canvas. The roads were hard to travel."

Oozalluc sat with her arms folded across her chest, listening eagerly.

"When we reached Lancaster," she continued, "we had to leave the wagon. There wasn't any more road, just a path of blazed trees. Together we rode on horseback, leaving most of our supplies in a farmer's barn."

"All except for what we carried on the drag," put in Amos Akers, who had joined his wife and Oozalluc.

"Until we finally came to North Stratford, a small settlement of log cabins," Blanche put in. "But they sure looked good to us."

"Why did you not settle there?" asked Oozalluc.

"We did stay for a few months and nearly settled there," she paused.

"But I wanted to keep going," Amos put in. "Heard this was beautiful country. And then I heard about this land grant, if we could put up a cabin and clear five acres of ground. So I burned off some timber and cleared the fields, and last year traded in our wheat crop for a cow, so now we even have milk."

"The little one wakes," said Oozalluc, bringing the child to his mother for feeding. She went to the kitchen to start supper while Blanche fed the baby.

She noticed that Blanche's husband appeared to be very nervous about something. He paced back and forth and finally went into the bedroom to talk in whispers to his wife. When he came out, he went about the kitchen methodically, taking his gun and a few supplies, not staying for supper.

"Be back tomorrow night," he said to his wife from the bedroom door.

"Be careful," she cautioned, her tone serious with concern.

Oozalluc wondered why he should be careful and where he was going in the dark. Strange people, these whites, going out to do their business in the evening. Wisely she asked no questions. Out the window she could see Amos heading in the direction of the village.

Blanche appeared fretful all the next day, jumping nervously each time the baby woke. He was a fine healthy boy who drank greedily of his mother's milk and slept most of the time. Blanche didn't hum to him as usual, just hovered around looking at the clock.

When evening came and her husband had not returned, she paced the floor, looking occasionally at Oozalluc. Finally she decided to confide in her.

"Amos went across the border into Canada," she said quietly. "The only way we can raise the money for taxes is from the sale of our potash. But of course it's against the law and Government agents patrol the waters between here and Canada." She laughed nervously. "I know it's silly, but I worry until he gets home."

189

"There was no moon last night," Oozalluc told her placidly. "Probably all went well and you worry for nothing."

"Oh, you make me feel so much better, Oozalluc." Blanche grew more talkative and explained that her husband always brought home a little salt, which was good for cooking and salting the meat.

Even Oozalluc grew concerned when darkness fell and still Amos did not return. Blanche stood anxiously by the window, not speaking.

"If Amos does not return soon, Oozalluc will fetch Metallak," Oozalluc offered.

Blanche burst into tears of gratitude.

Metallak too would like salt on his meat," added Oozalluc. "Next time Amos makes a trip across the border, they will go together in the canoe. In this way, they will not be caught."

As they spoke, the door opened and in walked Amos, breathless and carrying a small bag of salt. "Narrow escape," he said, "but we made it."

"Oozalluc says Metallak will go with you next time," his wife said, relief in her eyes.

"I'd feel much safer," he said turning to Oozalluc. "Much safer indeed. Fired two rounds of ammunition at us, but didn't hit anyone. Made it home through the woods and lost them."

Throughout the long winter, Metallak was seen occasionally pulling a sleigh across the Lake into Canada or riding his moose on a mild day. So popular was he with the children that often they would be seen riding the tips of his snowshoes. So none knew or suspected that there might be a bag of salt or cream of tartar hidden in his supplies. Everyone assumed he was just hauling potatoes as usual. Metallak knew that the settlers used the cream of tartar for making wine, and often they made him a gift of a jug in return for his help. Oozalluc claimed the wives used this powder to make light fluffy biscuits, but Metallak thought that was silly. He preferred Oozalluc's bread. Metallak was worried more about Oozalluc than about himself. Although she tried to hide it from him, he sometimes saw her grasp her side and her face tighten in pain. She had grown thinner too, though he brought her the fruits of the forest to whet her appetite.

He didn't even want to think of the emptiness of his lodge without Oozalluc there beside him.

"Let us drink the waters of Ne-bi-son-be," he told her in the spring. "The medicine water of our people will be good for Oozalluc."

"Does Metallak not see that his wife grows old?" she asked with a smile. "She is like the small poplar that bends with the wind."

He stood beside her, his arm about her tenderly. "But the great oak stands beside the small poplar to protect her from the wind."

He talked eagerly of their trip to the springs, and early next morning, cut her a sturdy stick of hemlock to use as a cane. They took the trip in easy stages, resting whenever Oozalluc grew tired. At the springs, he filled great vessels of the water for drinking and bathing. This seemed to revitalize Oozalluc, and Metallak gained confidence. Nothing must ever happen to Oozalluc. He had come to know that her beauty reached far below the surface, like the bottomless pool at the springs. She shared with him a great love for the simple and beautiful things in life, the stars in the sky, the sight of a rainbow, or watching Big Horn eat from Metallak's hands. With Oozalluc at his side, Metallak seldom thought about all that had passed, or his banishment and shame at not being able to clear his name.

When they returned up river, they saw signs of new settlements springing up. Metallak vowed to Oozalluc that he would honor the treaty of his father, but he would never give up his home. Now, more than ever, he knew he could never confine himself to the mission village with his Cowassuck brothers, or join the renegade tribes of Tom Hegan. He would rather stay here and live in the shadow of life as it used to be.

He had heard gossip about Tom Hegan, that he was still too lazy to work, and so had no money. He was still bitter against the whites, blaming them for the shortage of game, forcing his people to forage for good furs. His people had lost faith in his false promises, and many had returned to St. Francis. He made frequent trips to the trading post, not for supplies but for rum, and the more he drank, the more bitter he became, urging his people to strike back at the whites, who had taken over their lands.

Much as Oozalluc and Metallak missed their people, they hated the disruption Tom Hegan brought to their people, and cherished the privacy of their lodge. Here they would sit in the evening enjoying the solitude of the lake and each other.

One day as they sat near their lodge, they heard an old familiar whistle and time stood still for a moment. Metallak had scanned the countryside in vain for days on end, daring not speak his thoughts aloud to Oozalluc. Perhaps Parmachenee wouldn't come home for the summer. Perhaps she liked her new life in the village and no longer missed them.

But there she stood, beautiful as ever, at least three inches taller, drinking in the sight of the lodge. Metallak stood quietly, not betraying his joy at seeing her, but she dropped her satchel and raced to him, throwing her arms about him. Gratefully, he returned the hug, reluctantly letting go as she raced to Oozalluc.

"Mother, I have missed you so."

She had returned to them just as she left, dressed in deerskins and wearing moccasins, her fine clothes in her satchel.

"Parmachenee brings joy to our lodge," Metallak told her seriously, his eyes glittering with pride. For a while, Parmachenee chattered like a magpie, telling them the wonders she had seen and learned in the great city, and all about school and the strange ways of her white family.

"They clean and dust every day, mother," she told Oozalluc. "And sometimes they wash the windows inside and out. My hands are so clean they are losing their color." At this they all laughed, amused at the boundless energy of the white women and their war against dirt.

Oozalluc often sent them off together, knowing how much Metallak enjoyed his daughter's company. The summer would soon be over and she would be gone again before they knew it. Besides, she could no longer keep up with them and preferred to stay at home and relax.

Together, Metallak and Parmachenee explored the waters around Umbagog, caught fish, and tanned skins for the coming winter. He taught her his special way of tanning to get the finest and softest robes. His quick steps took on a new vigor when he walked beside his daughter, and Oozalluc realized how much he had missed her.

"Tell me about my brothers," she said one day. "Will they come home this summer?"

"They do not have summers off," her father said.

192

"But they like Wheelock's School and already they have learned to read and write." Proudly, he showed her the letters they had written. "Some words even Metallak cannot read," he told her, ashamed to admit that his eyesight was slowly failing a little.

"Let me read them to you, father," she said excitedly. And so throughout the summer months, she would read and re-read the letters from her brothers to Oozalluc and Metallak who took great pride in her progress at Squire Charles.

Parmachenee loved the water just as her mother had, and often teased to take the canoe out alone. Usually Metallak went with her, but more and more he trusted her to navigate the canoe, even over the small rapids. she showed great skill for one so young. In no time, she was as brown as her father, spending all her time outside with him. When they weren't working in the garden, they would go canoeing or take a swim near the lodge.

But Parmachenee would never forget the only mother she had ever known. She gathered sweet grass and helped Oozalluc make baskets, planning to take some back to her white family also. She too had noticed that Oozalluc tired easily, and made her tasks as light as possible.

She made a sketch of their lodge sitting on the lake, and gave it to them one night. "This is how I will remember you in the winter months," she told them shyly.

"How do you like your white family?" Metallak asked.

"Everything is lovely, father, but I miss you very much."

"Does Squire Charles ever speak of having you painted? I have heard this is a favorite past time of the whites, especially those with money."

"It is the most remarkable thing, father. Squire Charles has a portrait that looks very much like me. The girl is wearing a lovely blue dress and on her shoulder there is a small birthmark just like mine. I am sure you were right father, when you said that he is my great grandfather."

"Did you speak of this to Squire Charles?"

Parmachenee sat pondering the question, as though far away. "I think they must miss their daughter very much father, and I remind them of her. I think perhaps that is the reason for Aunt Carrie's moods. Sometimes when I am talking or drawing a picture, a tear will

193

run down her cheek. She brushes it away and pretends that all is well. She has told me several times that soon my portrait will hang beside that other portrait above the fireplace."

"That is fine, my child. We are pleased that your white family is kind and good to you."

"They are always kind, father, but I would rather be here with you."

This was what Metallak longed to hear, that his daughter would always think of his humble little lodge as home. He turned aside so she wouldn't see the relief in his eyes.

Oozalluc, too, made the most of their time together. She wasn't sure how many summers she would have left to spend with Parmachenee, and there was still so much to teach her. In the long evening hours, she taught Parmachenee some old Indian melodies, and Parmachenee sang them in her native tongue until she had memorized them.

With a deep sense of loss, Metallak returned her to her benefactor in the fall, promising her that the winter months would fly by quickly and soon they would be together again.

He kept busy every minute so he wouldn't think about her, and began chinking the lodge and preparing for winter. The root cellar was well stocked already, and Oozalluc had gathered in a great supply of berries with Parmachenee's help. He helped Oozalluc grind a good supply of corn too. Once a month, he took the sled to Andover to trade for tobacco, potatoes and molasses. Oozalluc always looked forward to a fresh jug of molasses.

Soon winter came with all its fury. Often the temperature dropped to twenty below zero and the huge drifts of snow were impossible to navigate without snowshoes. But Oozalluc and Metallak were comfortable and when the sun reflected on the crust of the huge drifts, Metallak often went walking, enjoying the crispness of the winter air. He cleared a path to Big Horn's pen and left plenty of food each day, then brought in dry wood for their fire.

One evening, as he sat comfortably before the fire with Oozalluc, a sudden squall blew up, sending great gusts of wind and snow in all directions. There was a howl in the wind that swept through the thick rafters in their lodge. Metallak tucked more furs around Oozalluc, then straightened up, listening intently. He thought he heard a strange, muffled cry. Hurriedly, he pulled on warm clothes and took up his gun. Perhaps some wild predator was attacking Big Horn,

194

or perhaps some smaller animal was caught in the storm and floundering through the snow.

A distant echo met his ears in the howling wind. It sounded hollow and far away, but it sounded almost human. There it was again. As the wind shifted its direction, he caught a glimpse of a figure far away, waving his arms. Metallak quickly made haste toward the sound. If the figure fell down, he would never find him in this blinding snow. But as he drew closer, he saw the staggering, blurry figure and made his way to the man's side.

The man gratefully followed Metallak to his lodge, barely able to keep going, his figure a white blur, stumbling behind Metallak. Once inside the lodge, Oozalluc got up and made hot rum while Metallak rubbed his limbs trying to warm him. At first the man was barely able to speak out loud, but as he slowly warmed, he told them what happened.

"Jonathan Leavitt's my name," he said, shaking hands with Metallak when he was finally able to speak. "I don't know how to thank you for saving my life. Been at the grist mill in Upton all day long," he said. "Slowest miller I ever saw. By the time I started home across Umbagog Lake, the squall blew up, and I've been wandering around out there for hours. I was just about ready to give up when you found me."

"Welcome to Metallak's humble lodge," Metallak told him. "You will be warm and dry here tonight, and make a fresh start in the morning." He extended a soft moosehide for a coverlet and made him a place by the fire. Jonathan was amazed at the texture and velvety touch of the moose skin robe.

"You tan this yourself?" he asked. Metallak nodded modestly.

"Sure would like that tanning recipe," he said.

But Metallak did not reveal his method of tanning. Instead he decided to give Jonathan the robe when he left in the morning. Jonathan slept as comfortably on the floor, deep in the furs, as he did in his own bed at home.

In the morning, all was quiet and clear, no evidence of the squall of the night before. All about them, the sparkling snow lay on the ground like a beautiful blanket. Jonathan started off eagerly, inviting Metallak and Oozalluc to visit them on the Megalloway.

"I'm deeply indebted to you," he said.

"Jonathan is always welcome in Metallak's lodge," he told him.

"Metallak makes many white friends," Oozalluc told him after Jonathan had left.

"White settlers are good friends to Metallak also," he said. "Better than some Abenakis who think Metallak would commit murder."

"Does Metallak never forget?" she asked quietly.

"Metallak cannot forget. Metallak's sons will carry this shame also."

"Has Metallak been happy with Oozalluc"

"Metallak lives only for Oozalluc," he told her. "She is the best friend Metallak ever had."

Oozalluc spoke no more of the past. There was nothing she would like better than to clear Metallak's name, but she didn't know how to even begin.

They did not make the trip to the mission village that winter to make peace with God. Metallak felt Oozalluc was too weak, but Sebattis and Moll Ockett brought news from the village in mid-winter.

"We bring letters from Olumbo and Parmagunnit," she said, taking them out of her pouch. Eagerly, Metallak opened the letters and read them aloud. Most of the words he could decipher. He looked around at the others.

"You heard that my sons wish to live at the mission village now, and stop their schooling."

"But they have learned to read and write, Metallak, just as you and I did many years ago," Sebattis put in.

Metallak was pleased that they had remained even for four years at the difficult school. They were young men, and it was time they made their way in the world. There would be good training in the village too.

And so the winter passed. Metallak, sitting quietly by Oozalluc in the evenings, waited impatiently for spring when Oozalluc could go out of doors and Parmachenee would return to light up their lodge.

Just before summer planting, that was the time they

agreed upon. He was at their meeting place at Umbagog before dawn every day that week and when she saw her father, Parmachenee waved gleefully from a distance.

As always, he was taken aback by her beauty and grace. Surely this had been a wise decision. Parmachenee would live with the whites long after he and Oozalluc were gone, and her white family might be useful one day. But for the summer months, he would not think of her white family again. He reached out his hand and she stepped into the canoe as delicately as a swan on the water.

"Let us make haste to the lodge. Oozalluc too is waiting," he told her.

It was a happy reunion as Parmachenee recounted her adventures in the city. She described the lavish dinners where they ate from beautiful plates, when her grandparents entertained, and the servants who did all the cleaning.

"And all we have for you is new moccasins," Oozalluc said shyly, groping for her basket.

Metallak reached for the basket in the twilight, and reached inside for the moccasins. Hastily, he pulled at the bone needle holding them together, his eyes resting on his beautiful daughter.

It happened so suddenly he was stunned for a moment, then cried out in pain. The needle broke as he pulled and flying up, punctured his left eye.

Parmachenee screamed at the sight of the needle protruding from her father's eye as he moaned, unable to remove it.

Calm as always, Oozalluc bade him to be still, her heart hammering with fear. Blood ran down her husband's face and he was unable to conceal the pain. Finally, with her sharp teeth, she was able to remove the needle. But one look at her husband and she knew he would never use his left eye again.

Tenderly, she bathed his face and Parmachenee, calm again, tended to his every need until he finally slept. He tossed and turned in his sleep, frightened. How would he manage with only one eye? What would become of his family?

CHAPTER TEN

In spite of the beautiful summer weather, Oozalluc continued to lose weight and strength rapidly. Metallak remained at the lodge as much as possible, to be near her. He recovered quickly from the loss of his left eye, but there was no question about it. His eyesight was failing in the right eye too. The fear he would go blind gnawed at him, making him short tempered. He lost weight, and ate sparingly. But with Oozalluc he grew more tender each day.

"Let us fish from Molly Oozalluc's Rock," he would say, and row her carefully to the large rock in Lake Umbagog, casting his fishing line from the rock in content. Oozalluc sat quietly by his side. Never had she been so happy as these last few years as Metallak's wife. One day she would have to leave him alone here, but he would be at peace now. It had been many months since he spoke of Keoka's death, or woke from a bad dream bathed in sweat. Her biggest regret was that she had not cleared Metallak's name. Try as she would, there had been no clues to uncover in the strange death that had blackened his name and the names of his children. True, most of the villagers did not truly believe Metallak to be guilty and would have welcomed him back as Chief, but Metallak's pride would not allow that, not without clearing his name.

When the pain was strong and she wished to be alone, she would send him away for the day.

"Parmachenee longs to climb to Table Rock," she would tell Metallak, and off they would go, the two of them. This was Parmachenee's favorite spot. From their small lodge near Errol, they looked up toward the Dixville range. The mountains seemed to close in on both sides of the road and they felt like tiny ants crawling through a niche. As they climbed higher, great jagged pieces of granite seemed to hang suspended from the sky. Some looked bottom side up, others like high turrets. Parmachenee climbed nearly as well as her father, and by noon they had finally reached Table Rock, extending like a huge table above the jagged pieces of granite all around them. Sitting on this large projecting rock high above the valleys and rivers, Metallak felt like the King of the forest, Lord of all he surveyed. The view was breathtaking. Tiny streams wound through the mountains, waterfalls sprayed below them. For as far as the eye could see, they gazed into the Abenaki territory, slowly becoming the land of the whites. Here and there they saw a new clearing of a cabin going up, or a settler clearing his fields. Far below in this valley Metallak's people had danced the Calumet and harvested their corn together. His daughter interrupted his thoughts.

"What do you think about, my father?"

"Metallak thinks about the Calumet Dance, that he saw here as a child."

"Tell me about it, please."

"Among our people," he said, "this was called the Dance of the Spirit, and the words of the song would invoke the Great Spirit. Sometimes the dance was performed to summon the souls of our enemies, other times to obtain good weather, favorable to the crops that grew."

"Was it ever danced in time of peace, father?"

"When the enemy sent a peace offering, this was a very important ceremony."

"Did everybody dance, father?" Parmachenee tried to imagine the dance, as she looked far below.

Metallak described the ceremony to her in great detail. First a spot would be cleared and surrounded with shade trees. Here was placed a god of the person who gave the dance, usually an animal or a bird, along with the calumet, and trophies of warfare. There was a space too, for the singers of the dance, because every step of the dance was very precise and must be in perfect cadence.

"You see, Parmachenee," he explained, "this was before my people learned of the true God, before the coming of the good fathers. One brave would begin the dance holding the Calument. Soon another brave would approach, holding a bow and arrow, and they danced as though in a duel. When they all grew tired, others took their places. When they grew tired of dancing, there was always a great feast, to celebrate the occasion."

"It must have been very beautiful," she said.

"It is a dance that must be buried in the past," he said. "And you my child, what are your thoughts?"

"Parmachenee thinks of our ships at sea."

"But surely Parmachenee should not worry about these things."

"You see, father," she said, "the British are kidnapping our sailors from their vessels, so they will have more men to fight France. Our ships are always in danger at sea, and already we have lost many men."

"Parmachenee says we," he said thoughtfully. "Has Parmachenee forgotten she is an Abenaki?"

"Parmachenee has a white family also," she said in a small voice. "Grandfather Charles has been very kind to Parmachenee and speaks often of this trouble on the high seas."

"Metallak does not like to have Parmachenee in any danger. Perhaps the English ships will attack."

"Nonsense, father, our lodge is well protected inside and out. Besides, the British have never attacked on land."

"It seems the British will never stop," he said with a sigh, hoping that war was not forthcoming. How long would the colonies allow the English to take advantage of them and seize their sailors? He thought of his own sons and was glad they were far away.

"Could we not go to the village, father, and see Olumbo and Parmagunnit?" she asked, as though reading his thoughts.

Metallak did not answer right away. "Oozalluc, too, wishes to return to the village," he said finally. "She wishes to see the priest and ask forgiveness of all her sins." He couldn't speak of Oozalluc's illness to Parmachenee and rose abruptly.

"We have a long descent, my child," he said. "Let us begin now, before sunset."

A few days later, on July 10, 1803, they set out, taking the trip very slowly so that Oozalluc would not get too tired. Up Lake Azicohoos, on to Lake Parmachenee, and up the small tributary of the St. Francis River. It seemed much longer than four years since they had seen the boys. Although he had given his consent for them to remain in the small village, Metallak had missed them very much.

"Father, look," said Parmachenee with excitement when she saw St. Francis. "We are almost there."

The village looked exactly the same, a forest of greenery shrouding the landing area, and insuring the privacy of their friends and relatives still at the village.

Metallak felt like a stranger as he neared the village center with his family. It seemed all the Abenakis dressed like their white brothers now. He alone remained in his deerskin clothing. Many old friends came forward to greet them, hospitably offering them the shelter of their lodges. Metallak learned that Chief Joseph Louis had long since passed on, and there was a new Chief in his place. The small new building he saw was a school, but little else had changed.

Metallak recognized his sons immediately, although they were taller now and weighed nearly as much as he. His sons shook hands solemnly, glad to see their father and Oozalluc, who greeted them warmly, even in her frail condition. They took in the sight of their father gravely, noting the sunken dead eye and silver threads of hair.

"This cannot be Parmachenee," exclaimed Olumbo, gazing at his beautiful little sister with awe. At fifteen summers, she was a lovely young woman, tall and slender, dressed in deerskin like her father. Although she loved the beautiful clothes she wore with her white family, they tore easily and she enjoyed the freedom of the deerskin that stretched with her movements. Then, too, she knew her father took pleasure in seeing her wear the fine skins he had tanned so painstakingly throughout the long winter.

"Come and see the new school," said Parmagunnit, taking her arm protectively, eager to show her around and speak to her privately.

"Is father happy now?" he whispered at the first opportunity. Has he finally forgotten the death of our mother? What has happened to his eye?"

Parmachenee spoke softly. "He loves Oozalluc very much. But she is not well and has little strength. Father sits by her side at the lodge all the time now. Oozalluc pretends that she grows old and needs her rest, but I don't think she will see another summer. Then father will be all alone."

She told him painfully about his lost eye. A dirty looking old man watched them from behind a tree, muttering to himself. They neither saw nor heard him, so absorbed in seeing each other that they chattered like children.

"The evil Spirit of Keoka returns." He rubbed his hands to warm them. "It is the Demon come back to life." He drew closer and shook a rattle at Parmachenee, still muttering.

"Who is that?" asked Parmachenee with a shiver.

"Pay no attention. It is the old Shaman, who talks to himself all the time now."

"Oh."

They visited some friends, examined the interior of the school, and went to find their parents and Parmagunnit. They were surrounded by villagers, who sought news of the white settlements.   Metallak told them of the difficulty with the English impressing American sailors, and of the smuggling across the border.

"Even though the settlers fear the English sentries along the border," he explained, "they continue to trade with their friends in Canada." He looked at Oozalluc, remembering his own activity along the border.

"Trading   causes warfare at   the   boundaries, sometimes even shooting." "And so they should give up this practice, father," put in Parmagunnit. "If not for the white settlements, we would occupy the lands of our grandfathers instead of this small village. At least the English allow us to stay here in peace."

"White   settlers are good people too,"   said Metallak, surprised at his son's attitude.   "They are like our own Abenaki brothers."

Metallak sensed his sons' loyalty to the English and spoke of other matters.

Metallak learned for the first time that another treaty had been written for the Abenaki territory and passed into the hands of three white men. It seemed each of these men, Bedell, Wales and Gibbs claimed one third of the land. Like the deed of his father, he would respect this deed, but still claimed the little parcel of land where he had made his home at Umbagog in Errol.

Later that evening he sat with his sons in the sweat lodge, as he had sat with his own father years ago, and they talked.

"What will Parmagunnit do here at the village?" he asked.

"Perhaps farm," he said, "and make baskets to sell. It is surprising how much these baskets will bring at the market."

"And you, Olumbo?"

"I wish to sail away, to see other lands across the sea," he said, his eyes full of excitement.

"And none but Metallak will live on the grounds of our fathers?"

"You are the last of the true Cowassucks, father," said Parmagunnit thoughtfully. "Even the elders say this. We could not live as you do, using old-fashioned tools and knives. We prefer the good rifles of our English friends, and the comfortable fashions of the whites."

"Besides, life would be lonely in the forest," added Olumbo. "Without our people, there would be nothing to do but hunt

202

and fish.''

Metallak fell silent, pondering their words. He knew there was truth to what they said. His sons and daughter belonged to a different world than he had known. The love of the ancestral land was not in their blood as he felt it. They preferred company while he preferred solitude, and they admired the material things they saw in the white settlements. The life they sought would force them to earn wages from the white settlers. They would never know true freedom such as he had known. And worse, they would forget their own heritage.

"Metallak is pleased that his sons will remain here at the village,'' he told them finally. "Here in Canada there is fine country too, good grazing land. Here perhaps one day you will take a wife. There are still many young women of your own village. The French settlements, too, have many handsome young women.''

"But father, I told you I wish to sail far away,'' protested Olumbo.

"That is true, that is true,'' Metallak answered, "but one day you will return to take a wife. I ask only that you do not take an English wife.''

Olumbo opened his mouth to speak, then changed his mind.

The boys said no more, not daring to arouse their father's wrath. Although he had never struck them, there was a deep tone he used that they had never questioned, not even as children.

After a short visit of two weeks, Metallak was ready to return to the comfort and quiet of his own lodge. True, the villagers had made him welcome, none of them even hinting at that tragic day long ago, but he longed for the solitude of his own lodge. Oozalluc, too, was eager to leave. All this visiting with old friends was tiresome. Besides, she had come to make peace with God and fulfill her religious duties. Now she was ready to return.

"Will you visit often, father?'' the young men asked hopefully. Deep down, they had hoped he would return to the village to be with them. But they should have known he would never give up his independence and live in the small village area.

"Metallak will try to visit often,'' he assured them, shaking hands.

"We will visit too, father, at least once a year,'' Parma-gunnit told them, "if only to admire our sister, who is sure to have many suitors.''

Parmachenee blushed at this and shyly said goodbye. She wondered when she would see her brothers again. They had questioned her for hours about her white family, and seemed impressed with all that she told them. They envied her life and her affection for her white family.

Metallak marveled at the growth and independence of these two young men, his sons who carried his blood. He had barely known them as children, before the death of their mother, and then had them only a few short summers before they went off to school. He couldn't believe they were young men of nineteen and twenty summers. They would soon be taking wives of their own, and he, Metallak, would be a grandfather. If only things had been different, the Cowassucks would follow Metallak to the ancestral grounds, his sons included, but there was no point in dredging up the past. What was done was done.

Parmachenee brightened up their return trip home, always exclaiming over the beauty of a simple flower or the sight of a new fawn running through the forest. She sensed Oozalluc's withdrawal from their company, probably lost in her prayers, but never spoke of this until she and Metallak were alone one day after their return home.

"Oozalluc needs me, father, and I am educated now. Please let me stay."

"Metallak too needs Parmachenee," he told her, giving her a big hug. "Perhaps in one more year."

"What if that is too late?"

"Metallak will care for Oozalluc now," he said, "as she cared for you many years ago. I will send for Moll Ockett if I need her."

"I love her too," said Parmachenee, tears in her eyes. "She has been a mother to me."

"All this is true," her father said. "Perhaps Metallak is selfish, but I wish to share Oozalluc with no one. In this last season of her life, I must be with her alone. Besides, your great grandparents also grow older, and they too long for the companionship of youth in their old age. I ask that you do this for me."

204

The pain in Metallak's good eye was more than Parmachenee could bear. She knew then without a doubt that Metallak cherished Oozalluc and loved her beyond all else. "If that is your wish, father," she said simply.

After she left, Metallak spent all his time with Oozalluc, bringing her fresh broth, tender fish, calling on Moll Ockett for special herbs and barks. With more tenderness than he had ever shown before, he bathed her daily and wrapped her in furs to prevent a chill. Sometimes if she felt like talking, he would sit quietly beside her and listen, holding her hand. Sometimes she told him stories of the children when they were little. Other times she spoke to Metallak of his own future.

"You are well liked in the white settlements," she told him over and over. "Let them give you work to do and put by some money, so you will be comfortable in your old age." He dared not to sleep, day or night, sensing that she grew weaker every day. He prayed to the Invisible God to be kind to Oozalluc, who had never hurt a soul on this earth. For himself, he asked nothing, only that Oozalluc would not suffer. To Oozalluc, he betrayed nothing, bringing hot broth as often as she had the strength to drink it. But she saw the pain in his eye, and knew that he loved her deeply. One night she asked him to brush her hair, and he brushed it until it shone, long and gray now, but still thick.

The next morning Oozalluc did not open her eyes. Her body was cold and still. The hair was like a veil of mourning over her shoulders. At first Metallak tried to awaken her, but he knew she would never waken again. It was the middle of winter, and he felt cold and empty, colder then he would be if the winds howled and snow crept up under the eaves of his lodge. He wanted to lie beside Oozalluc, in the cold face of the earth and never wake again.

There was no one he could call on for help. Moserill was way over in Andover, and he didn't want to leave Oozalluc, even for a minute. It would take hours by snowshoe to walk to the nearest village. He sat for hours with her head in his arms, thinking. There was no way to bury her body in the frozen ground, even if he had a good shovel. Already there was an odor in the lodge, and he knew he must do something.

He fondled the hemlock stick in his hands, the last thing Oozalluc had put into his hands. "I have nothing to leave Metallak," she said quietly, "no special memories of the past, except

205

this." As she pressed the hemlock stick into his hands she said. "Perhaps Metallak will keep a record of the years that pass when Oozalluc is no longer here." She knew that Metallak treasured records, and would keep the stick as carefully as he had kept the rocks and barks of his father.

At last he decided to wrap her body in a length of birch bark, which he tied carefully with withes. But he didn't know how to preserve it until spring when she could be buried properly. And then it dawned on him all of a sudden. He would place her over the smoke hole of his lodge where the slow flame would preserve her body all winter.

He climbed a tree near his lodge and tested the strength of the branches. Next he went and got Big Horn and with his help, mounted Oozalluc's body on one of the overhanging branches close to the smoke hole, thus preserving it until spring. Exhausted, he huddled in the lodge without a fire. Throughout that long winter, he ate very little and spoke not at all except to Oozalluc.

"Oozalluc was always loyal," he would say, "and never questioned the death of Keoka. She never asked anything of Metallak, and always kept him in fresh clothes carefully stitched. Metallak will never have another friend like Oozalluc."

In the spring, when the ice went out, he tenderly laid her body in his canoe, crossing the narrow straits and making his way on down to the Molechunkamonk, towards the rapids of Umbagog, where he nearly capsized. Somehow he managed to stay afloat. Down through the rapids and eddies he navigated with difficulty, on to the lower lake, and to the little island that Oozalluc had loved so dearly. Here, by the peaceful Umbagog, the crooning of the frogs would forever sing to Oozalluc in her sleep. After digging a shallow grave, he planted a paddle for a marker, having nothing better, and sat down by her grave, not leaving the spot until the third morning, praying for Oozalluc.

In his heartbroken state, Metallak lost all track of time. He built a small lodge near the grave, so he could protect and watch over it, leaving only when he ran out of supplies. Parmachenee remained alone in the lodge for a few days after her return home and then decided to try and find her father. She knew Lake Umbagog as well as her father, and quickly located the new lodge, where she joined him. He looked emaciated, as though he had eaten nothing all summer. Parmachenee made several trips for supplies, bringing comfort and food to her father. She even made a tiny garden for him.

Moserill was the first to learn of Metallak's loss and the only friend Metallak ever allowed to visit Oozalluc's grave. Moserill quietly observed the ritual Metallak carried out whenever he visited Oozalluc's graveside. First he would wash his hands. Then, moving carefully so as not to even break a twig, he would approach the grave, always from a different angle, never from the same path twice in a row. Sometimes he sat there for hours.

For the next three summers, Metallak lived as a hermit. Parmachenee hated to intrude on his privacy and stayed with her white family.

Moserill brought fresh vegetables, telling Metallak all the news. He felt sorry for his old friend.

"All supplies are cut off to England," he said one morning, "according to the Embargo Act."

"How will the settlers trade?" asked Metallak.

"Smuggling's worse than ever," Moserill told him. "People got to live, and pay their taxes. If they can't trade one place, they'll trade someplace else."

"Moserill too, is forced to smuggle?"

"Got to! Flour's worth only four dollars a barrel here in the states, but the price is nineteen dollars a barrel in Canada."

Slowly, that summer, Metallak came out of his lethargy. With all this smuggling, Parmachenee might be in danger, might even be trying to come home. He must return to his old lodge and await her.

He packed up and returned to his old lodge with Moserill, who stayed a few days to keep Metallak company. Secretly, he was delighted that Metallak had overcome his grief. Looking at him, you'd never believe Metallak was fifty years old. He had very little gray hair, and his body was as lithe and slender as always. Somehow, he had to get word to Parmachenee that her father was waiting for her.

"Why don't you come over to my place and spend a few days?" he asked. "The Misses will be glad to have you."

"Metallak will wait for Parmachenee," he told Moserill, thanking him for all his help.

After Moserill left, he set about cleaning up the debris around his lodge, which was over-run with weeds and bushes. He wanted all in readiness when his daughter arrived.

A dozen times a day, he ran to the water's edge to search for her. Ugly thoughts haunted him. He had neglected his little girl. What if she'd been hurt, or captured? He couldn't bear it if he lost both of them.

In a frenzy, he decided to go search for her. He would leave at first light. He had never felt so helpless lying there. He had already lost two precious loves - first Keoka - then Oozalluc. Would Parmachenee be next?

He awoke staring into a vision that looked like Parmachenee. Startled, he struggled to sit up. Parmachenee had brought home a beautiful silk scarf for her father.

"Where did Parmachenee get this?" he asked admiring the bright colors and tying it about his leathery neck. He just couldn't believe she was really home.

"From the Orient, father. Many ship captains return from the Orient and bring me gifts because they know my white family. But I worry about them. Many ships are seized by the barbary pirates and never return.

"Then they should seek trade elsewhere," he said emphatically.

"They must, father. No longer can we trade with England. They continue to kidnap our sailors and press them into English service."

"It seems the English always cause trouble," he said, "as long as Metallak can remember. I ask this of Parmachenee, never to marry an Englishman. Promise me this."

"I promise, father."

"Moserill tells me that all supplies are cut off to England."

"That is true, father," she said, "but the sailors are a hardy lot. Often, they set sail for a port in the states and find they are blown off course. This, of course, permits them to take refuge in a West Indian port and sell their cargo for repairs and passage back home. So you see, father, one way or another, they continue to trade without actually breaking the law.

To please her father, Parmachenee still wore the deerskin garments in the summer months. While he worked in the garden, she made him several shirts and leggings, enough to last a good long time. She had heard the compliments he received whenever they went into town, and how proudly he had said, "My daughter makes all my clothes, even the sign of the bald eagle." Now she took extra pains to stitch carefully so that Metallak would never be ashamed of her handiwork. Besides, she didn't want him using any more of the bone needles.

She was pleased to see Sebattis and Moll Ockett approaching in a canoe, and went running for her father. He too, was glad to see his old friend, who brought news of the mission village and of Metallak's sons.

"The new church is finally finished," Sebattis told them. "Let us hope this one will not burn."

"What of my brothers?" asked Parmachenee.

"Parmagunnit has a fine basket business," said Sebattis. "Olumbo, who comes and goes, has asked me to tell you that he plans to make a visit during the growing season.

"Father, did you hear?" cried Parmachenee, excited that she would soon see her brother. Metallak nodded, pleased also that he would see his son this summer.

"Let us celebrate!" said Sebattis, drawing forth his jug. Metallak refused to drink in his own lodge as always, afraid he might lose control and burn or damage his property. "Sebattis grows old now," confided Moll Ockett to Parmachenee. "It is the rum as always." Parmachenee had heard that Moll Ockett often struck off without him, spending the night in Bethel or Paris, making her calls on the sick.

After their visit, Metallak busied himself with making canoes. He had found that the whites admired his birch bark canoes and paid well for them. He had put by a large store of coins and counted himself lucky. If only he could prove his innocence in the death of Keoka, he would be a happy man.

That summer he and Parmachenee dwelt at Metallak Point on Richardson Lake, where he could visit Oozalluc's grave often. Already there were four notches on the old hemlock stick she had left in his care. He would make a mark for each year that passed without her. Parmachenee planted wild flowers over the grave, and Metallak planted bushes on the sides.

One evening they returned to the lodge after sunset and there stood Olumbo, waiting for them. "Olumbo," shouted Parmachenee, "you look so different."

His hair was cut short, and he was dressed in a fine suit. This displeased Metallak, but he shook hands cordially.

"I am proud that you keep your promise and visit

your father," he said. "Tell us news of the village."

"It is always the same, father. Nothing ever changes. Many, like Parmagunnit, are content to sell baskets for a mere pittance, while the white grow rich with trading."

"Most of the white settlers I know are very poor," said Metallak thoughtfully.

"How do you like my suit?" asked Olumbo, turning about and displaying his clothes. "For this suit, I made a birch bark canoe."

Already the suit had begun to collect burs and bits of brush from the forest. Within a few days, it would probably have to be thrown away. "It looks fine, Olumbo," said Parmachenee, afraid her father would show his disapproval. "But while you are visiting, you may wear some of these leggings." She went inside and got some of the garments she had been making.

"Just like a wife already, aren't you?" teased Olumbo, but he wore the clothing to please her.

"I'd like to spend a few days hunting with you, father, just like the old days."

At this, Metallak brightened. Perhaps in time his son would appreciate the riches of the great forest. They hunted all day, and at day's end, he showed Olumbo his store of skins and furs in the private cave.

Olumbo was quite impressed with his father's store of skins. "You could be a rich man, father. Why don't you sell all your furs?"

"They will be there when I need them," Metallak said. "I have no need of gold or riches."

He was strangely disappointed in Olumbo's attitude. He could see that his son still wished to be rich, and talked of far off lands and great riches with his head in the clouds. He was not interested in the canoe trade, though he knew his father made good wages from it. Baskets did not interest him either.

"Woman's work," he had said to his father.

Sometimes Metallak caught him telling lies about having checked the traps, and he would go out himself to check them again, often finding them full.

One day, they took their canoes out fishing while Parmachenee chose to pick berries. But Olumbo claimed to be having no luck.

"I will return and help Parmachenee with the berries. "Perhaps my luck will change." He headed back to their lodge early, and furtively packed the furs he had secreted out of the cave into a hiding place. He packed the canoe as tightly as he dared, and started off for the head of the lake before his father's return. With the price of these furs, he would be considered a wealthy young man. He would be respected as his father was, when he returned to the village dressed in fine clothes.

Metallak continued to fish, enjoying the beauty and solitude of the lake. He knew the days of solitude and privacy were numbered. Already the whites moved here in great multitudes, no longer fearing the Indians or the wild animals. This would be good for Parmachenee, who needed companionship.

He had an uneasy feeling that something was wrong. Olumbo had acted peculiar all day, refusing to look his father in the eye when they spoke. His mind seemed to be elsewhere. Perhaps he was in some kind of trouble and hesitated to tell his father. Metallak decided to return to his lodge and see what was going on. Perhaps he was imagining things, and the two of them would surprise him with their large quantity of berries.

First he decided to check on his cache of furs. He had planned to give some to Olumbo to take back with him. On finding most of them gone, he ran to the lake, and there paddling hard towards the head of the lake, was Olumbo. Enraged that his own son would steal from him, Metallak jumped into his own canoe and followed him, his anger mounting as he paddled.

In his whole life, Metallak had never stolen from another. His integrity was a matter of great pride to him, and word of this quickly spread through the white settlements. Metallak was an honest man and always honorably upheld his word. He was bitterly disappointed that his own son had betrayed him, willing to forsake his father's love for a few furs. The muscles in his powerful arms rippled as he gained speed on his son, slowly but surely overtaking him. Although he was close to fifty-eight summers now, Metallak was still lean and muscular, his body inured to the hardships of everyday living in the woods.

Olumbo was no match for his father. He had been spoiled among the villagers, leading a lazy life of ease. He grew nervous as he turned and saw his father gaining on him, and paddled harder. He approached the head of the lake, thinking he would escape just

211

in time.

For six miles, Metallak had paddled hard and just as Olumbo pushed into the shore of the lake, Metallak overtook him, leapt into his canoe and overturned it, with all its contents.

Olumbo found himself being pulled out of the water by two strong arms, and for the first time in his life was truly frightened. Would his father kill him?

Metallak proceeded to give him a good beating, making Olumbo wish he had never come for this visit. He feared for his life.

"Kill me," he gasped finally, "as you did my Mother!"

At this, Metallak froze, standing tall and straight, letting Olumbo go as though he held fire in his hands.

"Go!" he thundered. "Olumbo is piz-wat, like his mother. Good for nothing!"

Without waiting to right the overturned canoe, Olumbo ran off into the woods empty handed, wanting only to make his escape.

Slowly, Metallak repacked all the furs, after righting the canoes, and pulling one behind the other, made his way back to the lodge. His head was pounding. So even his own son thought he was guilty. The memories all came back in a flood, and for a long while, he sat with his head in hands, staring at the ground.

Parmachenee found him staring at the lake, and guessed what had happened when she saw both canoes. "Do not grieve, my father. Olumbo was always hasty and often regretted his actions after it was too late. One day he will come and ask your forgiveness."

For the next five years, until 1812, he lived almost as a hermit, seldom leaving his lodge except for supplies. Always loyal, Parmachenee came to spend summers with him, returning to Portsmouth for the winter months with her white family. She brought gifts to her father, and the *Falmouth-Gazette*, which she read to him often.

"Why do Sebattis and Moll Ockett not come for a visit?" she asked one evening.

"I had forgotten to tell you, little one. They are no longer together. Sebattis has a great weakness for the rum as you know, and Moll Ockett finally left him. He is a lonely man now."

"Father," she said, "White people call me Fluella, after my grandmother. Do you think it's a pretty name?"

"Fluella is all right," he said slowly. "But Parmachenee means Smiling Water. What meaning does Fluella have?"

"I do not know, my father, but I will never forget my people," she said seriously. "But few of us are left, and this is the white man's world now."

"That is so," he said quietly.

Sebattis came riding in hard one day to bring news. He lost no time in getting to the point.

"The Americans are at war," he said, dismounting. "The settlers have declared war against England for preying on their ships and blockading their ports. Sebattis rides to the village now to see what stand the Abenakis take."

Metallak was filled with anger, even though he had expected this for a long time. Would the English never stop bearing arms and causing discord? He thought of the smuggling in the old Abenaki territory, slandering the proud vestige of pines and beauty with their acts of violence across the boundary lines, causing men to lie and cheat to pay their taxes. He knew his sons were loyal to the English cause, and hoped they would not get involved.

Parmachenee was a great comfort to him. "Do not brood, my father," she said. "Surely Parmagunnit and Olumbo will return here to stay with us throughout the fighting."

But Metallak was not convinced of this. Long ago his people had pledged their loyalty to the English, and Canada was in the hands of the English. His sons were not American. Neither were they French farmers. Where would they go if the English renounced them?

Two weeks later, Sebattis returned with news. "Olumbo and Parmagunnit fight with the English," he told Metallak quietly.

"But do not think ill of them. The English have promised land and money to all soldiers. Further, the Abenakis like Sir Prevost. He is wise and kind, not like the old Governor Craig."

Parmachenee sat by her father's side, listening quietly.

"Besides, it has been many years since the Abenaki warriors go to battle. In this, we are united with our old enemy, the Iroquois, who wish also to fight. They will never forgive the American for attacking them and destroying their villages under the hands of

21.

General Sullivan. From their refuge along Lac St. Pierre, they come in droves."

Parmachenee interrupted. "But the Americans hope that Canada will join with them to repel the English. Surely the Canadians must know this."

"This will never happen," said Sebattis. "In all likelihood, the Americans will lose."

"And what of our people?" Metallak asked bitterly. "Will the English never stop making demands on the Abenakis?"

"The Abenakis march in two camps," said Sebattis. "Olumbo and Parmagunnit are together. They are stationed along the shores of Lake Champlain under Lt. Salaberry. Their company numbers one hundred fifty warriors."

"This many?" asked Parmachenee.

"The second band of Abenakis travels with General Brock."

"This is the work of mad men," said Metallak sadly.

"Some say it is the work of Tom Hegan," said Sebattis. "He stood with his war club, and asked for volunteers, telling them they would be rich with land and money after the war. Many of our young warriors stood up."

On hearing this, Metallak paced the floor of the lodge, not trusting himself to speak. He might have known his old enemy would turn his own sons against him.

"Tom Hegan is a thorn in my side, a troublemaker! Why did they listen to him? Haven't they had enough of his lies and promises?"

"Who knows why the young listen to Tom Hegan?" Sebattis said quietly, sorry that he brought this news to Metallak. "Perhaps they thirst for bloodshed and hunger for the land and riches that he promises. Perhaps they long to see a real battle. Up to now, they have only read about them."

Metallak spoke very little all day. He brooded and reflected, deep in thought. Finally, he made his decision.

"From this day forward, Metallak disowns Parmagunnit and Olumbo. No longer may they wear the sign of the eagle or visit the lodge of Metallak. Metallak has no sons!"

"Surely you do not mean this, my father. They only do what they believe is right. Let us pray for their safety instead."

"Metallak has no sons!" he said again, leaving the

lodge to sit by himself on Oozalluc's Rock. Sebattis tried to comfort Parmachenee, and then left to bring news to Moll Ockett.

Parmachenee sought news of the war from their neighbors and hurried home to her father. As they supped, she would tell him what she learned, knowing what he longed to hear but that his pride would not permit him to ask.

Try as he would to forget his sons and bury himself in seclusion, sometimes he would accompany her to the nearby towns of Canaan and Errol to get word of the war. Moserill, too, often came over to tell him the news.

"It is rumored that General Hull of Michigan has crossed the Detroit River and read a Proclamation to your people to win them over. For a month, he remained camped at Sandwich, and sent out many detachments, but the English defeated them. It does not go well for the Americans. I heard that Lt. Roulette, with only six men, boarded and took over an American ship filled with troops and baggage."

"What news do you hear of Hull?" asked Metallak. Of all the settlers, only Moserill knew that his sons fought alongside the British.

"He has retreated to Detroit, and General Brock has gone to drive Hull from his position. He has 1300 men with him, 500 of them your people."

"Tell Metallak no more," he said in a tired voice, not wanting to hear news of battle. Perhaps his sons were wounded, even dead, and for what? Would the English keep their promise to give them more land?

Months later, he went to Errol to pick up supplies, and heard the latest gossip from the farmers gathered there.

"Hull has surrendered his entire Army. Some say he has gone over to the British. All of Michigan is in the hands of the English."

It looked as though the Americans had no chance. Metallak felt a strong loyalty to these settlers he had traded and hunted with these past twenty years. They did not want war anymore than he did. Most of all, they didn't want to go back under English rule. More and more he sought the solitude and peace of his lodge. His loyal daughter kept him posted.

"The Americans have had a great disaster at Queenstown," she reported one day. "They lost over 300 men, with 1000 taken prisoner. Our people led the attack."

Secretly, Metallak was proud of his people, who marched bravely forth in the hope of gaining back some of their own lands. But he wished they had remained at their own little village, instead of getting involved in this bitter feud between the English and the Americans. They would gain nothing, he feared.

Throughout the war, Parmachenee stayed with her father, often speaking of a young beau named Moulton, a Canadian. Metallak had begun to think Parmachenee would never marry, and teased her about this Moulton.

"When will Metallak meet Moulton?"

"Soon, father, soon," she replied, as she wrote her beau another letter.

When her young man finally came to Metallak's lodge one day, she proudly drew him inside. "Father, Andrew has come to make a visit."

Hospitably, Metallak bade him enter, and made him comfortable. Moulton seated himself on the floor just as Metallak did, obviously wishing to be accepted. He complimented Metallak on the beauty of the lake and his lodge.

"Andrew wishes to learn the history of the Abenaki people from you," said Parmachenee, appealing to her father to accept the young man that she cared for.

Moulton's jet black hair reminded Metallak of his own hair many years ago, refusing to lie flat around the edges. His blue eyes were genuine and sincere as he spoke. His fondness for Parmachenee was plain to see, even with only one eye. Why would this young man yearn to know the history of the red man? Was it not already common knowledge?

"The young man may read in history books of the red man's fall from greatness, his defeats, and white man's flourishing, and the red man's fading. Now you have the history of the red men, and their sad history in this rich country."

Sternly he regarded the young man. "Does the young man understand the creed of our people?"

Moulton recalled the words of his grandmother, who had befriended an Indian in hiding. Her hay had been mysteriously cut and brought in by these same Indians that summer, who came and left as quietly as the wind, after the hay was piled in the barn. "An Indian never forgets a kindness," she had told her grandsons. "Remember that."

"I understand, sir, that your people always observe a kindness and that such kindness is never forgotten."

"This is true," said Metallak, "but neither is a wrong-doing ever forgotten."

"I will protect Parmachenee as you yourself would do," he said humbly.

Throughout the summer, Metallak watched and observed, glad to bring his thoughts away from the war. Moulton was good company, and Metallak taught him to build a canoe that would last many summers. Already Moulton could navigate the rapids, with caution. Together they spent many hours talking.

"Are you not the wisest red man in these hills?" he asked one day.

"Maybe so," answered Metallak. "Perhaps because I am the oldest red man in these hills. Once Metallak was mighty and stood like a tall lofty pine, laughing at the storms around me."

"You are still strong sir," said Moulton, admiring Metallak's strength and appearance.

Metallak laughed. "Now I am like the aged trunk, with his limbs crooked with age standing stiffly in the wind, but no longer bending with it."

"Will you not consider returning to Canada with Parmachenee and me to make your home with us?"

"No," said Metallak quietly. "Here, in this spot, I will die like my father and his father, in peace with the earth and forest, here where the Sokokis, the Anasquanticooks, the Kenabas, and the Wawenocks all met to smoke the Calumet and celebrate. Here, too, they defended their glory. But like the withered leaves of a ravaged forest, I will be the last. You will live in peace with the whites, and my daughter will be happy. She has been the light of my lodge and I will miss her sorely."

When fall came and Moulton made ready to leave, Metallak drew out a gift.

"Metallak has a gift for his future son-in-law," he said, proof of his approval and respect for Moulton. "Soon Metallak will have two lights to visit his lodge instead of one." He brought forth a hand-made tobacco pouch, embroidered long ago by Oozalluc in the sign of the bald eagle. "The young man is part of Metallak's family now," he said.

"I will carry it with honor, sir," said Moulton.

They parted, to meet again after the war. Parmachenee had refused to leave her father until peace was restored. She was already twenty three summers, considered aged for a bride, but she would not leave her father in his hour of need.

Secretly, Metallak looked forward to the wedding. Already, he regretted his rash decision to disown his sons. He longed to see them again, even Olumbo, and prayed that they were still alive.

CHAPTER ELEVEN

Metallak often meditated about the past, remembering the carefree days so long ago when all he had to worry about was hunting and fishing and playing with his children. How simple life had been then, before Keoka's death. She had captivated his heart, right from the start, even though he knew she was different from the women of his own tribe. He should have had more patience and accepted her the way she was. Taking her away to the wilderness had only caused the death of his first son and the life of solitude had eventually forced Keoka to turn to rum. And then the tragedy of her death and his banishment had caused him to shut himself off from the world of his people, the people he loved the most. Once again, he regretted his rash decision to disown his sons. Surely they thought they were doing the right thing, just as he did. What right did he have to judge them?

He was grateful for Parmachenee's comfort that summer and dreaded the day she would leave him forever. Still, he felt guilty that she remained with him when she longed to be with her beau. Parmachenee seemed to sense his despair and never mentioned her own plans for the future. From time to time, she went to pay a visit to Moll Ockett over in Andover, where she lived now at the home of Captain Bragg. Moll had been persuaded to spend her old age there in comfort, but even at her advanced age, she remained alert and had good sense. One particular day, Parmachenee returned earlier than usual, running to the lodge to find her father.

"It is the dreaded plague, father," she reported. "Moll Ockett has just heard the news. Some lie sick and dying, others have recovered. It is called the Spotted Fever."

Metallak remembered well the dreaded disease that had killed so many of his people. Sometimes there would be a severe headache, and pain along the back. Other times the victim would suddenly take a chill and begin vomiting. Ugly fever blisters covered the face. Dark spots appeared, faces grew bloated, and tongues became dark and dry. Often the sick ones had convulsions and a speedy death. Some, though, became delirious and had a long and painful death. Finally, the head would be drawn back and the muscles of the neck rigid before death finally struck.

"There is no one to care for the sick, father. And the settlements beg for assistance. Moll Ockett has told me the herbs and barks to use for this sickness."

Metallak paced the floor. "Parmachenee, too, will get the plague," he said. "Have you forgotten your wedding plans?"

"I am strong, father, and you know I never get sick. Please let me go." She looked at her father, her eyes full of compassion for the ill.

He could not bear the look in her eyes, and turned his back. But even then, he could not refuse his only daughter.

"Parmachenee is free to go," he said at last with resignation.

"Father is kind," she said softly. "No harm will come to me, and I will be back in just a few weeks." Quickly, she prepared to leave, taking a blanket, several pouches, and a loaf of bread. "Perhaps I will see a newspaper, and get word of my brothers," she told him, knowing that he worried about his sons even though he never mentioned them.

"Wli-nanawalmezi," she said, hugging her father.

"Wli-nanawalmezi, my child." He remained standing in one spot until he no longer saw her canoe and then slowly went inside, not daring to think what he would do if she got the fever.

Parmachenee was a welcome sight to Andover. There were no doctors for miles around, and Moll Ockett was too feeble to get out these days. Parmachenee visited the homes of the sick, first making a steam bath to bring on sweating. She brewed them warm drinks, sometimes causing them to vomit. She applied poultices to their extremities, then watched and waited, giving what comfort she could. Sometimes the sick ones would recover, days after she had left, not remembering all that had passed. Other times she lost them.

Sometimes the fever would pass over an entire township, only to strike the next town. Parmachenee followed the crooked course of the fever, going from one small town to another. As she traveled through the open fields, she gathered Indian tobacco, storing it away in her pouches. Only about a foot high, the plant contained a small fruit bearing tiny brown oblong seeds. The taste of these was like fiery hot tobacco. It took very little to bring on sweating, or to cause nausea. Parmachenee used it very sparingly. She had heard that the hill doctors often bled their patients, and sometimes even applied leeches, but she had never seen this done, and wondered at the strange ways of the whites.

She returned periodically to Andover to rest and consult with Moll Ockett, asking her advice. But when Parmachenee saw how feeble she was this last time, she remained with her for several days. Moll Ockett knew her time had come, and urged Parmachenee to return home.

"Old Moll has tried to walk straight for a good many years, my child," she said. "But on this night Moll wishes to lie outside under the stars." Parmachenee hurried to Captain Bragg with this last request, and they carried her tenderly out under the stars, where she breathed her last.

It wasn't long before Parmachenee had another blow. During the excitement of her old friend's funeral, she chanced to learn of another tragedy that struck while she was away caring for the sick. There had been a terrible fire in the town of Portsmouth. More than one hundred dwellings had burned to the ground, including the great mansion of her white family, her second home.

She learned too that Squire Charles had died fighting the fire, and that his fragile wife had suffocated in her bed. As soon as Parmachenee recovered from the shock, she went to the house, picking through the charred rubble, tears running down her face.

"You are Fluella, I believe?" she heard, and turned to face a stranger, an old friend of Charles, he told her, named Blodgett.

"Some of the articles were recovered from the fire, my dear. They have been put away for you. Will you come with me?"

In a state of shock and bewilderment, Parmachenee soon learned that all of the furniture that had been saved belonged to her, and that besides this good fortune, she was a very wealthy young woman, by today's standards.

"But I am soon to be married," she stammered.

"Then we shall call this your dowry," Mr. Blodgett told her, going through all the papers with her.

Parmachenee was speechless, first at learning of the death of her great grandparents, and now to learn that she was rich. Squire Charles had never once spoken to her of this inheritance and she was overwhelmed. She agreed to come for the furniture and portraits after her marriage, taking only small objects she could easily carry. She thanked Mr. Blodgett and set off for home, where she could think quietly.

Metallak was concerned, his daughter looked so tired and heartsick, and ate very little, sitting listlessly in the lodge.

"Parmachenee must think now of her own life," he told her. "For every old tree, a new sapling will soon grow." He decided she needed a change, and proposed a trip to Portland for the mail packet.

"Let us go through the mountainous notch called Dixville, and stop once again at the large rock," she said.

"Metallak has been looking forward to such a trip," he said, relieved that Parmachenee was coming out of her shell. "We will take Big Horn."

The two set off on Big Horn, taking a leisurely trip to Portland, enjoying the solitude of the forest and the busy sights and sounds of the white settlements. It seemed every settlement had at least one saw mill, and new houses going up every day. When the mail packet came, they learned that Parmachenee had a letter, the first she had ever received.

"To my lovely Fluella," she read. "I pray that you are well, and that your father is agreeable to our marriage plans. I bear good and ill tidings, that you may not have heard. But lest you not know, peace has been restored to Canada, six months past, and the Governor is proposing to reward the Abenakis for their heroic action. The wounded will receive one hundred twenty five dollars and the wives of the wounded twenty five dollars a year." She read on quickly, seeking news of her brothers. Then she gasped. "Olumbo is dead," she read. "And all who knew him say that he died with valor on the battlefield. Parmagunnit returned safely and has taken a wife at the village." Then he talked of their wedding and closed, "until our next meeting in the spring, my betrothed."

Slowly, Parmachenee read the letter to Metallak, feeling him stiffen as she read of Olumbo's death. "He begs us to come to the village, father, that we may be married this fall. Already the frame of the house is up." She blushed and looked toward her father.

When he didn't answer, she placed her hand on his in comfort. "I too, grieve for Olumbo, father, and I know your heart is sick. But I am pleased that God has spared one of my brothers. I am pleased, too, that Olumbo died gallantly on the battlefield."

Metallak cleared his throat. "Metallak is proud," he said, "of both his sons."

"Then let us go to the village, father, please."

222

Secretly, Metallak was delighted at the chance to see Parmagunnit again, although his expression betrayed nothing. Instead he said "Metallak's name brings shame to his family."

"But, father, you know that is long forgotten, and many of the villagers never believed you were guilty."

"What if Moulton finds out?" he asked. "Will he still marry you?"

"He already knows, and he does not believe evil of you any more than I do."

"Then Metallak will make the trip with Parmachenee," he said finally.

As they returned home to make ready for the trip, Parmachenee took note of the change in her father. There was a more lively spring in his step, and he looked much younger than his sixty winters. He packed many fine skins for Parmachenee's wedding, as well as for Parmagunnit and his new bride. Parmachenee thought this might be her last chance to speak about her mother.

"Am I like Keoka, father?" she asked him cautiously.

"Parmachenee is even more beautiful than her mother," he said looking at her. "And the beauty lies within and without." He paused and continued. "Tragedy and misfortune followed in Keoka's footsteps, mostly because of her white mother, who was treated as a slave. Keoka needed love and understanding, but Metallak was young and impatient. Still, we had many happy days together before tragedy struck, and the wolves took our firstborn. Keoka walked fine and straight on feet smaller than your own, feet that flew like the wind. She could bring down game with an arrow like a young warrior. Metallak loved her very much." Then he was silent.

Parmachenee was happier than she had ever been in her life. For the first time, they had talked of her mother openly and she didn't have to be ashamed of her mother's behavior. Many times she had heard others speak of her mother in whispers. Even Moll Ockett had never spoken to Parmachenee of her. And Oozalluc had always carefully avoided her questions, so that she felt a deep shame about her mother's past. But now her father told her everything, all about her mother being a Sauk, being taken prisoner, and how he had rescued her. He told her how bravely she had borne the death of their firstborn, and later of her taking to the rum because of loneliness. He even recounted the terrible night of her death, how he had cast her from his lodge and Keoka had been found dead next morning. But he swore to Parmachenee he had nothing to do with her death, but that he had wanted to clear his name before he passed on for the sake of his children.

"One day I will repeat this story to your grandchildren," she told him, tears in her eyes, "and they too will know you were innocent."

Metallak took out a roll of birch bark that he had carefully kept for many years. Inside the roll were the etchings Keoka had made, even the one of Metallak astride the great bull moose.

"Your mother too left you a dowry," he said. "So you see, it was your mother and not Metallak, who thought of taming Big Horn. This too, you may tell your grandchildren."

"Oh, father, you saved these for me?" Parmachenee was overcome with joy, and the look on her face did not go unnoticed by her father, who was pleased also.

Metallak slept well that night, content that his daughter knew and understood the past. He only regretted that he could not clear his name for the light of his lodge before her wedding day.

Joyfully, they set off for the village, stopping for many carries where the full streams had flooded over. Metallak still carried the canoe as easily as he had in his youth, and Parmachenee marvelled at his good health.

Old and familiar sights greeted them as they entered the village. There were many new faces not familiar to Metallak, and he felt like a stranger. Here and there he spotted an old friend, or recognized a widow wearing the black mantle of mourning. The War had taken many lives.

Parmachenee sought the village priest, who made them welcome.

"Why, you are pledged to young Moulton," he exclaimed, on learning her name.

Parmachenee blushed, giving her dusky skin a lovely glow.

"Do you know of my brother Parmagunnit?" she asked, knowing what her father desired to hear.

"Certainly, my child," he said, and pointed out the lodge of Metallak's second son. "Why, this must be Metallak," he said, noticing Parmachenee's father out in the road. He rushed out to shake hands, bidding Metallak welcome.

So far, everything was going very well. But Parmachenee was eager to see Parmagunnit. "Come, father," she said. "Parmagunnit's lodge is over there," and she pointed in the direction of the new lodge.

Metallak seemed hesitant and his face took on a stubborn look. "Metallak will wait in the church," he said. "I would like to say a prayer for Oozalluc." Parmachenee knew that Metallak was afraid to face his son and be rejected. True, Metallak had disowned his sons, but he didn't mean it. Surely Parmagunnit would make him welcome and let bygones be bygones. But still she wondered if Parmagunnit held a grudge after all that had happened.

She decided to go ahead and pave the way, and then come for her father.

"Stay in the chapel, then, father, and I will bring Parmagunnit to you."

And she hurried off to find her brother. She hoped she would recognize him after all these years.

"Parmagunnit," she exclaimed when she saw him. "You will never change." He had grown thinner, and walked with a slight limp now. But his body was still lithe and muscular, like his father's. A lovely woman walked at his side, and her brother proudly made introductions.

"My wife Theresa." Both girls smiled shyly. "And this is my sister Parmachenee," he said, grasping Parmachenee's hands. In no time the two of them were chattering about Parmachenee's wedding.

"What of our father? Has he not come also?" asked Parmagunnit impatiently.

"He waits eagerly to see you," explained Parmachenee. "But you know father. He fears you may not welcome him, though he won't admit it. Please join him in the chapel and make peace."

"Parmagunnit, too, has pride," he said, holding his head high.

"I ask you to remember this," said Parmachenee. "Our father has lost the sight of one eye, and grows older. Now he has lost two sons, one to wolves and one to war, and still he grieves for Oozalluc, who filled his empty life with meaning."

"Let us go to him," said Parmagunnit. "He is a man

225

of great pride," he explained to Theresa, who nodded agreeably.

Inside the chapel, they turned and greeted each other hesitantly, shaking hands quietly, but there was deep contentment in their hearts. Later they shared a pipe by the fire and Metallak observed Theresa as she brought forth their supper. She seemed eager to please and kept her lodge neat, as well as her garden. Metallak was pleased that Parmagunnit had chosen well.

"With my pension," explained Parmagunnit, "we will build a small farm not far from here."

Metallak nodded, deep in thought. This time he had been wrong and the English had kept their promise of more money and land. He was grateful that Parmagunnit did not mention this.

"Olumbo spoke of you often," offered Parmagunnit. "And the little dog. The one we called Moslem."

Metallak chuckled. "Moslem lived many years," he said.

"He told me about the furs," Parmagunnit said quietly. "And the shame he felt in betraying you."

"Metallak forgot this long ago," his father said. "Sometimes even the good are tempted. Did Olumbo suffer?"

"No, he died very quickly."

"That is good."

Parmagunnit looked to his sister. "Why does the young man not come?" he teased. "Perhaps he no longer wishes to take Parmachenee's hand."

Theresa whispered to Parmachenee that already Parmagunnit had sent a courier to the Moulton farm to fetch Moulton. He was pleased that at last his sister would be living nearby and they could visit.

They had several guests that evening, who came to call on Metallak and his beautiful daughter, much envied for her beauty and education. Parmachenee said nothing about her white family, or her dowry. One day she would tell Parmagunnit all about it, but for now she wished to think only of her coming marriage.

There were still a few old cronies in the village who took pleasure in gossip. They whispered among themselves. "She looks like Keoka, especially her hair. Let us pray she does not follow in her mother's footsteps."

Their whispers did not escape the unsavory ears of

Shaman Ignatius, although none sought him out. His health had steadily failed over the years, and the elders avoided his malevolence. Even the children feared him, in spite of his ill health, because he threatened them with tortures by the Demons if they did not bring him fresh fish and game, and carry his firewood. For hours at a time, he would sit among his gourds and pouches, wearing the stained garments of his animal helper, seeking a vision. And at last the vision had come true. The daughter of Keoka had returned, or was it Keoka's Spirit? Walking as though in a stupor, he skirted the village, circling Parmagunnit's lodge, hoping for a glimpse of the Demon. Once again his wrath against Keoka rose feverishly in his mind, as he conjured up his most daring plan. Keoka had ruined his entire life, made him a laughing stock in the village, an object of scorn to be ridiculed. And in spite of all the evidence against Metallak, stories came to their village of his bravery, of his popularity with the whites, of his great hunting skills.

He chuckled to himself. This plan would not fail. It would be his moment of triumph there in the village for all to see, even the children. His hooded eye darted from one lodge to another, and then he heard the laugh. It was the same tinkling laughter that had come to him countless times as he slept, a Demon's laugh.

Oh, yes, he had heard about Metallak's war aginst the wolf family, of the beautiful lodge where he dwelt, even of the white traders who spoke so highly of him. Angrily, he spat through his gaping teeth, brown with tobacco stains.

No doubt the girl was evil like her mother. He would be doing the village a great service if he could but summon the strength to get rid of her. He whispered his plans to his animal helper. This would be his shining moment, the moment of truth! And none would ever guess his plan. He rubbed his long dirty fingers, and from time to time, patted a basket that he kept at his side.

He laughed until he coughed and forced himself to sit quietly. But his plan was so clever. He would carry his rattlesnake to the wedding of Keoka. If it was merely Keoka's spirit in her daughter's body, that would be even more fitting. A beautiful bride, dressed in white, would go to the welcoming arms of the Devil to be consumed, and he, Ignatius, would be a hero! Saliva trickled down his dirty chin as he giggled over this final act of revenge. Had Keoka chosen to marry him, none of this would have been necessary, but in spite of all his cajoling, she had returned to Metallak. True, he had been able to lure her away once or twice with many promises of riches, but only for a swim. And when he had begged her to run away with him, she had laughed, that half-crazed tinkling laugh that drove him mad with hatred, and now she had returned from the dead in the guise of a young woman again. Surely the Devil was offering Ignatius another chance. He slept fitfully, impatient for the morning.

Early the next morning, Moulton arrived with horses and many fine gifts for Metallak. He was made welcome in Parmagunnit's lodge. They made plans for the wedding three days hence. The women whispered, making last minute preparations and gifts. Metallak visited old friends, still not comfortable in the mission village, but determined to stay for the wedding.

At last the wedding day arrived, the forest a rainbow of fall colors. Parmachenee dressed with great care in the gown Moulton had ordered for his bride, still not believing that the elegant gown was really hers. Great billowing folds of lace hugged her small figure, embroidered with hundreds of tiny seed pearls, and a long veil covered her long chestnut hair. Andrew too dressed with great care in his fitted black suit with red borders and great ruffled white waistcoat.

The villagers gasped when they saw the young couple approach the altar in the small chapel. Never had they seen a bride and groom attired in such splendor in their small village. Even Metallak was striking as he kneeled in his pew, wearing leggings as usual. But these were new, and made of the softest doeskin they had ever seen. The emblem of the bald eagle was carefully stitched on both sides of the shirt. The family of the bridegroom was dressed handsomely also, and had brought many gifts.

They were so spellbound by all this beauty that the stealthy movements behind the altar curtains went unnoticed. The priest began the mass in Latin, and finally it was time for the marriage vows.

The ring glittered on Parmachenee's finger and she smiled fondly at her new husband. As the priest pronounced them man and wife, a figure came flashing out from behind the curtains, half dancing, half screaming strange intonations, holding a small basket in his arms. He clutched the basket as a mother would hold a newborn, jumping about like a rabbit.

228

"Keoka lives again. Keoka must be punished. Rise and give witness, as I strike her down again."

The congregation rose hysterically, some screaming, others running outside the little church. Then Parmachenee screamed too as she saw the snake's head rise slowly from the basket. But Moulton was quicker than Ignatius, pushing the basket toward Ignatius, who lurched sideways, lost his balance and fell. As he fell on the basket he had guarded so zealously, the snake bit him in the chest. As he gasped convulsively, he whispered "Come to me, Keoka," beckoning with his long grimy hands. Then he shuddered once more and died while Parmachenee clung to her new husband hysterically. Metallak had already clubbed the snake to death, and stood by protectively lest there be more surprises in store for them.

The priest calmed the crowd and with Metallak's help, got the Shaman's body outside and disposed of the snake. Curious onlookers watched them, whispering and making comments on what they had seen.

The priest shook Metallak's hand and thanked him for his help. He clapped his hands and asked the people to come closer.

"We have all heard of the tragedy of Keoka's death," he began, and there was a sudden hush. "It is a great pleasure to proclaim Metallak's innocence on his daughter's wedding day," he continued. "By his own words, Shaman Ignatius was the guilty one who committed this act. For many years, Metallak has carried the shame of a crime he did not commit. I hope he will forgive all of us." All rose up and cheered, some throwing their hats into the air. Metallak was surrounded by old friends and villagers eager to make amends.

For Metallak, it felt like a giant beast had been lifted from his chest. He was grateful that the name of his children and their children would bear no evil stigma after he passed on. Now he could lie beside Oozalluc with pride until all eternity. He suddenly noticed that his family stood proudly beside him, Parmachenee and Moulton on one side, Parmagunnit and Theresa on the other. A tear slowly trickled down his cheek and his daughter tenderly wiped it away. Now at last he felt cleansed in the eyes of his children.

They feasted for many days, celebrating the double festivities with joy and abandon. But after several days, Metallak longed for the quiet and peace of his own lodge. Although Parmagunnit hospitably offered to share his lodge, urging his father to stay with him, Metallak wished to be close to Oozalluc. He invited all his friends and relatives to visit his lodge along Lake Umbagog, setting off one fine morning all alone, but promising to return often to visit his daughter and son.

After his return, he went straight to Moserill to tell him of all that had happened. "Now at last I can live in peace," he told him.

Moserill shared his friend's happiness. Better than anyone else, Moserill knew the despair and loneliness Metallak had suffered. "The truth always comes out, Metallak. It may take awhile, but it always comes out."

Metallak returned home to raise a small crop of corn and make up a supply of canoes to have on hand. He spent long leisurely days making baskets, visiting, and preparing for winter.

For some time, he lived in seclusion, visiting Oozalluc's grave, and going to Andover for supplies, always stopping in to see Moserill. It was one of the quietest times of his life, a time of contentment and peace. Except for the smuggling along the border, there was little activity around Errol.

Metallak was often in demand to make trips across the border, or take oxen across, bringing back less than he took, but never getting caught.

He did not see the thunder clouds brewing. Neither did the settlers. The summer of 1816 took them all by surprise. It was worse than the spotted fever or even the war. It was the summer of starvation. The summer of 1816 was one Metallak would never forget. Planting time came and went, but the frost on the ground was still hard enough to bear his weight. He watched the leaves of the oak tree, but he knew they would never grow to the size of a mouse's ear. Instead, they shriveled up and died. He decided to wait another month to plant, but on June 10, there was another heavy frost.

Thinking this surely would be the last of the frosts, he finally planted, and then waited for the sun in vain. With little else to do but study the skies, he kept a record of the frightening season.

"July 11, saw another heavy frost. Killed nearly all of Moserill's corn and apples. July 15, ice forming around Metallak's lodge. August 20, rain and snow fell. The seeds rot in the ground. August 22, heavy frost killed all of Metallak's corn." Metallak was puzzled and worried. His needs were simple, but already Big Horn had grown lean, and he worried about his people, as well as those of the white settlements.

The settlers too, watched the skies anxiously, hoping each day would bring a change in the cold dismal weather. Everywhere families were hungry, and their faces took on a grim harshness as the steady diet of oatmeal took its toll. They watched what remained of their gardens carefully, hoping some of the seeds would thrive, but cold rain fell from time to time, rotting what seeds remained in the soil.

Moserill came to seek advice of Metallak. He was completely bewildered by this long cold spell. "Ever see anything like this before?" he asked.

"Not in all my life," Metallak said, shaking his head sadly.

The sight was a poor one indeed. All around him berries lay green on their vines, dying from lack of sun and too much moisture. Apple trees had shriveled up and died. An ominous quiet greeted them from the forest. Even the birds had flown elsewhere seeking warmth and food. There was no chatter or activity from their friends in the forest, just grim silence.

As families became more destitute, tempers grew short, and the settlers pulled in their belts another notch. Some slaughtered their livestock to keep their children from crying with hunger. Many prayed feverishly, thinking that surely this must be the end of the world coming.

On days when the ponds were free from ice, Metallak fished, sharing his fish generously with Moserill and his friends. He treked near and far to dig wild onions and roots that were edible. But he feared for the coming winter. Game was scarce, even for a skilled hunter. One day he was lucky and spotted a small doe nibbling at a shriveled up apple tree. He quickly put an arrow to her heart and carried the bounty home. If he used the meat sparingly with his friends, it would last a long time.

After leaving the meat in Moserill's keeping, he set off in late August to see how others fared. He too prayed as he traveled, thinking perhaps he had offended God in some way. He prayed that he would find enough food to sustain himself and his friends. He stopped at Green's Trading Post to hear the news.

"Yes sir, there was ice on Wilson's Pond in Dover," said one man. "Seen it myself."

"Never seen anything like it," agreed his friend.

231

"If you ask me, it's a good time to move out of these parts," said another. "Go west and start all over again. I hear they have a coach in Concord that holds a dozen people."

"You don't say." He chewed his tobacco, then turned to Metallak.

"What do you say Metallak? Should we head west?"

Metallak's eyes were never more serious and the famine sweeping over New Hampshire had not changed his way of living. "Metallak will die here on the ancestral grounds of his people," he said quietly, and left.

"He ain't afraid of nothing, is he?" the man asked his friend, puzzled by Metallak's behavior.

"I guess you don't know Metallak," said an old settler. "He was born in these hills and he'll die in these hills. Never asked a favor of any man and he never will."

Metallak traveled south to Lancaster, studying the land, looking for signs of wheat or corn. What the settler told him back at Green's was true. He passed several families planning to head out west. Some even talked of taking a packet by steamboat in the spring. Hope showed in their faces when they described the great west, where a man could see for miles, and buy land for a dollar-fifty an acre. Metallak wished them luck.

Here and there a crop would survive somehow. Metallak stopped at a farm so that Big Horn could have water, and learned of such a farm.

"I hear there's a man named Reuben Whitten over in Ashland that raised 40 bushel of wheat. Raised it on a hill where the drainage was good, and then dried it around his fireplace. He gives a little bit to every man that comes to his door."

His wife came running out calling for her husband. "Silas, Silas, I've just heard there's corn in Egypt. Good corn for sale."

He turned to his wife, his voice ragged and tired. "But Elizabeth we have no money and . . ." Metallak rose quickly and spoke.

"Metallak has money," he quickly put in. "Together we will go on Big Horn for the corn."

"That's right neighborly of you," Silas told him. "I'm beholden to you."

So the two of them set off and before nightfall, reached Egypt. They spotted the field which boasted corn, growing

232

magically in the midst of all the barren stark grounds that surrounded it. It was like a miracle. Metallak drank in the sight of the huge abundant field and blessed himself. He was reminded of Joseph's brethren who were sent to Egypt to buy corn.

Silas bargained with the farmer who gladly shared his corn with them at a fair price. He too was puzzled that his field yielded what no others in the whole town had been able to produce.

In their joy and excitement, Metallak and Silas returned to Lancaster without resting, and reached Silas's home late that night. Elizabeth cried tears of happiness, and quickly made a bunk for Metallak by the open fire, both of the men damp and cold from their long ride.

After dividing the corn next morning, Metallak set off for home, confident that somehow they would survive the summer and the coming winter, and the summer after that. Though the fields that met his good eye were stark and barren, God in his mercy had granted them enough corn to survive. He no longer feared starvation. He stopped often to let Big Horn rest, and walked the last ten miles to ease the burden on his back. He and Big Horn had grown very fond of each other. Even the whites no longer feared his great bull moose, tame as a kitten now.

Early next morning, he headed for Andover, eager to share his bounty and good fortune with his friends. Moserill couldn't believe his eyes. He too had been lucky. In digging up the grounds around his home, found some edible carrots under the ground. That evening they had a great repast of corn bread and corn meal mush, eating until they were full.

When the shad came in, Metallak traveled to the Lakes Region for fish and brought home what he could carry. Somehow they lived through that desolate summer of the corn famine, only to worry about the coming winter.

With the first fall of snow, Moserill and Metallak set out on a hunting expedition. Moserill hoped to appease the hunger of his people and at the same time, think about the turmoil and disruption of his native state. He warmed to the subject easily, and over their camp fires, he would hash it over with Metallak.

"I tell you, Metallak, we want to have a state of our own. We don't need Massachusetts and we never did, that's what I say. What did they ever do for us in the War of 1812? Did they stop the blockade along our seaports? Did they carry goods overland to us by oxcart to help us in our time of need? No sir, we had to take care of ourselves, and we don't need them now."

Metallak was deep in thought. For as long as his people could remember, this had been their land, and now his white brothers argued about parceling it all up into territories called states. He understood none of this, but he was fond of Moserill.

"Moserill is right," he said emphatically. He hoped there would be no more fighting over this property line. Trouble enough along the northern borders. The Indian Stream Territory, the land of his people, was being claimed by New Hampshire, Massachusetts and Canada. This invisible boundary line was causing a lot of trouble. They fought especially over the big stands of timber, worth a lot of money in the states as well as Canada.

"And all because they can't find the head of the Connecticut River," fumed Moserill. "Seems like they'll never settle it. Where do you say the head of the river lies, Metallak?"

"This is very easy," said Metallak. "The water flows from Indian Stream and what the whites call Hall Stream." He paused, then continued. "Metallak's people traveled the waters long before the white men came. Always we shared the water and the fish too, then the white man came and took our beaver and our fish. Why should the law be any different for white men?"

"You're right, Metallak, you're right. We're fighting over something that ain't even ours."

Indian Stream had become a haven for refugees who were escaping their debts or hiding from the law. The land was a no-man's land, where they made up their own laws and enlisted no assistance. Metallak was glad his father couldn't see the greed and lawlessness that invaded the privacy of his old domain.

He knew that one day Indian Stream would be full of white men. Already there was a stage coach between Boston and Bangor. People came in droves to settle the land. Sheep and cattle were plentiful and carding mills were part of large communities. Life was changing rapidly, even in the hills.

After two weeks in the woods, they brought home fresh venison, enough to survive for a time. Carefully, they stored some in the river to preserve it, and divided the rest up among the villagers. Green was glad to get the skins and saved them for whatever he could get in the way of food.

Wolves and panthers were hungry too, in this

barren time. The settlers were constantly on the watch for them, protecting what was left of their livestock. As Metallak rode Big Horn to Moserill's one day, he saw a group of young children running wildly toward him.

"It's the panther," they screamed. "He's after the cattle." Heading in the direction of the barn where they pointed, Metallak soon spotted the panther. Jumping off Big Horn, he lunged at him, managing to sink his knife deep into the chest of the beast, who quivered and lay at his feet.

The children stood with their mouths open in awe, staring at Metallak. But Metallak quickly surveyed the ground. One cow lay helpless and in pain. He severed the vein in her neck and butchered her, putting her out of her misery. He quickly gutted and quartered the animal, handing the children great hunks of meat to bring home to their families, cautioning them to watch for wolves who might smell the meat.

Word spread of this tough old Indian, afraid of nothing, master of these hills, who rode a great beast and spoke to him in whispers. At his gentle whisper, the beast would nibble from his hand. It was unbelievable.

"Best trapper in these hills," they say with pride. "Lives out on Metallak Point near his wife's grave. Still rides his moose too."

As the soil became rich with fertility again, people still struggled, trying to build a life in the wilderness, building communities and starting schools. Usually the first building was a small church. Not for many years would these settlers forget the year that frost struck every month of the year, the year of the corn famine.

The years seemed to vanish, one after the other. Metallak became a grandfather, and though his hair turned gray and his leathery face showed wrinkles, his body remained lithe and muscular, as he continued to trap and kill all his own game, and tan his skins for his clothing.

Twice a year he dutifully visited the mission village to make peace with God. Steadfastly, he refused to hunt or fish on Sunday, making his dogs rest also. He took great pride in his grandchildren, and spent all his spare time whittling small toys for them, and tanning extra skins so they could be dressed as a true Abenaki should be.

The children took to him as readily as the children

of the white families, begging to ride on the tips of his snowshoes, clamoring for stories in the evening hours. Parmachenee thrived on married life, and although she aged after the birth of many children, their farm was affluent, thanks to Parmachenee's inheritance and her husband's eye for business. Metallak was pleased with Moulton, but never more pleased than when he saw the portrait of Keoka's grandmother hanging over her fireplace. This was the children's favorite story, the story of their great grandmother's captivity, and of their very own mother living in the same family. Over and over he told them this story as they sat on his knee before the fire. Parmachenee too, would slip in and listen, never tiring of the story either.

"Will you stay this time?" Moulton always asked.

But Metallak always declined. "Metallak wished to stay near Oozalluc," he would say, "and lie beside her one day. And Moserill is an old friend," he would add. But always he stayed long enough to teach the grandchildren to make a canoe, or lace a snowshoe. Although they were dressed in the latest fashion, they were fascinated by his clothing and teased to dress like their grandfather, so Parmachenee continued to make his fringed shirts and trousers, often making them for the children as well.

With Maine's statehood, there came more changes. The stagecoach was a common sight now, and people came to Maine just to hunt and fish. Metallak found himself more and more in demand as a guide and took his visitors to the choicest rivers and streams for their fish. They loved the excitement of traveling in his birch bark canoe, and coming back home to see Big Horn tethered in his pen. Sometimes Metallak even shared his modest lodge with them.

One day he had a visitor, a rather elegant visitor even for a white man. Obviously, from the cut of his broadcloth coat and tall hat, he was a man of substance. Metallak squinted through his good eye as the stranger spoke.

"Metallak, I've heard of you and I've come to ask a favor," the man said after dismounting from his horse. "They tell me you're the best hunter in these hills. That you know them like the back of your hand." The young man with him quickly tied the horse to a tree.

"Maybe so, maybe not," Metallak answered, feeling his way warily with this tall stranger.

"I need a retreat for a few days now and then, away from the confusion and noise of the city. May I stay with you and do

236

a little fishing and hunting?"

Metallak was puzzled. Why would this well dressed stranger want to share his simple hut?

"Metallak has little to offer," he said. "As you see, my lodge is small and simple, without even a bed."

"You know, of course, this is Governor Lincoln," put in the aide.

"Metallak is pleased to meet the Governor," he said, extending his hand.

"I'd like to see your lodge, Metallak," said the Governor, and they looked it over. The small structure was only ten feet long, but neat and clean, with plenty of cooking dishes and clean furs spread over the floor.

"This is just fine, Metallak, just what I was looking for. May I stay?"

"Metallak is honored that Governor Lincoln wishes to share his lodge," he said. "The door is always open."

"Then it's a deal, Metallak. I'll make it worth your while. And please call me Enoch if we're going to be friends." They shook hands and made plans for the Governor's first visit.

And so it was that Governor Enoch Lincoln spent many days in retreat with Metallak, coming whenever he had a few days off to relax in solitude and privacy, enjoying the fishing and hunting immensely.

Metallak was surprised that the Governor took such a great interest in his red brothers, but he patiently answered all the questions about his people that the Governor asked. Secretly, he was rather pleased that the Governor sketched just as Keoka had, on a piece of birch bark, and gladly posed for the sketches.

The Governor too was pleased with the whole arrangement. He trusted Metallak implicitly and never hesitated to get matters off his chest through the sympathetic ears of his friend.

"I tell you, Metallak, I need a rest," he would often say as he rode in.

"Governor Enoch should rest like everybody else," Metallak would say, tethering his horse and offering him a small drink of rum. A few days of hunting and fishing and the Governor looked like a different man, ready to return to business again and please the public. Then too, the excitement of bringing home a ten point buck and a few bear skins gave him added status. It wasn't long before he brought a friend, Congressman Mason, to visit also. They paid Metallak well for his friendship and help in the vast woodland. Metallak was always glad to oblige, helping them bring down whatever game they desired.

It wasn't long before Congressman Mason's entrance hall boasted a large moose horn coat rack, the envy of all his neighbors.

For several months, Metallak had been fascinated by the small knife that Governor Lincoln carried. There were so many different blades in the small pen knife that Metallak longed to have it. He thought it must be very costly and never mentioned to Governor Lincoln how much he desired the knife.

"Metallak will take Governor Lincoln to his private cave today." he announced early next morning. "No other white man has ever seen it."

"I am deeply honored that you share this secret place with me, Metallak," said the Governor when they arrived on the Little Island on the lake where Metallak stored his furs. "I shall tell no one of it."

Metallak weighed his chances, then spoke quickly.

"Suppose Metallak offered Governor Enoch twenty furs for the small knife?" he asked. Then he waited, listening intently for a reply.

"Oh, no, Metallak, I can't sell you the knife," protested Governor Lincoln.

Metallak was hurt. He had been so sure they would be able to strike a bargain, and he had grown fond of Governor Lincoln.

"Metallak will not carry you off the island if you refuse to sell Metallak the knife."

Though his face looked stern, the Governor did not fear Metallak. He chuckled and went to stand next to Metallak.

"I said I would not sell you the knife, Metallak, but I will give it to you as a present. Here you are." He handed over the small knife to Metallak. "You've given me much more than the value of a small present, Metallak," he added.

Metallak was immensely pleased. The Governor was indeed a good man. He too wished to make the Governor a present, and picked several choice furs and presented them to Governor Lincoln. When they returned to the lodge, each of them was content and pleased with the bargain.

Metallak found himself more and more in demand, thanks to Governor Lincoln's associates and friends. His little hoard of cash was growing. But even he was surprised when a party of engineers came to survey the land and talk about the great iron horse that would one day run through these hills, all the way to Portland. They too had a proposition for Metallak and they would pay him well to survey the land for the new railroad.

He began to blaze a trail for the Atlantic and St. Lawrence Railroad shortly after their meeting, following the upper Ammonoosuc up past Stark, a tiny hamlet on the banks of the river with a conspicuous cliff, known as the Devil's Slide.

Metallak stood poised at the base of the cliff and looked up, remembering the small boy who had sat spellbound while his grandmother told him the legend of this great cliff. Metallak had been only about six years of age, and he thought the cliff quite a formidable sight, impossible even to scale.

Here on this very spot, she told him, the invisible spirits who controlled the winds and storms had had a great quarrel and hurled thunder bolts at each other, leaving great splintered and jagged rocks exposed. The heavens too had become involved in this fight, and the atmosphere blazed from the warfare of these invisible powers, causing half of the mountain to sink down into the bowels of the earth, but leaving the barren side to remain.

Shrugging his shoulders, he continued to blaze his trail, following the Androscoggin River, where the passengers would one day see distant mountain ranges and pass by groves of slender white birches. Off in the distance, he could see Blind Cap Peak. All along New Hampshire's border, he followed the Little Androscoggin, blazing a trail that was easily followed, and would require the least woodcutting. He was happy that he was still needed, a man of sixty seven summers living in a world that was fading away. He knew that some of his red brothers were unable to find work, or buy the costly goods of the whites, to which they had grown accustomed, among them Tom Hegan, and it was no longer possible even for Tom Hegan to raid the well protected white settlements. So now he had taken on more treacherous work and all but a few of his red brothers had deserted him.

Years ago, Moll Ockett had discovered a plot laid by Tom Hegan to kill Colonel Clark of Boston. Moll had to warn the Colonel somehow, and hurried through the wilderness to save him from the massacre. She got to him just in the nick of time, and from that time on, even the Abenakis had lost all respect for Tom Hegan. Colonel Clark was a fair and just fur trader, who had always treated them kindly. Metallak chuckled as he thought of Moll Ockett going to Boston with the Colonel, dressed like a queen, to become a member of his family. But Moll couldn't leave the security of the forest any more than Metallak, and within a short time, she was back, dressed in her old calicos.

By late summer, he had blazed a trail all the way to North Stratford, and stopped in to see his old friend Jeremiah.

"Metallak," Jeremiah said greeting his old friend. "Good to see you. Come and sit a spell." Anxious to hear the latest news, Metallak found a spot on the floor.

"Where you been all summer?" asked Jeremiah. "Folks been worried about you."

"Metallak is well," he said firmly. "Well enough to blaze a trail for the new Iron Horse that will soon come through the wilderness."

"I should have guessed," said Jeremiah. "I heard there was talk of a railroad up here. Sure is different from the old days, isn't it?"

Metallak nodded.

"Metallak, I want to tell you that there's going to be trouble. Tom Hegan's killed two fur trappers and run away. He's a marked man, and they'll get him, sooner or later. There's a reward for him if you hear of his whereabouts."

"Metallak is not surprised," he said. "Tom Hegan is a trouble maker."

"Seems he got rummed up and said these trappers were trying to cheat him. Pulled a gun, said it was time they learned a lesson. Shot them down in cold blood."

"He will not come to Metallak's lodge for help. For many years, we have been enemies," said Metallak.

"Well, if you hear anything, you let us know," Jeremiah said as Metallak made ready to leave.

He traveled north to Umbagog, going on to Andover to pick up fresh potatoes, corn and other supplies. He had a long talk with Moserill, and just before he left, Moserill's wife gave him a fresh blueberry pie, one of his favorites. Carefully, he carried it home.

Just as he sat down to eat the pie, there came a rap at the door, muffled but distinct. Cautiously, he opened the door, a club in one hand. There, standing at the door, exhausted and dirty, stood Tom Hegan.

"Metallak, you got to help me," he pleaded. "The law's after me. Killed two dirty white trappers because they were stealing my furs. Couldn't let 'em git away with that. They won't look for me here. They like you."

"Tom Hegan is not welcome here," said Metallak, blocking the door. "Only Metallak's friends are welcome here."

"Metallak, we're brothers of the same father." His eyes darted around to see if others heard him. His eyes had a bright feverish look.

"Tom Hegan did not befriend Metallak years ago when he was banished." Bitterness and anger filled his voice and Tom Hegan took a step backward, frightened at the look of hatred on Metallak's face. "You are no brother of mine!"

"You had everything Metallak. But I was the half-breed that shamed my father. I wasn't good enough to live in his lodge, or stand at his side. But you were special, Metallak. I thought they'd forget about Keoka and let you come home."

Metallak felt himself weakening, hesitating. He spoke quickly.

"Tom Hegan knew Keoka had a weakness for the rum, yet he gave it to her and encouraged her to gamble and neglect her children."

"She begged me for it, Metallak, said you should never have married a half-breed."

"Tom Hegan is Magua," said Metallak. "Only a coward would try to steal another man's wife. Years later, you tried to rob Metallak of his sons by stirring up warfare. Metallak never saw Olumbo again. And now you come here like a sniveling dog and ask my protection. Go now, or I will kill you myself!"

"I'll get even with you, Metallak," threatened Tom Hegan. "Wait and see. I will tell Parmagunnit how you betrayed me and turned your back on a blood brother."

Metallak closed and barred the door, his appetite gone. Strange, but he no longer hated Tom Hegan. He felt only pity for this broken down man. Two weeks later, he heard the details from Moserill.

"Well, we won't have to worry about Tom Hegan from now on. Bound him to a stallion, they did. Thought a good ride would teach him a lesson. But the horse went completely wild, and plunged into an apple orchard. Bashed him to pieces against the trees.''

Metallak said nothing.

CHAPTER TWELVE

"I am an old man," thought Metallak, as he tethered Big Horn in his pen that evening. "Seventy seven is no longer young." All day he had tracked a moose, then lost him. For some years now, his vision had been failing, but he had spoken of this to no one. When Moserill rode in later that evening, he said in disgust.

"Metallak tracked a moose all day. Almost saw him."

"Weather was against you," Moserill commented, offering Metallak a smoke from his pipe.

Metallak hospitably accepted the pipe, meditating. "Couldn't even strike the doe," he said, describing his efforts with the gun he had recently purchased. "Never trusted these guns. When the gun is wet, it misfires and scares the animal away."

They sat comfortably together for some time, content now to sit idly by the fire. Although Moserill was nearly as old as Metallak, he wished Metallak would move into town, where he could keep an eye on him, but the old Indian was determined to live out here in the wilderness.

Metallak was determined to go out hunting that winter, to prove something to himself. Surely he could still see well enough to bring down a buck or a moose. He set out on snowshoes after a fresh snowfall. The air was warm and he enjoyed walking on the new snow. Luck was with him, and he brought down a great bull moose that day, the beast barely able to move through the deep snows of winter. It took him all afternoon to skin the animal and take off what meat he wanted. Then he rested.

Dusk was coming on, and he was weary. He decided to sleep in the woods in the warmth of the snow. Using his snowshoe for a shovel, he tunneled down through four feet of snow to build a fire. Then he laid a good bed of spruce boughs and cooked a little fresh meat. He slept well on his bed of boughs, covered with the warm skin of the animal he had just slaughtered. His self respect was restored and once more he was confident that he could bring down a moose, even after seventy seven winters.

He woke with a start, his arms and legs pinioned in a strong vise, gripping him painfully all over. "Metallak is caught in a trap," he thought, as he struggled and squinted in the semi-darkness to see what clutched him.

He imagined for an instant that he was in the hands of an enemy who wished to make off with his fresh meat, and had trussed him up with rope. But as he struggled, he realized the blanket which covered and pinioned him was the very one he had pulled over himself, the skin of the dead carcass. As he moved his neck warily against the stiffness of the skin, he chuckled. He had become like one of his own frozen carcasses, with the fresh moose skin tightening around him. Last night it had been flexible and warm as down, but now it was frozen around him like tight rawhide, cutting his arms and legs. He wriggled close to the embers of the fire and gradually warmed himself, stretching and loosening the skin a little at a time. After a long time, he managed to free himself, his arms and legs a mass of small lacerations.

"Tough skin will make a tough moccasin," he said of the treacherous old moose. He slit the hind leg down the front, leaving the hock joint for the heel of the moccasin, cutting the shank above the hock below his knee, and cutting it again below the hock for the foot of his moccasin. Then he trimmed it to fit his foot. Beginning at the toe, he made holes on each side and cut some long thin strips for laces, leaving the hairy side out.

Wrapping all this in the skin, he mounted his snowshoes and strode home to his lodge, content that he had not lost his abilities. To his surprise, Sebattis was there to greet him. For many years now, Sebattis had made his home at St. Francis.

"Sebattis finds Metallak on the hunt, as usual," he said, glad to see his old friend. Quickly he pulled on snowshoes and taking a sleigh, helped Metallak bring home his meat. Then they sat and ate.

"Parmachenee sent me," he explained. "Wants you to come to Canada for the winter. She misses you, Metallak. Why don't you come?"

But deep in his heart, he knew that Metallak would not be coaxed or persuaded to leave his home. "Metallak grows old and stiff," he replied. "But he can still bring down a moose. I wish to live here on the sacred ground of our ancestors, near Oozalluc. Tell Parmachenee to pay Metallak a visit in the spring time, and bring the grandsons with her."

Sebattis stayed for a few days, visiting, recalling the old days of his marriage to Moll Ockett. "Moll was a good woman," he said, "but she always gave orders. Sebattis couldn't please her. She spent all her days in the white settlements delivering babies." He offered Metallak rum from his bags, but Metallak refused.

Metallak had a quiet winter, going to Andover occasionally for potatoes and other supplies, hauling them home by sleigh, taking Big Horn out whenever the weather was fair.

When the trees cast aside their coat of snow in the warmth of spring, and buds peeked out of the ground, Metallak yearned to be outside again. Though he had plenty of wood, he took his hatchet and went out to chop down a tree. The exercise would strengthen his arms, after a long lazy winter. He walked further than he intended to, enjoying the spring weather.

After chopping down the tree, he placed the tump line around his forehead as he had hundreds of times in the past and started for home, dragging the large tree behind him. It was hard work, but he was still strong.

All of a sudden, the tump line snapped, and Metallak went sprawling into the mud. He landed face down in a pile of stumps, one of them very jagged, severing his right eye. He felt a tearing pain in his head, then fainted.

When he woke, the pain throbbed intensely. Then he remembered. The tump line had snapped and he had gone plunging into the brush. He strained to see where he was, but could see nothing. He felt moisture on his cheek and suddenly realized that his sight was gone.

This frightened Metallak. Never before had he been in complete darkness on a warm day. He calmed himself and said a prayer. Perhaps if he rested, his sight would return. No doubt tomorrow he would see as well as ever. The important thing now was to get to his lodge for shelter in case of wolves. Besides, he didn't know the time, and wondered if he would ever see the sun again. Pangs of hunger told him it was long past dark.

Painfully, he reconstructed his position. He knew about where his lodge was, having sighted the moose pen just before he fell. He crawled in the direction of BigHorn's pen and after nearly an hour, reached it. Yes, there was the gate, so this must be the front. The pen was fenced in with cordwood, so he dragged a piece with him. He would manage somehow to get a fire going. Perhaps that would ease the pain. But the cordwood released a lot of others, and they fell all around him, bruising his arms and legs. It was a great struggle getting into the lodge from the pen, but at last, half crawling and stumbling, he managed to get inside, find his bed of boughs and lie down, too tired to even think of supper or his fire.

The next day, he still couldn't see, but he knew he had to find food. He felt dizzy and sick to his stomach. Forcing himself to crawl to his root cellar step by step, he found some raw potatoes to eat, and clutching them, made his way back to his bunk, wrapping himself in a fur. As he lay there chewing on the cold potato, he thought he felt a breeze. He should get up to barricade the door, not even certain that it was closed tight against the wind, but too tired to make the effort.

He slept fitfully, all his senses alert to new found dangers, now that he couldn't see. He thought he heard the scratching of bears. Every howl of the wolves brought them closer to his lodge as though they could sense his helplessness. For three days, he lay in his bunk, too weak to rise.

"Perhaps Metallak will die like his first born," he mused, "at the mercy of the wolves." He shivered in despair.

But his early manhood training and courage finally returned, giving him confidence and strength. "Metallak is not a coward," he told himself. "He will die with dignity, even if the wolves do attack." He lay back, more relaxed than before.

Determined to live in spite of his weakness, he carefully conserved his strength, moving as little as possible, feeling about for the hemlock stick. He finally located it in his bed of boughs and fell asleep grasping it, counting the notches. It didn't seem possible. There were thirty notches now, thirty years since he and Oozalluc had shared this lodge. He fell asleep thinking of Oozalluc, wondering if they would be together soon.

But instead he woke to human voices and sat up, startled. Who could be here at his lodge?

"Peculiar tracks, if you ask me," a voice said. "Never saw Metallak walk like that. Think somebody broke in here?"

"Let's go inside. I don't like the looks of it."

"Metallak, Metallak, can you hear us?"

Metallak recognized the voice, John's voice. So help had come. Relief flooded over the tough old Indian, who called out feebly.

"Metallak hears your voice, John. But my sight is gone."

The two men peeked inside the lodge, and there lay Metallak, weak and thin, wrapped in his furs, the lodge a shambles from his efforts to find food and warmth.

"We'll get you out of here in no time, Metallak. Just hang on," Jonathan Leavitt told him, finding skins and rope to make up a bed of sorts to carry Metallak.

"Jonathan is a good friend," said Metallak. "Metallak has money to pay you."

"Now, now, none of that," said Jonathan. Didn't you save me thirty odd years ago in the middle of a blizzard? Why, if it hadn't been for you, I wouldn't be here today, and that's a fact."

In a short while, they had him bundled up and placed on a sleigh, dragging him the twelve miles or so to Lombard's, the nearest house.

When she saw the sleigh and Metallak on the bed, Mrs. Lombard greeted them with milk and whiskey, which quickly revived Metallak's strength and warmed the two rescuers. Suddenly Metallak sat up, remembering.

"Big Horn will starve in his pen," he said in dismay.

"Now, now, don't you fret none, we put him out to pasture," said Jonathan, lacking the heart to tell him the moose had escaped when Metallak pulled out the cordwood. Sooner or later, some hunter would get him.

Metallak stayed several weeks at the Lombard's, resting and regaining his strength. When his daughter learned of his condition, she immediately sent two of her sons to bring him home.

Metallak knew his days of independence were over. With a sigh, he asked for Moserill one evening, and Moserill came to visit.

"Metallak is ready to sign over his land," he told Moserill. "You write up the paper, Metallak will sign it." With a heavy heart, Moserill wrote down what he told him, and Metallak managed to scratch out his signature signing over the small parcel of land in Errol in the spring of 1836.

Moserill took Metallak's grandsons to his lodge and helped them pack up his personal things, his furs, skins and blankets. The hemlock stick Metallak carried himself, entrusting it to no one else, along with his pouch of coins, his life savings.

His grandsons were grown men now, and kind to him on the trip back to Canada. When they arrived at the Moulton farm,

247

Parmachenee gave him a beautiful room of his own with a feather bed. She described the room in detail to him, telling him of the view from the window of the apple orchard and the nearby streams where he could fish.

"Metallak has never slept in a bed. Never will," he said firmly, placing his coverlet on the floor. But he knew his daughter was trying to please, and he enjoyed the younger grandchildren, especially little Metallak, his namesake, and recounted many stories for him. His grandsons basked in this special attention and sat by his side much of the time.

But in spite of this, Metallak was lonely. He missed the lullaby of the frogs and the sight of the beautiful lake. Although he saw nothing, he could still picture it in his mind, the most beautiful lake in the world. He felt far away from Oozalluc now and wondered if the paddle over her grave was rotted out from the winter snows. He pleaded with Parmachenee to take him back for the summer to make a visit and replace the worn marker over Oozalluc's grave.

"But father, you know we have to harvest the crops, and Andrew has business. It is impossible. Besides, you are better off here than in that forsaken part of the country. Perhaps after the harvest we could go."

But that seemed a long way off to Metallak. He thought of the long lonely summer in the confinement of this house with all its luxuries. He missed the smell of the pines and the lap of the waves against the shore.

Often as he lay awake at night, he counted his coins, knowing he had close to five hundred dollars put aside. This would be his path of escape, the money. Slowly, he developed a plan. There was a half breed who frequently came to the farm seeking work, having no real home of his own, glad to make some money. He bided his time until one day he and the boy were alone.

"Metallak will pay you well," he told the boy in secret. "If you take me to Moserill's in Andover." He let the boy feel the coins through the pouch.

The temptation was strong and the boy wavered. Metallak knew he had won and gave the boy instructions.

"This must be kept secret," he told him. "We must leave in the night."

And so they conspired, the old man and the boy, each with his own secret plans. The boy longed to explore and make lots of money, and Metallak longed to see his old friend and be near Oozalluc. One night, under cover of darkness and a gentle summer rain, they made their way.

For many days they walked, the boy growing weary of his charge, no longer trusting Metallak's directions. He endeavored to find food, but was not skilled in the forest, having made his home with farmers. They made do with farm houses, buying what they could, killing an occasional squirrel or rabbit. At last they came down to a small town called West Stewartstown, not too far from the Canadian border. From the height of the tall hills, the boy could see for miles, even into Canada. Scattered farm houses provided light and security from the howling of the wolves.

"We walk through the ancestral grounds of my father," Metallak told the boy proudly, recognizing the lay of the land. "Many times the Abenakis have held great pow wows here."

So the boy felt less guilty about what he planned to do. Metallak had a daughter with money, and Metallak would not go hungry. Here he was among friends, who would take him in. Besides, he was an old man with his life behind him.

As Metallak bathed at the stream that night, the boy stealthily took his pouch of coins, and quickly replaced them with the rocks he had gathered along the way. Satisfied that they felt the same weight, he returned the pouch to Metallak's roll. Then he guided him to a farm house.

"I grow tired of this trip, old man. I leave you now within sight of a farmhouse."

"But Metallak is not there yet. We will reach Moserill's lodge in three days walk," he said. "Besides, you have not yet been paid." Metallak's heart hammered with fear.

Without a word, the boy turned and started back on his way. Metallak stood uncertainly, feeling forlorn and lost in the dark. Soon he heard the barking of dogs and sat down in weariness on the ground. A farmer with a lantern came to investigate the barking dogs and saw Metallak, then went running for his gun, thinking him to be drunk.

"Do not run away, it is only Metallak," he told him quietly.

"Metallak! Why I've heard of you. What on earth are you doing out here in the dark?" He went to give Metallak a helping hand.

"Why, bring him in, said Mrs. Blodgett, when she saw her husband leading the blind man. "The poor man has lost his sight." They made him comfortable by the hearth, and whispered after he slept.

"We can't turn him out, Howard. He's an old man and blind too."

"Reckon he can stay here, but it's another mouth to feed," whispered her husband.

Metallak's ears were keen and he heard her whisper. He proudly handed over his pouch of coins next morning as they talked. "Metallak has money," he said. "Can you fetch me a guide to bring me to Moserill's lodge?" He described Moserill's home in Andover, and how many days it would take to get there.

Mrs. Blodgett took the pouch and shook out the money, gasping when she saw the stones in the pouch. "Why, Metallak, this isn't money, it's a bag full of stones." Then she bit her tongue, wishing she hadn't told him.

"Metallak has five hundred dollars!" he shouted. "It must be the small guide who brought me here. If the money is gone, he took it."

"Why, this is dreadful, Metallak. But we don't know where to look for him. With that much money, we'll never see him again."

Metallak lost his will to live after that, broken and beaten by this last act of treachery. A town meeting was called to discuss the future of this proud haughty Indian, now a pauper in the hills that had long been his home.

"We must take him in. This is his home," said Mrs. Blodgett.

"We got funds in the treasury," said Mr. Fellows. "You make us a bid, Howard."

And thus it was that Metallak's future was placed in the hands of an auctioneer for the town poor and he was bid off to Howard Blodgett for $48.25 a year.

"You're to feed and clothe him, and keep him in tobacco," he was told, and Metallak became a resident of West Stewartstown.

He didn't resist when they told him he'd be staying on with them.

"Metallak will be a good boarder," he said. "Won't

make any trouble.''

"Now this is your home, Metallak,'' said Mrs. Blodgett. "If there's anything you need, you let me know. You'll be just like one of the family.''

Metallak said nothing, feeling utterly helpless, without sight or money, dependent on others for charity. Perhaps Moserill would hear of his whereabouts and come for him. Perhaps he would visit Oozalluc's grave once more if he could get his strength back.

Metallak turned his head gingerly as he came out of a deep sleep. Slowly the fuzziness of sleep left him and his mind was fresh and clear. He felt he had come through a long dark tunnel and the end was within sight. Yet he felt a sense of urgency, as though time was running out. Strange, because his body felt weightless, as though he rested on a cloud. He murmured.

"Tilda.''

Matilda rushed to his side, re-arranging his coverlets and trying to make him comfortable.

"Metallak, I have good news,'' she burst out, unable to wait. "Parmachenee is coming to see you.'' She saw the frown deepen in his gaunt forehead and continued. "No, no, I didn't send for her. Your grandson was here in town searching for you.''

"Grandson?'' he questioned.

"Your very own namesake, Metallak, and he looks like you too. Wanted you to know what a fine job he did making his first canoe.''

Metallak could sense Matilda's relief that his daughter was coming. He smiled with pleasure. So his grandson had made his own canoe. And Parmachenee was coming herself. Very well, let it be so. Secretly, he longed to hold her tiny hand once more before this weightless tide carried him away. Nervously, he reached up to smooth his shaggy hair, but his hand fell to the floor, useless.

Strange, but he had no desire to lift his arm again. He had never felt so contented or relaxed. For a moment he saw Oozalluc's shadow in the distance.

"Oozalluc,'' he murmured.

"I checked Oozalluc's grave just yesterday, Metallak,'' Leonard assured him. "And I put up a new marker for her too.'' He didn't add that he saw signs of tampering with the grave. Lots of times, strangers came up this way asking about old Metallak and his woman Oozalluc. No doubt one of them had searched the soil looking for something. Downright disgusting, it was.

Metallak tried to mouth the words, but they wouldn't come out. Watching his lips, Leonard made out "North Hill."

"You have my word, Metallak," Leonard told him. "Metallak will be buried on North Hill, facing the east and looking toward the river. Sitting up, too, just like you wanted." Leonard wiped his brow, wet with perspiration. He'd be glad when this was all over with. He squeezed Metallak's hand and returned to the kitchen, pacing the floor nervously.

"You go ahead, Leonard," Matilda said. "We'll be fine here and I know you're anxious to get over to that town meeting."

"Well, I suppose I could, if you don't need me," Leonard put in, quickly grabbing his jacket. He looked at Matilda sheepishly, wondering how it was that she seemed to read his mind. Then he tiptoed out.

Metallak fought sleep, though he could feel it creeping up and carrying him away, like a tiny leaf on a great tide of water. Where was Parmachenee? He clutched the hemlock stick, feeling the notches he had carved, with his left hand. The other hand still lay lifeless on the floor. He wondered if he made a mistake in counting the notches. Surely it had not been forty years since Oozalluc put the stick into his hands.

Someone was feeding him something in a spoon, sticky and sweet. He lapped the spoon and took more. It tasted like honey and rum, a lovely taste.

Then he felt a familiar hand on his brow. No, this was not Matilda's rough hand, it was an old familiar loving touch, soft on his temples and flickering through his hair. Tears ran down his face.

"Parmachenee," he whispered, his chin trembling.

"Ssshh," she whispered back, drying his face with a soft handkerchief that smelled like heaven.

Metallak sighed gratefully. The Light of his Lodge was here with him. She held his gnarled old hands firmly, giving him strength. From far away, he heard the murmur of her voice.

"You have many friends here, my father. Your name will long be remembered by your white brothers . . . your red brothers too."

Metallak summoned all his strength to mouth the

words. "Legacy all gone."

Tears ran down Parmachenee's face and spilled on his arm. "You leave a legacy of love, my father. That is far better than gold." Her voice cracked, as she remembered the day he placed her on the horse and bade her goodbye, in the village of Portsmouth. She knew then, and she knew now, the pain it had cost him.

He could hear the murmur of latin words, and someone touching his forehead. No doubt it was the priest. So Parmachenee had brought a priest with her.

Metallak felt a strong sensation in his body, giving him great strength. He was a young man again, astride a great bull moose, with two boys in back of him. Their laughter echoed through the vast forest. Their faces swam before him vividly, these young men who bore his name. He leaned forward to whisper to Big Horn, but he vanished out of sight.

There seemed to be a lot of commotion in the room around him. Several voices spoke all at once. He recognized the triumphant sound of Leonard's voice.

"You tell him, Parmachenee," he said eagerly. "No sir, Metallak ain't no pauper, and we'll see to it, one way or the other."

And then Parmachenee was close to his head, whispering into his ear.

"A town meeting has been held just in your honor, my father," she told him in a happy voice. "There will be a special legacy for Metallak, and his name will long be remembered. There will be a Metallak Pond, a Metallak Island, a place called Metallak Point also. You remember that one well, my father, it was our special place. There may even be a Metallak Mountain one day. Your grandchildren will be very proud of you."

Metallak's throat constricted, and tears ran down his furrowed face. Parmachenee felt a light squeeze from his left hand. So he had heard, after all. Her father had not lived in vain. She felt as though her chest would burst with happiness.

She heard a light sigh. Metallak was beginning to drift away. The hand in her grasp was growing cold. Through her own tears, she saw a coin fall onto the coverlet in front of her.

"Never paid you for those new snowshoes, Metallak." somebody said, and walked past them.

"I figger we owe you a lot more than this, Metallak," another voice said, as more coins fell on the coverlet. They spilled into a puddle as the line continued to file past them. Some of them said nothing, just pressed his hand, leaving a token of respect for an old friend.

Tremors shook Metallak's body as he felt himself being lifted gently, gently, up and away, his face a mask of peace and contentment. He tried to snap himself awake. He must say goodbye to Parmachenee.

"Wl..." he tried to form the word, but his mouth failed him. He tried again. "Wli...".

"Wli-nanawalmezi, my father," he heard her say, as the tide gathered him up at last.

Sometime later that night, they placed a penny over each eye and prepared him. He was buried sitting up, just as he requested, in the North Hill cemetery, in a special grave.

He is remembered affectionately as Metallak, the last of the Cowassucks.

Afterword

At the corner of Route 145 and Creampoke Road, in West Ste-wartstown, a marker has been erected for Metallak, often called "The Lone Indian of the Megalloway," indicating that he is buried in North Hill cemetery nearby.

Very little is known about Metallak. Kenneth Poore, son of the sexton who buried Metallak, was certain that Metallak attended Dartmouth, although he never had graduated. Kenneth recounted the story of Metallak's attack on a wolf which saved several cattle. This story apparently was published in *Youth's Companion* in the early 1900's.

As to Keoka, Metallak's first wife, the spelling of her name would indicate Sauk origin, a tribe she was allegedly banished from for her unseemly conduct. Although Metallak loved her dearly, his second wife, Molly, was his greatest love. She was his companion in all things, while the children from his first wife grew up elsewhere. Parmachenee, his daughter, was educated by a white family, although she was very devoted to her father and visited often.

Although it is well documented that Metallak "laid away" his first wife for her "unwifely" behavior, and for this or some similar incident was banished from his tribe, there is reason to question his involvement. Metallak himself conveyed that he was banished from his tribe for rescuing a white prisoner, which sounds more in keeping with his character. In fact, his popularity with the whites as well as his own blood brothers, made him a sought-after guide and hunter. His sincerity made him respected by all, contrary to the way the whites felt about Tom Hegan, who led the raid on Bethel in 1781.

From all accounts, Metallak was a very religious man, and perhaps that helps explain the confusion regarding his marriages. Some evidence indicates that he was married three times, but I believe this might be inaccurate. During the research process, I learned that most female converts chose to take the baptismal name of Mary, pronounced "Molly" because the Abenakis did not have a letter "r" in their alphabet. I believe that Metallak's first wife was baptized in the Christian faith as Maryeunice, or Molyeunice, and that Keoka and Maryeunice are one and the same, and that Metallak was actually married only twice.

The King Philip's Land Grant was recorded in 1796, a short time before Pial's death. Since Metallak is recorded as having been either the brother or son of Pial, one would assume that he was the son, judging by the dates involved.

Metallak's prowess as a skilled hunter and guide made him invaluable to the white community. Thus, he was chosen to survey for the Atlantic and St. Lawrence Railroad, also known as the Grand Trunk.

He did indeed disown his sons for their allegiance to the British during the War of 1812, and lost one son in that battle.

He was a registered member of the village of Odanak, on the St. Lawrence River, in the census taken in 1812. The religious ceremonies described in this book are based on actual fact, translated from early missionary records there at the village. The accounting of the treasury and reading of the wampum are also documented.

It is true that Metallak's first son was killed by wolves, and that he took vengeance on the entire wolf family. I used the name Paugus for this first son because there is reason to believe that Metallak was actually related to Paugus, although they were from different tribal origins.

255

Metallak accomplished many unusual feats during his lifetime, including the taming of several moose. His endurance, even at an advanced age, was such that he was able to sleep out in the open with nothing but a moose skin wrapping--which froze over his body during the night.

Sad but true, he did lose sight in his old age, and signed over his remaining small parcel of land in 1836. He later became a pauper in his own kingdom, dependent on others for the necessities of life. A stone was erected for him in 1915.

Although my story is fiction, it based on the life of Metallak, and portions of the story are authentic.

About the author

Alice Daley Noyes was born in Lemington, Vermont, and educated in Colebrook, New Hampshire, near the site of Metallak's grave.
After working several years at the V.A. Medical Center, she decided to pursue her writing career by taking a night writing course at University of New Hampshire. Her first fiction endeavor was *Metallak, his legacy*, which was the basis for this book.
Alice is presently a realtor in Manchester, New Hampshire; she has also completed a textbook on typing (now in its fourth year of publication), and plans to continue writing in her spare time.

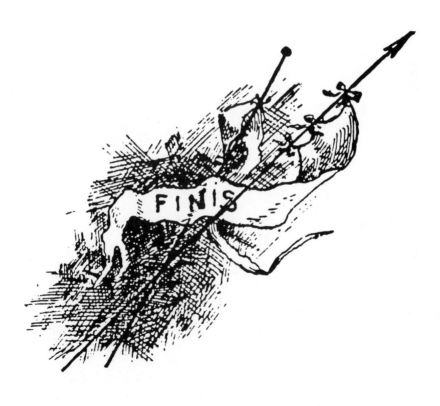